BONES IN THE WELL

BOOK NO. 3 – FOLEY & ROSE SERIES

GARY S. GREGOR

GW00499973

ACKNOWLEDGMENTS

A number of people play a role in getting an author's story from an initial idea to a published book. For some of them, that role is small, for others it is significant. All who contribute in some way, regardless the level of input, are important to me, and although it might be cliché, it is true that this book would never have seen the light of day without each of them.

If I must nominate just a few, I would start with my former colleagues in the Northern Territory Police Force. You wonderful folk are the inspiration for my characters and, while those characters are fictional, I occasionally draw on the personality traits of some of those I have met in the job. If you recognise yourself in any of them, please remember that you are there because you inspire me.

My beautiful wife, Lesley, who tolerates my long hours in front of the computer without complaint, I love you and I thank you, although I still insist my love of writing is not an obsession.

Last, but by no means least, I thank all at Next Chapter Publishing. The Next Chapter team took a punt on an unknown, and that's rare in this business. I hope I can justify your gamble. I know I'll never stop trying to honor that leap of faith; thank you.

This book is respectfully dedicated to the memory of police officers everywhere who have paid the ultimate sacrifice in the service of their communities.

1
_____

A hand snaked over Miranda Winters' shoulder and grabbed her roughly from behind. She cringed as the strong fingers, smelling heavily of nicotine, slammed painfully across her mouth. She tasted her own blood as her teeth cut into her lip. She tried to scream, managing only a muffled, garbled cry. Immediately she regretted the effort, as the hand tightened even further across the lower half of her face.

A second strong arm encircled her waist pinning her arms in front of her, then yanked her backwards. Her backward momentum was suddenly halted as she crashed into the chest of someone behind her. She felt the hot, foul smelling breath against her cheek. In an instant, her feet left the ground, and she felt herself carried backwards. Palpable fear, gripped her tighter than the arms embracing her. She could not move her head in any direction. She darted her eyes crazily from side, to side, searching for someone, anyone, who might see she was in trouble. She saw no one.

Earlier, before the sun sank behind the Devil's Marbles, there were people everywhere, tourists mostly. Many strolled casually through the area looking at the amazing rock formations, while others relaxed at their respective camp sites, animatedly discussing the spectacle of a glorious sunset over the Marbles as they enjoyed their ritual happy hour.

A few, like Miranda, were young, most were middle-aged, and a few were elderly. All were filled with wonderment at the red, yellow, and orange, hues, draped like a fine, transparent curtain across the western sky as the hot central Australian sun slowly settled below the distant horizon.

Formed by the combined processes of weather, and erosion, over tens of millions of years, the Devil's Marbles comprised hundreds of granite boulders, scattered over a large area approximately one hundred kilometres south of Tennant Creek, and three-hundred-and-ninety kilometres north of Alice Springs in the heart of Australia's Northern Territory. Some of the boulders balanced precariously on top of one another, appearing as though they may topple at any moment. Others appeared to have been cleaved neatly down the middle by the unpredictable forces of nature. A short, gravel, access road from the Stuart Highway running from south, to north, through the centre of the formation, led the inquisitive traveler to the basic campground on the eastern fringe of the area.

Managed jointly by the traditional aboriginal owners and the Territory Parks and Wildlife Service, and now officially known as Karlu Karlu/Devil's Marbles Conservation Reserve, the area attracts over one-hundred-and-forty thousand tourists every year, many of whom are back-packers, just like Miranda Winters.

For those traveling on a shoe string budget, also like Miranda, there are no outrageously overpriced accommodations designed to separate the traveler from his, or her, holiday dollars. Folks who visit Devil's Marbles either drive motor-homes, tow caravans, carry tents, or sleep in their vehicles. There is also no power connected to the area, and ablution facilities are limited to two basic, biochemical, composting, unisex toilet blocks.

———

Now it was dark, and no one was around, at least Mandy couldn't see anyone within the scope of her vision given the limited movement of her head. She was in trouble, deep trouble. Surely someone would see her predicament. Just a short while ago, before the sun set, there were people all over the place. Now there was no one.

Mandy had heard a few horror stories about girls, and sometimes boys, who came to Australia in search of adventure and fun. And, perhaps for those so inclined, a holiday romance. She supposed backpacking in a foreign country, wherever it may be, came with potential risks, particularly for a young, attractive female. She had plenty of family and friends back home in London eager to point those risks out to her, and not the least vocal was her mother and father.

Australia had an ignominious reputation for backpackers going missing, even murdered. But, Mandy figured the sheer number of young, high spirited tourists who sought adventure in the land-down-under offered her more than acceptable odds against her becoming one of the unfortunate statistics. Besides, she liked to think of herself as a thrill seeker. Since she arrived in Australia, she had bungee jumped from a bridge, tandem parachuted from a plane, snorkeled on the Great Barrier Reef, taken a fast lap in a V8 Super Car around the famous Bathurst racing circuit, climbed Ayres Rock, and even tried rock climbing in the Summer Day Valley in Victoria's Grampian Ranges.

Mandy did not consider herself immune from danger, it was more she figured the potential risk of her falling victim to danger was minimal. If she was going to take the plunge and spend the money to travel to the other side of the world, she was determined to get value for her money.

She had a small number of friends who had visited Australia, and not one of them had anything adverse to say about the experience. To the contrary, each of them pestered her, almost to annoyance, insisting she should go. Inwardly, she was jealous of them all, but ultimately, she decided she simply had to go and experience it for herself. Despite the warnings of those few loved ones.

All she had to do was save the money required for the return airfare, plus a bit more to sustain her until she could get a part-time job. As a trained nurse, she figured it would take her eighteen months to accrue the required funds, but, such was her determination and enthusiasm, it took just twelve.

———

Mandy struggled to breathe. The hand across her face slipped upwards a little and now crushed against the lower half of her nose as well as her mouth, making it difficult to suck air into her lungs. She moaned again, struggling frantically against the anonymous force

4

carrying her backwards. She desperately needed to breathe, and waves of panic washed over her. *Is this what it feels like to drown*?

From sheer panic, Mandy made the decision to fight back. If she didn't, she was sure she would suffocate. Her legs swung free of the ground, and she tried to kick backwards, hoping to score a hit hard enough for her attacker to loosen his grip and allow her to take a much needed breath. Anticipating her resistance, her attacker slammed her feet hard on the ground. He leaned close and hissed in her ear.

"You try that again, and I will kill you right here, right now!"

———

Initially, traveling to the other side of the world alone was a source of nervousness for Miranda, much more so for her parents, but of those she would have chosen to travel with, all had already been to Australia, which left her no alternative but to go alone. She'd hoped she would meet another like-minded Brit also traveling alone; a nice English boy would be perfect. They could team up; safety in numbers, she reasoned. The idea eased her parents' concerns, albeit minimally.

As it transpired, Mandy did meet another backpacking Brit. Lillian Clutterbuck was an extroverted, opinionated, twenty-two-year-old from Hartlepool, in England's northeast. Mandy met Lilly in Sydney, and they traveled together for several weeks until Lilly met Michael, a typical sun-tanned, surf loving Aussie boy. Lilly elected to part company with Mandy and continue her travels with her new found love, following the surf breaks up and down the east coast.

Initially, Mandy was disappointed about the prospect of continuing her travels alone. Having someone else to talk to, as well as to share traveling expenses as they crossed the seemingly endless kilometres between towns and cities, was nice. Eventually, however, she settled into a routine and, for the most part, she was comfortable with her own company, until now.

Mandy was trapped within the strong arms. She was not a big girl; the contrary was the case. But whoever was carrying her to God knows where seemed to be doing so with such ease she might have been no heavier for him than a small child.

She certainly wasn't helping him; it was impossible with her legs dangling, and swinging crazily beneath her. Somehow, she managed to get one arm free, and she grabbed at the hand across her mouth, trying desperately to pull it away from her face. She needed air.

The man stopped, and lowered Mandy until her feet just touched the ground. "I won't tell you again!" he spat into her ear. "If you want to die here, I'm okay with that!"

Mandy stopped struggling. The man lifted her again, and continued to walk backwards. Every step he took, she could sense the distant campsite getting further and further away. She looked in its direction, nestled peacefully behind the shadowy shapes of the domed granite rock formation silhouetted against the dark eastern skyline. Help was right there. So close.

In the darkness, any hope of assistance from any of the many tourists, who were by now settling down for the night, was rapidly disappearing. A blanket of hopelessness, heavy and suffocating, settled over her.

She realised with a resigned finality, all hope was lost. She thought of her mother, and her father, and hoped they would forgive her.

After what seemed an eternity, but was in reality no more than a few minutes, her captor spun her around. They were in front of a large, dark vehicle. She didn't know what type of vehicle it was; motor vehicles were nothing more than a mode of transport for Mandy, and not something she needed to be particularly knowledgeable about. She could see it was big, and it loomed in front of her, a big, dark shape against the surrounding blackness of the night.

Without warning, the man slammed her against the side of the vehicle, and her forehead cracked against the side window. A sharp pain streaked across the front of her head, and what little air she still had in her lungs was expelled with a loud *Whoosh!*

Before she could recover, her arms were yanked roughly behind her, a knee was rammed roughly into her buttocks forcing her body even harder into the side of the vehicle, and her hands were bound tightly together with something she guessed was plastic cable ties.

Mandy began to sob. "Wh... what do you want?" she stammered.

"Shut the fuck up!" the mad hissed.

Then, he covered her mouth with a smelly, dirty rag, and tied it behind her head. It tasted of oil, or grease, and she gagged, as she struggled once again to breathe. A solitary tear escaped from her eye and rolled down her cheek.

Her captor dragged her roughly to the back of the vehicle and opened the large rear access door. A light came on, and she immediately recognised the vehicle as a large four-wheel-drive.

Rough, strong hands shoved her into the rear cargo compartment; her backside fell hard onto the floor, and her legs dangled out the back of the vehicle. She was wearing a light, summer dress that rode up high, almost to her thighs, briefly exposing a glimpse of white panties. Her captor paused, stared for a few seconds at the enticing view, and smiled. Mandy thought she heard a soft moan. She tried to slither backwards, deeper into the vehicle, hoping her dress would come down, preserving her modesty.

The man grabbed her legs and pulled her forward. With one big hand, he held both her feet tightly together, slipped a cable tie over them and yanked it tight, securing her legs together. She felt the thick, plastic tie cut deep into her ankles.

Then, he lifted her legs, swung them round, and pushed her onto her back in the cargo bed. He stepped back, leered at her for a moment, and then slammed the door shut.

Mandy lay on her back across the cargo bed with her head hard against the driver's side of the confined space, with her arms secured painfully beneath her. With difficulty, she managed to turn onto her side. When she tried to stretch, she found she couldn't extend her legs, so she drew her knees up to her chest and lay in the fetal position.

Never having felt at ease in confined spaces, Mandy sensed a panic attack coming, and sobbed involuntarily. She had to control it. She had to overcome the urge to scream. Besides, no one would hear her, anyway. She remembered reading something, somewhere, about the relationship between fear and panic.

When fear overrides the ability to think clearly and rationally, it becomes panic... or something like that. At this point, a panic attack was the last thing she needed. *Get a grip!* she urged herself silently, as she struggled to control her breathing and focus her thoughts on how she was going to get out of this mess.

She heard her abductor get into the driver's seat, slam the door behind him, and start the engine. Then, the vehicle began to move away. Where was he taking her? How far would they go? Was she ever going to see her parents again? Was she even going to live through the night? These were the thoughts crowding Mandy's consciousness as she felt the vehicle bounce across the rough terrain.

They were on a dirt road; she could smell the dust seeping into the vehicle. She thought about her car, back at the Marbles. She'd left it parked and locked, in the main campground while she walked through the magnificent rock formations, where, captivated by the beauty of the place, she lingered too long after the sun had set.

Her car, an old but functional Ford Festiva, had by necessity become her accommodation as well as her means of transport. Everything she owned was in the car; her clothes, her passport, her mobile phone, her meager food supply of rice crackers, instant noodles, tea bags, and a few pieces of fruit; each of which seemed to be the staple fare of back-packers such as herself.

She wondered if anyone else camped at the Marbles would notice she was missing. She thought not. She had not befriended any of her fellow travelers other than to say "Hi" to a few as their respective paths crossed while wandering through the Marbles, snapping photographs and wondering at the amazing balancing act of many of the huge boulders. Accordingly, she doubted anyone would even notice she had not returned to her car. She was alone, gagged, trussed hand and foot, dumped into the back of a car, and was being driven to a fate upon which she did not want to speculate.

———

Wherever her abductor was taking her, it seemed to be taking many hours, but Mandy guessed it was less than an hour. Her abductor played country music loudly, and occasionally she heard him singing softly along with the tune. Mandy had never been a fan of country music; it was the music of hicks, and mountain dwelling, in-bred folk. The quality of her captor's voice did nothing to assuage her dislike of the genre.

She began to count the number of songs played, mentally figuring three minutes per song. At one point, she lost count but decided it was close to twenty. By her estimation, they had been traveling for approximately one hour, perhaps an hour and fifteen minutes. She usually wore a watch, but had left it in her car; she wouldn't be able to read it anyway, with her hands trussed behind her back.

They were still traveling on rough dirt roads, she deduced, given the jolting and bouncing her body was forced to endure. Her fingers were becoming numb, and she wriggled them in a vain attempt to relieve the tingling. A persistent ache in her shoulder where she lay on it promised to spread to her neck, and back. She considered turning completely over but, to do so would leave her with her back to the rear cargo door of the vehicle, an option she quickly dismissed. If they stopped, and the stranger opened the rear door she wanted to be facing him and whatever he might have in store for her.

Mandy closed her eyes and tried to shut out the awful music pounding through the vehicle's sound system, and the equally awful vocal accompaniment of the man who now had total control over her life.

Eventually, the vehicle slowed, and stopped, and, thank God, so did the music. As Mandy lay in the cramped, uncomfortable space, waiting for whatever was to follow, she heard the crackle from the engine compartment as the motor cooled in the cold night air. She focused intently, listening for any other noises which might give her an idea of where they were. She heard only the engine crackle.

She waited, expecting to hear the driver moving about, opening the driver's door and shutting it behind him. Was he coming to drag her out of the back of the vehicle? Nothing! Mandy heard not a sound.

The driver must be sitting quietly in the front seat. What was he doing? What was he going to do? She found herself hoping he would do something, anything. Waiting for something to happen, was worse than the prospect of dealing with it when it finally did. Then, she heard him speak.

"It's time, my precious," the man announced in a tone, not loud, and not so soft she couldn't hear, but in a normal, controlled speaking voice, as though he might be ordering a litre of milk from the local corner store. So unassuming was his announcement, Mandy could almost imagine him smiling.

The driver's door opened, the interior light came on, and the front seat squeaked as the man got out of the car. He shut the door, and suddenly the vehicle interior was plunged into darkness. Mandy listened. She heard footsteps approaching the rear of the vehicle, and then the door swung open. The interior light flashed on again, and Mandy looked up at the man standing in the open doorway. Beyond where he stood smiling down at her, she saw only blackness—no street lights, no house lights, no corner store, nothing.

"Get out," the man ordered.

Mandy lay still, staring wide-eyed and afraid at the stranger.

"Get the fuck out!" he yelled. His voice seemed to echo in the still, black night air.

Mandy started at the shrillness of his voice. She tried to move forward, towards the open door, but it was difficult with her hands and feet bound. She sobbed involuntarily behind the gag in her mouth, and tried harder to move.

Eventually, the man reached inside the vehicle and grabbed Mandy roughly by the upper arm. He dragged her forward, and she almost fell from the car. He changed his grip from her arm to her feet, swung her legs outwards, and left her half lying, half sitting, on the edge of the cargo compartment. All concerns of modesty were gone. Mandy's short dress was now well above her thighs. Her captor stared lustfully.

"You sure are a pretty one," he declared. He fumbled in his pocket, and produced a pocket knife. He opened the blade, and Mandy's eyes widened with fear. The man reached down and, with one deft stroke, cut the cable tie binding her feet.

Mandy felt a sudden rush of pain in her feet and ankles as the blood began to run unrestricted to them. The man again gripped her upper arm, and yanked her from the vehicle. When her feet touched the ground, she tried to stand but her feet were still numb and she fell against the man. Her face crashed into his chest, and he held her roughly against him. Mandy heard his breath quicken, and one hand moved to her backside where it rested for a moment, and then began to knead her buttocks.

Mandy wanted to throw up. She fought desperately to quell the urge lest the dirty gag in her mouth cause her to choke on her own vomit. She moaned loudly.

As if he had just remembered the gag, the man grabbed at the rag and pulled it free of her mouth. Now it hung loosely around her neck, and Mandy immediately took several deep breaths of fresh air. She pushed against the man's chest, and shuffled backwards until she hit the vehicle and almost toppled back into the cargo bay. Regaining her footing, she looked up at the man. His features were dark, and vague, in the half-light emanating from the vehicle's interior.

"What do you want?" she sobbed.

The man stared at her and smiled. "You'll find out soon enough," he said quietly.

"Wh... who are you?" Mandy stammered.

"My name is not important," he answered. "What is *your* name?"

Mandy paused, not sure what she should admit to. "My name is Miranda... Miranda Winters," she said finally.

"Miranda... Miranda," the man said. "Miranda... that's a pretty name."

"What do you want from me?" Mandy asked again.

"I have no money," she offered, almost as an afterthought.

"Do you think I'm a thief?" the man queried.

"No... no," Mandy said, hurriedly.

"I don't want your money," the man shrugged.

Mandy paused. "What then?" she asked, positive she knew the answer.

"All in good time," the man smiled. "Right now you need to sleep." He took her by the arm and steered her away from the vehicle.

"Wait there," he ordered, forcing her to halt. He let go of her arm, and fumbled in the rear of the vehicle. A storage compartment on the inside of the rear door dropped down, he reached in and grabbed a torch. He switched it on, and shone it in Mandy's eyes. Mandy turned her head, avoiding the bright light.

The man shut the rear door and spoke. "Okay, let's go."

"Where?" Mandy asked.

"Turn around and walk, straight ahead," he ordered. "Remember, I'm right behind you, so don't try to run."

Mandy turned slowly, paused, and looked into the darkness ahead of her. The man stepped up close behind her and shone the torch at the ground just in front of her. Up ahead, in the near distance, she saw a large, dark, shape. At first, she couldn't make out what it was. It looked huge; a big, high, black, shape looming out of the darkness. Then, as she stared at it, she realised it was a house.

The stranger pushed Mandy gently in the back. "Start walking," he commanded.

Mandy froze, afraid to move. She did not know

what evil awaited her inside the house, and she did not want to find out.

The man leaned forward, his mouth close to her ear. His lips brushed lightly against her lobe. "If you don't start walking, I am going to kill you," he whispered.

His breath was warm and moist against her cheek.

She jerked her head away from the terrible smelling breath. "I don't want to go in there," she sobbed.

"Okay, have it your way," the voice said.

Suddenly Mandy felt the sharp, point of a knife blade against the back of her neck. She flinched involuntarily, and tried to step away from the threat. A hand grabbed her by her hair.

"I don't want to use this, but if you don't move your pretty little arse you will die, right here in the dirt, and your body will lay here all night for the dingoes to feast on."

Mandy gasped aloud. "Okay... okay." She stumbled towards the dark shape. "I'm going... I'm going," she sobbed. "Please don't hurt me."

"I thought you might see it my way eventually,"

Her captor kept a tight grip on her hair as she walked tentatively towards the house.

The house was huge. Even in the dark, with just the torch light to guide her, Mandy could see it was a big homestead with a very wide verandah running all the way along the front. She supposed it would also surround the entire building. There were steps, several of them, leading up from ground level to the verandah deck. Mandy paused in front of the bottom step and looked up.

"Go ahead, up the stairs," the man prompted from

behind her. He nudged her with a light tap on the back of her head.

Mandy began to climb, slowly, stopping briefly at the top of each step. There were railings on either side of the wide stairs, but with her hands bound behind her she was unable to balance herself, and ascending the stairs was not easy. Then, there was the unknown; a fate she did not want to contemplate awaiting her at the top of the steps. A feeling, a premonition she had never experienced before, washed over her, and suddenly she was certain if she entered the house, she would never again come out, at least not alive.

"Get up there!" the man insisted. He shoved her again, more forcibly this time.

Mandy stumbled, regained her footing, and climbed the last step to the landing. In front of her was a large pair of double doors. Partially lit in the glow of the torch light she could see the doors were closed and the top half of each contained an ornate stained glass panel. The door handles were large, round, carved knobs, and her eyes were drawn to them as if she half expected them to start turning by themselves.

Then, she felt the knife blade at her hands, and suddenly the plastic tie fell away. Pain rushed to her fingers as the blood was again free to flow. She brought her hands to her front and massaged them in an attempt to get the feeling back.

"Open the door, it's not locked,"

The voice startled Mandy. She stepped forward, and stopped in front of the doors, reached out, and grasped one of the knobs, her tiny hand barely covering it. It turned easily, and she gently pushed forward. The door swung open and creaked loudly in the stillness of the night.

Before she stepped inside, she looked around her, estimating her chances at making a run for it. She hoped to see lights from nearby houses. Somewhere she could run and scream for help. There were no lights. As far as she could tell in the enveloping darkness there were no neighbors. She was alone, in the middle of nowhere, at the mercy of a stranger who obviously had plans for her she did not want to think about. She stepped forward and entered the homestead.

The man flicked a switch just inside the doors and the room was suddenly flooded in light. Mandy blinked against the light, and looked around. She was in a wide, long hallway made to look deceptively bigger by the lack of any furnishings along its length. There were doors along both sides of the hallway but she did not have time to assess where they might lead. The man shoved her roughly forward, and she stumbled along the hallway towards the rear of the house. About half way along the hall, he grabbed her from behind, forcing her to stop in front of a closed door which had a sturdy bolt complete with a padlock securing it.

The man grabbed Mandy's arm, thrust her aside, and produced a key from his pocket. He fumbled with the padlock, slid the bolt, and unlocked the door. He placed the key back in his pocket and pulled on the door handle. The door opened outwards and a deep, uninviting blackness appeared beyond.

"Shoes!" he demanded.

"Wh... what?" Mandy stammered.

"Shoes... take them off."

Mandy paused. "My shoes? You want my shoes?"

"Take your shoes off, or I'm gonna hurt you," the man threatened.

Mandy kicked off her shoes.

"Get in the room," the man ordered.

"Wh... why," Mandy stammered.

"You heard me. Get the fuck in there." He shoved her roughly into the room. Before she could react, the door slammed shut behind her, and she heard the bolt slide and the padlock click.

Terrified, Mandy turned in the dark, and threw her body against the door.

"Please... please... don't lock me in here. Please!" she cried. She heard footsteps fade into the distance. The man was gone. She was alone. She fought against the rising panic threatening to overpower her. She banged on the door with closed fists and sobbed loudly. No one came.

With extreme difficulty, she managed to regain a small degree of control, and scrambled in the dark, feeling around, on both sides of the door, searching for a light switch. Finally, she found it and flicked it. Nothing happened. She flicked it up, and down, several times. The darkness remained. Despair threatened to consume her. She leaned forward and her forehead banged against the door.

"Please... please," she sobbed. "Please don't leave me here." Then, from somewhere behind her, she heard a voice.

"He took the globe."

Mandy spun towards the voice in the dark, and almost fell. "Wha... what? Who's there?" she cried.

"He took the globe," the voice repeated.

The voice belonged to a girl, and it carried the pitiful, mournful tones of someone totally defeated.

"Who are you?" Mandy called.

"My name is Veronica," the girl answered softly.

"Where are you?" Mandy asked.

"Over here, to your left. Follow the wall. There's a mattress on the floor," the girl named Veronica instructed.

Mandy moved cautiously, feeling her way around the wall to her left. Eventually, she stumbled on something soft on the floor. She knelt down and fumbled with her hands, and found a mattress. She collapsed onto it, and drew her knees up, her hands clasping them tight to her chest.

"Where are you?" she asked again.

When Veronica spoke, her voice was close, and it startled Mandy.

"I'm right here, next to you. There's another mattress, on the floor."

Mandy reached out in the dark and her hand touched Veronica. She felt a naked shoulder and moved her hand upwards until she felt her face, and then her hair. The girl's hair felt oily and dirty.

Veronica pulled her head away from Mandy's touch. "Please, don't touch me."

"I'm sorry," Mandy apologised. "Where are we? What is this place?"

"I don't know where we are," Veronica said. "I haven't been outside since he brought me here."

"Who is that man?" Mandy asked.

"I don't know. He won't tell me his name."

"How long have you been here?" Mandy probed.

Veronica hesitated, and then said softly, "I don't

know. I gave up trying to keep count of the days. About three weeks... I think."

"Three weeks! Jesus what does he want?'

For a long time, Veronica did not answer.

"What does he want?" Mandy asked again.

"Sex," Veronica answered, finally.

Mandy's heart sank. Her worst nightmare was now a reality. "Oh God!" she moaned. "We have to get out of here."

"We can't get out," Veronica said. "There's only one door, and it's always locked."

"We have to try!" Mandy insisted.

"We can't get out," Veronica repeated. "Others have tried."

"Others! What do you mean others?" Mandy asked.

"There were others before me... and you," Veronica said.

"Jesus, how many?"

"I don't know."

"Where are they?" Mandy asked.

"I don't know," Veronica answered.

"Did they escape?"

"No."

The finality of Veronica's response caused Mandy to shudder involuntarily. "Did he let them go?"

Veronica did not answer.

Mandy reached out in the darkness, put her arms around Veronica, and pulled her close. "I'm Miranda," she said. "Call me Mandy."

Veronica clung to Mandy and began to sob, quietly at first, and then louder until her weeping became un-controllable.

"Shh... shh," Mandy crooned. Veronica's sobbing

was contagious, and Mandy fought hard not to lose control herself. "It's okay. We'll get out of here," she said with little confidence.

"I'm next," Veronica said finally, between deep sobs.

"What?"

"I'm next. The girl who was here when he brought me here has gone."

"Gone where?"

"He took her out and she never came back," Veronica explained.

"When did he take her out?" Mandy probed.

Mandy felt Veronica shrug. "I don't know... a few days ago... maybe a week," she paused. "At any one time, there's never more than two of us here. The last girl... her name was Janice... she told me another girl was here when she came, and eventually she never came back. When he took Janice, she fought like mad, but he is too strong. I think she knew what was going to happen."

"Rape?" Mandy asked.

"Worse than rape. He did that all the time, and always brought us back after."

"What do you think happened to the others?" Mandy asked.

"I think he killed them," Veronica said amid a renewed bout of sobbing.

Mandy held her tight and suddenly realised Veronica was almost naked. "Where are your clothes?" she asked.

"He took them, soon after he brought me here. He left us wearing only bra and knickers. He'll come for yours... probably in the morning."

2

———

S am Rose woke slowly, turned his head, and looked at the woman sleeping next to him. He watched as her chest rose, and fell, rhythmically, the bed sheet just covering the gentle swell of her breasts. Her hair, long, and blonde, splayed haphazardly across the pillow, and one wisp fell across her cheek. The fine, light tip waved almost unperceptively as she softly exhaled.

There were only two occasions in Rose's life where he had grown more than fond of a particular woman, and Sarah Collins, sleeping peacefully beside him, was one of them. Love was an unfamiliar emotion for Sam. He was, of course, aware of the concept of love and all it entailed in respect of the partnership between a man and a woman, but until Sarah came into his life he came close to experiencing it himself on only one other occasion. Like any new, exciting experience, it was going to take getting used to, he thought.

Careful not to wake her, he rose on one elbow and stared at the woman who had, in recent months, become such an important part of his life.

For Sam, confirmed bachelorhood was never a

conscious decision reached after having given due consideration to the benefits as well as the negatives. Rather, he could well be described as a devotee of the brotherhood of single men, were such a brotherhood to exist. He was considered by many of his colleagues to be the epitome of a lady's man. Indeed, it would be fair to say of Sam, one-night stands had become somewhat of a stock in trade.

Since the onset of puberty, when he first came to the realisation there were very distinct differences between the male and the female of the species, he had more than his share of girlfriends. Long term physical, and emotional attachments to members of the opposite sex were not something he purposely set out to avoid. It was simply one of those things which, for one reason or another, rarely happened for Sam. He never considered himself out of step with his male counterparts, and it wasn't something he should be particularly concerned about.

Sam Rose and Sarah Collins were both cops—Northern Territory police officers to be precise. Sam was a Detective Sergeant attached to Major Crime in Alice Springs, and Sarah was the Officer in Charge of Yulara Police Station, five hundred kilometres to the south west of Alice Springs. They met when investigating a series of murders at Lasseter's Cave, west of Yulara. Over the period of their investigation, a mutual fondness developed culminating in the inevitable physical consummation of their relationship.

Both Sam and Sarah were single; Sarah was married once, but the union ended in divorce when she discovered her husband enjoying an afternoon delight with her next door neighbor. Her involvement with Sam was the first with any man since her divorce, and initially, she was surprised to find herself attracted to him given his reputation as a skirt chaser. The last thing Sarah wanted, or needed, was to get involved with another man with a wandering eye and a penis that followed.

She was well aware the police force had more than enough testosterone dripping, knuckle dragging Neanderthals. She swallowed her disgust whenever she passed within ten metres of them as they sucked in their bellies, puffed out their chests, and played with the back of their short necks so their biceps bulged. Sam Rose, to Sarah's relief, was not one of them.

Since getting to know him however, she had decided his reputation, although almost certainly having a degree of truthfulness to it, was not something by which she should judge him. He was a single man; a free agent. He was a good-looking man, without being drop dead gorgeous. He was tall and had a body commensurate with his height and weight. He made her laugh, and he was good to her, and for her. It was easy to understand why any woman would be attracted to him. He possessed the physical, and personality, traits she found sadly lacking in the majority of men she came into contact with, and that was always going to be a plus.

They were together a few months, and although he worked in Alice Springs, and she at Yulara, Sarah had no reason to suspect, or evidence to suggest, he might be cheating on her. It comforted her to assume his apparent monogamous behavior might be attributed to his feelings for her.

Men, many of them, had declared to her, she was beautiful, Sam being one of them, but beauty was not something which preoccupied Sarah's thoughts any more than as a passing interest. She was not ugly, she knew that much about herself. She accepted she was probably pretty, but she had always prescribed to the theory, real beauty originated from the inside. The visible, physical image was merely window dressing and of little consequence when assessing an individual's overall character, and of no consequence at all when measuring one's ability to attract a member of the opposite sex.

Despite Sam's good looks, Sarah discovered he had qualities far more attractive than mere looks, and while she was not in love with him, she was well aware, as their relationship progressed, she might very well be before much longer.

———

Sarah opened her eyes and saw Sam resting on one elbow watching her.

"Hi," she murmured sleepily.

"Good morning," Sam smiled.

"How long have you been laying there staring at me?" Sarah asked.

"A while," Sam answered.

Sarah stretched and yawned. "What are you thinking about?"

"I was wondering whether you might be interested in good morning sex," Sam answered.

Sarah raised her eyebrows. "You woke me three times last night," she declared. "Aren't you tired?"

"Well... to be fair," Sam reminded her, "One of those occasions you woke up to go to the loo and, if you recall, *you* took advantage of *me* when you came back to bed."

Sarah raised herself onto her elbow and brought her face close to Sam. "And, if *you* recall, you never objected."

Sam smiled and kissed her lightly. "I might be silly, but I'm not a total idiot."

Sarah kissed him back. "Well we don't have time. I have to go back to Yulara this morning. I need to shower and get dressed."

Sam lifted the bed sheet from his body and looked down at his groin. "What am I going to do with this?"

Sarah followed his eyes. "Oh dear... that looks nasty... you really should get that looked at. Is it painful?"

"A little, but you could ease the pain," Sam suggested.

Sarah looked down again. "Mmm... maybe I could make time to administer pain relief." She moved her leg across his body and sat astride him, the bed sheet sliding away from her naked body. "Be brave... I'll have you fixed up before you know it."

"Take your time," Sam said.

————

Russell Foley opened his desk drawer and took out the holstered Glock .22 semi-automatic pistol, clipped it onto his belt, and adjusted his jacket so it concealed the weapon. Foley, a Detective Inspector, and Officer in Charge of Major Crime in Alice Springs, made a point of completing a tour around the city and suburbs of the Alice as often as he could. The time constraints of his position made it difficult to do regularly, but he was conscious of the need to stay in touch with the streets and the people on it.

Foley loved his current position, but he missed working at the coal face of the job. Out on the street, reacting accordingly when drunken Joe Citizen was smacking the daylights out of his wife, or one of his kids. Or, when he decided sex with his spouse, or with anyone, was a right and not a privilege, and was there to be taken, by force if necessary, as opposed to being consensual.

Russell Foley had been on the job long enough to know there were streets in any town or city which had become the breeding ground for lowlife scum who considered themselves above the law. Alice Springs, in the heart of the Northern Territory was no exception. Foley considered the Alice, as it was affectionately known, and indeed most towns in the Territory, was at a distinct disadvantage from most other major cities in Australia. It was isolated, at least geographically speaking, and it was populated by an eclectic mix of races and cultures, too many of whom considered themselves to be more deserving of hand-outs than others like them.

Despite benefits, government or otherwise, being available for everyone entitled to receive them, it seemed there were always going to be those who considered themselves deserving of even more, and were inclined to take it illegally. These folk were the reason Foley joined the police force in the first place, over twenty years ago. There had to be something intrinsically wrong with people who chose to steal that which belonged to another, those who laid claim to a benefit to which they were not entitled, or those who, be it pre-meditated or otherwise, took the life of another.

Russell Foley not only loved his job, he was good at it. Was his contribution making a difference? The short answer was, probably not. He knew nothing he alone did in relation to his job would bring the crime rate down. While that was disappointing, those statistics were never going to change until member numbers increased proportionately with those willing to chance their luck and break the law. Foley took little consolation in the realisation that, government budgets being what they were, there was not likely to be an increase in member numbers any time soon.

He was about to leave his office when the telephone on his desk rang shrilly. Given the nature of his job, a ringing telephone was rarely good news. "Shit!" he cursed aloud, and stepped back into his office.

————

Russell Foley knocked on Sam's door. While he waited he looked at the front yard of the modest, police department subsidised home. The lawn, small and compact, was in need of mowing, and the narrow garden bed running the length of the low front fence was bereft of anything resembling flowers, and crowded with everything resembling weeds.

He heard the click of the door lock and turned to see Sam Rose, standing in the doorway looking casual and relaxed in a fleece tracksuit which looked like it could well be a relic of the nineteen-seventies. Foley slowly, and deliberately, eyed Sam's attire from head to toe. "Been shopping at St. Vincent De Paul again?" he said.

Sam paused, and fixed Foley with a look which displayed offence. "I'll have you know, St. Vinnies have some very good stuff... and it's cheap. What are you, the fashion police now?"

Foley pushed past his friend and stepped into the house. "It's very fetching," he scoffed.

"Please, come in," Sam said sarcastically as he closed the door and followed Foley into the small lounge room. "You insult my choice of off-duty attire, and now I suppose you want coffee?"

"No time for coffee," Foley shrugged. "We have a job."

"What's this '*we*' business?" Sam said. "I'm on my days off. I told you Sarah was coming in from Yulara."

"How is the lovely Sarah," Foley asked.

"She's gone back. Left about an hour ago, and she's fine, thanks for asking."

"Have a nice time?" Foley smirked.

"None of your bloody business... but for the record yes, we had a nice time."

"You're a lucky man," Foley said. "I hope you know that."

"I do know that," Sam nodded. "What's the job?"

"We're going on a road trip," Foley answered.

"Where to?"

"About an hour west of Wauchope," Foley said.

"Where's Walk Up?"

Foley shook his head. "Not 'Walk Up' you uneducated moron. It's Wauchope... one word... Wauchope! It's up near the Devil's Marbles."

"Now I really am insulted," Sam said. "You criticise my choice of wardrobe, and now you call me an 'uneducated moron'. I went to high school... I'm well educated."

"Sorry," Foley laughed. "I stand corrected. You're a very intelligent moron."

"Apology accepted," Sam said. "I do know where

the Devil's Marbles are," he added, eager to demonstrate his limited geographical knowledge.

"Ever been there?" Foley asked.

"No."

"For someone born and raised in the Territory, you haven't seen much," Foley said.

"You've pointed that out to me before," Sam responded. "What have we got up there at this 'Wauchope' place?"

"Bones at the bottom of a well," Foley smiled.

"Oh, that's great," Sam said. "Bones at the bottom of a well... probably a bloody kangaroo fell in getting a drink of water. It's my day off!" he moaned.

"What else would you be doing, besides recovering from what has obviously been a strenuous couple of days?" Foley winked.

"Something wrong with your eye?" Sam asked sarcastically.

"My eye is fine," Foley smiled. "Go pack a bag."

"Pack a bag! How far away is this place?"

"Wauchope's about four hundred kilometres north, and the well is another hour east."

"I shoulda hid under the bed when you knocked," Sam murmured as he stalked off to his bedroom.

When he returned a few minutes later, he had an overnight bag draped over his shoulder. "You know I get paid extra for sacrificing my day off."

"Tell it to the Pay Office," Foley said, crossing to the door.

They stepped outside, and Foley indicated the unkempt garden. "Your lawn needs mowing, and you need to plant flowers in the garden bed."

"I've never owned a lawn mower in my life," Sam said dismissively. "I can't see myself changing now."

"You could pay someone to mow it for you," Foley suggested.

"Then I gotta pay every few weeks for the rest of my life," Sam scoffed. "I'm gonna get a few head of cattle, they'll keep the grass down."

Foley laughed. "What about flowers?"

Sam began walking towards the unmarked police car parked in the driveway. "The cows will crap on the lawn, I'll shovel the shit on the flower bed, and flowers will grow all year round."

"Do you even own a shovel?" Foley asked, following along behind.

"No, do you?"

"Of course I own a shovel," Foley answered.

"Then why the fuck do I need one?"

———

Russell Foley turned right from Sam's street, and merged into the traffic building rapidly towards the morning peak hour.

"Have you two made any plans?" he asked, as he swerved around a slow moving, heavily loaded utility.

"Plans?" Sam said, looking across at Foley.

"Yes, plans," Foley said. "You know, plans for something more permanent in regards to your relationship."

"More permanent than what?" Sam asked.

"More permanent than seeing each other more often than once every now and then," Foley explained.

"No," Sam answered.

"Really?"

"Yes, really," Sam said.

"You like her don't you?" Foley asked, concentrating on the traffic ahead.

"Yes, I like her," Sam agreed.

Foley glanced quickly at Sam. "Why don't you marry the girl?"

Sam looked again at Foley. "What... you're my mother now?"

"A blind man can see she's perfect for you," Foley added.

"Maybe the blind man should marry her," Sam said.

"What?" Foley cried, surprise evident in his tone.

Sam shifted in his seat. "Look, Russell, I appreciate your concern, I really do. I'm fond of Sarah... I might even be falling for her, but I'm not the marrying kind. Marriage scares me." He paused. "You know better than most, police marriages are, in the majority, doomed to failure."

"Only when one half of the partnership is in the job," Foley explained. "You and Sarah are both cops, you both know what the job involves."

"Can we talk about something else?" Sam asked, feeling decidedly uncomfortable.

"Sorry," Foley shrugged. "None of my business, I just thought I'd ask. I'd kinda like to be best man before I'm too old to stand at the altar with you."

Sam smiled. "Best man! Don't you think you're being a bit presumptuous?"

Foley looked back at Sam. "Why, who else have you got in mind?"

Sam reached across and patted Foley on the shoulder. "No one else, Russ, if and when I ever decide to get married, you're the man, buddy."

"I think I'm gonna cry," Foley said.

"Please don't," Sam smiled. "Tell me more about the bones in the well," he suggested, changing the subject.

"The Tennant Creek chaps are at the scene. The well is located on a cattle station out beyond an old tungsten mine east of Wauchope. A boundary rider was checking out the well and discovered a body at the bottom. He contacted Tennant Creek, and a couple of uniform blokes attended, had a look, and called it in."

"Why are we going? It sounds straight forward?"

"It looks like there may be more than one body," Foley said.

"How many more?" Sam probed, his interest aroused.

"I don't know," Foley shrugged.

———

On arriving at Wauchope, Foley stopped at the fuel pumps in front of the hotel. While he filled the tank, Sam stepped out of the vehicle and stretched. He looked around at the tiny settlement consisting of a solitary hotel and very little else which could be considered inhabitable. He wondered why anyone would even want to live in such a lonely looking place. At first glance, apart from the hotel, there seemed to be absolutely nothing to offer even the most enthusiastic traveler.

Wauchope was a few hundred metres off the main tourist route. Russell Foley explained during the four-hour drive to get to this point, Wauchope was once a thriving township servicing the now abandoned tungsten mine further to the east. When the mine closed in

1941, the population plummeted, and now just a few hardy souls remained.

Fifteen kilometers to the south, was Wycliffe Well, a much more popular stopover point. Wycliffe Well boasted a spacious caravan park offering a variety of accommodation options for the weary traveler. Also on offer were fuel supplies, and a roadhouse with a basic, clean, dining room where hungry tourists could enjoy a meal, a cold beer, and a glass or two of wine while reading the many articles adorning the walls claiming it to be the UFO capital of Australia.

Well marketed, and equally well managed, Wycliffe Well had long ago outstripped Wauchope as the preferred place for the traveler to break his journey. As an added incentive, there was always the possibility of seeing a genuine UFO. However, in the event a tourist was unfortunate enough not to see a UFO, he or she could, by way of consolation, have their photo taken with their face stuck through the life size Alien cut-out on display outside the entrance to the roadhouse.

Sam walked around the vehicle, stopped in front of the hotel, and cast his eyes about. He did not see a soul anywhere, not even another vehicle. He turned to Foley who was almost finished filling the fuel tank.

"Does anyone live here?"

Russell Foley glanced at the immediate area. "I guess so, I'm getting petrol out of this pump so I expect someone is watching me."

"I suppose real estate would be cheap," Sam surmised.

"Are you considering a tree change?" Foley kidded.

Sam paused. "If I was, I think I could find somewhere with a little more life."

Just then, a black dog appeared from around the side of the hotel, stopped, cocked its head to one side, and studied Sam, and Foley, with momentary interest. The dog lifted a leg, peed against the corner of the building, and then disappeared back around the corner of the hotel.

"That reminds me," Sam said. "I need a leak."

Foley hung up the fuel nozzle. "We need to leave the car here. Someone from Tennant Creek is meeting us here with a four-wheel-drive vehicle. Apparently it's a rough, dirt road out to the well. I'll talk to the hotel manager and find out where we can leave our car."

"How far do we have to go?" Sam asked.

"About another hour," Foley answered. "

Foley, and Sam, removed their weapons from their belts, locked them in the glove compartment of the vehicle, and walked towards the hotel entrance.

"Are you hungry?" Foley asked Sam.

Sam looked at his watch and shrugged. "A little, but I'm not in the mood for road-house take-away. Bloody stuff will clog up your arteries quicker than cement."

"Since when have you been health conscious?" Foley said. "Some of the shit you eat would kill a horse."

"A man can change, can't he?" Sam answered.

"It's Sarah, isn't it?" Foley prodded Sam.

"What?"

"It's Sarah. She's got you eating healthy food at long last."

"I've lost weight," Sam said, patting his belly.

"How much weight?"

"A couple of kilos," Sam said.

"Good for you, Sam," Foley smiled. "Good for you. Has she got you jogging yet?"

"I'm health conscious, not suicidal," Sam stepped in front of Foley, and pushed through the door of the hotel.

3

M iranda Winters slept fitfully, and woke with a
start. For a moment, confused and disorientated, she struggled to comprehend where she was.
Suddenly, reality hit her and she sat bolt upright. She
was on the floor, on a dirty, uncomfortably thin, foam
mattress, with a single, barely adequate blanket covering her. She turned her head and looked through
sleepy eyes at the girl laying close by on another mattress. The girl; her name was Veronica, Mandy remembered, was still asleep. In the dark, half-light,
Mandy strained to focus on the form next to her.
Veronica moaned softly in her sleep, and occasionally
her hands, and feet, twitched involuntarily, as though
she was trapped in a bad dream.

Slowly, in all their terrifying detail, the events of
the night before came back to Mandy. She was kidnapped; snatched from Devil's Marbles, and thrown
into the rear of a large vehicle and transported to this
place. She did not know where she was, or who the
man was who brought her here. She remembered he
was very strong, had bad breath, and he threatened to
kill her. She shuddered at the recollection of the terror

she felt as the man trussed her hands and feet and pushed her bodily into his vehicle. At the time, she truly believed she was going to be killed.

She looked around, at the room which had become a prison, and wondered what time it was. When the man shoved her into the room last night, it was dark, and although the early morning light penetrated faintly from somewhere behind her, it was still difficult to see clearly. She determined, more by sense rather than by actual vision, the room was big.

She removed one arm from under the blanket, and touched the floor, rubbing her hand over the surface. The floor was devoid of any covering; just bare wooden floor boards. Despite the mattress beneath her, her back and shoulders ached where she lay through the long night with her slender body pressed against the hard, unforgiving floor.

Long, restful nights of deep, undisturbed sleep were few and far between since Mandy left her home and embarked on the adventure of her young life. A downside to the back-packer lifestyle was the *'party long, hard, and often'* mindset which seemed to be a mantra for the many thousands of young folk who chose to embrace the relatively inexpensive option of traveling abroad.

The suffocating, debilitating tiredness she felt now was not, however, a result of drinking and partying all night with other carefree, like-minded travelers. Rather, it was as a result of tossing and turning, seemingly every few minutes, throughout the night, while trying to make sense of what was happening to her; and anticipating what horrors awaited her in the coming day.

The things Veronica had told her haunted her

every restless minute of the night. There were other girls before… and now they were gone. Gone where? Were they dead, as Veronica had suggested? Did they escape? How many were there? Did the man kill them? Was he going to rape her? Was he going to kill her? The questions came, and went, then came again, all night long. Now, Mandy was tired. So tired she wanted to lie back down, fold her arm under her head, and surrender to long, blissful sleep. Although the weight of her weariness pressed down on her like a fog getting heavier, and darker, by the second, she knew the blessed oblivion of sleep was not going to happen for her. She wondered if she would ever be able to sleep peacefully again.

As she strained her eyes against the dim light, she began to see the dark silhouette of things in the room. Across the room, opposite where she and Veronica lay, was a small round object, against the far wall. Mandy focused on it and tried to determine what it might be. She stared at it until it morphed from a small, dark, indistinguishable shape in the corner into something she recognized. A bucket. A common household bucket one might use for collecting and carrying water. As she stared at it she wondered what it was for. Water for drinking perhaps? Or for washing?

Eventually, undecided as to the purpose of the bucket, she turned her attention to the rest of the room. She slowly moved her head, following the line of the walls all the way to the door she was thrust roughly through the previous night. She remembered the sound of bolts, or padlocks being clicked shut after the man slammed the door behind her. She made a mental note to check it later.

Her eyes moved slowly past the door, and con-

tinued around until she was staring at the wall just beyond where Veronica slept. The other girl's mattress
butted up against the wall, and Mandy reached across
Veronica and felt the wall surface was smooth, and
cold. It must be an outside structural wall, she
thought. She had been in Australia long enough to
know, at this time of the year, in central Australia, the
nights were freezing. She shuddered, pulled her hand
back, and lifted the blanket higher around her body.

Eventually, she turned and looked at the wall behind her. Her eyes were drawn immediately to a
window almost directly behind her, its base about half
way up the wall and the top approximately a metre
below the ceiling. Drapes, ragged and dirty looking,
hung down from a pelmet above, and fell to the base
of the window sill. Light from the breaking day outside seeped into the room through a narrow gap
where the drapes did not quite meet in the middle.
Mandy felt a glimmer of hope flash through her.

Careful not to disturb Veronica, still sleeping, and
moaning softly beside her, Mandy kicked off the blanket, got cautiously to her feet, and stepped over to the
window.

She reached out and parted the drapes. The
window was filthy. Dirt and grime, obviously built up
over a very long time, caked the glass making it difficult to see clearly what lay beyond. Not so difficult to
see however, were bars, long, thick, heavy bars, covering the outside of the window. She placed her face
close to the glass and peered through the layers of
grime.

Full daylight was still sometime away, and she was
unable to distinguish anything outside other than
dim, blurred shapes she decided were trees and

shrubs which might have, at one time, been a garden of sorts. She looked beyond the supposed garden, but was unable to see anything else recognisable.

Disheartened, Mandy let the drapes fall, and continued her examination of the room. To the right of the window, she moved along the wall and stepped onto a smooth, cement hearth in front of a fireplace. Under her bare feet, it was cold, and she stepped back onto the naked timber floor.

The fireplace was empty. There were no ashes which might signify a recent fire had blazed, and no signs of any dry wood nearby with which they might be able to light a fire. Mandy hugged herself and shivered.

That was it. There was nothing else in the room. A big, cold, empty room. One locked door, and one heavily barred window. A sense of hopelessness washed over her as she turned full circle, taking in the barren, hollow spaciousness of the place which had become her prison.

Her eyes were drawn again to the bucket. Silently in her bare feet she padded across to the far corner of the room, leaned over, and looked into the bucket. At the bottom there was a small amount of liquid few centimetres deep. She reached down, picked it up, and looked closer. Suddenly, an odour she recognised immediately wafted in her face. Urine. The bucket contained urine. A piss bucket! That's what they had for a toilet, a piss bucket!

Disgusted, Mandy placed the bucket down on the floor and stepped away from it. A soft moan escaped her lips. God, what was happening to her? She hurried back to her mattress, dropped down onto it, curled her body into the fetal position, and pulled the blanket back over her body. She began to sob, and rocked back and forth as she felt herself beginning to lose control.

————

Mandy must have fallen asleep. This time when she woke, Veronica was sitting on her mattress watching her.

"Hi," Mandy said sleepily.

"I've been waiting for you to wake up," Veronica said.

"How long have you been awake?" Mandy asked, sitting up.

"Not long," Veronica answered.

"Do you know what time it is?" Mandy asked.

"No, I don't wear a watch," Veronica replied.

Mandy reached out and touched Veronica's hand, squeezing it gently. "You moaned a lot in your sleep."

Veronica lowered her eyes. "Sorry, did I keep you awake?"

"No," Mandy said hurriedly. "It's okay, I couldn't sleep anyway."

"I have bad dreams," Veronica explained, starting to sob quietly.

Mandy squeezed her hand again. "It's okay. Really, it's okay. I understand."

Veronica looked up at Mandy. "He'll be here soon," she said.

"The man?" Mandy asked.

"Yes."

"What will he do?" Mandy asked, a new wave of fear washing over her.

"He'll bring us food... maybe."

"What else?" Mandy asked tentatively.

"Sometimes that's all. He'll put the food on the floor, just inside the door, and then he'll leave."

"Sometimes?" Mandy asked.

"Other times he will take you out and... and... make you have sex with him."

"He rapes you?"

"Yes."

"Can you fight him?"

"He's too big, and strong," Mandy explained. "We all tried... the other girls... and me. You soon learn if you fight him he'll hurt you... bad."

"You just give in to him?"

"You have to," Veronica nodded. She tossed her blanket aside and got up. "I need to pee," she said

Mandy looked across at the bucket. "In that?"

"Yes. it's all we have."

"What about... you know...," Mandy raised her eyebrows.

"The other?" Veronica asked.

"Yes."

"You call out to him, and if he comes he takes you to the main house toilet, and he stands outside and waits for you to finish."

"What do you mean 'if he comes?'" Mandy asked.

"Sometimes he doesn't come. Then you have to hold it, or go in the bucket."

"That's disgusting," Mandy declared.

"Just pray you don't have to go when he's not here," Veronica advised.

"How often does he leave?" Mandy asked.

"I don't know," Veronica shrugged, and walked across to the bucket. She looked small and vulnerable in just her bra and panties.

43

Mandy turned her face to the wall while Veronica relieved herself.

"He never tells us when he's going somewhere, and I've never heard him leave," Veronica said from across the room. "Sometimes he doesn't come back all day. Those days we go hungry." She finished what she was doing and returned to sit on her mattress, pulling the blanket over her near nakedness.

"We have to get out of here," Mandy stated.

"There's no way out," Veronica said. She indicated the window behind them. "The window's barred, and the door's locked. There's no way out."

"We have to try," Mandy insisted. "Is the man here alone, or are there others with him?"

"I've never seen, or heard anyone else. He's alone, I'm sure of it."

"There's two of us," Mandy said, "and one of him. Together maybe we can overpower him."

Veronica shook her head. "He's too strong. We can't overpower him... no way!"

"We have to try," Mandy declared adamantly. She got up from her mattress and moved to the window. She drew the drapes apart, and sunlight, diffused by the grubby window glass, filtered into the room.

Full daylight had broken, and she squinted through the grime, looking for the position of the sun. If she could see where the morning sun was she would know which way the window faced. Way off, on the horizon to her front, the skyline was darker than it was immediately outside the window. She could not see the sun, in any direction she looked. Accordingly, this combined with the darker, distant horizon, led her to the assumption she was facing west. The morning sun would be behind her, on the opposite side of the

house. Tennant Creek would be to her right, she figured, and Alice Springs hundreds of kilometres to her
left. How knowing what direction the room faced, or
how far away a town might be was of any help to her,
or even if it did help her, she had no idea. She
dropped her head in frustration.

Veronica, the blanket clutched tightly around her
body, stepped up behind Mandy, reached out, and
placed a comforting hand on her shoulder.

"Are you okay?" she asked.

Mandy shook her head as if to clear it, and returned her gaze to the scene outside the window.

"I was supposed to meet my friend Lillian today,"
she answered. She turned to Veronica and the two
girls hugged tightly.

"Where?" Veronica asked.

"At Tennant Creek," Mandy said.

"When you don't show up will she report you
missing?" Veronica asked hopefully.

"She'll try to phone me first," Mandy responded.
"But my phone is in my car, its parked at Devil's
Marbles."

"That's good," Veronica said, trying to sound positive. "She'll report you missing, the police will find
your car, and then they'll start looking for you."

"I hope so," Mandy said. "What about you? Surely
someone has reported you missing by now?"

"I promised to call my parents in Tasmania every
week. The man took my phone, and the last time I
spoke to them was from Alice Springs. They'll be beside themselves. I'm sure the police are already
looking for me, as well as the other girls, but no one
knows where we are, or where to start looking." She
began to cry and clung tighter to Miranda.

Mandy patted her warmly on the back. "We will get out of here," she promised.

"How?" Veronica sobbed.

"I don't know, but we will get out." Mandy answered.

Veronica pulled away from Mandy, returned to her mattress, and sat down. "He'll be here soon," she said, looking at the locked door.

"I know," Mandy said. She reached into the pocket of her dress and took out a bunch of keys. "I need to hide these," she said.

"Car keys?" Veronica asked.

"I have a car. It's parked... and locked, at Devil's Marbles," Mandy answered.

A sudden noise from outside the door made both girls turn quickly. Hurriedly, Mandy shoved the car keys under her mattress as there came a rattling, the sound of a lock being opened. The door swung open on hinges which squeaked loudly, and a narrow shaft of light flooded through the gap. Then the man stepped into the open doorway.

Mandy remembered he was a big, strong man, but seeing him now, in the day light, brought a fear to her perhaps even greater than she felt when he grabbed her at Devil's Marbles. He was huge, and his body almost filled the open doorway, shutting out most of the light emanating from behind him. He stood motionless for a moment, and stared at both girls, huddled together by the window on the opposite side of the room. Then he smiled.

Veronica hugged Miranda tighter and, clad only in her underwear, tried to hide behind Miranda. She dropped her eyes, afraid to look at the man standing in the doorway leering at them. Had the time she dreaded finally arrived? Was he here to take her away to somewhere from where she would never return? She whimpered involuntarily, and attempted to squeeze her body even further between Miranda and the wall.

Mandy reached back and patted Veronica on the arm. "It's okay," she whispered in a vain attempt to reassure her. She focused on the man. She wanted him to know she was not intimidated by his presence, despite being scared to death. She hoped her fear was not obvious but felt herself trembling, which had to be a dead giveaway.

"What do you want?" she heard herself ask, curious she was capable of speaking at all given the terror raging inside her.

The man looked directly at her, the sickly, leering smile, the catalyst for a wave of nausea rising from deep in her belly up to her throat. She swallowed against the urge to throw up.

"Your clothes," the man said, the smile getting wider.

"Wha... what?" Mandy asked, knowing full well what he said.

"Your clothes," he repeated.

Mandy remained silent, physically revolted at the sight of the grinning face staring at her from across the room.

"I won't ask again," the man said, his voice both monotone and threatening.

"Ta... take them off," Veronica's voice trembled from behind her. "He'll hurt you." Mandy remained motionless.

"I'd listen to Veronica if I were you," the man said.

"She's right. I will hurt you if you refuse to do as I ask." He took a step further into the room.

Mandy shrank back, her mind racing as options came and went from her mind with every beat of her pounding heart. Then, before she even realised what she was doing, her hands went to the straps of her dress, and she began to lower it from her shoulders. She heard herself sob loudly. She lifted her buttocks from the mattress, pulled the dress from under her, and tossed it aside.

She looked down at the crumpled frock, crossed her hands across the front of her panties and stared at the discarded dress. She wanted to raise her eyes and look at the man but she could not. Her shame, her embarrassment, and her fear rendered her helpless.

"Pick it up and bring it over here," the man ordered.

Mandy could not bring herself to look at him. She leaned over, picked up the dress, and hugged it to her body.

"Over here," the man said.

Mandy climbed awkwardly to her feet, and took a couple of tentative steps forward, her eyes downcast and focused on the floor in front of her.

"Good girl," the man said softly. "Bring it to me."

Mandy slowly crossed the floor, and stopped a couple of metres in front of the waiting man. She did not want to hand over the dress, and clasped it tighter to her torso.

"Give it to me," the man directed.

Mandy paused, slowly lifted her eyes, and looked at the man in the doorway. Her eyes rose slowly up the length of his body, from the floor to the top of his head. He was indeed, a big man, standing almost two metres tall. His legs, clad in faded, soiled, blue denim jeans looked strong and poised, ready to react in an instant should he need to.

A plaid, long-sleeved shirt, even dirtier than his trousers, was tucked into the belted waist of his jeans, and Mandy, surprised and sickened that she would think of the body beneath the clothing, suspected he would not be carrying an ounce of unwanted flab.

His shoulders were broad, and his hair, showing thick strands of grey at the sides and appearing greasy and in urgent need of a wash, grew down to touch the tops of his ears. He was unshaven, and although his beard was not shaggy and unkempt, it did give his face an unclean appearance. His eyes immediately sought hers, and she noticed, as well as obvious signs of redness to them, a web of crow's feet lines extending out from the edges.

He was still smiling broadly at her, and her mind immediately returned to the previous night and the foul breath wafting in her face as he breathed close to her. His teeth were rotten. They were heavily discoloured with what appeared to be nicotine stains, and Mandy immediately dropped her eyes from his face and focused again at the floor in front of her.

"Give me the dress," the man ordered, louder this time.

Reluctantly, Mandy slowly moved the dress away from her body and held it out in front of her. Suddenly it was snatched from her grasp and she was left standing before him in her underwear.

Mandy had never considered herself a prude, and although there were times, albeit very few, when she found herself naked, or near naked, in front of members of the opposite sex, this was different. Never before in her life had she ever felt as helpless, as vulnerable, or as ashamed and embarrassed as she did at that moment. She swallowed hard again against the bile rising in her throat and threatening to spew forth all over the floor.

"You sure are a pretty one," the man said. He reached out and touched her face. Mandy recoiled in horror, and scurried back across the room to where Veronica sat hugging her knees on her mattress. She plopped down next to her and buried her face in Veronica's shoulder. Her whole body began to shudder. Veronica hugged her protectively and whispered in her ear. "Shh... shh. It's okay."

"Good news, girls," the man announced from the doorway. "Today is a day of rest. Relax, but don't get too comfortable, I'll be back later tonight." He turned to leave the room.

"We're hungry!" Veronica called to him over Miranda's shoulder.

The man turned his head, smiled a stained-tooth smile, then walked out the door, shutting it behind him. The sound of the lock clicking home came clearly through the closed door.

4

The circular well was enclosed by a stone wall approximately a metre-and-a-half high. Toward the top, on one side, several stones had fallen from the wall and lay scattered haphazardly on the ground at its base. Extending about a metre above the inside wall of the well, the top of an aluminum extension ladder protruded.

Next to the well, running at ninety degrees out from it, was a long water trough, which had fallen into disrepair and had, at a point long after its useful life, collapsed in the middle. The section remaining relatively intact was beset with rust and threatened to join the middle section at any moment. Weeds, rooted in the now dry sludge in the bottom of the trough, struggled to survive in the harsh, waterless conditions. On the opposite side of the well, a windmill, in even worse condition than the trough and missing all but one of its vanes, leaned perilously close to the point of toppling over on top of the well.

On the ground, a few metres from the base of the well, five body bags lay adjacent to each other in an orderly line. Each of the bags was zipped closed, and most looked to be almost flat, as though they might be empty. One was different however; the first one in the line. It lay a little higher than the others, as though it might contain something more substantial than the rest.

Sam had seen many body bags in his career, and had many years ago become inured to their purpose. He stepped away from the four-wheel-drive police Toyota which brought Foley and himself to the scene, and looked across to the line of body bags. He didn't have to reach far back into his memory to know he had never seen this many in one place at one time.

Including himself, and Russell Foley, there were a total of ten police officers gathered around the well. Most stood casually, talking quietly among themselves, including three plain-clothes detectives gathered in a huddle. Another was occupied taking photographs of the well and its surrounds. Each cop glanced briefly at the new arrivals, and then continued with what they were doing. Sam looked at the faces of his fellow officers, and was surprised to see he did not recognise any of them.

A fourth plain clothes detective stood apart from the others, talking to a man dressed in jeans, plaid, long sleeve shirt, and wearing a dirty, deeply sweat stained, western style Akubra hat. This had to be the man who found the bodies in the well, Sam guessed.

Near to where the detective was talking to the man, an old model Nissan four-wheel-drive tray top was parked. One fender, on the driver's side, was a different colour to the rest of the vehicle, and large areas of rust were evident at the bottom of the driver's door. As Sam cast his eyes over the vehicle, he doubted it would pass even a casual road worthy inspection.

Besides the vehicle in which Sam, and Foley had come across the dusty, corrugated road to get to the scene, there were three other police vehicles parked near the well including two marked police four-wheel-drives similar to the one Sam and Foley came in, and one unmarked, conventional two-wheel-drive sedan.

A uniformed officer, wearing the chevrons of a Senior Constable, stood sentinel over the bags, and watched Sam approach.

Sam reached out his hand and introduced himself. "Sam Rose,"

"Peter Critchley," the uniformed cop said, shaking Sam's hand.

"Five," Sam said, staring down at the body bags.

"That's it," Critchley confirmed.

Russell Foley stepped up alongside Sam. "G'day Critcher," he shook hands with Critchley.

"It's been a while... Sir," Critchley said, tentatively.

"Out here it's Russell, Critch. We've known each other too long for the '*Sir*' business."

"Okay, thanks," Critchley said.

"What have we got?" Foley asked.

"Five bodies," Critchley announced, indicating the body bags. "All brought up from the bottom," he tilted his head towards the well.

"Male, or female?" Sam asked.

"Definitely one female," Critchley answered, pointing to the biggest of the body bags. "But, given the clothing on the remains, they are almost certainly all female."

"Clothing?" Foley looked at Critchley.

"They are all almost naked, just wearing scraps of underwear... bras, and knickers."

Sam exhaled through clenched teeth. "Jesus!"

Foley stepped closer to the largest of the five body bags. "What's the deal with this one?"

"Obviously the latest," Critchley said. "The others are mostly skeletal remains. Patches of skin, and hair, on bone. Fell to bits when we brought them up. It's gonna take someone a while to determine which bones belong to which girl." He paused, and indicated the bag at Foley's feet. "That one has only partially decomposed. She's definitely female. Hard to tell, but she's probably been in the well a couple of weeks. We'll have a better idea of a time line after the autopsy."

"Any ID?" Sam asked.

"We've still got a man down there," Critchley looked across at the well. "So far, nothing. We'll put a rush on DNA checks, and have a close look at missing person reports. Hopefully we will get a hit on one or more of the bodies."

"Were they killed here, or somewhere else and then dumped in the well?" Foley quizzed.

"Too soon to tell," Critchley answered. "There are dark stains on the stonework at the top of the well which could be blood. We've taken scrapings, but again, we won't know until we get test results."

"Who's the lead on this?" Foley asked.

As if he might have overheard the question, a plain clothes detective stepped up to the small group and stood between Critchley and Foley. "I'm Detective Sergeant Terry Potts." He offered his hand to Foley.

Russell Foley shook the proffered hand. "Detective Inspector Russell Foley," he smiled and indicated Sam. "This is Detective Sergeant Sam Rose."

Potts shook hands with Sam, and turned back to

Foley. "I was informed you would be attending," he announced. "We seem to have things in hand here, and I can bring you up to speed on developments so far."

"That's good to hear," Foley said.

"I understand you will be taking control of the investigation," Potts said.

Foley paused, and cast his eyes towards the well. "I have a feeling I'll live to regret it, but yes, I am." He turned his attention to the civilian being questioned by one of the detectives. "Who's the cowboy?"

Potts followed Foley's gaze. "His name is Thomms." He flipped through the pages of a notebook he took from his shirt pocket. "Michael Thomms. He's a boundary rider... works for Neutral Junction, a cattle station south of here."

"He's a long way from home," Foley observed. "Neutral Junction is down near Barrow Creek, isn't it?"

"Just north of Barrow Creek," Potts nodded. He swept his arm in a large arc. "This land is part of an old station... abandoned years ago. The owners of Neutral Junction bought it recently at a fire-sale price with intentions of extending their holdings." He looked back at Foley. "Apparently he's up here doing the rounds of the numerous fences, and bores, assessing what needs to be done to get the place up and running again as a working cattle station."

"He find the bodies?" Foley asked.

"Yeah. Says he was checking the well, windmill, and trough, assessing the chances of getting it all operational again. Smell got him... thought an animal might have fallen in. He had a torch in his vehicle... took a look, and found the bodies."

"Any water down there?"

"No. Been dry for years, it looks like," Potts said.

"He call it in?" Sam asked.

Potts nodded. "Yeah. There's no mobile phone reception out here, but he carries a satellite phone, supplied by his employer. This is hard country. If he is injured, or has vehicle trouble, he's a long way from help. A sat phone is a must-have accessory."

Sam glanced over at the boundary rider's vehicle. "More likely to be car trouble I think," he mused.

"In his defence," Potts said, "he's only a boundary rider, I don't suppose they would provide him with a Mercedes."

"Is he a suspect?" Foley enquired.

"Not at this stage. Tennant Creek is running a background check on him at the moment. He looks a rough nut, and probably is, but if he killed these girls," Potts indicated the body bags, "I don't see him contacting us and telling us where to find the bodies."

"Stranger things have happened," Foley said.

"How long has he been out here?" Sam asked.

Potts looked at Critchley. "I've got a chap talking to him now, getting a detailed statement, but Critch spoke to him earlier."

All three men looked at Critchley, who adjusted his utilities belt, cleared his throat noisily, and spoke.

"It's a bloody big property," he confirmed. "Nearly a million acres. He said it takes a couple of weeks to get around all the bores and fences. He's been out here a week already. Camps out of his truck... sleeps in a swag on the ground. He brings all his supplies... food, and water, and so forth with him."

"Is there any indication as to how the victims were killed?" Sam asked.

Potts glanced at the body bags and then at Sam. "It

appears they were shot in the head. They all have a hole in the back of the skull. We'll know more after the autopsies."

"He have a gun?" Foley inclined his head towards the man in the cowboy hat.

"Remington .308," Potts answered. "Fully registered, and he has a current shooter's license. Says it's for putting down injured stock. He claims he fired it yesterday. Had to dispatch a kangaroo after it jumped in front of his truck. Said it had a broken leg." He paused. "We have it now, and we'll do the ballistics tests when we get back to Tennant Creek."

"Did you find anything here... spent cartridges for instance?" Sam asked, hopefully.

"Nothing up top," Potts answered. "We have a chap down in the well now, searching the bottom. So far he's found nothing."

"You know," Sam said, looking towards the horizon and distant hills silhouetted against the skyline. "If this is an old cattle station there must be a homestead somewhere."

"Burnt down years ago," Critchley confirmed. "A large fire went through the place and burned the house, and a number of sheds and outbuildings to the ground. Lucky no one was living there at the time."

Foley turned to Sam. "Are you getting at something?"

Sam shrugged. "I dunno... but look at this place. Look at where we are... miles from anywhere. There's nothing here." He looked down at the body bags. "These girls did not just happen to be out here, they had to have been brought here. If a killer wanted to dispose of a body, or bodies in this case, why bring them all the way out here?"

"Because it's isolated, and not likely to be stumbled upon," Foley suggested.

"Mmm... maybe," Sam pondered. "But, I think the killer knew the well was here. I don't buy he was driving around out here in this God-forsaken place hoping to find somewhere suitable to dispose of a body. Regardless of where he's from, there must be a thousand places on the way here he could bury a body where it would never be found. I'm guessing he knew this place was here, he knew it was long abandoned, and he didn't expect anyone... like the cowboy dude over there for instance, to stumble across it."

Foley thought about Sam's theory for a few moments and then responded. "You're right, there are any number of places out here where he could dump a body, so why choose this place?"

Sam shrugged. "Because we never saw anything anywhere else on the way out here, except lots of open space. He would have to bury a body, deep probably, to prevent dingoes from scattering the bones all over the countryside where they might be found one day." He scraped at the ground with the toe of his shoe. "This ground is as hard as cement. Who would want to dig a deep hole in this, let alone *five* deep holes?"

"Good point," Foley acknowledged. He turned to face Critchley, and Potts.

"Are there any people living anywhere within close range of this place?"

Potts and Critchley exchanged glances. "Not that I'm aware of," Potts said. "But then I'm not familiar with this country. I've been up and down the track a number of times in the two years I've been at Tennant Creek, but I've never had reason to travel too far off the highway."

"Me either," Critchley agreed.

All four men turned towards the well as the cop assigned to scour the bottom for evidence appeared at the top of the ladder. He was a big man, wearing police issue overalls he had donned over his uniform. Obviously hot, and uncomfortable down in the depths of the well, damp perspiration stains were evident beneath his arms, and across his chest. He wore a basic first-aid-kit face-mask and, as he surfaced from the well, he paused at the top of the ladder, pulled at the mask, cast it casually aside, and sucked in clean air.

Carrying a large Dolphin torch, and moving with obvious caution lest he lost his footing, he swung his legs over the side of the well and sat for a moment on the edge of the crumbling stonework. With the back of his hand he wiped at the sweat running freely down his forehead, pushed himself off the wall, and leaned against it. Another uniformed cop stepped over to where he rested and handed him a small, plastic bottle of water which he consumed in a matter of seconds.

Potts, Foley, and Sam moved over to the well. The cop in the overalls watched them approach, wiping again at the perspiration on his face.

Potts introduced Sam and Foley. "Ben Adams, meet Inspector Foley, and Sergeant Rose. Adams shook hands with Sam, and Foley, and then proceeded to remove the sweat drenched overalls.

Russell Foley gave him a moment to gather himself and then asked, "Anything of value down there?"

"If you call half-a-metre of dry, hardened sludge valuable, there's plenty of it," Adams answered. "But there is no evidence I could find, other than bones."

"No spent cartridges, personal belongings?" Foley pushed.

"I'm sorry," Adams shrugged. "Everything I found down there is in those bags," he inclined his head towards the body bags.

Sergeant Potts faced Foley. "What's the next step?"

Foley looked around the immediate area. Everyone seemed to have completed whatever task Potts had set for them. Even the detective talking to the boundary rider had finished his interview, and now stood just a few metres away. Foley looked at each man individually for a few seconds, and then turned to face Potts.

"Do you have a plan to get the bodies back to Tennant Creek?"

"In progress," Potts nodded. "A van left Tennant about an hour ago."

"Excellent," Foley said.

"Thomms wants to go," the interviewing detective said.

Foley looked across at the boundary rider, lounging against his vehicle smoking a cigarette. "You've got a detailed statement?" he asked.

The detective waved a notepad. "Three pages," he confirmed.

"Got a contact number for him?"

"His mobile, and his sat phone numbers, as well as contact details at Neutral Junction Station," the detective said.

"Well done," Foley nodded. "Send him on his way, and tell him we may need to speak to him again."

Foley turned back to Potts. "We need to conduct a thorough ground search... everybody in. We'll move in an ever widening circle out from the well... out to about one hundred metres. Obviously the gap between us will get wider as we go, so keep your eyes peeled. Try not to get ahead of the chap next to you. Look for anything that doesn't belong. Gum wrappers, cigarette butts, spent cartridges... anything. If you are not sure of something you find, pick it up, bag it, and tag it. We'll assess its worth later."

"Will you and Sam be coming back to Tennant Creek?" Potts asked.

"No," Foley said. "You can drop us back at Wauchope. We'll stay there and make further enquiries with the pub owner. In my experience publicans are notoriously good sources of information. Our vehicle is there, and we'll make our own way to Tennant Creek tomorrow."

———

By late afternoon, Sam, and Foley were back at Wauchope. They booked into very basic, old, but clean accommodation behind the Wauchope Hotel, and were enjoying a quiet drink before their evening meal.

Sam lifted his first glass and took a long, slow drink of the amber fluid. "Shit that's good!" He lowered the half empty glass to the bar and smacked his lips.

Russell Foley took a somewhat more tentative sip of his beer, and also replaced his glass on the bar. "Nice and cold," he said.

"Sam swiveled on his bar stool and stared at Foley. "Is that all you've got to say... 'nice and cold?'"

"You've known me long enough to know I'm not a big drinker," Foley said, taking another delicate sip.

"It's nice and cold, *and* bloody beautiful!" Sam declared. He drained his glass and signaled to the bartender, who also happened to be the pub owner. "I'll have another beer, if I may."

"Comin' right up," the publican smiled.

"I've been thinking about what you said out at the well... about the killer knowing the well was there," Foley said quietly. He glanced around the small bar. There were eight people in the bar including the publican, himself, and Sam, and he preferred their conversation not be overheard.

"It makes sense," he continued in hushed tones. "But who would know about it? Apparently the place hasn't been a working property for years. It's a long way out there. Whoever dumped those bodies must have known the well was there."

"Did I do good, Boss?" Sam drank from his second beer.

"I would have guessed it myself eventually," Foley smiled.

"I never doubted it for a second, Russ. That's why they pay you the big bucks."

Foley ignored his friend's sarcasm. "So who would know?"

"The boundary rider," Sam suggested.

"Yes, he would know," Foley agreed. "Who else?"

Sam leaned closer to Foley. "The publican?" he suggested covertly.

Foley shrugged. "Maybe."

"And, anyone else who has lived in the area for any length of time," Sam added.

Both men looked around at the other people in the bar. Four drinkers, two men, and two ladies. All appeared to be in their late twenties, or early thirties, and were gathered around a small table at the opposite end of the room from where Sam, and Foley sat at the bar.

Occasionally, a bout of raucous laughter, obviously fueled by copious quantities of alcohol, erupted from the group as one of their number regaled the others at the table with a story they found outrageously humorous.

At the bar, directly opposite Sam, and Foley, a man on his own, lovingly nursed a rum and coke; mostly rum and very little coke, Sam couldn't help but notice. He was of indeterminable age due to a full-face beard, completely disguising any facial features which might, had he been clean shaven, offer a reasonably accurate estimate of how old he was.

His hair was long also, and both the beard, and the hair, appeared in need of a wash. As if to verify this, the man scratched first at his scalp, and then at his beard, with a grubby finger sporting an even dirtier finger nail. Obviously satisfied, he examined the finger, flicked something onto the floor, and returned his attention to his drink.

Despite the smoking laws in effect throughout the Northern Territory making it an offence to smoke in hotels, restaurants, and clubs, the man was either blissfully unaware of the regulations, or simply chose to ignore them. He fumbled in his pocket, removed a packet of tobacco, and expertly rolled a cigarette which he proceeded to smoke, exhaling a cloud of toxic smoke which hung in front of his face, and then began to dissipate under the effects of a ceiling fan turning lethargically high above his head.

"Maybe the old codger at the end of the bar," Sam offered.

"Do you think he could lift a girl over the wall, and drop her down the well?" Foley asked.

"Perhaps not," Sam answered.

"Let's have a word with the publican," Foley suggested.

Shortly, the publican made his way casually to where Sam, and Foley sat. As he approached, he wiped at the bar top, marked with scratches and stains of indeterminable origin, and which could easily be eons old. He stopped in front of Sam and Foley, but continued to wipe the bar in front of them.

"You boys having dinner?" he asked.

"Yeah," Foley said. "What looks good tonight?"

"You're lucky," the publican answered straight-faced. "Tonight we have a choice... steak, egg, and chips, or chips, egg, and steak."

"Wow," Sam smiled. "Tough choice."

"If I were you, I go for the steak, egg, and chips," the publican showed no expression. "Name's Bob," he introduced himself, offering his hand, and shaking with both Sam, and Foley before continuing his bar wiping routine.

Foley sipped at his beer, the glass still more than half full. "Been here long?"

The publican stopped wiping. "Too bloody long," he stated. "But what else am I gonna do? Who'd buy the place? Besides, even if a buyer came along, I'd have to give half what I get to the bloody missus. She took off months ago. Long distance trucker paid her a compliment and swept her off her feet."

"Maybe she'll come back," Sam said.

"I hope not," the publican resumed his wiping. "I miss *him* though, he was a good customer."

Sam, and Foley laughed.

"You two boys are cops, right?" the publican asked.

"Yeah," Foley confirmed. "We're up from Alice Springs."

"Been cops in, and out of here all day, something going on?"

"A bit of trouble out west of here," Foley confirmed.

"Anything you can talk about?"

"Not just yet," Foley said.

"Gonna be staying long?"

"Tonight at least," Foley answered. "We'll reassess the situation tomorrow."

"Well, it's nice to have you with us. If there's anything I can do to help, you just have to ask."

Foley paused. "Maybe there is something you can help us with."

"Shoot."

"How many people live here at Wauchope?" Foley asked.

"The number fluctuates a bit," the publican said. "At the moment there's four of us. Me, old Kenny down there at the end of the bar, and I've got two back-packer girls been working here for about a month now... cooking and cleaning the rooms. They don't stay long. Put a few bucks away to finance the next leg of their trip, and then they move on."

Sam looked passed the publican, at the old man at the opposite end of the bar.

"What's Kenny's story?"

"Kenny's my boots-barman... does all the odd jobs around the place. Unloads the delivery truck, stocks the cool-room, keeps the generator running, keeps the water up to the garden... such as it is. I provide free room, and board, and a small wage in return for his help."

"Has he been with you long?" Sam probed.

"He was here when I bought the place six years ago. He lives in an old donga out the back, past the camp ground."

"What do you know about him?" Foley asked.

"Not much. He's not much of a talker. Some folks would call him a barfly. When he's not out the back working, he's in here drinking. I fixed his room up a bit when I first came here, it was almost falling over. In a box behind a cupboard, I found some old military medals. I asked him about them, and he told me he served in Vietnam, but that was all he was prepared to tell me. Keeps to himself and seems to prefer it that way."

"Does he ever leave the place?" Foley continued to probe.

The publican shrugged. "Once, or twice a year, he goes to Tennant Creek to see a doctor, and fill prescriptions, but he never goes on his own. He doesn't drive. I take him, or one of the staff will drive him there and back. He had a car, when he first came here. Apparently it shit itself a few k's down the track. He managed to get it going, and stopped here. He's been here ever since.

"His old car is out the back, someone pinched the wheels off it years ago, and now it's got weeds growing up through it. I always meant to get rid of it, it's a bit of an eyesore. One of those *must do* things that never gets done."

"You trust him?" Foley asked.

"Like I said, I don't know much about him, even though he's been here for years. He's just... you know...

here." He paused. "But I've never had any reason *not* to trust him... why? Do you suspect him of something?"

"No," Foley said hurriedly. "We're just trying to get a picture of who lives here. Has he got a surname?"

The publican raised his eyebrows. "Of course he's got a surname, everyone's got a surname, unless you're one of those eccentric, no-talent rock star types; most of them have only one name... like Madonna... Prince... Sting, and Bono. What the fuck's that all about?"

"How about Kenny?"

"Watt," the publican said.

"Kenny," Foley repeated. "What's his surname?"

"Yes," the publican nodded.

"Yes what?"

"Yes, Watt," the publican said, his face showing mild confusion.

Sam decided it was an appropriate time to enter the conversation before both men became totally befuddled.

"You two sound like you're doing the old Abbott and Costello skit." He looked at the publican. "How about you spell Kenny's surname for the Inspector... then perhaps we can all move on."

The publican looked from Sam, then to Foley, shrugged and spelt "WATT. His surname is Watt."

"Oh," Foley presented an abashed smile. "Now I'm with you."

"Anyway," the publican continued. "You're barking up the wrong tree if you're looking at Kenny for anything. He's harmless."

"That's good to know," Foley said.

"Happy to help," the publican moved quickly back around the bar, wiping the same area he had just completed. Occasionally he glanced back over his shoulder, and threw a confused frown at Russell Foley.

When the publican had moved out of earshot, Sam looked at Foley. "What do you think?"

"About Kenny?"

"Yeah, about Kenny W-A-T-T," Sam spelt the surname.

"He's probably harmless, like the innkeeper said," Foley shrugged, ignoring Sam's sarcasm. "Still, we might have a word or two with him later."

"Lookin' at him," Sam decided aloud, "the only thing he could kill would be another bottle of rum."

"He has got that look about him," Foley agreed. "What is it about a lot of the Vietnam blokes? That skirmish must have really fucked them up."

"Yeah," Sam said. "And Kenny could well be the poster boy for the FITH."

"Fifth? What is that?" Foley asked.

"Not fifth, as in the number five. It's an acronym," Sam explained. "Stands for *Fucked In The Head*." He looked at Foley. "Not unlike some of the characteristics you display from time to time."

"Is that an attempt to lighten the moment?" Foley enquired.

"If you want it to be," Sam smiled.

"It's not working," Foley announced.

5

Mandy and Veronica filled monotonous hours talking, getting to know each other, and intermittently dozing. They were both hungry and thirsty. Mandy hadn't eaten since lunch time the previous day. She intended to heat a packet of instant noodles when she returned to her car after strolling through the Devil's Marbles, but the stranger put a terrifying end to those plans.

They were sitting on their respective mattresses when they heard the sound of the lock being turned. They clasped hands, and turned to stare, wide eyed and terrified at the door. Not yet dark in the room, the light was fading, and it would soon be difficult, and eventually impossible to see clearly.

A beam of light from the hallway flooded in, casting a narrow, illuminated strip across the wooden floor. The man stepped into the beam, and stopped just inside the room, one hand on the door knob, the other holding a plastic, two litre bottle of water.

"Good evening, ladies," he smiled.

Mandy and Veronica remained silent, their hands

clasped tightly, almost painfully, and stared at the grinning face across the room.

"I thought you might be getting thirsty," the man said. He leaned down, and placed the water bottle on the floor at his feet.

"We're hungry," Mandy said, her voice cracking a little.

"Hungry?" the man said.

"We haven't eaten all day," Mandy added.

"Maybe I'll feed you tomorrow," the man smiled. "If you are good."

"What is that supposed to mean?" Mandy dared to ask.

The man shrugged. "It means maybe I'll feed you tomorrow." He turned his attention to Veronica. "Come with me Veronica."

Veronica whimpered softly. "No, please," she begged.

"Come with me," the man repeated.

Veronica drew even closer to Mandy, and squeezed her hand until Mandy almost cried out with the pain.

"Please... please... please don't take me," Veronica sobbed.

Mandy shook her hand free from Veronica's grasp, and climbed awkwardly to her feet. "Leave her alone," she said to the man.

The man turned his attention to Mandy. "Well, well," he leered. "Just as I suspected, you have guts, girl." He looked back at Veronica, cowering on her mattress. "Get up, Veronica. Don't make me come over there!"

Mandy stepped in front of Veronica, and glared across the space between herself and the man. "Take me... leave her alone."

The man's eyes lingered on Veronica a few seconds longer, and then, he slowly turned his head to stare at Mandy.

"Don't push your luck with me, Miranda," he said threateningly. "Sit the fuck down, and stay out of it! This is between Veronica, and me."

Mandy remained standing. "She's had enough; take me," she insisted.

The man shrugged. "Okay, I was becoming bored with her," layin' there all limp as a rag doll. Might be time for a change... that's why you're here. I was gonna keep her for a bit longer, 'cause she's a pretty good looker. Not as good as you, but not bad. You interest me; you are full of spunk. I like my women with a bit of attitude." He looked back at Veronica. "You lucked out, Veronica. You get a reprieve... for now."

Veronica slumped on her mattress, her back resting against the wall. "Thank you," she murmured softly.

"What was that?" the man asked.

"I wasn't talking to you," Veronica said, slightly louder.

Mandy looked down at Veronica, and nodded, almost unperceptively.

"Thank you," Veronica mouthed, as tears rolled down her face.

Mandy tried to smile in response. She leaned down, and patted Veronica on the shoulder, an action which served only to promote more tears from the other girl.

"Come with me, Mandy," the man ordered.

Mandy looked back at the man standing in the doorway.

"Now, Mandy!" he said, louder this time.

"And if I refuse?" Mandy asked. She tried to sound defiant, but it was difficult when all she could feel was paralysing fear.

"I will come over there, and drag you out of here by the hair. I will beat the crap out of you until you wish you were dead." He paused. "Then, I will fuck you so bad it will take you a week to stand!"

An audible moan escaped Mandy's lips. "You... you don't have to do this," she stammered.

"No I don't," the man smiled. "But I do so enjoy it. Besides, it gets lonely way out here. It's nice to have feminine company."

"Please," Mandy said. "Just let us go. We'll not talk to anyone."

"Yeah, right," the man chuffed. Then he screamed across the room. "GET THE FUCK OVER HERE!" Flecks of spittle flew from his mouth.

Mandy jumped, and she heard Veronica sob loudly behind her. "Okay... okay," she said. She took a few tentative steps toward the door.

As she approached the man, his eyes wandered over her body. One bra strap had slipped off her shoulder, and he lingered on the bare swell of her breasts beneath the constraints of the lacy undergarment. Then, he lowered his eyes to her crotch. Her panties were a pale pink in colour, and very brief. He licked his lips as she stopped a metre in front of him, and crossed her hands in front of her abdomen.

"Wow," the man whispered between pursed lips. "You *are* lovely. This is going to be a fun night." He stepped aside, and beckoned for Mandy to walk through the door into the adjoining hallway.

Mandy hesitated, a delay she instantly regretted.

The man's hand snapped out, grabbed a handful of her hair, and pulled her savagely through the door.

Mandy yelped in pain, and stumbled out into the hallway, collapsing to her knees on the floor. Then, she felt a foot in the middle of her back, and she was forced face down onto a very dirty, smelly, threadbare carpet. Her face rubbed painfully against the rough, gritty carpet pile, and she exhaled loudly as the air was expelled involuntarily from her lungs. The man's foot pressed hard into her back, and she heard him fumbling with the lock as he secured the room, once again locking Veronica inside.

"Okay, Miranda," the man said when he had locked the door. "I'm gonna take my foot from your back now. I want you to stand up, and do exactly what I say. Do you understand?"

"Yes," Mandy mumbled.

"Good girl."

Mandy felt the man's foot lift from her back, and she breathed a little easier.

"Get up," he ordered.

Getting to her feet from her position face down on the floor was awkward and ungainly. It was going to be far worse, and far more indelicate wearing nothing but her underwear.

Mandy turned over, and rose to a sitting position. She rubbed at her face where dirt, grit and Lord knows what other indescribable matter, including carpet mites and bugs, adhered to her face. She tried to stifle a sob, but it escaped, loud and mournful, from somewhere deep inside her. It made her angry. She did not want to show the man any weakness, but she was failing miserably.

"Get up Miranda!" he ordered again.

Mandy looked up at the man, hoping a look of defiance would show the man she was not afraid, despite being more terrified than she ever thought anyone could be. Whatever it was he saw in her eyes, he failed to recognise as defiance, and it served only to make him smile even more lustfully down at her.

"You're trying to be brave," he said. "That must be so hard for you to do given the situation you find yourself in." He leaned forward until his face was very close to hers. "If you don't get up, right now, I promise, you will regret it."

The man's hot, foul breath washed over Mandy's face, and she felt she was going to vomit. She turned her face away from his, and slowly began to push herself up from the floor. He reached down, and offered his hand. Mandy ignored the gesture, and struggled clumsily to her feet. She stood directly in front of him, and, to avoid looking at him, she cast her eyes along the length of the hallway.

———

Mandy remembered little of the hall from the night before when the man brought her here, it was dark then, and her mind was on things other than the decor. Like the room she and Veronica were locked in, this hall also had no furniture. In the centre of the ceiling, which was made of pressed tin and discoloured with age, a single light globe burned dimly, casting deep shadows into the recesses along the length of the passage.

"Turn around, Miranda," the man ordered.

Mandy turned her head, and looked at the man. For the first time, she *really* looked at him, forcing herself to study him as deeply as her circumstances, and her fear, would allow.

He was a big man; tall, and obviously strong and well-built beneath the dirty, unwashed clothing hanging loosely from his frame. She remembered how easily he was able to control her as she struggled against him when he grabbed her at Devil's Marbles.

He wore his hair long, more as a result of neglect as opposed to style, Mandy thought. It hung in lank, greasy, uncombed strands to a length where it touched his ears. The ends were ragged and uneven, as though he might have cut it himself.

His face was unshaven, also an example of poor grooming, Mandy decided. This man could not possibly have a wife, or indeed anyone in his life who cared for him, she thought. If he did, surely such a person would have encouraged him long ago to pay more attention to his personal appearance. His unkempt, disheveled appearance made it difficult to determine his age, but, if she had to guess, she would put him somewhere between forty, and fifty years old.

When he smiled, it was not a smile of a friendly, personable being, but a lust filled leer of a man obviously afflicted with an unhealthy sexual obsession with young women. His teeth were stained a patchy brown colour which might easily have come from years of disregard for the benefits of regular dental hygiene. His breath was not just bad, but seriously so.

As she studied him, he smiled the telling, unctuous smile. Mandy steeled herself, looked the smiling face squarely in the eye, and knew instantly he was a man devoid of a soul, and who would hurt her badly, maybe even kill her in an instant, if she ignored his demands. The very thought of the horrors she was confident he was capable of chilled her to the bone.

"Turn around, Miranda," he said again.

Mandy turned her back on the man, and faced the opposite end of the hallway. In front of her she saw the two large double doors she was forced to enter the previous night. The doors stood open, offering a wide exit to a large, covered verandah leading to the outside of the premises.

In another era, these doors might have offered a welcoming entranceway to a sprawling homestead. Now, they looked old, dirty, and forlorn; a portal to un-thinkable horrors. The stained glass panels in the top half of the doors, obviously a once colorful and elabo-rate addition, were now ingrained with dirt and grime accumulated over many years and now resembled something one might associate with an old, aban-doned haunted house often seen in horror movies.

Mandy felt a hand in the middle of her back, and the man's hot breath against her ear. "Let's go outside, Mandy," he said quietly.

The hand pushed her toward the doors, and Mandy almost stumbled. She began to walk slowly towards the exit, wondering what horrors awaited her outside. Was he taking her outside to kill her? Would she get the opportunity to make a run for it? The man was big, and strong, but was he fit?

Mandy knew she was very fit. She always looked after herself, and could outrun most people, except perhaps a trained athlete. Could she outrun this man? If she tried, where would she run? She didn't even know where she was, or how far she would have to run to reach help.

As if he was reading her mind, the man said, "don't

even think about it, Miranda. You are in bare feet, and wearing just your underwear. You would cut your feet to ribbons on the stony ground, and freeze to death in your undies, and that's if I don't catch you first."

Mandy reached the open doors, and paused. To her right, a single door, also open, led to a kitchen. A light burned in the room, and Mandy could see an old wooden table, two chairs and beyond that, a stove. Her vision of the room was fleeting, but she saw enough to determine it was messy. The room seemed to be filled with rubbish, piles of it.

She felt a cold blast of air blow through the wide doorway, and shivered involuntarily. A hand reached out and grabbed her shoulder.

"Outside," the man ordered.

"It's cold," Mandy complained.

"Of course it's cold, this is the desert," the man explained. "The days are hot, and the nights are freezing. I don't know how long you've been in the Territory, but you should have worked that out by now."

"I would like to put something warm on," Mandy said. "Can I have my clothes?"

"No," he responded. "Just get outside."

Mandy took a few tentative steps, and found herself on the threshold of the open doorway; not in, and not out. She stopped, and peered out into the dark night beyond.

In front of her was a wide expanse of veranda. She estimated the distance from the doorway to the outer edge at approximately three metres. At the far outer edge of the veranda, opposite the doors, a set of steps, she was unable to count how many, led to nothing beyond she could recognise other than darkness.

A dim light burned in the underside of a gal-

vanised iron, bull-nose roof covering the veranda, and
a waist-high wooden railing ran for what she could see
of the length. She stepped out onto a coarse mat, in
front of the entrance way. The mat was rough, and
prickly under her bare feet. She stepped off it, onto
slatted, timber floor boards.

Immediately to her left was a small, round, table,
and two metal chairs. On top of the table there stood a
bottle of Bundaberg Rum, two glasses, a packet of tobacco, and an ashtray filled with cigarette butts. The
top of the table was Formica, chipped, cracked and
peeling. It looked as if it had not been cleaned, or even
had so much as a cursory wipe down, in a very long
time.

"Sit down." The man's voice startled her in the
stillness of the surrounding night.

"Wha... what?" Mandy stammered.

"Sit down," the man repeated, pushing her in the
back again.

Mandy stepped across to the chair closest to where
she stood in the doorway. She paused, and moved
to sit.

"Not there," the man said. "Sit in the other chair."

Mandy looked at him questioningly, moved to the
other chair, and sat. She took a moment to look out to
her front. The sky was dark now, and getting darker by
the minute, too dark to distinguish anything further
than a few metres beyond the veranda railing.

There was nothing. No outbuildings she could see,
no vehicles, nothing but a cold darkness descending
rapidly like a dense fog over the house. And, it was
cold. The man was right, she had been in the
Northern Territory long enough to know, at this time
of the year, in this part of the country, the temperature

at night regularly dropped to freezing, or below. Mandy shivered, and wrapped her arms around her upper body in a vain attempt to warm herself against the chill.

The man sat in the chair opposite, and poured two glasses of rum from the bottle. Mandy watched him pour, and couldn't help but notice the glasses looked smudged and dirty.

"Cheers," the man said, lifting his glass in a salute.

Mandy sat stoic, and silent, staring out at the blackness.

"Have a drink, Miranda," he invited, nodding at the glass in front of her.

"No, thank you," Mandy said.

"You don't drink?" he asked.

"Not rum," Mandy said.

"What do you drink?"

"Som... sometimes wine," Mandy mumbled.

"Sorry, I don't have any wine. Drink the rum."

"No," Mandy said, louder than she intended.

The man took a long sip of his drink, smacked his lips, placed his glass back on the table, and leaned across the gap separating them.

"Drink the fuckin' rum!" he snarled.

Mandy shrank away from his leering face, and his rum tinted breath. "I... I don't like rum," she stammered.

The man sat back in his chair, picked up his glass, and took another drink. "I don't care if you like it or not. Drink it. We are having a nice night together. Just you and me. I want you to enjoy yourself. Have a drink with me. It will make me happy."

The last thing Mandy wanted to do was make this man happy. Albeit having dedicated her short working life to date tending and caring for the sick and injured, right now she wanted to kill him, and she felt if the opportunity arose she would not hesitate. She looked down at her glass, and tentatively picked it up. As she brought the drink closer to her face she could smell the sickly sweet aroma of the rum, and see grubby finger marks all over the glass. If the rum didn't make her sick, the germs in, and on the glass, would, she thought.

She lifted the glass to her lips, closed her eyes, and took a small sip. She held the warm liquid in her mouth for a moment, reluctant to swallow. Eventually she had to take a breath, and the rum slid down her throat, burning all the way to her gut. She gagged, and almost brought it back up. She coughed, spluttered, and speckles of brown syrupy saliva flew from her lips.

"See, that wasn't so bad, was it?" the man asked, seemingly enjoying her discomfort. "Have another one, it gets better," he smiled.

"No... no thank you," Mandy said. "I can't... I don't like the taste."

"Don't make me come around there and pour it down your throat," the man threatened.

Mandy took another cautious sip.

"There you go. I knew you would enjoy it." He fumbled with the packet of tobacco and rolled himself a cigarette.

"Please... it's cold. I want to go inside," Mandy pleaded.

The man lit his cigarette, and took a deep drag. "I know you do, and we will. Soon. I promise. Finish your drink, and we will go inside. Tonight is going to be so special."

His words sent a new wave of dread through

Mandy. What did that mean? What horrors awaited her when they went back inside the house? She raised her glass to her lips, and pretended to take another sip of the rum. She stared out into the darkness in front of the house, and briefly thought about leaping over the railing and making a run for it. What if she hurt herself jumping over the railing? What if she broke her ankle, or worse? She quickly discarded the idea. She had no idea exactly where she was, or which way to run if she did survive the jump unscathed. Besides, the man was right; she wore no shoes, and she was dressed in her underwear.

Perhaps she could delay the inevitable. Perhaps she could get drunk on the rum, and pass out. Maybe then he wouldn't touch her. She glanced across the table at him. He was watching her with the same lecherous, sickening smile, displaying his black, rotting teeth. She dry-retched, and turned her head away. Tears began to fall from her eyes, and run down her cheeks.

The man stubbed out his cigarette in the overflowing ashtray, picked up his glass, and drained the contents in one long swallow.

"Okay, Mandy. Let's go inside."

He stood, moved around the table, and stood in front of her. "Come on, we'll have fun. You'll be nice and warm soon." He reached down and grabbed Mandy by the arm. As he did, Mandy's drink spilled, and rum slopped onto her bare thigh.

"Oops!" the man smiled. "You spilled your drink. Never mind, I'll lick it off for you."

Mandy immediately rubbed vigorously at her thigh. "No... no, it's all right," she said. "I've got it." She sobbed aloud, Her body involuntarily followed the momentum of the man's pulling, and she rose from her chair. The man released his grip on her arm, took hold of her hand, and squeezed hard. Mandy tried to pull away. The man squeezed harder, and she yelped loudly with the pain.

The man dragged her roughly back into the house. Mandy resisted but knew it was hopeless. The man was just too strong. This was it. This was what Veronica warned her about. The man was going to rape her. Mandy wanted to scream, but no one would hear her—no one except Veronica, securely locked in the other room. Screaming was not going to alter the situation she found herself in, other than to antagonise the man even more.

The man dragged Mandy back into the house. With his foot, he kicked the double doors shut behind them, and pulled her along the hallway.

"Please... please don't do this," Mandy begged when he stopped in front of the room she feared was his bedroom. It had to be his bedroom, she decided. That was all it could be. She assumed she and Veronica were being held in one bedroom, and the house had to have at least another. The man had to sleep somewhere.

Ignoring her pleas, the man shoved her roughly into the darkened room. She stumbled forward, almost falling. Suddenly, the room was flooded with light. He had followed her inside and flicked the light switch.

Mandy gasped in horror at what confronted her. Directly to her front, just a metre or so away, was a large, four-poster bed. Like something from a gothic film set, everything was black; the canopy over the bed, the bed head, the bed spread, even the carpet covering the floor was mostly all black. Hundreds of tiny, red, diamond shaped symbols forming a mosaic type pattern across the carpet were the only things breaking up the ugly, uninviting blackness of the floor covering.

Mandy looked back at the bed, and stared at the pillows; four of them, two on each side, one black, and one red. She could be exhausted to the point of collapse and she could never sleep in this bed, she thought.

She door closed behind her, and she spun around. He was right there, grinning madly at her, unbuttoning his shirt. Mandy glimpsed a tuft of chest hair exposed beneath.

"Oh no... don't do this," she cried.

The man continued unbuttoning. "Take your underwear off, Mandy," he breathed heavily.

"No... please," Mandy shrank away until her backside hit the foot of the bed.

"Take them off, or I will," he demanded. "If I take them off, I will rip them to shreds, and you will remain naked for the rest of your time here."

Mandy dropped her head. Tears ran freely, and she sobbed mournfully. Defeated, she moved her hands to her bra straps, and lifted them from her shoulders.

6

The rooms at the rear of the Wauchope Hotel consisted of a row of tiny box-like structures containing nothing more than a single bed, a small bedside table, one chair, and a small screen television mounted on a bracket attached to the wall opposite the bed.

Originally built to house workers from the Wolfram mine, these were not four or five star accommodations, and in most cases hardly two-star. There were no facilities to prepare a cup of coffee, or even a sink with a tap to get a drink of water. As for bathroom amenities, when a guest decided to retire for the night, he or she had to make sure they used the toilet provided in a small ablution block attached to the back of the hotel, or they would have to go out in the cold if the urge to pee came during the night.

Sam Rose was one of those unfortunate souls who had to avail himself of these amenities in the very early, cold, pre-dawn hours, and doing so did nothing to enhance his already negative impression of the Wauchope Hotel and the questionable facilities it offered the weary traveler.

He woke early, and lay, uncomfortable on the lumpy mattress watching the early morning news broadcast on television. Frustrated following a sleepless night, he tried watching television. The picture pixilated and flickered erratically and eventually dropped out completely leaving him staring in anticipation at a blank screen. As his frustration peaked, he got up, and quickly dressed in the cold morning air. He grabbed a small toiletries bag from his luggage, and exited his room, making for the bathroom, thirty metres from his door.

When he entered, Russell Foley was at one of the hand basins, shaving. He looked up when the door opened.

"Good morning, Sam," he greeted, his tone light, almost jovial.

"Hmph!" Sam chuffed.

"Tough night?" Foley asked.

"Bloody lucky if I got more than three hours sleep," Sam complained. "Mattress had more lumps and bumps than the road out to the well we traveled yesterday. And," he added, "I had to get up twice for a piss. Try doing that at three o'clock in the morning when it's minus a thousand-fuckin'-degrees outside."

Russell Foley smiled and resumed shaving. "I don't suppose the beer you drank last night had anything to do with that?"

"Yeah, probably," Sam nodded. He placed his toiletries bag on a sink next to Foley, and crossed to the urinal. "How did you sleep?" he asked Foley.

"Like a log," Foley answered. "My bed was soft, and comfortable, and I never had to get up once."

"Bastard!" Sam cursed. He finished what he was doing, and returned to the sink. "What's the plan?"

"No plan," Foley announced, rinsing his razor. "I'm hoping we will hear from Potts with a preliminary Coroner's report, and go from there."

———

Russell Foley's phone rang. He fumbled in his pocket, flipped the phone open, and spoke. "Russell Foley."

"Inspector Foley?" a voice on the other end asked.

"Yes," Foley confirmed.

"Sergeant Potts here."

"Good morning, Terry, what have you got?" Foley asked.

"Well, it's early days yet, but I requested a rush on pathology, and we have a preliminary report."

"Excellent, that's quick work," Foley said. "What do we know?"

"The report covers just one set of remains, and the autopsy is not complete, so it's preliminary, and short on detail," Potts stressed.

"Give it to me anyway," Foley ordered.

"Okay," Potts began. "The report is for the last body, the partially decomposed remains. The girl has been dead for about a week to ten days, it's too soon to determine an exact time of death, and besides, the pathologist thinks the body being down in the well would have protected it somewhat from the elements, and would have had an effect on the decomposition rate."

"What else?" Foley probed, jotting notes in a small notebook.

"Obviously female," Potts continued. "Approximately eighteen to twenty-five years of age, it's too early to tell more accurately. She died from a gunshot wound to the back of the head."

"Did he find the bullet?" Foley asked.

"Yes," Potts confirmed. "I have sent it to ballistics for identification but it looks like twenty-two calibre."

"A bloody pea shooter," Foley commented.

"Powerful enough to kill at close range, particularly a head-shot," Potts said.

"Anything in Missing Person reports?" Foley asked hopefully.

"We have been going through them, and a list of possible names is being prepared as we speak. I'll have it sent down to you as soon as it's completed. Are you still at Wauchope?"

"Yes," Foley answered. "We'll be here for another day or so. I think the killer has to be someone from the area, someone with a bit of local knowledge."

"Sounds plausible," Potts said. "We can spare a couple of guys if you want extra feet on the ground."

"Thanks, Terry," Foley said. "Sam and I have it under control for the moment, but I'll call you if we need help."

"There is one peculiar thing about the bodies," Potts said.

"What's that?" Foley asked, his interest piqued.

"It seems they were dressed only in their underwear when they were thrown in the well. I'm not sure what that tells us about what might have happened to them prior to them being shot"

"We can only imagine," Foley commented.

"We recovered five pairs of lady's knickers, and five bras," Potts continued.

"No other clothing?" Foley asked.

"No," Potts confirmed.

"Sounds to me like the work of a sexual predator," Foley speculated.

"We are looking through our records for any registered sex offenders living anywhere in the area."

"Any history of such a character in the area?" Foley probed.

"Nothing that stands out," Potts answered. "Apart from the occasional sexual assault case, of course. We have people going through old files as we speak, but so far we have no single offender with multiple offences to his name."

"Keep looking, Terry," Foley instructed. "There has to be something, somewhere."

"Okay, will do," Potts said. "Those reports will be with you soon."

"Oh, one more thing," Foley said hurriedly.

"What's that?" Potts asked.

"Run a name check for us will you?"

"Sure, what's the name?"

"Surname is Watt; Whiskey, Alpha, Tango, Tango. Christian name probably Kenneth... goes by the name, Kenny."

"Middle name?" Potts asked.

"Not known," Foley answered.

"Okay, I'll run it through the system and let you know."

"Thanks again, Terry. Stay in touch. I'll talk to you later."

Russell Foley disconnected the call, looked at his notes for a moment, and then at Sam, who sat opposite him at a small table in the hotel dining room. They had just finished breakfast, and were lingering over their second cup of coffee for the morning.

Sam was slowly beginning to show signs of recovery from his sleepless night. "Any developments?" he asked.

"One partial autopsy completed at this stage... on the most recent body," Foley said. He referred to his notes. "Female, eighteen to twenty-five, gun-shot to the head, possibly a twenty-two calibre. A list of reported missing persons will be down here in a couple of hours."

"That's it?" Sam asked. "What about the 'sexual pervert' thing?"

Foley looked back at his notes. "As we discovered yesterday, all the remains were virtually naked, dressed only in knickers and bras."

"Why do I get the feeling this is not going to be a slam dunk?" Sam said.

"How many 'slam dunks' do we get in this business?" Foley asked.

Sam nodded. "Not many." He swallowed the remains of his coffee. "So what now?"

"Now we wait for the preliminary reports to arrive from Tennant Creek. In the meantime, we can nose around the area, turn over a few rocks, and see what crawls out."

"This is a great job, isn't it?" Sam suggested, mildly sarcastically.

———

Kenny Watt heard Sam and Foley approach. He was emptying one of the several rubbish bins strategically placed throughout the camping ground into a large dumpster behind the hotel. He never looked up from his work. Kenny was not the type to invite or attract attention. He was a loner, and he preferred it that way.

Kenny was one of those people who seemed to be perfectly comfortable with his own company. He decided long ago, talking was for those who had something interesting to say, or for those who simply liked the sound of their own voice. Besides, he prescribed to the theory, most people, at least most of those with whom he had ever conversed at any length, seemed to talk a lot but say very little of any significance.

The two strangers who arrived yesterday were cops. He could pick a cop a mile away. Who dressed the way these two did out in this country if they weren't cops? He figured they would be wanting to talk to him sooner or later. It wouldn't be the first time he had spoken with members of the constabulary. He seemed to attract them. Had to be the way he looked. He was hardly the poster boy for the quintessential, clean cut Aussie male.

He banged the bin on the lip of the dumpster, shaking loose the last of the contents sticking persistently to the inside. He looked inside and, satisfied the bin was empty, swung it down to his side, and stepped away from the dumpster. The two cops stood in his path.

Kenny side-stepped, intending to walk around the cops. One of them stepped in front of him, blocking his path. Kenny stopped, and looked the cop in the eye.

"Excuse me," he said quietly and stepped around the cop.

Sam stepped with him, and again blocked his path.

"Kenny," he said. "Can we have a word?"

"I'm busy," Kenny said.

"I can see that," Sam said. "We won't keep you

long. We would like to ask you a few questions." Sam flashed his identity card. "I'm Detective Sergeant Sam Rose," he indicated Foley. "This is Detective Inspector Russell Foley."

Kenny glanced at the identity card. "You don't need that thing," he scoffed. "You two characters stand out like a dog's nuts."

Sam looked at Foley. Foley winked at Sam. Sam looked back at Kenny.

"Dog's nuts?" he asked.

Kenny shrugged. "You know what I mean... your choice of occupation is obvious."

Guessing Kenny's age would be just that, a guess. Given the publican indicated he was a Vietnam Veteran, he had to be over sixty years old, probably closer to seventy, Sam thought. His face, partially obscured by a beard, thick but not lush, would likely present an impression to the casual observer that Kenny had not shaved, nor groomed his whiskers for a considerable time; perhaps not since the eighties, Sam thought. Tiny specks of unidentifiable matter clung to the beard at the edges of Kenny's mouth; the remains of a meal hastily consumed, Sam continued to speculate. Kenny was a man who obviously held little regard for self-image.

At the outer edges of his eyes, deep, weathered lines, the valleys dark with built up grime, radiated outwards, and downwards, almost disappearing behind the scruffy whiskers. Sam guessed, without the beard, Kenny's face would resemble a map of the rough, hard roads he had traveled in getting to this place.

"I understand you've been here a few years," Sam said.

"That a question, or a statement?" Kenny wondered aloud.

"Let's call it a question," Sam smiled.

"In that case, yes."

"Yes? Yes, what?" Sam asked, becoming a tad frustrated.

Kenny shrugged. "Yes, I've been here a few years."

"I suppose you have seen a lot of people come through here," Sam said.

Kenny remained silent. He stared blankly at Sam.

"Well?" Sam asked.

"Well what?"

"I suppose you have seen a lot of people come through here," Sam repeated.

"Oh," Kenny said. "I didn't realise that was also a question. I thought you were making a statement."

"Are you trying to antagonise me?" Sam asked, a serious edge developing in his tone.

"No, Sir," Kenny shook his head. "I don't reckon there's a lot to be gained by antagonising a police officer."

Sam smiled. "You got that right, Kenny."

Kenny lowered the bin to the ground, and fumbled in the pocket of a faded, baggy pair of shorts, below which two very scrawny, weathered, and tanned legs protruded. Eventually he produced a half smoked cigarette, put it to his lips, and relit it with a lighter he found in the same pocket. The cigarette, bent in the middle, hung from his lips, and a thin tendril of smoke wafted in front of his face.

"What do you want to know?" he asked.

Russell Foley stepped forward, and stood next to Sam.

"Is there anyone, a man, a loner maybe, living on

his own, who frequents the area?"

Kenny looked stony faced at Foley. "You mean a man like me?"

"Well... yeah... kinda," Foley sounded embarrassed.

"People come, and people go," Kenny shrugged. "Some stay a day or two and then move on. They come mostly to see the Devil's Marbles."

"You mean tourists?" Foley asked.

Kenny threw Foley a look which said *what a dumb question.* "Yeah... tourists," he said.

"Anyone who might *not* be a tourist?" Sam posed. "Anyone who comes back every so often?"

Kenny shrugged. "Ringers, maybe... you know... station hands."

"Yeah, we know what a ringer is, Kenny," Sam said. "Is there any *one* ringer who springs to mind?"

"No. They come in, get drunk, sleep it off in one of the dongas, and leave the next day," Kenny explained.

"What do you do here?" Foley asked, changing tack.

"Odd jobs," Kenny shrugged.

"For board, and keep, right?"

"Yeah."

"You've been here a long time... you know, just doing odd jobs," Foley observed.

Kenny offered another of his shrugs. "I like it here. It's quiet. And..." he looked from Foley to Sam... "generally nobody bothers me."

"You married, Kenny?" Sam asked.

"Not anymore." Kenny answered.

"Did it end badly?" Sam probed.

Kenny paused "You could say that."

"Was there someone else?"

"No."

"What happened?" Sam pressed.

"I'd rather not talk about it." Kenny lifted his eyes and stared at Sam.

"Why not?"

"Because I don't see what it has to do with anything."

"You should let us decide that," Sam advised.

Kenny shrugged.

"What happened?" Sam asked again.

"She died," Kenny said.

Sam shuffled uncomfortably. "I'm sorry."

"Why? It wasn't your fault." Kenny picked up the rubbish bin, stepped aside, and walked away.

Foley and Sam stared at Kenny's back as he walked away.

Foley turned to Sam. "Nice job, Sherlock."

"I'm tired," Sam offered, as though it might offer mitigation for his line of questioning.

"Now I'll ask you the same question you asked me. What do *you* think about Kenny?" Foley probed.

"I think he's a broken down old digger who has seen more than his share of the worst life has to offer. Then, on top of all that, he lost his wife, and this is how he deals with it. I'm gonna apologise to him again later."

"Good for you, Sam," Foley smiled. He reached out and patted Sam on the shoulder. "You're not the insensitive bastard people say you are."

Sam looked at Foley. "Do people really say that?"

Foley started to walk towards the hotel. "Only every day."

———

Foley fumbled with the large, brown envelope, ripped open the seal, and took out the preliminary report he and Sam were waiting on. It arrived mid-morning, hand delivered by a uniformed patrol officer from Tennant Creek.

Foley flipped through the pages, giving them a cursory glance before taking a longer, more focused look at the contents. As he completed a page, he handed it to Sam.

Foley's phone rang. "Russell Foley," he answered.

"Terry Potts again, Sir."

"Hello, Terry," Foley greeted.

"Have the reports arrived?" Potts asked.

"Just now," Foley confirmed. "We are going through them as we speak."

"Have you noticed the pattern?" Potts asked.

"Pattern?" Foley queried.

"With the Missing Person report," Potts said.

Foley flicked through the pages he still held, looking for the Missing Person details. "No. They arrived a few minutes ago, and we haven't had time to study them in detail. Why?"

"There appears to be a pattern in regards to girls going missing in the area dating back twelve months or so," Potts announced.

"That's interesting," Foley said. "Fill me in."

"Well," Potts began, "it seems there are at least six young women who have gone missing from the area. Their details, sketchy as they are, are in the report. We are working on a more detailed analysis at the moment, and I will get back to you as soon as we know something more definite."

"Six?" Foley said. "There were only five bodies in the bottom of the well."

"That's correct," Potts said.

"What do you make of that?" Foley asked.

"Maybe the sixth girl is not missing, and is frolicking happily on a beach somewhere," Potts offered.

"I hope you're right," Foley said. "Sam and I are going to have a close look at the list, and please call me as soon as you have anything further."

"Will do," Potts agreed.

Russell Foley disconnected the call, and turned to Sam. "The plot thickens," he said.

"Do tell," Sam responded.

"We have six girls, all reported missing over the last twelve months, and all went missing from somewhere in the area," Foley reported as he rummaged through the papers.

"This will be it," Sam said, holding up a two-page Missing Person report. He started to read aloud.

"Astrid Bengtsson, twenty-five-year old Swedish back-packer. Last seen at Tennant Creek while hitch-hiking to Alice Springs to meet up with a traveling companion. Next was Susan Mitchell, twenty-three-years-old from Brisbane. She was working as a cook at Wycliff Wells." He paused, and read a little further. "Next was Karin Albrecht from Hamburg in Germany. She was traveling with her boyfriend when she disappeared from Barrow Creek. Then Gabrielle Didier, twenty-two-year-old French back-packer traveling with her nineteen-year-old sister also disappeared from Wycliff Wells. Followed by twenty-year-old Janice Clarke from Adelaide, traveling alone. Her car was discovered broken down, thirty kilometres south of Tennant Creek. Lastly, Veronica Cooper, another Aussie girl, from Tasmania. She was reported missing three weeks ago." He paused looked at Foley. "Six MP's and only five bodies."

"Maybe there's no connection with the sixth one... what's her name?" Foley paused.

Sam referred to the Missing Person report. "Veronica Cooper."

"Right," Foley said. "Maybe there's no connection with Veronica and the five bodies."

"We've both been on the job long enough to know coincidences like that are rare," Sam said.

"Yeah, I know," Foley nodded. "If she's another victim, the perp either still has her, or he dumped her body somewhere else."

Sam agreed. "Either way, we have to find her, and soon."

"We need to go back out to the well," Foley said. "We need to go over the place with a fine tooth comb. There has to be something there we missed."

"We are going to need more manpower," Sam suggested.

"Yeah," Foley agreed. "I'll contact Alice Springs, and see if we can get the Task Force up here."

"Bloody Task Force," Sam chuffed. "Couldn't find their dicks on a dark night."

"Be that as it may," Foley responded. "We need feet on the ground up here."

Russell Foley took a few moments to read the autopsy report on the most recent victim.

"This is brief," he said. "But it says the latest victim has been dead for about a fortnight. It's too soon to be certain, but if she turns out to be the last missing person on the list, I'm willing to bet the other bodies will match four other names on that list."

"Leaving us one MP unaccounted for," Sam suggested. He quickly scanned the Missing Person report. "If the latest victim is Janice Clarke," he continued. "twenty-years-old, from Adelaide. Then we are looking for Veronica Cooper."

"Yeah," Foley nodded. "If it turns out the latest victim *is* Janice Clarke,

"Curious," Sam suggested.

"Indeed," Foley agreed. "But let's not jump the gun. Let's wait until we get a more detailed report, and then we can decide what our next move will be."

"Can we at least work on the assumption the perp is local?" Sam asked.

"Yes, we can," Foley agreed. "The trouble is, local can mean anywhere between Tennant Creek and Alice Springs. Where do we start?"

"You're asking me?" Sam smiled. "You're the one getting paid the big bucks, remember?"

"Be careful," Foley warned. "I have the power to have you transferred back into uniform."

"You might have the power," Sam agreed. "But, you can't do this without me, who's going to do all the dirty jobs you blokes with a couple of dobs of bird shit on your shoulders think are beneath you now you've reached the dizzy heights of officer rank."

Foley looked long, and hard at Sam. "You're right," he nodded. "And, when we go back out to the crime scene, I'm gonna make you go down in the well."

"Why don't I buy you a cup of coffee?" Sam asked.

Foley patted Sam on the shoulder. "Now you're getting the idea. It's called brown-nosing to the boss. Can you afford a nice blueberry muffin as well?"

"Okay, but I have my limits, so don't be pushing your luck beyond coffee and a muffin."

"Sounds like a plan," Foley smiled

7

Miranda groaned. The pain was excruciating. It came in throbbing waves, washing over her in a seemingly endless succession of stabbing pains deep in her groin. She found it difficult to stand, and she wanted desperately to lie down and never get up.

The man gripped her arm tight, and shoved her in front of him as he guided her towards the door to what had become her prison. Locked in a fog of pain and a deep sense of incomprehension, she seemed to have lost all sense of reality. All she could think about was the unrelenting pain.

As if she had mentally stepped aside from reality, and was mysteriously conveyed to another place, she hardly noticed as the man unlocked the door, and shoved her forcefully into the room. When she stumbled, and fell heavily to her knees, she fully realised where she was.

She hugged her stomach against yet another wave of pain, and fell forward until her forehead cracked hard on the floor. Seconds seemed like minutes until she heard the door lock behind her, and she finally, slowly lifted her head, and squinted into the gloom embracing the big room.

Outside, dawn was breaking. A thin shaft of early morning light filtered in through the window at the far side of the room, and as Mandy stared into the darkness, she became aware it was beginning to lighten gradually. Had she been with the man all night? She couldn't remember, didn't want to remember.

All she knew was the man raped her. Not once, but over, and over, until she could no longer remember how many times the brutal abuse continued. Somehow, the night had passed without her realising it. She had managed, somehow during the assault, to disassociate from the reality of what was happening to her. That had to be a positive thing, she thought.

Through the gloom, she saw a shape across the room. As she watched, the darkness in the room faded gradually, and she saw Veronica sitting on her mattress watching her.

Mandy stared across at Veronica, and an involuntary sob emerged from somewhere deep inside her. She wanted to vomit. And one hand shot to her mouth as she began to dry heave. Desperate, she looked around the room, hoping to see the toilet bucket.

Then she saw the small, dark shape in the darkest corner on the other side of the room. She focused on it for a moment, and wondered if she could even make it across there. She had to move, if she didn't she was going to throw up on the floor. Carefully, painfully, she crawled on her hands and knees towards the bucket, her knees scraping painfully on the hard wooden floor.

Finally, she was there. She leaned forward over the

top of the bucket, and retched noisily. A thin, watery stream of hot bile gushed from her mouth, and splashed into the bucket, mixing with the urine it already contained. It seemed her retching would never stop, and it continued, exacerbated by the strong ammonia stench emanating from the bucket, until she felt her insides would surely spew from her mouth, and drop into the disgusting container.

When the retching finally slowed, and eventually stopped altogether, she collapsed, exhausted and defeated onto the floor, next to the stinking bucket. She drew her knees into the fetal position, sobbed loudly, and silently prayed she would simply die and the nightmare would be over.

Veronica got up from her mattress, and padded across the room to where Miranda lay. She knelt next to Mandy, and gently rubbed her bare shoulder. Mandy lifted her head, and rested it on Veronica's knee. Both girls remained silent; words somehow seemed unimportant and unnecessary. Eventually Mandy forced herself to a sitting position, and leaned heavily into Veronica who immediately embraced her, and held her tight. Both girls began to sob softly.

"Shh... shh," Veronica crooned. "It's going to be all right. The pain will stop."

"Wh... when?" Miranda sobbed.

"In a little while," Veronica reassured.

"It hurts," Mandy moaned.

"I know... I know," Veronica said, holding Mandy tighter. "Come on, come back to the bed and lie down. You need to sleep."

Veronica helped Miranda to her feet, and guided her slowly, gently across to the mattresses.

"Here, lie down. Close your eyes. Try to sleep." She

gently lowered Mandy to the mattress, sat down next to her, and held her hand until she finally fell into a fitful, dream disturbed sleep.

————

Miranda opened her eyes, and blinked against the light flooding into the room. For a few moments, she was confused and disorientated. She rubbed at her eyes, forced herself to focus on her surroundings, and saw Veronica, sitting very close to her, watching her.

"Hi," Veronica said softly.

"What time is it?" Mandy asked.

"I don't know," Veronica shrugged. "About noon, I think... or early afternoon."

"How long have I been asleep?"

"Five... maybe six hours," Veronica answered.

"Has he been back?"

"No, but he will be. We need to eat. We need water to drink... and we need to empty the bucket," Veronica said.

Mandy forced herself to sit up. "What do you mean?" Mandy asked.

"We have to do it," Veronica confirmed. "He makes one of us take it out and empty it."

"How often?"

"Every couple of days."

"Maybe that's our chance to escape," Mandy suggested, a tiny glimmer of hope developing in her mind.

"He only takes one of us, and he locks the other one in here," Veronica explained. "He waits outside the toilet while the bucket is emptied, and then he brings you back here. It's hopeless."

Mandy laid back down and closed her eyes.

"How are you feeling?" Veronica asked.

"It still hurts," Mandy said.

"It will get better," Veronica promised.

"Only until the bastard does it again," Mandy supposed aloud.

"I'll be next," Veronica's voice seemed distant.

Mandy sat up, and reached out to Veronica. "Maybe not," she tried to sound reassuring.

"Yes I will," Veronica explained. "He knows he hurt you. He hurts us all. That's why he mostly has two of us here. So he can let one rest while he has his way with the other one."

The two girls embraced.

"We have to get out of here," Mandy said, determinedly.

"There's no way out," Veronica insisted. She looked up at the window. "Believe me, I've talked about it with the girl before you. There's no way out."

Mandy looked around the room. She cast her eyes up and down the walls, across the high ceiling, over to the door, and then back to the window. Nothing immediately sprang to her mind, so she repeated the process, taking longer this time, her eyes lingering long, and intense on every square inch of the room. Then, she studied the floor, looking for a weakness, any weakness; a loose floor board, a hole in the floor boards, anything which might offer hope. She found nothing. Even when she encouraged Veronica to help her move the mattresses so she could look at the floor underneath, she found nothing, only her car keys she had hidden beneath her mattress. Dejected, she tossed the keys aside, and slumped back on her bed. "There has to be something... some way we can get away from this place," Mandy insisted.

"There's no way," Veronica said. "It's hopeless."

They sat in dispirited silence; each lost and pre-occupied with their own personal thoughts. Both girls started when they heard the lock on the door slide open.

———

The man stood in the open doorway. He placed a large, five litre plastic water bottle on the floor just inside the door. Then he produced a wrapped parcel, and put it down next to the water bottle. He looked across the room at both girls and smiled.

"Lunch is served, ladies," he announced. He stepped back out of the room and began to close the door.

"The bucket needs emptying!" Veronica called.

He stepped back inside the room. "Bring it, Veronica," he ordered.

Veronica got up from her mattress, hurried across the room, picked up the bucket, and moved over to the door. She stopped in front of the man who leaned sideways, and looked around her at Miranda.

"How are you, Miranda?" he asked.

Miranda met his eyes from across the room. "I'm hurt. You hurt me you arsehole!" she spat.

The man smiled. "You'll get over it, my dear. Then you'll be back for more."

"No I won't. You touch me again... or Veronica... I will kill you!"

The man laughed. "Really... and exactly how are you going to manage that little feat?"

Mandy glared at him across the space separating them. "I don't know how, but I *will* kill you!"

The man reached out and grabbed Veronica roughly by the arm. Veronica jumped, and a small amount of the contents of the bucket slopped over the side, onto the floor. The man raised his free hand, formed a fist and drew it back to punch her.

Veronica tried to shy away from the pending punch. "No... no don't," she moaned. "I'll clean it up, I promise. Please don't hit me."

Miranda pushed herself to her feet and took a step toward the door.

"Stop, Miranda!" the man cried. "Stop right there. One more step, and Veronica gets hurt... bad!"

Mandy stopped. She raised her hands defensively. "Okay... okay... don't hit her... don't hit her," she pleaded.

The man paused, and glared across at Miranda. "Smart girl, Miranda. Smart girl." He turned his attention to Veronica, and pulled her through the open door. Just before he slammed it shut, he looked back at Miranda. "Enjoy your lunch, Miranda." He leered across the distance. "I made it with love."

Miranda watched the door close, and heard the lock slide shut, locking her alone inside the room. She waited for a few moments, staring transfixed at the locked door. She wondered if Veronica was going to suffer the same fate she had just been through, and then wondered how it could be possible.

She did not know how many times the man had raped her; she stopped counting, and caring, after the third time. Surely he had to be just as tired as she was. Surely he wouldn't... couldn't, do that to Veronica so soon after the monstrous events of the previous night. The bastard never stopped. Where did he get the stamina? He had to be taking something, drugs maybe, illegal or otherwise. Nobody could be that brutal, that cruel and sadistic, and not be on a chemical stimulant of some description. Could they?

———

Veronica was gone just a few minutes when the door unlocked and swung open again. Shoved from behind, Veronica stumbled awkwardly into the room. She carried the empty toilet bucket, and when she had regained her footing she carried it back across the room and placed it in its usual place on the floor. The water bottle, and wrapped package were still where the man had put them. Veronica crossed back to the door, grunted with effort as she lifted the heavy water bottle and, with her free hand, picked up the package. She crossed to where Miranda sat cross legged on her mattress.

"Are you okay?" Miranda asked, looking up at Veronica.

"Yes, I'm okay." Veronica put down the water bottle and sat next to Miranda. "This will be sandwiches," she said, handing the parcel to Miranda. She reached for the water bottle, and unscrewed the plastic cap. With effort she lifted the container and took several big gulps. Her thirst quenched, she offered the bottle to Miranda who handed the parcel back to Veronica, and drank herself.

"No glasses?" she asked, wiping water from her chin.

"No," Veronica said. "We used to have plastic cups,

but he got angry one day and took them away. He never brought them back."

"What did he get angry about?" Mandy asked.

Veronica unwrapped the parcel, and handed a sandwich to Miranda. "I don't know, I can't remember. He's always angry about something." She took a large bite from her sandwich.

Miranda looked suspiciously at her sandwich, lifted it to her nose, sniffed it and then peered at it again.

"It's a sort of meat, and cheese," Veronica explained. "It's always the same, meat and cheese."

"What sort of meat?" Miranda asked.

"I don't know. Camp Pie I think."

"Camp Pie?"

"Yes," I've seen a lot of it in the shops here in the Territory. Apparently the aborigines eat a lot of it because it's cheap."

Mandy lifted one corner of the bread, and peered at the meat underneath. "Looks about as nutritious as cardboard," she observed.

"I think cardboard might taste better," Veronica suggested.

Both girls smiled, an incongruous reaction, Miranda thought, given their current predicament, and the likely ultimate outcome.

They ate in silence. Both girls were hungry, given it was the first time either of them had eaten anything since Miranda arrived, and it was difficult not to wolf the sandwich down, but they forced themselves to eat slowly, making the experience last as long as possible. One sandwich each was nowhere near adequate to appease their hunger, but it was something. How long such a meager meal would sustain them, and how long it would be until he fed them again was an unknown but, despite the unappealing taste and the scant quantity, they lingered, occasionally taking a sip of water between bites.

When they had finished eating, Veronica screwed the cap back on the water bottle and put it aside. "We have to conserve the water," she explained to Miranda. "He doesn't refill the bottle often."

"Jesus!" Miranda cursed. "Who is that bastard?"

Veronica fell silent and dropped her eyes. "Soon he'll come for me... and I won't be back," she said almost in a whisper.

Miranda reached out and took Veronica's hand. "Maybe he won't," she suggested.

"Oh, he will," Veronica insisted. "It's what he does. When a new girl comes, it's only a few days before the old one is taken away... and never comes back."

"We have time," Mandy said.

"Time for what?" Veronica asked.

"Time to think of something," Mandy did not sound particularly reassuring.

"It's hopeless," Veronica shook her head. "There's no way out of here."

"We'll find a way, we will, we'll find a way."

Mandy got carefully to her feet, grunting with the effort. She stood unsteadily for a moment as a wave of dizziness came over her. The pain in her groin had eased, albeit slightly. Earlier, when the man took Veronica out to empty the bucket, she examined herself and found traces of blood on her panties. She didn't think she was seriously injured, but the blood, and the pain was enough to steel her determination to get out of this place, and, if she had to kill the bastard to do so, so be it. Mandy rather looked forward to the opportunity to do just that.

When she was satisfied she was not going to collapse, she turned, and stared around the room. She had done this before, and found nothing offering even the tiniest shred of hope. But Mandy was, if nothing else, a determined person. She was not, and had never been, one to back away from a challenge. Hence the bungee jumping, the sky diving, the rock climbing, and the other adventurous pursuits she had embarked on since she arrived in Australia.

As her eyes slowly scanned the room, they stopped when they came to the large fireplace. Something about the fireplace intrigued her. Slowly, she walked across the room, and stopped on the cement hearth directly in front of the empty space where a metal grate would have once sat.

Normally in a home with an open fireplace there would be a container next to it holding fire tongs and a poker. Here, there was no such container. Something about the plain, unobtrusive fireplace drew Mandy's attention.

She leaned forward at the waist, and looked closely at the three walls surrounding the space. They were made of stone, the same as the external surrounds which would once have been an attractive feature of the fireplace; something a family might have sat around on a cold winter's night, and talked of happy times. There was nothing attractive about the fireplace now, and Mandy guessed much time had elapsed since anyone gathered around it and talked of such times. There had been no laughter in this room for a very long time, she figured.

She got down on her knees, and stuck her head

completely into the open fireplace. She was looking down, facing the bottom of the space, where the metal grate on which the wood would have burned, once sat. She twisted her head in an attempt to look up, into the chimney. Impossible. She would have to lie on her back.

She called out to Veronica. "Veronica, my car keys, can you bring them here?"

Veronica fumbled in Mandy's bedding, found the keys, and took them across to where Miranda was now laying on her back, the top half of her body inside the fireplace.

Mandy peered up into the chimney. She saw daylight up there; blue sky, way up there, at the very top of the chimney cavity. Mandy dared to embrace a tiny glimmer of hope.

Veronica placed the keys in Miranda's outstretched hand. "What are you doing?"

"I don't know, yet," Mandy answered.

Mandy's key ring contained, along with her car keys, a tiny, single battery torch, no thicker or longer than her pinkie finger. She bought it at the airport when she first arrived in Australia. She knew when she bought it, being so tiny, the battery life would be extremely limited, but it was a nice little trinket, and it was cheap, -if airport souvenir shops could ever be considered cheap. It had come in useful on a few occasions, especially when she slept in her car and had to fumble in the dark amongst her stuff looking for a bottle of water.

Mandy fumbled with the torch, thrust her arm upwards into the chimney cavity, and flicked the switch. The beam was weak and illuminated just a small section of the inside of the chimney. The walls were black, thick with years of built up soot and ash. She waved the torch around slowly, splaying the narrow shaft of light on each of the chimney walls.

With her free hand, she reached up, closed her eyes, turned her head to the side, and rubbed at a small section of the interior. Soot and ash fell into her face, and she closed her mouth and held her breath, so she wouldn't be forced to swallow, or breathe any of the black, possibly toxic remnants of long ago fires.

After a short while, she stopped rubbing, waited a moment for the last of the soot to settle, and then opened her eyes, and looked at the area she had rubbed clean. Here, inside the chimney, the walls were never meant to be seen, so it was not necessary they be finished to present an attractive feature. The small section of wall she had rubbed relatively clean, showed the interior stonework was craggy, rough, and uneven. As Mandy studied the chimney walls, her eyes slowly rising up the length until she once again saw blue sky, she felt her mood lighten ever so slightly.

She pushed herself backwards, out of the fireplace, and got awkwardly to her feet. Veronica stood next to her, and helped her to stand.

Veronica was smiling, and Mandy looked at her. "What are you smiling about?" she asked, slapping at the soot and ash on her upper body.

"You look like Al Jolson," Veronica said.

"Who?" Mandy asked.

"Your face," Veronica pointed. It's black... like Al Jolson, the American entertainer."

Mandy wiped at her face with her hand. "I've never heard of him," she said.

"Never mind," Veronica said, dismissively. "He's

been dead for decades." She indicated the fireplace. "What were you doing down there?"

"Looking for a way out," Miranda answered.

"Up the chimney?" Veronica asked, incredulously.

"Sure," Mandy said. "I could see daylight up there."

"You are joking," Veronica decided.

"No, I saw daylight."

"No, not joking about the daylight, joking about going up the chimney," Veronica said.

"Why not," Mandy shrugged. "The walls are made of stone. It's all rough... lots of foot holds, and hand holds."

"I can't climb up the chimney," Veronica complained. "I can't climb a ladder!"

Miranda reached out and grasped Veronica by the shoulders. "We can do it, Veronica. I've done a bit of rock climbing since I've been here. I was pretty good at it. It's not far. I can teach you."

Veronica shook her head. "Oh no... no! I could never climb up there. It's so small. What if I get stuck in there?"

"You're not going to get stuck," Miranda insisted. "It's a big fireplace. It's a big chimney. "You can do it... *we* can do it! We have to try. You said yourself, there is no other way out of here."

Veronica looked down at Mandy's near naked, soot covered body. "Look at us. We've got no shoes, and we are wearing our underwear. What do we do even if we were to make it out?"

"We have to try, even if we are near naked. We have to try. We'll get out on the roof, and then climb down and make our escape."

"Where to?" Veronica asked.

"Anywhere," Mandy said. "As long as it's away from here, what does it matter where we go? We'll keep going until we find help."

"And perish in the bush trying," Veronica suggested pessimistically.

Miranda was beginning to get angry. "The alternative is to stay here, and wait for him to take us away, permanently. Is that what you want?"

Veronica paused. "No," she said, finally.

Miranda moved back to the mattresses, picked up the bottle of water, and took a long swig. Veronica followed her. Mandy turned to the other girl, and handed her the light blanket covering her mattress. "Here, wipe the soot from me. I don't want him to see what I've been doing."

Veronica took the blanket and wiped vigorously at Miranda, removing all traces of soot and ash. "Do you really think we can get out that way?" she asked Mandy.

Mandy took her hand. "Yes, I do. I really do. We have no choice. If we stay here, sooner or later we are going to die. That animal is going to kill us both. We have to try. We have nothing to lose, and everything to gain."

Veronica dropped the blanket back onto the mattress, and looked at Mandy. "All right, I'll try. I'm scared, but I don't want to stay here."

Mandy smiled, hugged Veronica and said, "good girl."

"When will we go?" Veronica asked.

Mandy looked across at the fireplace. "Soon," she said quietly.

"How soon," Veronica asked. "He'll come for me soon."

Mandy squeezed Veronica tighter. "I know," she nodded. "We have to wait for night. It's broad daylight out there now, and he might see us. "Does he ever come in here late at night?"

Veronica shook her head. "He never has since I've been here."

"Good," Mandy said. "We'll go tonight."

"Tonight?" Veronica sounded alarmed. "It's too soon. I can't learn how to climb a chimney in a few hours."

"Yes you can, Veronica. I'm going to show you how."

Veronica hesitated, glanced nervously across at the fireplace and shuddered. "O... okay."

8
_____

Sergeant Terry Potts was alone in a police four-wheel-drive. He pulled up in front of the Wauchope Hotel, retrieved a file from the passenger seat, and got out of the vehicle. Russell Foley and Sam Rose, watched him from the hotel verandah as he approached. Potts had a steely, determined look on his face; a look both Sam, and Foley, had seen many times, and recognised as not the look of a man bearing good news.

Potts halted in front of Sam and Foley. "Good morning again," he greeted.

"Your being here indicates to me this is not a social visit," Foley observed. "We weren't expecting you. We were just about to head back out to the well."

"Sorry," Potts apologised. "I could have called, but this is too important," he waved the file.

"What have you got?" Sam asked.

"A seventh missing person," Potts answered.

"Tell us you're joking," Foley said.

Potts frowned and handed the file to Foley. "I wish I was. Her name is Miranda Winters, a nurse from London. She was reported missing yesterday, at Tennant Creek. The file came to my notice a couple of hours ago." He paused.

"Tell us more," Foley insisted.

"Winters was reported missing by another Pommy backpacker, Lillian Clutterbuck. She was supposed to meet Winters yesterday, at Tennant. Winters never showed."

"Maybe she's running late," Sam suggested.

"She hasn't answered any of Lillian's text messages, or voice calls, in the last two days," Potts added.

"Where was she two days ago?" Foley asked.

Potts paused, looked at Sam and then at Foley. "This is where it gets interesting," he announced.

"You have our undivided attention," Sam said.

"Winters last sent Clutterbuck a text message, accompanied with a photo, from Devil's Marbles, two days ago. There's been nothing since."

"And...?" Foley pushed.

"Miranda Winters was traveling alone since she parted company with Clutterbuck in Sydney a few weeks ago. She bought an old Ford Festiva, and continued her travels alone. They agreed to meet up in Tennant Creek, and were in touch by either text message, or phone call almost every day. Clutterbuck claims it is totally out of character for Winters not to respond." Potts explained.

"What about Devil's Marbles?" Sam probed.

"Her car is there," Potts said. "I called in there on my way here, but there's no sign of the Winters girl. I left my partner there. I figured you would want to attend and check it out for yourselves."

"How far away is Devil's Marbles?" Sam asked.

"Nine kilometres up the road," Potts confirmed.

"Let's go," Foley said.

———

Sam looked out of the car window at the amazing formation of rocks. "I've never been here before," he announced.

"Never?" Potts asked.

"I drove through here when I transferred down to the Alice, but I never stopped," Sam explained.

"Why not?" Foley asked, astounded. "One of the Territory's greatest tourist attractions and you never stopped for a look?"

Sam reached across from the rear seat and patted Foley on the shoulder. "I was in a hurry to get to Alice Springs, I missed you Russ."

"You're so full of it, Sam," Foley announced.

Potts drove slowly along the entrance road, and into a large, open, designated camping area on the eastern side of Devil's Marbles. Sam was amazed to see how many recreational vehicles of varying shapes, sizes, and configurations were parked there. There were caravans, motor homes, a couple of huge fifth-wheelers, and even several tents, all gathered together at the far northern end of the area.

Scattered about at strategic locations were a number of wooden picnic tables and wood burning barbeques. On the far eastern edge of the area stood a public toilet block, used, Sam guessed, by the tent dwellers and those who did not have the luxury of en-suite facilities in their holiday homes-on-wheels.

"Busy place," Sam observed aloud.

"Always is at this time of the year," Potts announced. He slowed, and stopped behind a small Ford Festiva sedan parked between two large, dual-axle caravans.

A uniformed police officer sat on a low, wooden, single-rail fence running the length of the camping area, delineating its front edge, and preventing vehicles from encroaching any closer to the rock formations. Every ten metres or so, a small gap appeared in the fence allowing foot traffic access to a number of walking trails weaving like a spider web through the entire formation.

The cop got up from his perch, and approached the four-wheel-drive as Sam, Foley, and Potts got out of the vehicle and stepped across to the small Ford. Potts introduced the uniformed officer, and Sam and Foley recognised him as the cop who'd climbed out of the well after recovering the remains of the five dead girls.

"This the car?" Foley asked.

"Yes," Potts confirmed. "The registration checks out. It belongs to Miranda Winters. It's all locked up, and is packed with personal belongings."

"No sign of the keys?" Sam asked.

"No," the uniformed cop answered. "I checked everywhere. She must have had the keys with her."

"Makes sense," Foley commented. "You're going for a look around the area, you lock your car, and take the keys with you."

"I've ordered a truck to come out and convey the car back to Tennant Creek," Potts said. "Should be here any time now."

Russell Foley stepped up to the driver's-side door, and tried the handle. The door was locked. "We need to take a look inside," he said.

"We have probable cause," Sam offered.

"Yes we do," Foley agreed.

"Shall I?" Sam asked.

"Please," Foley said, stepping aside.

Sam stepped up to the door, turned his back to the vehicle, drew his arm forward and, with great force, thrust his elbow backwards into the driver's side window. Nothing happened.

"Fuck! Fuck! Fuck!" Sam howled. He jumped up and down, clasping his elbow. "Shit, that hurt!" he cried.

From the caravan parked immediately next to the Festiva, the sound of muffled laughter drifted across the immediate area. Sam stopped hopping about for a moment, and looked up at the caravan. An elderly lady stood in the open doorway of her caravan, chuckling at his misfortune.

"That's not funny, Ma'am," he said, rubbing vigorously at his elbow.

"I'm sorry, officer," the lady giggled "but it is a *little* funny." She ducked back inside her caravan and reappeared a moment later carrying a small hammer. "Would you like to borrow this?" she smiled.

Sam stepped across to where the lady stood in the caravan doorway. The step up into the interior was high, and, from her vantage point, she was slightly taller than Sam. She turned the hammer around, and offered him the handle end.

Sam reached up and took the hammer. "Very kind of you, thank you. Oh, and sorry for my language," he said, shaking feeling back into his arm.

"I've heard worse," the lady smiled. "Don't break the hammer," she cautioned. "My husband only bought it a couple of weeks ago." She tried unsuccessfully to stifle another chuckle.

Sam gave her a look severe enough to send most people scurrying for cover, but not this lady. She looked at him, and offered him another smile warm enough to melt the heart of the hardest of hard men.

Sam dropped his eyes and turned away. "I won't break it, Ma'am," he promised in a quiet, softly spoken voice.

He stepped back to the Festiva, and was confronted by his three colleagues, all grinning at him widely.

"What?" he said.

Russell Foley stepped aside, allowing Sam to get close to the car window. "Nothing," he said. "Don't break the lady's hammer."

"If you three don't stop grinning at me like loons on the run from the nut house, I'm gonna break your heads with the lady's hammer," Sam said, shaking the hammer at them. He paused in front of the car window, rubbed his throbbing elbow for a few moments, raised the hammer, and smashed the glass.

The window shattered, spraying glass into the front seat of the Festiva. Sam reached inside and unlocked the door manually.

"There," he said, stepping back from the car. "Nothing to it."

"Be a good boy, and give the lady back her hammer," Foley said.

Sam moved back to the caravan. Now, the lady's husband had joined her. They had both stepped out of their caravan, and were standing beneath the van's awning, drinking coffee, and watching the activities.

"Been here a couple of days," the lady's husband said, nodding towards the Festiva.

Sam handed him the hammer. "Really? Was the car here when you arrived?"

"Yeah," the man said. "Arrived a couple of hours

before we did." He put the hammer down on a small table and offered his hand to Sam. "Ralph Browne... with an E," he introduced himself, and inclined his head towards his wife. "The bride is Kath."

"Nice to meet you," Sam smiled, and shook hands with both of them. "Did you see the driver?"

"Had a cuppa with her," Kath answered. "Pretty young thing, from England she said. Miranda her name was."

"You spoke with her?"

"Of course," Kath shrugged. She pointed at the car. "She parked right there. We are caravanners, we meet people all the time... fellow travelers, you know. It's what makes this lifestyle so enjoyable."

"What did you talk about?" Sam probed.

Kath shrugged again, more demonstrative this time. "Stuff... where she was from, places she had seen, where she was heading... you know, travel stuff. She was lovely. Said she loved Australia and was having a wonderful time."

"Was she traveling alone?" Sam asked.

Kath's husband, Ralph, fielded the question. "Yeah... bloody dangerous that, I reckon."

"Oh, Ralph," Kath chided her husband. "They do it all the time. Young ones have no fear. There must be hundreds of young backpackers wandering all over the country. They're having a wonderful time."

Suitably chastised, Ralph leaned back against the side of his caravan, and sipped his coffee in silence.

"What did she say about where she was headed?" Sam asked.

"She was meeting someone in Tennant Creek. Said she was leaving the next day," Kath said.

Then, as if realising for the first time, four police

officers gathered around Miranda's car and smashing the window to gain access might indicate a problem, perhaps something sinister, Kath looked around Sam, at the Festiva.

"Oh dear, has something happened to that lovely girl?"

"We don't know, Ma'am," Sam hastened to inform her. "The lady she was supposed to meet reported her missing, and we are just following up on that."

The husband, Ralph, deciding this was getting interesting, pushed himself upright, and stepped closer to his wife.

"Four of you... two detectives... two uniforms? Smashing the car window? Sounds a tad like overkill to me. for a missing person that is."

Sam ignored the speculation. "When was the last time you saw Miranda?" he asked.

"That same day," Kath answered, sounding concerned. "She went off for a walk through the Marbles, just as it was getting dark. It's lovely here at night... much cooler, and it's so nice to walk through there in the evening." She gazed at the nearby formation.

"And you never saw her again?"

"Now you mention it, no," Kath answered, returning her focus to Sam. "I never really thought about it. I thought she must have decided to stay out there a bit longer. It's so pretty here. You could walk for hours, and hours, through the Marbles. I guess I just assumed she was still out walking, taking photos and stuff." she glanced at the Marbles, just a few metres from where they stood.

"Where did she sleep? Did she have a tent?" Sam asked.

Ralph must have decided it was his turn to speak.

"She said she slept in the car," he answered. "Dunno how they can do that," he added.

"They're young, Ralph," Kath interjected. "Young ones can sleep on a barbed wire fence. You were young once."

"Can't remember that bloody far back," Ralph resumed his position, leaning against his van. "And I never slept on a barbed wire fence."

"Oh, stop it, Ralph. Now you're being silly."

"Did you see her come back to her car, at any time?" Sam probed.

"We don't spend all day and night watching the comings and goings of folks parked next to us," Ralph answered. "Got better things to do," he added as an afterthought.

His comments drew a look from his wife, leaving him with no doubt he was going to hear more from her later.

Sam paused, and looked at Ralph, wondering just how much enjoyment the man got from traveling around the country in a caravan with just his wife for company. Should be called Grumpy Ralph, he thought.

"I'm going to ask one of the other officers to take a statement from you," he said. "Are you both okay with that?"

Kath put her hand to her mouth. "Something's happened to that lovely young girl, hasn't it?"

"Right now she is just a missing person," Sam said hurriedly. "But we would like to get all you can remember about her in a statement."

"We're leaving a bit later today," Grumpy Ralph hastened to add. "We're booked into Tennant Creek for a few days."

"It won't take long," Sam said.

"Of course," Kath answered for both herself and Grumpy Ralph. "Anything we can do to help find her. She was lovely, really lovely. I hope she is all right."

Russell Foley, and the two Tennant Creek cops were occupied picking through Miranda'a belongings when Sam stepped back to the Festiva. Foley stopped what he was doing and looked at Sam.

"Making new friends?" he asked.

"Yeah," Sam nodded. "Grumpy Ralph, and his lovely bridezilla, Kath."

"Grumpy Ralph?" Foley raised his eyebrows.

"Never mind," Sam said, shaking his head. "We need a statement from them."

Terry Potts heard the conversation, and turned to his colleague. "Ben, can you get a statement from the folks in the caravan?" he indicated the van where the two were still watching proceedings at the Festiva.

The uniformed cop, Ben, looked across at the two grey nomads. "Sure," he said, as he started to move across to the caravan.

Sam grabbed Ben by the arm and halted him. "Take the statement from the lady, not the man," he instructed quietly.

Ben shrugged. "Okay."

"What did you find out?" Foley asked Sam.

"The girl was here when they arrived, two days ago. Everything seems to fit with what we already know. Driver was a young girl... name of Miranda. She indicated she was staying one night, and then meeting a friend in Tennant Creek the next day. She said she was going for a short night walk through the Marbles, and they haven't seen her since."

"And they weren't concerned she didn't come back to her car?" Foley asked, incredulously.

"It seems they never really thought about it. When her car was still here, they figured she changed her mind about meeting her friend and decided to stay a little longer," Sam explained.

"Where did they think she was for two days?" Foley asked.

"Out walking," Sam said. "They really didn't seem concerned."

"Really?" Foley exclaimed. "What the fuck's wrong with people? All sorts of crap going on in the world, and no one seems to give a shit!"

"Careful, buddy," Sam cautioned. "Remember your blood pressure."

"I don't have blood pressure," Foley said, indignantly.

"I'm very glad to hear that," Sam smiled. "Find anything in the car?"

Foley reached into the vehicle, and picked up a few items from the front seat. "A passport, in the name of Miranda Winters, a purse containing a driver's license in the same name, about one-hundred-and-twenty dollars in cash, a couple of credit cards. There are clothes, and bedding in the back seat... it looks like she slept in her car."

"Yeah, that fits with what Darby and Joan said," Sam nodded.

"Darby, and Joan?"

"Forget it," Sam said.

"There was a mobile phone in the glove box," Foley continued. "She was trading text messages with her friend, Lillian Clutterbuck."

"The girl who reported her missing," Sam concluded.

"We'll have a good look through the phone, who knows? We might get lucky," Foley said. "We'll get the car back to Tennant Creek, and go through everything with a fine toothed comb."

Sam stepped away from the car, and looked around, slowly perusing each of the many different recreational vehicles. Eventually he turned back to Russell Foley. "I have a bad feeling about this, Russ," he announced.

"Me too, mate," Foley said. "Me too."

"How many people would have come, and gone, from here in the last two days?" Sam asked.

"Too many to think about," Foley answered.

"Any one of them could have seen something," Sam added.

"There's a self-registration site on the road in," Foley explained. "Visitors are supposed to provide their details. Their name, vehicle registration, how long they intend to stay. And, they have to pay a nominal amount per vehicle, per day. It's an honor system."

"Finding them all, and checking them out, would be a nightmare," Sam said. "They could be anywhere by now."

Russell Foley paused for a moment. "I don't think our perp is a traveler," he decided. "The missing girls date back twelve months. He has to be from the area. We have seven missing girls, and only five bodies. Where are the other two?"

"You're assuming there's a connection between the sixth, and seventh girls, and the five bodies from the well," Sam said.

"It's too much of a coincidence for there not to be," Foley answered.

"I agree," Sam nodded. "Now all we have to do is find them."

"If they're still alive," Foley said.

"Even if they're not," Sam said.

9

Miranda spent the remaining hours of daylight instructing Veronica in the basics of rock climbing. Mandy was not an expert, far from it, she had rock climbed in Victoria, in an area renowned for climbs of varying grades of difficulty from beginner to downright hazardous, and while her experience at the art had never ventured much beyond beginner, she did find she seemed to have a natural ability for it.

Had time been on her side, she felt she would have liked to attempt a couple of climbs of greater difficulty but it was not to be. She satisfied herself with the self-promise she would pursue the sport when she finally returned home to England. The UK had a number of famous climbs she was looking forward to attempting.

Convincing Veronica climbing out of the house by way of the chimney was their best, if not their only way of escaping whatever horrors the man still had in store for each of them was not easy, but she had to try. She was determined she was leaving this place as soon as she could, and she did not want to leave without Veronica. Leaving the timid, terrified girl here alone was simply not an option.

Veronica cried a lot, and complained constantly she could not do it, and while Mandy would have preferred she practice with a couple of exploratory climbs of just a few metres, there was no opportunity to do so. The man could come into the room at any time, They would have one shot at it, and they had to wait for night fall when they could make their move under the cover of darkness.

Mandy explained the process of using the feet, and the back, to gain purchase, and accordingly, momentum when climbing. The chimney was large, but not overly so. The internal walls were rocky and uneven, offering foot and hand holds all the way to the top. She explained, when standing upright in the fireplace, with head and shoulders protruding upwards into the cavity, she had to reach up, find a hand hold on the facing wall, grip it tightly, and bring her knees up to her chest. Then, feel around with her toes, find a foot hold, lean back against the back wall, and push up with her feet. This maneuver would lock her tightly into the chimney flu, and then she had to reach up again, find a new hand hold and repeat the process.

At first, progress would be slow, perhaps as slow as a few centimetres at a time, Mandy explained. But, as long as she didn't panic, and as long as she pressed hard against the back wall, she would soon become more proficient, and the rate of progress would improve. She would have loved to have demonstrated the procedure for Veronica, but she was afraid of getting caught. If the man were to come into the room while they were practicing, the consequences were something she did not want to think about. This was going to have to be done on the fly, and in the dead of night.

She would never admit it to Veronica, but Mandy

held reservations of her own. Veronica had been a captive for three weeks, perhaps even longer, and she was not as strong as she would have been when she was first brought to this place. Daily meals were scant, if they came at all, and if what they ate today was an example of the norm, they were of little benefit in regards to their nutritional value. Mandy wondered if Veronica, undernourished and weak, would have the physical strength required to climb the chimney.

Then, there was the years of built up soot, and ash caked thick on the chimney walls. It would be unavoidably dislodged during the climb and, consequently, breathing the dust in would be unavoidable. A coughing fit mid-way through the climb was likely to have hazardous consequences.

Veronica assured Mandy she was not claustrophobic, but it was an assertion yet to be tested, and the panic factor had to be considered. An attack of the horrors half-way up the chimney would surely result in failure, and almost certain discovery by the monster lurking nearby, perhaps in the very next room.

Mandy was confident she would not slip and fall, but she could not hold the same degree of confidence in Veronica. A fall down the chimney could easily result in broken bones, or worse. She would have to send Veronica up first because she could not be sure she would follow if Mandy preceded her. If she chickened out, Mandy would have to decide to either go on alone and leave Veronica to her fate, or go back down the chimney.

The more she thought about it, the longer Mandy's mental list of things which could go wrong, grew. She decided to try not to focus on the negatives. Spending time thinking about the possible pitfalls meant she had less time to concentrate on the benefits of escaping the room and putting as much distance between themselves and the man as they could.

Preparations had to be made. They had no food to take with them, and just half a bottle of water to sustain them on their audacious bid for freedom. They would wrap themselves in their blankets for the climb. Although thin, and barely adequate, the blankets would hopefully help prevent injury to their backs as they climbed up the rough, uneven stonework forming the inside of the chimney. Mandy was under no illusion it was going to be difficult, even painful at times. They would have to lean back, hard against protruding lumps of stone, but, foot, and hand holds should be plentiful, and she considered the ragged interior had to be a plus, despite the obvious difficulties.

Then, there were the prevailing weather conditions to consider. The nights were cold in this part of the country at this time of the year, and, the blankets would offer at least a degree of protection against the chill of the night as well as from the heat of the day to follow. Dressed only in their underwear, their skin would burn quickly in the hot sun without protective covering.

In which direction to walk once they were out was also problematic. When the man threw her in the back of his vehicle two nights ago, she guessed he drove for about an hour, maybe two, before arriving at the house, but she had no idea in which direction he drove.

She had been in the Territory long enough to know, should the inadequately prepared and provisioned dare to venture too far off the major highway, there existed a whole lot of nothing for as far as the eye could see, and people often perished in this unforgiving, inhospitable landscape.

Footwear, or the lack of it, also presented a problem, one Mandy had no answer for. Presumably they had to cover a lot of ground before they reached help, and in their bare feet this could potentially be even harder on both of them than the actual climb up the chimney cavity. Perhaps they could tear strips from their blankets, and wrap their feet in the scraps of threadbare material. Hardly a satisfactory solution, she thought, but one worth considering given the alternatives were either to strip the soles of their feet to shreds, or stay put and abide whatever atrocities their captor had in store for them.

As hastily conceived as Miranda's plan was, it was a plan nonetheless. They would start the climb late at night, when they could be reasonably certain the man was not going to come into the room. Veronica said he never came in during the night, at least he hadn't in the time she had been there, so Mandy figured escaping late at night had to be their best chance of success.

They were not likely to be visited in the middle of their climb, and the darkness would cover their flight once they were out of the room. As for where, and in which direction they walked, or even how they were going to get down off the roof presuming they made it out of the chimney, was something they would have to decide on once they were out and were more able to assess their surroundings. The first and most important objective, as far as Mandy was concerned, was getting out of the room. Everything which followed could be faced as it came.

She got up from her mattress, and crossed to the

fireplace. Squatting on her haunches in front of it, she studied as much as she could see of the inner walls. They would be taking a huge risk, but it was a risk they simply had to take. They could not turn back. They would go tonight.

Mandy returned to where Veronica dozed on her mattress. "Are you awake?" she asked.

Veronica stirred, and opened her eyes. "Yes," she answered sleepily. She sat up and reached for the water bottle.

Mandy reached out and placed her hand over Veronica's stopping her from removing the cap.

"No," she insisted. "We need to conserve the water. It's all we have, and we don't know how long it will be before we can get more."

"Sorry," Veronica apologised.

"It's okay," Mandy said. "Are you ready to go tonight?"

"No, I'm crapping myself. I've been lying here thinking about it, and I'm scared."

Mandy took her hand. "I know you are, so am I. But, we can't stay here. It's our only chance to get away."

Veronica nodded. "I know it is. I just hope I can do it."

"You can do it," Mandy insisted. "I'll be right there. I'll guide you through it. It's not far up there."

"It's dark, and filthy dirty," Veronica announced.

"Yes, it is," Mandy nodded. "But it's only going to be that way for a few minutes... and, I have my little torch," she lifted her key ring and waved it at Veronica. "If we stick together we can do this, I know we can."

Veronica paused, fear plainly evident in her eyes. "Okay," she said, finally. "I'm ready."

Mandy patted her hand. "Good girl. Now, let's get some rest. It's going to be a long night once we get outside."

———

He came at dusk. Mandy and Veronica heard the door lock slide, and then he was there, standing in the open doorway leering across the void at them. For a long time, he stood there, staring at them, his eyes swinging from Veronica, to Miranda, and then back to Veronica; as if he was making a choice.

Veronica reached out, clasped Miranda's hand and squeezed it tight. "What does he want?" she whispered.

"I don't know," Mandy answered. "What do you want?" she called out to the man.

"Are you hungry?" he asked.

Mandy paused. "Of course we're hungry," she said. "We've had one sandwich in two days."

"I'll bring food tomorrow," he smiled.

"Why not now?" Mandy asked.

"Because I'll bring it tomorrow," he repeated.

"What do you want?" Mandy asked.

"I came for Veronica," the man said.

Veronica squeezed Mandy's hand harder making Mandy flinch with the pain. Mandy did not let go.

"Pl... please, no," Veronica sobbed.

"Why?" Mandy asked the man.

The man ignored Mandy and fixed Veronica with an icy stare. "Come with me, Veronica," he ordered.

"No... no, please... no," Veronica begged.

"She's staying here!" Mandy spat at the man.

"Veronica, come with me," he demanded again.

"Oh God," Veronica breathed. "He's going to kill me."

"No... no, he's not," Mandy said. "She's not going with you!" Mandy fired back at the man.

The man paused for a moment, and then stepped further into the room. He swung the door shut behind him, and was across the room in seconds. He halted in front of the two girls, sitting cross legged on their mattresses and without any warning he swung his arm, and hit Mandy on the side of her head with a clenched fist. Mandy reeled sideways under the force of the blow. Unable to control her momentum, she fell across Veronica, and they both collapsed onto the mattresses.

Initially, Mandy felt no pain. Then, it hit her; her head felt as though it was cleaved in two. The pain, savage, and worse than anything she had ever experienced, radiated outwards, and backwards, from her temple to the top of her head, across her brow to the opposite side of her head, and then down her face, until even her teeth ached. She felt herself slipping into unconsciousness, and tried desperately to fight it. Then, a nauseating throbbing started, and her vision became blurry and indistinct. She tried to raise her hands to her head, but they would not move. From somewhere, far, far away she thought she heard Veronica's voice, calling her. Then, there was nothing.

———

When Mandy finally regained consciousness, the room was dark. Confused and disorientated, it hurt just opening her eyes. She was lying awkwardly across her own mattress, the top half of her body encroaching onto Veronica's bed. Her head throbbed, and as she tried to move, the pain stabbed savagely, mercilessly behind her eyes, threatening to send her back into the black oblivion from which she had just emerged. A part of her, somewhere deep within her being, would welcome it; it was pain free in that place.

Cautious not to make any sudden movements which would exacerbate the pain screaming through her head, she reached out and felt around in the dark. Very slowly awareness dawned on her. She was alone.

"Veronica," she whispered. "Veronica, where are you?"

No response came. "Veronica! Veronica!" she called again, a little louder this time. Silence surrounded her in the darkness. She closed her eyes, and moaned. "Oh... God... no. Please don't let me be alone. Veronica! Veronica!"

Carefully, and excruciatingly slowly, she pushed herself into a sitting position, and fumbled in her bedding. looking for her car keys. She could not find them, and she felt herself beginning to panic. They had to be there. For a few anxious moments her desperate searching became more frantic, and then, there they were, buried under her mattress.

She clutched them hurriedly, flicked the switch on the tiny torch, and shone it around the room. The beam was not strong enough to illuminate the far corners of the room, but it was sufficient to confirm she was alone in the room. Veronica was gone.

Slowly she began to remember. The man had hit her, punched her in the head. He came into the room. He wanted to take Veronica. Veronica begged him not to take her, and Mandy remembered protesting to him. Then he stormed across the room, and hit her. That was all. She remembered nothing else.

The bastard took Veronica. Was he out there now, in his room, doing to Veronica the things he did to her? Would he bring her back at dawn? She closed her eyes as disjointed, sick and twisted images flickered across her mind in a macabre slide show running in uncontrolled fast-forward mode.

She wanted to vomit, and tried to stand. The effort, clumsy and uncoordinated, initiated a new wave of excruciating pain. It seared across her forehead, and pounded behind her eyes. Her feet became tangled in the bedding, she stumbled backwards, and her shoulder crashed into the wall beyond Veronica's mattress. She moaned loudly, and leaned heavily against the wall, waiting for the pain to subside.

As she leaned unsteadily against the wall, she began to sob. Deep, gut wrenching sobs echoed in the big, empty room. Was this it? Was this where it all ended? Was the man coming for her next? She didn't want to go through the horror again.

Where was Veronica? Was she even going to come back? Had the man taken her away, never to return, just like the girls who came before her? What did it mean? Were they all dead, every one of them, even Veronica? The very thought precipitated a renewed bout of chest heaving sobbing. She slid down the wall, and collapsed onto the mattress, her sobs becoming muffled as she buried her face in the bedding.

Eventually, she fell into a restless, exhausted sleep. When she finally woke, dawn was once again struggling to make an impression in the room. Thin shafts of dull light shone weekly through the window, barely penetrating the cold morning darkness.

The pain in Mandy's head had eased, but was aggravated by sudden movement, so she was mindful of the need to move slowly and precisely. She needed to pee, and she used the wall as support as she made her way slowly around the room, passed the locked door, and relieved herself in the bucket. On her way back to her bed, she stopped in front of the fireplace and stared into the empty space.

They should be out of the house by now. She and Veronica would be hours away from this terrible place had they been able to go through with their plan. Now she was here in the room alone, with no idea when, or if, Veronica would be back.

A large, painful node had developed on the side of Mandy's head. She gently massaged it, and wondered; should she go alone? She would be able to make much quicker time without having to coax Veronica up the chimney. Immediately overcome with strong feelings of guilt at the very thought of going alone, she quickly dismissed the idea. What if Veronica came back and discovered she had been abandoned by the one person who had promised to save her? She could not leave. She could not abandon Veronica.

Besides, she thought, it was dawn. Soon it would be full daylight and way too risky to attempt an escape. The man could come into the room at any time during the day. She did not want to think about what he might do to her if he came while she was still inside the chimney.

She would leave, however. Of that she was certain. She had no idea what fate had befallen all the other girls, and now maybe Veronica, but she was determined she was not going to become victim to the same fate. The chimney idea was still her best shot at freedom. She was confident she could climb it. Now it was just a case of determining when.

She would wait until nightfall. Just one more day to get through, and then she would go. If Veronica was not back by nightfall, she could assume she would not be coming back. A terrible thing to have to consider, she thought, but, whether or not Veronica came back was something she had absolutely no control over. If she came back, they would leave together as previously planned. If not, she would go alone. She was not going to die at the hands of the monster lurking on the other side of the locked door.

Mandy made her way cautiously back to her mattress, and found the bottle of water. She held it up to the slowly brightening light and checked the level. The bottle was half full. She took a small sip, screwed the lid tight, and placed the bottle next to her bed where she could easily find it in the dark of the coming night. Carefully, she lowered herself to her mattress, curled into the fetal position, and closed her eyes, willing herself to ignore the throbbing ache in her head. She needed to sleep. Getting out of the house, and as far away from this horrible place as she could, was going to take a long, sleep deprived night.

As she lay awaiting the blissful onset of sleep, her mind raced with a mental inventory of the things she would take with her. If the man brought food, she would save it, she had no way of telling when she would next eat once she was out of the house. She would ask him for more water, the days were hot, and she would be moving as fast as her bare feet would allow, water was essential for survival. Then, there was a blanket, she would need her blanket to protect her back during the night climb up the chimney, and then from the hot sun of the day.

The plan was audacious, and it would be hard, maybe even impossible, but the alternatives, more vicious sexual abuse for Lord knows how long, followed by death, did not bare thinking about. She would rather die out there, in the harsh Australian outback, than at the hands of the sick bastard on the other side of the door.

10

The Police Tactical Group, one component of the Territory Response Division and commonly referred to as Task Force, arrived from Alice Springs just as Sam, and Foley were finishing their breakfast.

The Lenco BearCat armoured vehicle pulled up at the southern end of the access road leading to the Wauchope Hotel. Eight crew members, all clad in black tactical clothing complete with balaclavas covering their faces, climbed out and immediately formed themselves in defensive positions surrounding their ride. To anyone other than a member of the police force—an unsuspecting tourist perhaps—it had to be an intimidating sight.

Responsible for such things as counter terrorism duties, hostage rescue, bomb response, counter disaster operations, and close personal protection, among other duties as might be required from time to time, the Task Force was a highly trained, crack force of extremely fit and dedicated police operatives. However, it was incongruous, and unmerited, that their members were often the butt of jokes and unfair criticism from police members outside the close-knit group.

Given the unit was, more often than not, called out to incidents which turned out to be of a benign nature, such criticism probably had something to do with the intimidating outfit they wore, and the aggressive nature of their preparedness at any time.

On occasions such as this, their presence at a scene was often seen as overkill and the catalyst for unwarranted denigration which seemed to follow the group wherever, and whatever the situation might be requiring their attendance.

A sergeant, wearing the regulation black outfit, complete with balaclava, stepped out in front of his unit. His men surrounded the armoured vehicle, facing outwards. They carried high-powered, semi-automatic rifles, and Glock pistols holstered low on their thighs. The sergeant turned and spoke to his men, and then walked slowly but purposely towards the hotel entrance.

Sam Rose and Russell Foley watched through the dining room window as the sergeant marched purposely across the car parking area, his gait erect and alert. As he approached, he occasionally glanced to his left, and then to his right, as if anticipating trouble. This was a man who was not going to be caught unawares. He was in an open area, exposed and vulnerable, and he was obviously mindful danger could come from anywhere at any time.

Sam turned to Foley and smiled. "Who is this rooster?"

"That's Wayne Donaldson," Foley explained. "He's been with the Task Force for several years. He's a bloody good operator."

"I'll bet none of those dudes out there are married," Sam commented. "They wouldn't have any love left for anyone else."

Foley frowned. "Be nice, Sam."

"I don't have to curtsy, do I?" Sam asked.

"No," Foley said. "They prefer you to genuflect."

"Yeah, right," Sam chuffed. "Like that's gonna happen."

Sergeant Wayne Donaldson entered the hotel dining room, paused just inside the door, and cast his eyes quickly over the room. Satisfied no immediate threat existed, he spotted Sam, and Foley, and headed over to their table.

"Inspector Foley," he greeted. "Wayne Donaldson," he offered his hand.

Foley pushed his chair back, and got to his feet. He took Donaldson's hand, and the two men shook firmly.

"Hello Wayne," Foley smiled. "Thanks for coming. Want a coffee?"

Donaldson stood rigidly, soldier like, in front of Foley. "No, Sir. Thank you."

Foley indicated a vacant chair. "Take a seat."

"I'm fine, thank you, Sir."

"Suit yourself," Foley said. He sat back down, picked up his coffee cup, and sipped.

"Why are we here, Sir?" Donaldson asked, sounding mildly bemused at the apparent casualness of the two detectives.

Foley lowered his cup, wiped his mouth with his napkin, and looked up at Donaldson. "We have a situation, Wayne," he said.

"A situation?" Donaldson questioned.

"Yes, a situation," Foley repeated. "You see, there's this well... about an hour's drive west of here."

"Well?" Donaldson interrupted.

Sam Rose decided this would be an appropriate time to join the conversation. "Yeah, Wayne, a well... you know, one of those holes in the ground where they store water."

Donaldson gave Sam a condescending look. "You're Sam Rose, right?"

"Got it in one," Sam smiled, offering his hand.

"I know what a well is, Sergeant Rose," Donaldson scowled dismissively. He shook Sam's hand, more out of courtesy than any sense of respect or admiration.

Donaldson had never met Sam before, but he was familiar with his reputation. He was comfortable acknowledging Sam as a good cop with an enviable record, but he was not a fan. The police force was no different from any work place where a large number of employees had the opportunity to exchange gossip, rumor, and innuendo. Warranted or not, Sam happened to be the subject of a good deal of all those things. This did not sit well with Donaldson. He returned his attention to Russell Foley.

"What about the well?" he asked.

"We found bones in it," Foley said.

"Bones?" Donaldson threw Sam a warning scowl in case he was inclined to explain what bones were.

Sam drained his coffee, picked up the last remnant of toast from his side plate, looked at it suspiciously, promptly popped it into his mouth, and glanced at Donaldson.

"What?" he asked the Task Force Sergeant.

"Nothing," Donaldson answered.

"We found bones," Foley continued, breaking the

tense interaction between Sam and Donaldson. "Human bones. Five sets of human remains, in the bottom of the well."

Donaldson, obviously comfortable with one word questions, said, "Five?"

"All female," Foley nodded.

"Female," Donaldson said, it was not a question this time.

"That's correct," Foley nodded. "Five sets of female remains."

"In the bottom of the well," Sam added for good measure.

This time Foley glared his disapproval at Sam, who shrugged with indifference, and leaned back in his chair.

"What would our role be in the investigation?" Donaldson said more in that one question than he had said since he arrived.

"We are going out to the well," Foley began. "Sergeant Rose, myself, and you and your chaps."

"Okay," Donaldson said. "When do we leave?"

How does right now suit you?" Foley asked.

"Fine," Donaldson answered. "My men would like to use the facilities before we leave. We haven't stopped since we left Alice Springs."

"How about fifteen minutes from now?" Foley suggested.

"Ten will be fine, Sir," Donaldson said.

"Ten it is," Foley smiled. "We'll meet you outside."

Donaldson turned sharply, and marched regimentally to the exit door.

When he had left the room, and was out of earshot, Sam looked questioningly at Foley. "What's with those blokes?"

"What do you mean?" Foley asked.

"They're Task Force," Sam said. "I thought they could go two weeks without a piss."

Foley pushed himself to his feet. "You know, Sam... when we get out there, I'm *am* going to send you down the well *with* Donaldson."

"Good idea," Sam said. "He'd get lost down there on his own."

———

Sam and Foley, with Foley driving, led the way out to the well in their conventional drive, unmarked police sedan. The ride was rough across the dusty, corrugated road, and several times the Task Force armoured vehicle encroached a little too close to the sedan's rear bumper for comfort, as if they were encouraging Foley to get a move on.

They arrived at the well mid-morning and, as the heavy BearCat discharged its cargo of enthusiastic Task Force members, who immediately assumed their defensive positions circling their vehicle, Sam and Foley got out of the sedan, and casually leaned against the bonnet.

Donaldson approached Foley, and stood to attention in front of him.

"How would you like my men deployed?" he asked.

Foley indicated the well, thirty metres to their front. "That's the well," he said. "We'll start with a ground search, beginning at the well and radiating outwards for at least fifty metres."

"What are we looking for?" Donaldson asked.

"Anything that doesn't belong," Foley said. "The

chaps from Tennant Creek did the area over pretty well when they recovered the bodies, and found nothing," he paused, and cast his eyes over the intended search area. "But, there has to be something. A footprint, a cigarette butt, a gum wrapper... anything out of place."

"Okay," Donaldson said.

"You got a ladder in that thing?" Foley jerked a thumb towards the BearCat.

Donaldson looked mildly offended at the question. "Yes," we have anything you need inside the vehicle.

"And a torch?"

"Of course."

"Good," Foley said. "I want one man down in the well. Go over every square inch of the base."

"I'll organise the scuba gear," Donaldson said, a little too excitedly for Foley's liking.

"You won't need it," Foley said.

"Oh," Donaldson frowned, his enthusiasm obviously dampened somewhat.

"It's a dry well," Foley explained. "Been dry for years, apparently. Nothing but dirt down there."

"And maybe a lingering bad smell," Sam mentioned across the bonnet of the car.

Donaldson ignored Sam and looked at Foley. "We'll get right on it." He turned smartly, walked back to his vehicle, and began issuing instructions to his men.

Foley turned and glared at Sam on the other side of the car. "You *wanna* go down the well?" he hissed.

Sam raised his hands in mock surrender. "No... please... not the well."

Foley was about to respond when his phone rang.

He retrieved it from his pocket and flicked it open. "Russell Foley," he answered.

"Terry Potts again, Sir," the Tennant Creek Sergeant said.

"G'day Terry. What have you got?"

"A couple of things," Potts informed.

"Hang on a sec," Foley instructed. He switched his phone onto speaker and laid it on the bonnet between himself, and Sam. "Go ahead, Terry, you're on speaker."

"We have a positive ID on the most recent body," Potts said.

"Who is it?" Foley asked, looking up at Sam.

"The twenty-year old girl from Adelaide, Janice Clarke. She got done in South Australia a couple of years ago for possession, a small quantity of marijuana. Her finger prints were on record down there."

"She's the girl whose car broke down, right?" Sam asked.

"Yeah," Potts confirmed. "About thirty k's south of here. We have her vehicle in our compound here at Tennant."

"Next of kin been notified?" Foley asked.

"The South Aussie chaps are on it as we speak," Potts answered.

"What else you got?" Foley asked.

Potts paused on the other end of the line. "The media," he said eventually. "They're starting to gather."

"How the fuck did that happen, Terry?" Foley sounded annoyed.

"I'm not sure. I suspect it started with the girl who reported Miranda Winters missing, Lillian Clutterbuck. She's still here in Tennant Creek. She denies it, of course, but I think she went to a local bloke who hosts a community radio program here, playing all that Slim Dusty country music crap. The local folk go mad for it. She must have aroused his curiosity, and he's been nosing about asking questions."

"He the only one she spoke to?" Sam asked.

"I can't be sure," Potts answered. "I've been fielding calls from a couple of media outlets up in Darwin. It's only a matter of time, and I suspect we are going to be inundated with the press."

"Okay," Foley said. "Keep them at bay for as long as you can. We don't want the media descending on us yet. Get onto our Public Relations sections in Alice Springs, and Darwin, and inform them of what we've got here, and then you can divert any enquiries to them."

"I'll do my best," Potts agreed. "Unfortunately it's not just the media descending upon you, you need to be concerned with."

"Why do I get the feeling I don't really want to hear this?" Foley said.

"I expect you are going to get a visit from the Clutterbuck girl," Potts said. "She's like a dog with a bone, she won't let go."

"Shit!" Foley cursed. "That's all we need, a hysterical friend of the MP harassing us."

"What would you like me to do with her?" Potts asked. "Besides shoot her."

"Shoot her if you have to, Terry," Foley joked. "I don't much care what you do with her. Just keep her away from me. I'll talk to you later." He retrieved the phone from the car bonnet and disconnected the call.

"This is getting a little messy," Sam said.

"You think?" Foley chuffed. "What we need is a break." He turned, and looked across at the well as two officers from Task Force prepared to lower a ladder.

One of the officers leaned over the wall of the well to steady the ladder as his colleague lowered it. Suddenly he raised his hand, and called for his mate to stop. He unclipped a powerful Maglite torch from his utility belt, and shone it down the well. Suddenly he turned, and called out to his boss.

"Sarge, you need to take a look at this!"

Sergeant Wayne Donaldson was briefing the remainder of his crew when he heard the call. He turned, and crossed from the BearCat vehicle to the well.

"What is it?"

"There's something down there," his subordinate said, indicating the interior of the well.

Donaldson took the torch from his colleague, leaned over the top of the wall, and focused the beam down the well.

"Holy shit!" he exclaimed. "Inspector Foley!" he called to Foley. "I think you might want to see this."

Foley, and Sam hurried across to the well.

"What is it?" Foley asked.

"We've got another one," Donaldson answered.

"What? Another what?" Foley asked.

"Another body," Donaldson confirmed.

"I don't think this is the break you were hoping for," Sam said to Foley, as they leaned over the wall of the well and looked down.

Foley took the torch from Donaldson, and illuminated the interior of the well. A female body clad in her underwear lay in a crumpled, disheveled heap at the bottom of the well.

"You have got to be fucking kidding me!" Foley cursed.

"You got a camera in your vehicle?" Sam asked Donaldson.

"Of course," Donaldson answered. He turned to one of the ladder bearers. "Johnno, grab the camera from the truck, will you?"

Johnno, dropped his end of the ladder, and hurried back to the Task Force vehicle. He was back less than thirty seconds later, and handed the camera to his Sergeant.

Foley and Sam pulled back from the edge of the well.

"Get the ladder down there, Wayne. ... and send one of your chaps down to get photos, lots of them. Be careful not to disturb anything," Foley ordered.

"Give him a body bag as well," Sam suggested. "We need to get her up here ASAP."

"Get the rest of your lads to start a grid search," Foley ordered. Start here, at the well, and work your way out to about fifty metres."

Suddenly, the well and its surrounds became a hive of activity—disciplined, well-practiced, regimented activity. The Task Force members were well trained in this type of work, and they set about their respective duties with expertise and precision. Foley and Sam moved back to their vehicle, and waited for the body to reach the surface.

Foley and Rose were good investigators, both of whom enjoyed the unspoken envy of their fellow investigators, many of whom, although they would never openly admit it, worked hard at attempting to emulate their abilities. This of course, made for a competent crime investigation unit, the efficiency of which did not escape those far more senior in the ranks than Sam, and Foley.

Both Sam, and Foley had, over their respective time as detectives attached to Major Crime, received a number of commendations as a result of cases they had solved. successful outcome of cases being attributed to their personal involvement. However, neither of them had ever worked in Task Force, and they never ceased to be impressed at the way the crack unit carried out their duties, regardless of how mundane, or distasteful those duties might be at any given time.

Leaning against their sedan, watching the Task Force at work, might be considered to be the epitome of conceited laziness, but both Foley and Rose knew there were horses for courses, and it was always best to leave certain work to those best suited to carry it out. Besides, Foley figured if he waited for Sam to go down the well and retrieve the latest body, the remains would be nothing more than bones, and tiny scraps of rapidly perishing underwear.

"You want to speculate on who that is down there?" Sam nodded towards the well.

"Either missing person six, or seven?' Foley posed.

"That would be my guess," Sam agreed.

Foley fumbled in his pocket for his phone. "I'll call Potts, and get him to send a vehicle to take the body back to Tennant Creek,"

"The coroner up there is going to wish he'd chosen another profession," Sam suggested.

"This'll make up for the weeks, or maybe months, he sits around waiting for someone to die so he's got something to do," Foley said as he found Terry Potts's name, and hit redial.

"Potentially," Sam speculated, "There may still be

one more to come, we've got seven girls missing."

When Terry Potts answered, Foley asked, "Have you got photos of the two latest missing girls?"

"Yes," Potts answered. "We've got photos of them all. Not all recent, but we've got them all in our files."

"Can you e-mail me photos of the two latest girls," Foley fumbled in his notebook. "Veronica Cooper and Miranda Winters."

"Sure," Potts answered. "Give me a few minutes to get them out of the files, and I'll send them straight away. Why, what have you got?"

"Another body," Foley frowned.

"No way!" Potts responded. "Where?"

"In the bottom of the well," Foley said.

"In the well! In the same well?" Potts sounded astounded.

"The same well," Foley confirmed.

"Are you there now?" Potts asked.

"Yeah. We've got the Task Force retrieving the body as we speak," Foley said.

"What else do you need out there?" Potts asked.

"We need a vehicle to convey the body back to Tennant Creek for an autopsy," Foley said.

"I'll get right on it," Potts responded. "Do you want any more personnel?"

"No, Terry, thanks. We've got plenty here at the moment. Send me those photos so we can confirm an ID at this end."

"You'll have them shortly," Potts said.

"Thanks, Terry. I'll talk to you soon." Foley hung up the phone, and dropped it back in his pocket. "Photos should come through shortly," he said to Sam.

"I'll go and see how the retrieval is going," Sam said.

"Okay," Foley nodded. "I better call the boss back in Alice, and bring him up to date."

———

Thirty minutes later, the body, enclosed in a black body bag, lay on the ground at the base of the well. Russell Foley squatted at the head end of the bag, and reached for the zip running its full length. With his hands encased in white surgical gloves, he unzipped the bag in one swift motion, exposing the body of a young girl, dressed in soiled bra and panties.

"Pretty," Sam murmured, leaning over the open bag.

"Yeah," Foley agreed. He reached into the bag, gently turned the girls head to one side, and leaned closer. "Looks like a bullet wound to the back of the head," he observed aloud.

"Same as all the others," Sam said.

"Yeah," Foley said. "Same as all the others."

"We need to find this mongrel before he kills again," Sam declared.

"Yes we do," Foley nodded.

Foley's phone signaled an incoming message. He got to his feet, flipped open his phone, and retrieved the message; two photos were attached. He squatted back on his haunches, looked closely at the first photo, and then at the body. Then he advanced to the second photo, and glanced again at the dead girl. He paused, his eyes jumping from the photo, to the body, and then back to the photo. Satisfied, he got to his feet.

"Veronica Cooper," Foley said, handing his phone to Sam.

"The sixth missing girl," Sam commented, comparing the photo to the body.

"We have to find number seven," Foley declared. He turned to Donaldson. "How long can your chaps stay out here?"

Donaldson glanced back at the Task Force vehicle. "We are equipped with enough rations to last a week, ten days at a push," he said.

"What about fuel?" Foley asked.

"We have long-range fuel tanks fitted," Donaldson answered. "We can travel another thousand kilometers before we need to refuel. What are you asking?"

Foley scanned the surrounding area. "I want you to camp here for a few days. Drive out from here in a different direction each day. Cover perhaps a fifty-kilometer radius out from the well."

"What are we looking for?" Donaldson asked.

"A building... a shed... a house... anywhere someone might be able to keep a person captive for extended periods without coming to notice."

Donaldson slowly looked around, casting his eyes out to the distant horizon. "There doesn't seem to be anything as far as the eye can see," he observed.

"There has to be something," Foley said. "Six bodies have been dumped in this well. The killer must have held these girls captive somewhere before he killed them."

"If there's something out there, we'll find it." Donaldson programmed Foley's phone number into his mobile phone, and hastened away to join his men in the search cordon.

Foley reached down, and zipped the body bag closed. He faced Sam. "Let's get back to Wauchope," he said.

"Good idea, I could use a cold beer," Sam responded.

"I was thinking more about having another chat with Kenny, the barfly," Foley said.

"You looking at him for this?" Sam asked

Foley shook his head. "No. I think Kenny left his killing days behind him, in the jungles of Vietnam. He's been around a long time, and although he's not particularly forthcoming with information, I think he is our best source of local knowledge. The perp has to be from around here, or at the very least, familiar with the area. There has to be somewhere he could keep his victims prisoner without raising suspicion."

"Take a look around, Russ," Sam said. "There has to be millions of acres of wide open spaces out here. Where could he possibly keep them?"

Foley looked out across the vast, open land, extending to the far horizon. "I don't know," he said. "I don't know... but maybe Kenny does."

———

Kenny Watt sat on a low, post and railing fence, in the relatively cool shade of a huge Morton Bay Fig tree which cast a deep shadow across a large part of the caravan and camping area behind the Wauchope Hotel. He casually rolled a cigarette, and watched as Sam and Foley approached.

"Good afternoon, Kenny," Foley greeted the crusty old veteran.

"Hmmph!" Kenny grunted as he licked the edge of his cigarette paper, sealed it, and plucked at loose strands of tobacco protruding from both ends. Indifferently, he examined the finished product, and placed it between his lips.

"Warm day," Foley said, glancing at the sky.

Kenny fished a lighter from his pocket, lit his cigarette, and blew a stream of blue smoke into the air. "I've known warmer," he commented.

"I thought we might have a word with you," Foley said.

"Just one?" Kenny chuffed.

Sam leaned forward, towards Kenny. "Do you have a problem with the police?" he asked.

Kenny took another long drag on his cigarette. "I have a problem with anyone who encroaches on my privacy." He looked at Sam. "You two being police officers is irrelevant."

"All we want to do is ask you a couple of questions," Foley interjected. "And we apologise in advance for any inconvenience."

Kenny looked at Foley. "You do?"

"Yes," Foley said. "We do... both of us."

Kenny glanced at his watch. "It's almost rum o'clock, make it quick."

"We're looking for a house," Foley said.

Kenny looked first at Foley, and then at Sam. "Really? I wouldn't have taken you two for wanting to buy a house together."

"Oh, no," Foley said, a little too quickly. "We don't want to *buy* a house. We are looking for a house. Possibly off the beaten track. Somewhere, where most people would never know it existed."

"This about them girls?" Kenny asked.

"What?" Foley asked, the surprise evident in his tone.

"Them missing girls," Kenny continued. "This about them?"

"Missing girls?" Sam said. "What do you know

157

about missing girls?"

Kenny pinched the lit end of his cigarette, and tucked the butt into his shirt pocket.

"I might look like an old fart who doesn't give a shit," he said, glancing from Sam, to Foley. "And maybe that ain't too far from the truth, especially the part about not giving a shit, but I ain't stupid. I've been around the area long enough to hear the talk about girls going missing in the area."

"What have you heard?" Sam probed.

Kenny shrugged. "Just talk. Bar room talk. Bloody backpackers come out to this country, travelin' alone. Need their bloody heads read, you ask me."

"Anyone in particular who talked about missing girls?" Foley asked.

"Nope, just people passing through. Heard somethin' down the track somewhere, and yacked about it over a beer or two. Need to mind their own business, you ask me." Kenny pushed himself up from the fence rail. "Reckon I'll go in and have a drink now. Nice talkin' to you." He stepped around Sam and Foley.

"Wait," Foley said, grabbing Kenny's arm.

Kenny stopped, looked down at Foley's hand gripping his arm, and stared at it until Foley let go. "What?" he asked, sounding belligerent.

"What about a house... or a building of any sort... somewhere out of the way?" Foley pushed.

Kenny paused. "Might be a few. Either side of the highway. Some old mine buildings out at the old Wolfram mine site, about a half hour east of here. An old deserted station homestead or two, out to the west. Been empty for years." He walked away, towards the hotel and a waiting bottle of rum.

11

Miranda did not hear the man return. When she awoke, it was late in the afternoon. Dark shadows, created by the fading light outside the solitary window, had already begun to creep across the bare floor towards the far corners of the room. Over by the door, she noticed a small parcel. The man must have come back when she was asleep. She was surprised she did not hear him unlock the door.

Mandy pushed herself into a sitting position, and gently rubbed at the lump on her forehead. Mostly, the pain had subsided to a dull ache, and she was relieved there seemed to be no serious, long term injury to her head; at least nothing so serious it would prevent her from her escaping from the hell hole she was in.

Not long now, she thought. Just a few hours more; until it was late enough, and dark enough, for her to make her bid for freedom. Although she harbored fears about her plan, a small part of her looked forward to the escape attempt. It was not so much the climb up the chimney she found daunting, she was reasonably confident she could manage that part, it was more the flight once she was out of the house.

Where would she go? Which direction would she take? Would she make it in bare feet and just her underwear? These were doubts she tried unsuccessfully to put out of her mind, but they kept coming back at her. Questioning her. Challenging her. Filling her with self-doubt.

Carefully she got to her feet. Anticipating an accompanying dizzy spell, she paused for a moment. When no such spell materialised, she padded slowly over to the door and picked up the package. By the weight and the shape, she could tell it contained a sandwich. She hadn't thought about food for a while; the pain from the man's brutal attack on her overrode any desire for food. Now, as she turned the package over in her hands, she felt the first pangs of hunger deep in her belly, and was tempted to open the package and eat whatever it contained, regardless of how un-appetising it might appear.

She crossed back to her bedding, sat down, and lifted the blanket on Veronica's mattress. She placed the package on the mattress, and carefully arranged the blanket on top of it, hiding it from view. Out of sight, out of mind, she thought. Her plan was to take the sandwich with her when she escaped. It would be all she would have to sustain her for however long it took her to find help.

The water left in the bottle was hardly enough to quench her thirst out there in the heat of the day, or days, to come, and she looked back across the room to the door just to satisfy herself she hadn't missed a fresh bottle the man might also have left. There was nothing there. She lifted the half empty bottle, and looked at the water remaining. It would have to do, she thought.

Mandy laid down and closed her eyes. It would be nice to get more sleep before she left. She did not know when she might get an opportunity to rest again after she left the house.

———

The sliding of the door bolt roused Mandy from a restless sleep. She sat up quickly, and hugged the blanket to her body. In the darkness, she could not see the door; she peered into the blackness in the direction she knew the door to be. It swung open, and a pale shaft of light snaked across the floor, illuminating a path across the room from the door to her mattress. Then, a dark shape stepped into the shaft of light.

"Hello Miranda," the man greeted.

The voice sent a chill through Mandy, and she shuddered involuntarily.

"Wha... what do you want?"

"Come and have a drink with me," the man responded.

"Where's Veronica?" Mandy asked hesitantly.

She's not here," the man said.

"Where is she?"

"Gone."

"Gone where?"

"It is not important where," the man said. "All you need to know is she's gone."

"She... she's dead, isn't she?" Mandy sobbed.

"Don't worry your pretty head about Veronica, Miranda. Come over here."

"No," Mandy said, trying in vain to sound defiant.

"If I have to come over there and get you, I am going to hurt you again. Do you want me to hurt you again, Miranda?"

Mandy remained silent.

"Answer me Miranda. Do you want me to hurt you again?"

"No... no," Mandy sobbed.

"Then come over here. NOW!" he screamed.

Mandy shrunk back at the sound of his voice as the man screamed across the room at her. He was going to come in and hit her again if she disobeyed him. She touched her aching temple gingerly. She had no choice, she decided. She would have to get up, and go to him. The thought of what awaited her sent a shiver of dread through her body. She slowly rose to her feet, pulled the blanket tighter around her body, and began to shuffle across the room.

"Leave the blanket," the man ordered.

Mandy stopped. "What?"

"You heard me. Leave the blanket," he repeated.

"Please don't do this," Mandy begged as a tear rolled down her cheek.

"We are going to have a nice drink, Miranda. A nice quiet drink together. It'll be nice, you'll see. Leave the blanket, and get over here."

Mandy let the blanket fall from her shoulders, stepped over it, and walked slowly across to the door.

————

Once again out on the verandah, Mandy sat opposite the man. He smiled across the small table separating them. She looked out to her front, beyond the verandah railing, into the darkness, and then to her left, and her right, towards each end of the long, wide verandah. Unable to see anything further than the ends of the verandah, she had no better idea than the last time she was out here what lay beyond the limits of the house.

"Isn't this nice?" the man smiled. "It's just the two of us now." He poured a generous amount of rum into the same dirty glass he offered her last time she was in this situation. "Don't you think this is nice?"

Mandy met the man's eyes across the table, and hoped she could hold her nerve as she glared at him.

"No," she said. "It's not nice. It's cold. I want to know where Veronica is, I want my clothes, and I want to leave this place."

The man sipped his rum and smiled. "That's not going to happen, Miranda. This is your home now. I'll take care of you. Have a drink," he indicated the glass on the table in front of Mandy.

Mandy glanced down at her drink. "I'm not going to drink it. I told you before I don't like rum."

"Do I have to remind you, there is no way out of here? No one knows where we are. *You* don't even know where we are. No one is coming for you, Miranda. You might as well sit back and enjoy yourself. You know things will go much better for you if you cooperate. Surely you don't want me to hurt you again, do you?"

Mandy looked away from him. "No."

"Good. Now, have a drink, and relax. Enjoy the evening. I know I am." He lowered his eyes, and looked at Mandy's heaving breast.

———

The attack that followed was worse than the first. He was brutal, and it seemed the more pain he inflicted, the more aroused he became. When it was over, the man shoved Miranda cruelly into the prison-room, and locked the door, leaving her on her knees on the hard floor, clutching her lower abdomen, and grimacing in pain.

This time, however, Mandy was overcome with an emotion which, while it didn't obliterate the pain, it seemed to take precedence over it, at least in her mind. She was consumed now with hate. She could not think of a single person who had entered her young life up to this point who she could honestly say she hated, until now. The monster beyond the locked door was to be reviled; he deserved nothing less.

Mandy had never been a particularly religious person. As a young girl, she was encouraged by her parents to attend Sunday School every week, but it was not a practice she continued once she reached an age where she was able to make decisions for herself. Since becoming a nurse, she struggled to reconcile the sickness, misery, and heartache she had seen in her short life with God's supposed loving, caring, nurturing embrace of all human kind.

Now, as she thought about the despicable excuse for a human being who found pleasure in the disgusting, degrading, painful things he subjected hers, and the girls who came before her to, she decided God's judgment really had to be questioned. Particularly when he allowed a monster, a creation of something so alien it was difficult for her to comprehend, to breathe the same air as the rest of mankind.

If nothing else, the humiliation, the pain, and the

sheer horror of the things he did to her reinforced Mandy's determination to escape from this evil place.

In the darkness of the room, she felt her way on hands and knees to her mattress. The urge to drink the remaining couple of litres of water, and rinse the foul, lingering taste of him from her mouth was strong, almost too strong. She fumbled in the dark, found the bottle, and unscrewed the cap. As she raised the bottle to her mouth, something deep inside her she could not explain halted her hand, and she paused, the bottle touching her lips. Slowly, she lowered the bottle, and screwed the cap tight.

Mustering courage she never thought she possessed, Mandy found her tiny torch, and aimed the light at the chimney a few metres away. This was it. It was time to leave this place. She got unsteadily to her feet and crossed to the fireplace. She would have liked more time to consider every aspect of her escape plan, but there was no time. She was not going to go through the horror of the man's assaults one more time. It had to be now. It had to be tonight. She silently prayed she had the strength.

————

Frida Steinberg was never going to know just how lucky she was. Six, or seven more paces deeper into the tree line, closer to the man waiting for her, would ensure she would never return to her family back in Germany.

Suddenly, Frida paused; not from fear, or indeed anything ahead giving her cause for concern about continuing, it was the time. She had stayed too long in the roadhouse bar with the young man she met earlier in the day, and now it was late, after midnight. She was not drunk; Frida had always been careful in regards to how much alcohol she consumed, but she was interested in her new acquaintance, and she enjoyed his company to a point where she simply lost all track of time.

Also, there was the familiar stirring deep inside her, aroused when she met someone she felt she would like to get to know better. A part of her wanted to stay longer, maybe even go with him to his room. A few weeks had passed since she last had sex. She was a young, vibrant, carefree woman, in an exciting country where the men were fit, tanned, funny, and, for the most part, very nice looking. Something more powerful, however, something more attractive, overriding any carnal urges she felt, fluttered deep in her belly.

Frida had originally intended to leave the bar much earlier than she eventually did, and the lateness of the hour now meant she could spend less time out in the night than she would have otherwise, but she was nonetheless determined to make the most of the time she had.

The night was clear, and lovely, with very little breeze, and the sky was filled with millions of stars, perfect for what she hoped might occur. A distinct chill in the air hovered around her, typical of the outback nights at this time of the year, she had come to understand.

Frida never got tired of looking at the sky in this place. Night, or day, she, spent hours simply staring up at the broad, endless sky. She was enthralled with the history of this place, and hungered to learn as much as she could about it before she would have to leave.

It was not so much the geographical history of

Wycliffe Well that fascinated her, but the much-advertised history of UFO sightings associated with the area. Heavily marketed as the UFO capital of Australia, Frida was determined to visit this place from the moment she first Googled UFO sightings from her home in Hamburg in Germany.

Frida had a lifelong fascination, many of her friends back home would describe it as an obsession, with all things alien. Alien spaceships, alien sightings, secret government installations believed to house the remains of crashed alien craft, as well as their deceased alien occupants, and indeed anything remotely resembling, or suspected to be of alien origin was a source of never ending interest for Frida.

She decided before she left her home to travel to the other side of the world on what she called her 'extra-terrestrial adventure', Wycliffe Well would be at the top of her list of places to visit.

Frida arrived three days ago, and had yet to see a UFO. She was disappointed, but not deterred. There was so much UFO memorabilia scattered about the roadhouse and its attached caravan park directly relating to her fascination, she guessed she could easily stay a few weeks and not become bored.

Not for a moment did she believe all the memorabilia installed throughout the grounds, and the hundreds of newspaper clippings adorning the walls inside the roadhouse, were examples of man-made advertising hype designed to entice the traveler to stop and stay. Frida was so deeply enraptured with the whole alien, UFO, outer space concept, it didn't matter how many voices she heard to the contrary; she was never going to be convinced aliens had never visited earth.

Soon after arriving at Wycliffe Well, Frida had learned there was a large clearing beyond the lake on the other side of the tree line from where she stood. Should she continue? She was tired, and it was late. Perhaps she should head back to her room and try again tomorrow night. She looked at her watch, and then up at the sky glittering with stars visible through the canopy of trees. Reluctantly Frida turned, and walked away. She would never know the decision not to continue saved her life.

The man, waiting and watching from his vantage point deep in the tree line almost sprang from his hiding place and chased the girl. He had been watching her covertly for several hours. He first noticed her in the roadhouse, drinking and laughing with a young man who seemed to have captured her interest. She was pretty. very pretty.

He checked himself, ducked back behind the tree where he waited, and watched her walk away, out of the trees and towards the main roadhouse campground. He was angry. Furious. She had been so close. When she was gone, he hurried back to his car, climbed in, and slammed the door loudly. He banged his fist hard against the steering wheel, cursing vehemently.

The man sat in his car for a long time, in the dark, smoking cigarettes, and drinking Bundaberg rum directly from the bottle. Instead of making him sleepy, the rum fueled his anger. Hours later, when, in the distant eastern sky, the very first hint of the coming day began to materialise, he started the car, and drove away from the roadhouse and the pretty girl he wanted so badly.

———

Mandy hurried back to her mattress, and hastily gathered her own, and Veronica's blankets. Preparing herself was not a time-consuming job. She envisaged the whole process in her mind many times in the last twenty-four hours. Unlike when she rock-climbed in Victoria, there was no equipment to check and prepare.

She did not have the luxury of ropes, climbing shoes, helmet, or safety harness at her disposal, as she would if she were about to attempt a typical rock climb. She would be doing this without the security of the regulation safety devices so essential when rock climbing. But, thinking about, and ruing what she didn't have, was energy wasted, she deemed. She had what she had, and had to deal with it.

There were other unknowns, of course, like how to get off the roof once she successfully climbed out of the chimney. Could she climb down, or would she be faced with having to jump? All the effort would amount to nothing if she broke a leg, or worse. Then, there was the question of which way to walk if she was lucky enough to get off the roof injury free. She would just have to wing it, and hope for the best.

She tied both blankets around her neck, so the length of them hung over her shoulders, and down her back. She yanked on the loose ends hanging down, satisfying herself they would not come undone during the climb. Then, she picked up the bottle of water, ensured the cap was secured tightly, and retrieved the small package containing the sandwich.

Her car keys, with the torch attached, she would have to carry in her teeth. She was going to need the

GARY S. GREGOR

torch both during the climb, and then to find a way off the roof. Thankfully, there were only two car keys and the torch on the ring, so she figured she could carry them clamped tightly between her teeth without too much difficulty. She placed the keys in her mouth, and bit down on the ring. The torch, and the keys, dangled against her chin, and she moved her head about to satisfy herself she was going to be able to manage.

Immediately, she walked back to the chimney, crouched low, and stepped into the space where the fire grate once stood. Carefully, she stuck her head into the chimney cavity, and straightened her legs.

Suddenly, the water bottle, and the sandwich parcel, became problematic. She needed both hands free to reach up, find suitable hand holds, and then bring her feet up beneath her. She couldn't do this while holding onto the water bottle and the packaged sandwich. The weight was not her concern; the items were was more awkward than heavy.

For a brief moment, Mandy felt a tiny feather of panic stirring deep inside her. She took a couple of deep breaths, and focused on steadying her rapidly beating heart. No time like the present, she thought. If she hesitated and thought about the difficulties, she might not go at all.

She gathered the trailing ends of the blankets hanging to a point way below the back of her knees and tied them in a knot in front of her belly. The result was a very simple carry bag, not unlike the wrap-around, shawl type sacks women sometimes carried their babies in. She tucked the water bottle and the sandwich into the sack and pushed down on them to ensure they were snug and not going to fall out during the climb. Effective in its simplicity, she decided.

Steadying herself, she took the keys from her mouth, shone the torch up into the chimney cavity, and studied the interior wall directly above, and in front, of where she stood. Finding two rough, protruding pieces of stonework, she memorised where they were, switched off the torch, and placed the key ring back in her mouth.

Raising her arms to full stretch, she reached up into the black, stuffy space above her head, felt around for the two pieces of stone, and gripped them tightly. Her grip was tentative at best, with not much more purchase than by her fingers. Carefully, she tested the strength of her grip, and more importantly, the strength of the stones, by lifting first one leg, and then the other. She hung suspended for a few seconds, all of her body weight held by her fingers, and pulling down against the stones. The stones held. Her fingers ached.

Carefully, she lifted her legs until her knees came up into the chimney cavity. She pulled them in tight against her chest and felt around the wall directly in front of her with her toes, searching for a foot hold. Just as she thought the strain on her arms was too great and she would have to let go, she found a toe hold, and tensed her legs tight against the wall.

Pushing against the wall with her feet, she leaned back hard against the wall behind her, locking her body against the front, and back wall of the cavity. Satisfied she was not going to fall, she relaxed her grip, shook her hands, and massaged her fingers. So far, so good, she thought.

She took the key ring from between her teeth, and shone the torch further up into the chimney, scanning the wall in front of her. When she found another two suitable hand holds, she returned the torch to her mouth and repeated the process, her body rising another few centimetres higher into the cavity.

At this point, Mandy was beginning to have second thoughts. The climb was the least of her problems; it was the distance she still had to cover, and the unknowns in the darkness above. Spiders, and indeed bugs of any description, were not Mandy's favorite things to encounter, even in broad daylight, let alone in the dead of night, part way up an old fireplace chimney.

She shuddered involuntarily at the thought of the creepy crawlies climbing and falling on her.She paused for a few moments to re-assess her situation. She had two alternatives. She could keep going up and accept whatever scurrying, scampering nasties she might encounter on the way, or go back down and await the next episode of brutal, painful, sexual abuse at the hands of her gaoler.

For a few brief moments, she allowed herself to think about Veronica and what might have happened to her. She had to believe Veronica was not coming back to the room. Veronica was almost certainly dead, as were the girls who came before her. If Mandy went back down, she was going to die also, it was not a matter of if, but when. Ultimately, the decision was obvious, and she silently cursed herself for wasting time thinking about it. She had to keep climbing.

Steeling herself, she placed her hands flat against the wall behind her, pushed once again with her feet and her hands, and rose deeper into the black void above.

When her face met the spider web she very nearly lost it. She flailed wildly at the soft web fibres stuck to her face, her eyes, and her mouth. She emitted a stifled cry of horror, and the key ring, with torch attached, fell from her lips. Her knees knocked together painfully in a reflexive reaction as she attempted in vain to catch it before it clattered to the empty fireplace below. She listened as the torch hit the slab at the base of the chimney, rolled once, and fell silent.

Mandy closed her eyes and sobbed. Her whole body began to shake uncontrollably and, for a moment, she felt she was going to fall, but managed to jam her feet hard against the wall to her front, and lock her body tight. The thin, threadbare blankets around her shoulders offered little protection, and the rough, uneven surface behind her dug painfully into her back.

She slapped, and wiped at the remnants of spider web clinging stubbornly to her face. The musty, acrid taste of soot and ash filled her mouth, and she turned her head and spat into the void below. With a determination sourced from a place she could not identify, she breathed deeply through her nose, and pushed.

She lost track of how many times she pushed herself upwards. Her legs screamed in protest, and her back hurt so bad she cried out every time she slid up against the rough stone wall behind her. She could feel moisture beneath the blankets, and she wondered if it was perspiration, or blood oozing from where the skin had rubbed from her back.

Twice she had to stop and rest until she recovered from a coughing fit when the stinking, black soot was sucked deep into her lungs as she gasped for air following each renewed effort. At one point, she began to giggle hysterically as she thought about the irony of getting out of this hell hole and subsequently dying from a serious lung infection.

Regaining her composure, she set about psyching herself up for the next push. Suddenly, she tensed. Something from above touched her hair, and ruffled it ever so slightly. She felt herself beginning to panic and slapped at the top of her head. She lifted her head as far as she was able to, and stared into the blackness above.

A low, mournful moan escaped her lips. She was going to let go. She could go no further. Her body had had enough. Her mind had had enough. She could not do this anymore. She closed her eyes tightly, but was unable to stop the tears escaping and running down her cheeks.

Then she felt it. It came from above. Air! A tiny, gentle, feather soft wisp of air brushed against her closed eyelids. Then, another. Mandy snapped her eyes open, and peered intently into the darkness above. She held her breath, and waited. It came again! Another soft, whisper of air washed gently over her upturned face, and Mandy laughed. "Yes! Yes!" she cried softly, triumphantly.

With renewed vigor and hope, she pushed again. This time she did not rest between efforts. She pushed once, twice, three times and then, her head poked out the top of the chimney.

Cool, sweet, beautiful air washed over her, and she took a moment to luxuriate in the rejuvenating smell and taste of it. She inhaled, taking long, slow, glorious mouthfuls deep into her lungs. She could feel the revitalising effects immediately. Although it was still dark, she could see out here. The moon, high in the sky, cast a soft, delicate light across the roof of the house.

Mandy took a moment to take in her immediate surroundings. The chimney rose about two metres above the roof of the house, and she would have to be careful getting down from her precarious position. If she fell onto the roof, the noise would surely arouse the man inside, and getting caught now, after all the energy-sapping effort of getting this far, was not an option.

Carefully, she lifted her arms out of the top of the chimney, and gripped the exterior of the walls tightly. Pushing again with her feet, and pulling up with her hands, she was able to get her shoulders out, and then the rest of her body followed. In an ungainly display of contortionism, she had to turn her body as it came out of the chimney or she would find herself in a head-down position, with the distinct possibility of falling head first onto the roof.

A difficult maneuver at any time, an indelicate balancing act, but she tackled it slowly, and deliberately. Eventually, she found herself in a position where her legs were wrapped around the chimney below her, and her arms were wrapped around the top in a bizarre display of chimney hugging. With the water bottle and sandwich squeezed between her waist and the chimney wall, she lowered herself, centimeters at a time, until she felt her feet touch the cold surface of the galvanised iron roof. She lowered herself into a sitting position, the cold roof a comfort against her thinly veiled buttocks.

For a long time, Mandy sat there, her face raised to the sky, taking deep breaths of the sweet tasting night air. She lifted the blankets from her shoulders, and placed her meager rations next to her, again resisting the urge to drink deeply and rid herself of the lingering taste of soot and ash. The icy chill of a gentle, pre-dawn breeze wafting across the rooftop washed over her bare, scraped and bleeding back. She closed her eyes and welcomed the mild relief it offered.

———

Mandy must have slept, although she could not remember doing so. She had no way of knowing what time it was. but the sky was lighter, now. She cursed silently, and rose unsteadily to her feet. She had to get off the roof, and as far away from this place as she could before daylight made flight impossible. Careful not to make a noise, she padded in her bare feet across the roof to what she thought was the rear of the house. She stopped just short of the roofline, leaned out as far as she could, and peered through the gloom at the ground below. She guessed she was just above the barred window of the room she had escaped from.

The ground seemed a long way down. This was an old home, with high ceilings, and a high roofline designed to take advantage of any breeze on offer. There appeared to be nothing she could cling to and climb down, and it was far too high to jump without injuring herself. Dejected, Mandy padded around the roof line, stopping every few metres to lean out and assess her chances of getting down. As she proceeded, she became more and more dejected. Surely after all she had gone through to get out of the house she was not going to be stuck up here on the roof!

Then there it was! She was now on the opposite side of the house, above the verandah where she was forced to sit and drink disgusting rum with her captor. The verandah roof was just a metre or so below where she stood. She could climb down onto it, and then shimmy down one of the posts supporting it.

She looked back up at the sky, and saw it was even lighter than it was a few minutes ago. Dawn was going to be upon her soon. She had to get down before daybreak. She padded back to the chimney, gathered the blankets, the water, and the food, and hurried back to the front of the roof.

For the first time since she emerged from the chimney she really noticed the cold. This was outback country. The nights were cold, sometimes dropping below freezing, and the days were hot. Mandy shivered, and hugged herself. Standing on the roof in the pre-dawn chill dressed only in flimsy underwear, presented an incongruous picture. She wrapped the blankets around her shoulders, pulling them tighter around her near-naked body, and returned her supplies to the hastily fashioned pouch.

Hesitating was not an option. The sky was getting lighter by the minute. She had to get off the roof. Carefully she climbed down onto the verandah roof, silently praying the man was not an early riser. Was he sitting at the table on the verandah just below where she now stood? Could he hear her above him? She shook her head in an effort to dismiss the negative thoughts.

Slowly, quietly, she stepped across to the leading edge of the verandah roof, leaned out, and looked down. She was directly above one of the support posts. Without any further hesitation, she sat down and, careful not to crush the water bottle, turned over onto her stomach, and lowered her legs out over the edge. Sliding on her belly, she pushed herself backwards, feeling with her legs for the post. Finding it, she wrapped her legs around it, locked her ankles together, and pushed herself over the lip of the roof. Just like a fireman on the station-house fire-pole, she slid silently down to the ground.

She felt the ground beneath her feet, and let go of the post, steadied herself against it, and stared at the front door just a few metres from where she stood. The door was closed, and she could see no light from any windows along the length of the verandah. Got to go, she thought. Without delay, she scurried to the very end of the verandah, and darted around the far end of the house.

In the dim light, she did not see the rain water tank, and she collided with it. Located at the corner of the house, she crashed head-long into it, and fell heavily to the ground. Pain, like hot needles cruelly inserted into her eyes, raged through her head. She grunted aloud, clenched her teeth in an attempt to muffle the noise, and clasped her head in her hands.

Her head still ached from where the man had hit her, and now the excruciating pain was back, worse than ever. She rolled onto her side, and sobbed softly. A wave of despair washed over her, and she silently considered surrendering to the hopelessness of it all.

Mandy's will was strong, however. Something, from somewhere deep within her being, would not allow her to quit. She rolled onto her back, and stared into the star-filled sky high above her, waiting for the pain to subside to a tolerable throb. She had come too far to quit now. She had to keep going. She was out of the house. She could still get away from this awful place.

Then, she felt it. A cold, wetness against her stomach. Instantly she knew what it was, and she scrambled to remove the water bottle from the folds of the blanket. She could feel, and hear, water sloshing in the bottle, but the level had dropped considerably. Panic engulfed her again as she felt all over the bottle, searching for the leak. A split in the plastic, just above the base of the bottle, allowed most of the contents to leak. The remainder was spilling out as she watched. The bottle must have been ruptured when she collided with the rain water tank.

As quickly as she could, she unscrewed the cap, and swallowed the remaining contents in several deep gulps. It tasted beautiful. Sweet, cool, and soothing in her parched throat. As she swallowed, she sobbed, and tears ran freely from her eyes leaving wide tracks down her dirty, soot-covered cheeks.

She got to her knees, discarded the ruptured water bottle, and looked around, taking in the surroundings in her immediate vicinity. Now all she had was a soggy sandwich parcel, and no water. She was on her knees, right next to a large rain water tank containing Lord knows how much life-giving water, and the only container she had to store it in lay broken on the ground.

Through the dim light, approximately thirty metres away she saw the dark shape of a large building; a shed, she decided. Using the tank stand as support, Mandy climbed to her feet, and stared intently across at the shed. Perhaps there would be something inside she could use to store water, she thought. Making a snap decision not to hesitate, she pushed off from the tank and sprinted clumsily in her bare feet for the shed, her gait awkward, and ungainly, as the rough, stony ground dug into the bare soles of her feet.

She reached the shed, and stopped in front of a pair of large double doors. She glanced back at the house, expecting to see the man had discovered her escape and was right behind her. She saw no one, and sighed with relief. When she returned her focus to the shed, she noticed the doors were slightly ajar, offering just enough of a gap for her to squeeze through and enter the shed.

The night was evaporating quickly. Mandy glanced up at the sky, and knew instantly she had to find a hiding place. As desperately as she wanted to be far away from this place, she knew she could not attempt to flee in the daylight. In her bare feet, flight would be slow and cumbersome. She could not possibly hope to be far enough away where the man would not find her. Turning sideways, she put one leg through the gap in the doors, squeezed her body through, and stepped into the dark interior.

The morning light rapidly descending outside had not yet penetrated the interior of the shed, and the space she found herself in appeared cavernous and dark. Mandy waited for a moment, allowing her eyes to adjust to the darkness, and then, she moved cautiously, one step at a time, with her hands thrust out in front of her, deeper into the inky blackness.

12

Sam stepped from his room and was confronted by a small group of people gathered together in a cleared area, half way between the accommodation rooms and the hotel. He knew immediately who they were. He paused on the tiny, covered landing in front of his door, and almost turned and hurried back into his room. If it weren't for his bladder insisting on urgent relief, he might have taken that very option, but chose instead to continue to the ablution block on the other side of the gathered throng.

By the very nature of his job, Sam often found himself in contact with the various arms of the media machine, either voluntarily or otherwise, and he had never been comfortable with the pushy, competitive, intrusive manner in which many of them went about pursuing a story.

When one of their number noticed him standing on his doorstep, the small group moved en-masse. They pressed forward, thrusting cameras, microphones, and hand-held tape recorders before them, each jostling for front position. Questions came at him from every voice present. All he heard was a jumble of indecipherable babble.

A man in front of the pack came to a sudden stop at the foot of the small landing. Those pushing forward behind him tumbled into him, and subsequently into each other.

Sam frowned down upon the group. A few he recognised as representatives of the various Alice Springs media outlets, and those he had never seen before he assumed were from Tennant Creek, or beyond.

His eyes were drawn to one lady reporter in particular; an attractive, thirty-something, journalist who worked for one of the Alice Springs commercial television stations. Rebecca Anders and Sam were an item for a brief time, about two years ago. Sam smiled at Rebecca as she pushed and jostled her way, seemingly undaunted by the tightly compressed mass, closer to the front of the pack.

"Hello, Sam," Rebecca greeted, her voice rising above the others.

"Hello, Beccy," Sam acknowledged, smiling down at her. "Lovely to see you."

"I guess you know why we are all here?" Rebecca queried.

"A journalist's convention in the Australian countryside?" Sam suggested with undisguised sarcasm.

"Sergeant Rose!" a voice called from the middle of yammering pack. "What can you tell us about the bodies in the well?"

Sam raised his hands, and called for calm. "Whoa! Stop. Slow down." he demanded. "One at a time, please!"

The clamor of questions and demands for answers

slowly faded to a dull drone. Sam waited for a few moments before proceeding. He looked at Rebecca, inviting her to go first. "Miss Anders?"

Rebecca Anders glanced at a notebook she held, and then looked up at Sam. "Can you confirm eight bodies have been located at the bottom of a well near here?"

Sam smiled. "No, I cannot confirm that," he answered.

The dull murmur from the group rose in intensity immediately, and another voice from the middle of the pack called. "What *can* you confirm?"

Sam lifted his gaze to the man who asked the question. "Who are you, Sir?"

"Frank Coustos!" the reporter answered loudly.

"Thank you Mister Coustos," Sam said. "I can confirm *six* bodies have been located in a well near here." He looked back at Rebecca. "Not eight, as Miss Anders has suggested."

The revelation sent the media scrum into another feeding frenzy. "Who are they?" someone called.

"Where's the well?" someone else yelled across the top of the pack.

"Is it true they are all young women?" a female asked, her voice rising above the insistent crowd.

The questions came thick, and fast; too fast for Sam to respond to each one individually. He waited until the mob had quieted somewhat, and then continued.

"This is an ongoing investigation," he said. "I am not at liberty to offer any more detail other than what I have already confirmed. As soon as we are able to release further information, our public relations department in Alice Springs will be available to respond to your questions." He paused, cast his eyes over the group. "Thank you for your interest, but that is all I can tell you at this time."

He stepped from the top of the steps, and pushed his way through the throng. The hungry, inquisitive pack of media hounds, loudly voicing their disappointment, continued to hurl questions at his retreating back as they doggedly followed him across the open area.

At the door of the hotel ablution block, Sam turned and faced the small group. "I need to use the bathroom facilities," he said, "and I prefer to do that alone."

"Where is Inspector Foley?" one of the reporters called.

Sam paused, located the man behind the voice. "He is down the track, at Wycliffe Well, investigating a tip off from a member of the public," he lied.

"A 'tip off'?" someone said.

"Yes," Sam said. "Now if you'll excuse me." He opened the door, stepped inside the ablution block and closed the door behind him.

When Sam emerged a few minutes later the media group had gone; all except for Rebecca Anders. Rebecca was alone, waiting outside, leaning casually against the wall of the building.

"Hello again," she said as Sam stepped outside.

"Hello," Sam said. "I had a feeling you would still be here."

"Am I that predictable," Rebecca asked.

Sam ignored the question. "Where are all the others?" he asked, looking around.

Rebecca followed his gaze. "I suspect they are all

on their way to Wycliffe Well," she smiled. "That was pretty quick thinking," she added.

"Whatever do you mean?" Sam asked, feigning surprise.

"Where is Russell Foley, *really*," she asked.

"Russell is probably in the dining room having breakfast," Sam said. "He's an early riser."

"We checked in there first," Rebecca said. "There is no one in the dining room."

"Probably saw you all coming and hid in the kitchen," Sam speculated. "He's about as keen on the media as I am."

"We are not bad people, Sam," Rebecca said. "All we want to do is inform the public about what is happening."

"Some of you are bad people," Sam said.

"Don't throw out all the apples just because there are a few bad ones in the barrel," Rebecca cautioned.

Sam smiled. "Why are you still here, and not with the rest of them scurrying off to Wycliffe Well?"

"Have you forgotten? I know you, Sam," Rebecca said, a hint of seductiveness in her voice. "You and Russell are best friends, and have been working together for a long time. If he was in Wycliffe Well, you would be there too."

"Now *I'm* being predictable," Sam laughed.

"Tell me about the bodies in the well," Rebecca pushed.

"I've told you all I can," Sam shrugged.

"You've told me all you want to tell me," Rebecca said. "But not all you know."

"I'm sorry, Rebecca," Sam apologised. "I really can't talk about it."

"Is there any link to a number of young girls reported missing in the area?" Rebecca continued to probe.

"I'm sorry," Sam shrugged.

Rebecca stepped a little closer to Sam, and looked up into his eyes. "You know, we were pretty close once," she smiled.

"Yes, we were," Sam agreed. "And it was very nice, as I recall."

"Can't you give me anything? For old time's sake?"

"If I could, you would be the first to know," Sam nodded. "But I can't, and I won't." He stepped around Rebecca. "Now, I'm hungry. I need to have breakfast."

"I'm not going away," Rebecca said, defiantly.

"I can't make you go away, Rebecca. Stay as long as you like," Sam said. "Now, if you'll excuse me, I'm going to eat, and then I've got work to do." He turned his back on Rebecca and walked away.

————

Russell Foley was seated at a small table at the back of the dining room. Sam spotted him, crossed the room to where an urn with tea and coffee makings stood, made himself a mug of coffee, and took a seat opposite Foley.

"Good morning," he greeted Foley.

"Who was that?" Foley asked.

"What, no 'good morning?'" Sam asked.

"Good morning," Foley said. "Who was that?"

"Rebecca Anders," Sam said.

"The journalist?" Foley asked.

"Yes," Sam nodded.

"You two used to date, right?"

"A long time ago," Sam offered in explanation.

"Where did all the others she was with go?" Foley asked. "They jumped in their vehicles and headed south real fast."

"They went to Wycliffe Well," Sam said, sipping his coffee.

Foley looked at Sam suspiciously. "Why?"

"Why what?" Sam asked.

"Don't be a dick," Foley ordered. "Why did they go to Wycliffe Well?"

Sam shrugged. "I don't know. Chasing up a lead I guess."

"A false lead you tossed them?" Foley asked.

Sam shrugged again. "I was just feeding the chickens."

"You do know, as soon as they get there, they're going to know you sent them on a wild goose chase?"

Sam winked at Foley and ignored the question. "I'm hungry, let's eat."

A young Irish girl, working in multiple roles including waitress, cook, roadhouse attendant, and house-maid, came to their table, took their breakfast orders, and hurried out of the room towards the kitchen. Sam watched her leave, and when she had disappeared into the kitchen he looked across the table at Foley.

"How did you know there were other reporters with Rebecca?" Sam asked.

"I saw them," Foley answered.

"From the kitchen?" Sam asked.

"Yes," Foley confirmed. "Where is the lovely Miss Anders now?"

Sam shrugged. "Outside somewhere. Don't worry about Rebecca. She won't bother us."

"Are you sure?" Foley asked.

"I'm sure," Sam nodded.

"Good," Foley said, "Because we have more important things to worry about than a nosy journalist."

"Like what?" Sam asked, his interest aroused.

"I just got a call from Terry Potts," Foley began. "He has a preliminary pathology report on the body we found yesterday."

"And...?" Sam asked.

"There are signs the girl was subject to repeated, violent sex, anal as well as vaginal, over an extended period, possibly several weeks. Her genitals were torn up pretty badly. There were also deep ligature marks on her wrists and ankles. It appears she was bound hand, and foot, probably while being brutally raped."

"Jesus!" Sam cursed.

"That's not all," Foley added. "The most recent of the other five bodies, although it was partially decomposed, shows similar signs of violent sexual abuse."

"We have to find the Winters girl," Sam said. "Before we find *her* in the bottom of the well."

"There's more," Foley said. "It seems we are about to have another visitor."

"Really, who?" Sam asked.

"Lillian Clutterbuck, friend of the latest missing girl, Miranda Winters," Foley explained. "She reported Winters missing."

"She's coming here?" Sam asked.

"On her way as we speak," Foley nodded.

"What does she want?" Sam asked.

"She wants us to find her friend."

"Oh, is that all?" Sam said.

"Apparently, she's heard stories about dead girls in the bottom of a well, and she thinks we are not doing enough to find Winters," Foley elaborated.

"Should we hide in the kitchen?" Sam suggested.

Foley drained his coffee cup, and rose to get himself another. "I was thinking," he began. "You seem to have done such a good job at distracting the media, perhaps you could talk to her when she gets here."

"Can't do that, Russell... I'll be busy hiding in the kitchen," Sam said dismissively.

———

Lillian Clutterbuck was furious, and the intensity of her anger was increasing proportionately with the lack of information provided by the police. Her friend Miranda was missing, and she was no closer to finding out where she was, or what might have happened to her, than when she first arrived in Tennant Creek, excited to be catching up with her friend again.

Her frustration was exacerbated by stories she heard, and was still hearing, about young girls, girls just like herself, who simply vanished while traveling around Australia. Now, in the last twenty-four hours she was hearing even more stories in the media, and in the Tennant Creek back-packer's hostel where she was staying, about a number of bodies having been found in the bottom of a well somewhere in the remote outback near the tiny outpost of Wauchope.

Lillian was no shrinking violet. She was a tough, outspoken, no nonsense girl, who had never been in the habit of allowing herself to be dissuaded from any course she set for herself. The task foremost in her mind now was to find her friend Miranda Winters and, if the police couldn't, or wouldn't do it, she would hound them until they did. Determined to get the answers she could not get from the Tennant Creek police, she decided she would get them from the police officers in charge of the case.

She drove into the customer parking area in front of the Wauchope Hotel, stopped a few metres from the front door, and sat for a moment looking at the hotel and its uninspiring surrounds. Eventually she got out of her vehicle, locked the door, and walked purposefully to the entrance.

She recognised the police almost immediately. They were the only two people in the dining room, and they had cop written all over them. She strode determinedly to where they sat at the rear of the dining room. Their breakfast order had arrived, and they were both eating.

"Which one of you is Inspector Foley?" she asked sternly.

Sam pointed to Foley, and Foley pointed to Sam. "He is," they said in unison.

"Very funny," Lillian said, sarcastically.

Sam lowered his fork, laden with eggs, to the side of his plate. "What makes you think either one of us is an inspector of anything?" Sam asked the girl.

Lillian fixed him with a look which left Sam with no doubt his tongue-in-cheek repartee was not going to be accepted with the same good humor with which it was delivered.

"You have to be kidding," she said. "A blind man would have picked you two for cops a mile away."

"You know," Sam said. "You're not the first person to tell us that."

"I'm Inspector Foley," Russell Foley said, diverting the girl's attention away from Sam. "And who might you be?"

Lillian turned her attention to Foley. "Don't treat

me like a fool, Inspector. I expect you know who I am, and I expect you have been forewarned by Officer Plod in Tennant Creek that I was on my way here."

"Officer Plod?" Foley raised his eyebrows. "I assume you are referring to Sergeant Terry Potts."

Lillian shrugged. "Potts... Plod... what's the difference?"

"The difference is, his name is Potts, not Plod." Foley stared directly into Lillian's eyes. "And," he continued. "I would appreciate it if you would try to be a little more respectful. Sergeant Potts is a highly respected police officer with many years of distinguished service behind him."

Lillian, determined not to appear chastised, glared back at Foley. "My friend is missing. I want to know what you are doing to find her."

Foley picked up his coffee cup, took a long, slow sip, and gently placed the cup back on the table. "Miss Clutterbuck, I presume?" he asked.

"You presume correctly," Lillian confirmed. "What are you do—"

Foley raised his hand. "Just one moment, please, Miss Clutterbuck," he said. He indicated Sam, who had resumed eating his breakfast, and was busy chewing on a piece of bacon. "This is Sergeant Sam Rose. Sergeant Rose and I are currently investigating, among other things, reports of people who have gone missing in the area. Can we assume that is the nature of your enquiry?"

Lillian Clutterbuck fixed Foley with the same withering look she had earlier offered Sam. "What are you doing about finding my friend? You won't find her sitting here feeding your faces."

"Your friend would be who?" Foley asked.

"Miranda Winters," Lillian answered. "And don't you get all condescending with me!"

"Condescending?" Foley raised his eyebrows.

"You heard me... *condescending*," Lillian repeated. "You do know what that means, don't you?"

Russell Foley took another sip of his coffee, wiped his mouth with a serviette, and cast it aside. "Miss Clutterbuck," he said quietly. "Sergeant Rose and I are enjoying our breakfast... or at least we were before you so rudely interrupted us. Unfortunately, now it seems I've lost my appetite, so why don't you get yourself a cup of coffee, pull up a chair, and sit down."

"I don't drink coffee," Lillian said.

"Of course you don't," Sam muttered softly over a mouthful of thickly buttered toast.

"I beg your pardon?" Lillian swung her eyes to Sam.

"I said 'I haven't'" Sam said.

"You haven't what?" Lillian asked.

"I haven't lost my appetite," Sam said. A forkful of scrambled eggs followed the toast.

"You are a very rude man!" Lillian declared, glaring at Sam.

Foley glared across the table at Sam. "That's true, Miss Clutterbuck. Sometimes Sergeant Rose can be a *very* rude man." He returned his focus to Lillian Clutterbuck. "Please sit down." He indicated a spare chair at the table.

Lillian pulled out the chair, and sat. She turned sideways, facing Foley, her back to Sam, "I will repeat my question," she said. "What are you doing about finding my friend?"

"Well," Foley began. "We are doing everything we can to find her."

Sam spoke to Lillian's back. "We can't do anything more, other than all we *can* do."

In case Sam had missed it the first time, Lillian spun around, and gave him another of her peel-the-paint-off-the-wall looks.

"I wasn't talking to you!" she hissed through clenched teeth. "And, I don't *want* to talk to you!"

"I suppose dinner, and a nice bottle of red is out of the question?" Sam smiled.

"Sam!" Foley cautioned. "Let me handle this." He touched Lillian on the hand to divert her attention from Sam.

"Miss Clutterbuck."

Lillian turned back to face Foley, a red blush of rage lingering on her cheeks. "What?" she asked.

"When was the last time you saw your friend?" Foley asked.

Lillian paused, taking a moment to regain her composure. "A few weeks ago," she answered finally. "In Sydney."

"And you've kept in touch ever since?" Foley continued.

Lillian nodded. "Every day."

"When was the last time you heard from her?"

"Six days ago. She sent me a text from Alice Springs. She was looking forward to us getting together again. I sent her a text when I arrived in Tennant Creek," she paused. "Five days ago. We were supposed to meet there. She never answered my text, and she never showed up in Tennant Creek."

"Perhaps she decided to continue on her own," Foley suggested.

"No," Lillian shook head. "Absolutely no way. I told you, she was really excited about meeting up again.

Something's happened to her, I just know it. She would have let me know if she wasn't going to show." Lillian's eyes were showing signs her resolve might be starting to crumble.

"Was Miss Winters... Miranda, traveling alone?" Foley asked.

"Yes," Lillian answered. "She never mentioned anyone else."

"And you haven't seen her since she left Sydney?"

"Yes, I told you already," Lillian insisted.

"There was no male friend in her life?" Foley continued.

"No! No! There was no one," Lillian was adamant.

"Do you know which route she intended to take to get to Tennant Creek?" Foley asked.

"Is this really relevant?" Lillian complained.

"Humor me, Miss Clutterbuck. Which route?"

Lillian paused. "When she left Sydney, she was headed for Melbourne, then Adelaide, and then up the Stuart Highway to Alice Springs."

"Which way did you come?" Foley asked.

"What?" Lillian sounded incredulous.

"I said, which way did you come?"

"What difference does that make?" Lillian complained.

Foley shrugged. "Maybe none, but you need to let us be the best judge of that."

"You and *him*?" Lillian thrust a thumb behind her, directed at Sam.

"Yes," Foley nodded. "Me and him. Which way did you come?"

"I came across the Barkley Highway, from Queensland," Lillian finally confirmed.

"Thank you," Foley said.

"I've been hearing stories," Lillian announced, her voice several decibels quieter than it had been up to this point.

"Stories?" Foley questioned.

"About bodies," Lillian expanded. "Young girls' bodies... in a well."

"Where have you heard that?" Foley asked.

Lillian shrugged. "You know, around... in the back-packers hostel in Tennant Creek, in the pub. People are talking about it. Is it true?"

Russell Foley took a few moments, and looked into Lillian's eyes. "It's true, we have found a number of bodies," he confirmed. "And it's true they are the remains of young girls."

Lillian put her hand to her mouth and gasped audibly. "Is one of them Miranda?"

Foley reached out and touched her hand once again. "We are still waiting on forensic results, but I don't believe Miss Winters is one of the victims."

Lillian exhaled with relief. "Oh thank God," she whispered. "Thank God." She lifted her eyes and looked at Foley. "Her parents are coming," she added, almost as an afterthought.

"Miranda's parents?" Foley asked.

"Yes," Mandy gave them my contact details weeks ago. They are on their way out here."

"To Tennant Creek?" Foley asked.

"Yes. I've booked a room for them at the motel."

"When do you expect them here?" Foley continued.

"Tomorrow... maybe the day after," Lillian answered. "They are going to want to talk to you."

"I'm sure they will," Foley nodded.

"They'll want answers," Lillian suggested.

"I'm sure they will."

"Will you have the answers?" Lillian pushed.

"I hope so," Foley said. "In the meantime, we will continue to look for Miranda. Perhaps it would be better if you went back to Tennant Creek to wait for her parents."

"Are you trying to get rid of me?" Lillian asked suspiciously.

"No, not at all," Foley lied. "But we do have work to do."

Lillian fumbled in her purse, found a scrap of paper and a pen, and scribbled down her mobile phone number. She handed it to Foley. "I expect you to call me as soon as you know something," she insisted.

"Thank you," Foley said.

Lillian waited a few moments and then said, "Well?"

"Well what?" Foley queried.

"Are you going to call me?"

"Miss Clutterbuck," Foley began. "Procedure dictates, in matters such as this, we communicate with the next of kin. I assume that would be Miranda's parents." He handed the scrap of paper back to Lillian. "If you write *their* number down, we will contact them should we have any more news on the whereabouts of their daughter."

Lillian's look left little doubt she was unimpressed with Foley's response. She snatched the paper, scribbled down another number, presumably from memory, and pushed it across the table in front of Foley. Then, in one swift, noisy movement, she pushed her chair back, and stood. Foley did the same, and offered his hand.

Lillian glanced at the proffered hand with disdain, turned, threw a withering *'fuck you'* look at Sam, then turned and walked away from the table.

Foley remained standing, watching Lillian as she retreated from the room, his hand still partially extended.

"I don't think she's gonna come back and shake your hand," Sam said.

Foley sat down, and looked across the table at Sam. "What *was* that?" he asked.

Sam picked up his coffee cup, took a sip and lowered it to the table. "That, Inspector, was Miss Lillian Clusterfuck."

"She seems fond of you," Foley said. He looked down at his plate. "Now my breakfast is cold. I hate this fuckin' job."

13

Miranda progressed slowly and cautiously, deeper into the shed. In the dim light there appeared to be no windows, and just a tiny amount of dawn light penetrated the darkness through the small gap in the doors. She felt her way, hoping she would not crash into something and hurt herself again. Suddenly, directly in front of her, a dark shape loomed out of the gloom. She stopped, and stared intently at the shape.

It was long, and rectangular, and low to the floor, reaching only as high as her knees. Carefully, she reached out and touched it, and the feel of it was foreign to her. She moved her hands along its length, and slowly, recognition began to dawn on her. She was standing in front of a battery. More accurately, a large bank of batteries, linked together in a series. She paused, and wondered what its purpose could be, and then it came to her. All the power to the house had to come from this large bank of batteries. Somewhere outside, on the roof perhaps, there would be a series of solar panels directing power from the sun, into the batteries, and subsequently to the house.

The house had to be too far away from the main power supply to receive power from the national grid. She could not recall hearing the sound of a generator running at any time, so this had to be the main electricity supply. She dragged her hand along the top of the battery bank, and followed its profile until she had completed a full circuit. It was becoming a little lighter inside the shed and she was able to discern there appeared to be little else stored in here which would be of any use to her. She wanted a container she could fill with water from the tank outside. She turned slowly, peering intently through the dim light, and there, neatly stacked in one corner of the shed, she saw plastic containers, lots of them.

———

Mandy crossed quickly to the corner, and noticed some of the containers were empty, and others were full. She picked up an empty container, unscrewed the lid and sniffed the neck. Unable to determine what the container might once have held, she put it back down, lifted a full one, and repeated the process of unscrewing the cap and sniffing the contents.

The liquid was clear. It had no identifying odor, and looked exactly like water. Suddenly, there it was! Batteries needed water! Distilled water! There had to be a hundred litres or more here, all conveniently stacked in the corner of the shed. Mandy smiled. A degree of hope flickered; a sign of things to come, she dared to wonder.

A low, rumbling noise from outside filtered into the shed. Mandy froze. She tilted her head and listened. Suddenly, she spun around, and stared at the doors, and the tiny gap between them. A car was approaching!

She froze, listening to the sound of the vehicle coming closer, suddenly realising she never saw a vehicle when she escaped from the house. Where was the man's car? He had a car she knew that; he brought her here in a car. Why had she not seen his car when she climbed down off the roof of the house?

Mandy hurried over to the doors, and peeked out through the gap. There, in the distance, coming closer, and closer, a car was indeed approaching. At the moment, it was just a dark spot in the distance, but it was coming fast. A thick cloud of dust followed the vehicle as it sped towards the house.

Panic gripped her. It had to be him. He was not even here when she climbed the chimney, and clambered down off the roof! The bastard was not even here! She could have made as much noise as she liked! She could have gone back into the house, and searched for food. To search for her clothes... any clothes. She might even have found a weapon... a knife perhaps... anything she could use to defend herself if he came after her... no, not *if* he came after her, *when* he came after her. Mandy cursed silently ruing the missed opportunity.

As the vehicle rapidly approached, Mandy hurriedly looked around her. She had to hide. There had to be somewhere in the shed she could hide. When the man discovered her gone, he would come looking for her. If he found her he would kill her, of that she was certain. He was mad, crazy, bonkers, insanely mad.

Veronica was dead, she was sure, and so were all the other girls. The mad man used them for his own personal, depraved sexual pleasure, and then he killed them when he became bored with them. Then, he went out and found another girl. Mandy did not want to be the next one to die.

All she saw in the shed was the bank of batteries, and the store of distilled water. If he came in here he would find her for sure. She had to find somewhere else to hide. She turned back to the doors, and looked out again. The car was still a way off. Could she get out of the shed before he got here? Her heart pounded in her chest.

She had to decide, and she had to decide now. But, where would she go? If she ran she would be out in the open, exposed. In her bare feet, she would not get far enough away before he arrived at the house. He would see her running, and would be on her before she got more than a few hundred metres.

The house! She had to go to the house! Mandy looked again at the distant vehicle. The dark shape was getting closer, and growing in size. Could she get to the house before he saw her? If she did, where would she hide? What if the front doors were locked? She would be stuck on the verandah, in plain sight, trapped, like a rabbit in a spotlight.

Instinct kicked in, and Mandy ran. She squeezed through the gap in the doors, and charged for the house. Stumbling awkwardly over the rough ground, she thought for a moment she was never going to make it.

Then she was there. She scrambled up the steps, and crashed heavily into the closed front door. She grabbed for the door knob, and turned. Nothing! She turned the knob the other way. Nothing! Mandy began to hyperventilate. "Oh, no! Oh, no," she moaned loudly. "Don't be locked... please don't be locked!" The door was locked.

She looked over her shoulder. The dust cloud following the vehicle was much larger now, and at the base of the dirty cloud, the vehicle was just beginning to morph into recognisable form.

Mandy cursed. "Shit! Shit!"

She cast her eyes around wildly, looking for an escape route. She wondered if she had time to make it back to the shed. She would have to take her chances, and hide behind the batteries, and hope he would not look in the shed. No, he would look. He would look everywhere. The shed would probably be the first place he looked. Her heart was crashing so hard against her rib cage she felt it would surely burst inside her chest. At least the end would be quick, she thought; she hoped.

Then she noticed it. Without a second's hesitation, Mandy ran to a window further along the verandah. She reached out, and grabbed the base of the window, and heaved upwards. It did not budge. Mandy groaned with despair, glanced at the approaching vehicle, and then heaved again, with a strength that surprised her.

The window moved just a little, just a few centimeters. Heartened, Mandy planted her feet firmly, and lifted again, with renewed enthusiasm. The window opened, offering enough room for Mandy to climb into the house she had just escaped from. She gathered the trailing ends of the blankets around her, and threw herself head first into the room beyond. Before she could even take in her surrounds, she jumped to her feet, and slammed the window shut.

At best, Mandy figured she had a few minutes to

find a place to hide. The only light penetrating into the interior came from the window she had just climbed through. Her eyes darted around the room. She was running out of time. The man would be here soon. She had to find a hiding place, and there was nowhere to hide in this room. It contained a small settee in the middle of the room, and not much else. She ran from the room, into the long hallway. Immediately to her left she saw a kitchen. He would find her in there, she reasoned. Down the hallway she saw more doors. She hurried along the wide hall, glancing left, and right. She paused in front of the locked door where she and Veronica were held captive.

To her right was the man's bedroom. Mandy looked at the darkness beyond the open door and shuddered. This was the room where he did the terrible things he did to her. Her breath caught in her throat as memories of the atrocities he subjected her to came flooding back.

.Where to hide? Where to hide? She wondered, casting her eyes along the hallway. Somehow her attention kept returning to the man's room. She could hear the sound of the approaching vehicle louder now, much louder. He had to be very close. Once again, instinct kicked in, and Mandy found herself in the man's bedroom. She saw the bed, and the ropes he used on her discarded casually across the bedding. She hesitated, suddenly not wanting to go any further into the room.

Then, she noticed the silence. She listened. There it was; nothing but silence. She could no longer hear the vehicle engine. He was here. She heard a car door slam loudly. Even here inside the house, with the doors and windows closed, the sound startled her.

Mandy darted forward, and in one fluid motion, she dived under the bed and slid out of sight.

———

The man slammed the car door with such force it flew back open and crunched against the limit of the hinges. He lashed out furiously with his foot, intending to kick the door. He missed, and almost lost his balance.

"FUCKIN' HEAP OF SHIT!" he screamed at the car. He stormed towards the house, climbed the steps, and fumbled in his pocket for the key to the door.

The first time he tried, his hands shook so badly with pent up rage he could not get the key into the lock hole. Struggling to control the internal fire of rage blazing within him, he cursed loudly and tried again. This time the key slid home, and he unlocked the door.

He strode purposely, and directly, to the kitchen, threw open a cupboard door and grabbed a bottle of rum. He unscrewed the cap, cast it aside, and raised the bottle to his lips. He took a long, deep swallow and coughed as he felt the rum burn his throat.

"Fuckin' women!" he spat. "Fuckin' bitches!"

Missing the opportunity to grab the German girl ignited a fury inside him he was unable to moderate. Exacerbated by way too much alcohol, his anger flared like an out-of-control fire. He was so close. The girl only needed to come a few metres closer, and he would have had her.

Carrying the rum bottle by the neck, the man walked from the kitchen, and stood in the middle of the long, hallway. He stared at the locked door behind which Miranda waited. She would have heard him arrive. Bitch would be cowering under her blankets. He took another mouthful of rum, and wiped his mouth with the back of his hand. Someone had to pay, he thought. He was so close to having another girl... so close. Someone had to pay.

He took a step towards the door and paused. He had never used any of the girls during daylight. It would be a change of habit for him. Might be a nice change, he pondered. Why did it always have to be at night? Sex in the daylight might be even better; if it was possible to get any better. He took another step towards the locked door, and paused again.

He looked at the bottle of rum, took another swig, turned and hurried back to the kitchen where he placed the bottle on the sideboard. From the same cupboard where he kept the rum, he removed a padlock key and grunted with a mixture of satisfaction and anticipation.

———

When he entered the room, he immediately noticed the two mattresses—and nothing else. Confused, he stormed across the room, halted at the place where the girls always slept, and stared in disbelief at the bare, stained mattresses. His mind, befuddled by alcohol, could not comprehend Miranda was gone.

"What the fuck...," he muttered. He spun around, his eyes searching the room. Miranda was gone. How could it be? The door was locked from the outside! How did she get out?

If the man was angry before he entered the room, his mental state had now deteriorated to a point far beyond anger. His mind could simply not fathom why Miranda was no longer in the room. He rushed over to the window, and pulled aside the drapes. The window was intact. The glass was unbroken, and the bars were still secure. She did not get out through the door, and she did not escape through the window. Where was she?

"Fuckin' impossible," he fumed.

He looked up, and turned in a full circle, studying the ceiling. He saw no way out of the room. In a furious rage, he stormed around the perimeter of the big room. As he passed the toilet bucket used by the girls he lashed out with his foot, and kicked it half way across the room, spilling the stinking contents onto the floor.

"Jesus Fuckin' Christ!" he yelled. "I'll fuckin' kill you, you bitch!

On his second rage filled circuit of the room, something shiny, caught his eye as he stormed passed the fireplace. There, at the base of the chimney, what was it? He stared down at the keys for a moment while his brain scrambled to analyse what he was looking at. Then, he stooped low and picked up the keys with the tiny torch attached.

"Bloody bitch," he muttered. She must have had the keys on her all the time, he figured. Where did she hide them? Must have had them in the pocket of her dress, he deduced.

"Should have searched her. Should have bloody well searched her," he mumbled.

Then his attention was drawn to the chimney. He leaned in over the fireplace and craned his neck to peer up into the darkness of the chimney cavity. Remembering the keys in his hand, he flicked the switch on the torch, and directed the dull beam up into the chimney. The torch light was too weak to penetrate all the way to the top, but the tell-tale scuff marks were clear at the bottom end of the cavity.

She climbed out the chimney! The fuckin' bitch climbed out the bloody chimney!

"Oh, you clever little bitch," he said softly. He turned and faced the open door behind him. "YOU KNOW YOU DIE FOR THIS!" he screamed at the top of his voice. He flung the keys violently into the bottom of the fireplace, and noticed for the first time, the soot and ash scattered there.

The man charged out of the house, stopped, and stood in silence at the top of the steps. He stared out across the open landscape to his front. Above the sound of his racing pulse drumming loudly in his ears, he heard the crackling of the vehicle engine as it cooled rapidly in the early morning chill.

He cast his eyes across to the distant horizon, and then back again. It looked the same as it always did, endless kilometers of dry, dusty ground where occasionally, a stunted, spindly, thirsty shrub, struggled to survive.

As the man looked around, his attention was drawn to the shed. He raced down the steps, and ran across to the shed, flinging open the doors. Light from the outside flooded in, and illuminated the vast interior. He crossed to the middle of the shed, and circled the battery bank. Nothing. Mandy was not in the shed. Still mumbling incoherently, he left the shed and headed back to the house.

He saw the water bottle and almost walked right past it before recognising it for what it was. He stopped, and stared down at the bottle laying discarded next to the rain water tank. A small, wet patch of ground at the base of the tank, and several scuff marks in the dirt, indicated she had been here, he deduced. The bitch was here! He stooped low and picked up the water bottle, fingering the obvious split at its base. The bitch was here, and now, she had no water, he smiled.

How the bottle came to be ruptured was of little consequence to him. the important thing was, she had no water. He had lived out here for a long time, and he knew a person would perish quickly in this country without adequate water. He walked around the tank, and then around the entire perimeter of the house, and the shed, alternately scanning the horizon, and the ground in front of him. He found nothing.

———

Mandy cringed in abject fear, huddled beneath the monster's bed. What was he doing? Every time she heard him scream obscenities she clasped her hands tightly over her ears and tried desperately to stifle the sobs rising from deep within her.

Sometimes his voice seemed close, and then further away. Where was he? She swallowed hard and bit down on her lip in an attempt to suppress the sounds of her terror escaping from her throat. Her breath came, and went, in a staccato series of spasmodic, gasping sounds. When she inhaled, the smell, and taste of dust, stale unwashed bedding and clothing invaded her nose and throat, leaving her fighting against the urge to throw up.

Then, she heard him enter the house. He was there! Right there in the house! Mandy listened to his footsteps coming closer to the bedroom. Then, he was there! She could see his ankles down to his filthy boots, as he stormed around the room. He cursed loudly, his filthy obscenities interspersed with bouts of incoherent muttering.

She stared, mesmerized with fear, at the man's feet. When he moved close to the bed Mandy held her breath, not daring to exhale until he moved away again. He crossed to what she recognised, from what she could see of it, as a large, free standing wardrobe. He flung open the doors, and fumbled around inside.

Mandy saw a rifle. At least, she saw part of a rifle, the butt and the trigger assembly. Carrying the weapon by the barrel, the man crossed back to the side of the bed and stood motionless. Mandy held her breath until she felt her lungs would burst. Did he know she was under the bed, so close all he had to do was bend down and look underneath?

She did not dare close her eyes, although she desperately wanted to. She stared at the gun. She knew almost nothing about guns except they came in many different types and configurations. She had never in her life, ever been as close to a gun as she was at this moment. This one, so close she could reach out and touch it, was a rifle; that much she did know. On a few occasions in her career as a nurse she had seen the damage guns can do to the human body, but never in her wildest imagination did she ever think she might one day be this close to becoming a victim of such a terrible weapon.

The urge to flee was almost overpowering. Maybe she could roll out from under the bed, on the opposite side, and make a desperate run for it. She very quickly abandoned the thought. She was in her underwear, had no shoes on her feet, and had two blankets tied around her neck. He had a gun. He would shoot her before she got as far as the double doors at the end of the hallway. Silently she prayed he would not look under the bed.

Just when she thought it was over, when she thought he had figured out she was under the bed and was now toying with her, he left the room. Mandy watched his feet as he walked away from the bed. She listened to his footsteps as he left the bedroom and strode along the hall and out onto the front verandah.

She heard the front doors slam shut, and a few moments later she heard the rusty squeaking of what she assumed was the car door. Was he leaving? Mandy lowered her head onto the dirty, mildew smelling carpet and fought back tears. She stayed that way, for hours it seemed. Then, she heard the car engine start. From her hiding place beneath the bed, she listened intently until the sound of the engine faded into the distance.

Even after the noise of the vehicle engine was no longer audible, Mandy stayed where she was. Was he really gone? Did she dare emerge from her hiding place? She had to be sure he was gone.

14

Russell Foley and Sam Rose returned to Devil's Marbles and spent several hours walking through the popular tourist attraction. The travelers they met at the site when they first came, had moved on, only to be replaced with just as many, perhaps even more, newcomers. Interviewing any of the current group would be unproductive given none of them were at the Marbles when Miranda Winters went missing.

On their third walk through, Foley suddenly stopped and looked at the stunning rock formations. He turned to Sam, "We are wasting our time," he declared.

"I'm beginning to feel the same way," Sam responded. He wiped a bead of perspiration from his forehead and flicked it away.

"Somebody snatched Miranda Winters from here," Foley continued. "How do you grab someone, who had to be resisting, and take them away without being seen? There are people crawling all over this place." He studied the ground at his feet. "Any evidence will have been trampled into oblivion by thousands of feet. He had to have a car... how do we decide which tyre tracks are his out of the hundreds all over the place? A million footprints, any one of which could belong to our man. We are not going to find anything here."

"What do you want to do?" Sam asked.

Foley thought about the question for a few moments as he stared off into the distance. "We need to get off the popular tourist route," he said finally.

"Where?" Sam asked.

Foley shrugged. "I don't know. The perp has to be somewhere, out there," he indicated the far horizon. "He has to be hiding the girls somewhere. There has been six of them... maybe seven if we assume the Winters girl is another of his victims. If we accept he abuses them over a period of weeks, he has to have them locked up somewhere no one knows about. Somewhere which won't attract attention."

"That would be like looking for a needle in a haystack," Sam suggested.

"I don't think so," Foley said. "Look out there," he waved his arm across the horizon. "There's nothing out there for as far as the eye can see. Surely it can't be difficult to find one house, or a structure of any kind, where he could keep someone locked up without raising suspicion."

"It's a lot of country to cover," Sam suggested. "It could take weeks, or months."

"If we were driving," Foley agreed.

Sam suddenly felt uncomfortable. "Are you suggesting what I think you are suggesting?"

"We can fly over it," Foley said. "We could cover hundreds of square kilometers in a matter of a couple of hours."

Sam Rose had never been comfortable about flying anywhere, either in a large, fixed wing passenger airliner, and even less so in a helicopter. He eyed Foley hesitatingly.

"A chopper?" he queried.

"Yes," Foley nodded. "We can get one up from Alice Springs... they might even have one in Tennant Creek. I'll ring Potts in Tennant first." He dug into his pocket for his mobile phone.

Sam began to perspire more heavily. Flying petrified him. There were occasions in the past when he had to fly somewhere in the course of his job, and there was the time he flew in a domestic passenger plane from Darwin to Alice Springs when he was on leave from his position in Darwin, but flying thousands of feet above the solid, hard, unforgiving ground in a long, narrow, machine built of large pieces of metal riveted together and carrying extremely heavy jet engines on wings which flexed alarmingly, scared the living daylights out of him. Helicopters were even worse. Tiny, flimsy capsules, held aloft by a large fan spinning at a ridiculous rate on a spindle he could wrap his arms around.

"Done," Foley announced.

"Wh... what?" Sam stammered.

"The chopper," Foley said. "Terry Potts is going to send one down from Tennant Creek. It belongs to a mining company. They use it for flying over prospective gold bearing country to study the terrain and determine the likelihood of it being worth closer examination."

"Oh," Sam uttered.

"Apparently, it hasn't been used for a while, as the company suspended all mining operations after a dispute with the traditional landowners started to turn ugly and looked like costing millions. Potts said he will talk to the pilot, he has been living in town waiting for word to fly it back to the Alice."

"How long?" Sam asked.

"How long what?" Foley asked.

"How long since it's been flown anywhere?"

"A couple of months," Foley answered. "But Potts said it should be fine."

"Potts said 'it *should* be fine'?"

"Yes, what's the problem?" Foley questioned.

Sam shrugged. "Maybe we should ask the *pilot* if it will be fine."

"You, Sergeant Rose, are a worry wart," Foley said. "Come on, we need to get back to Wauchope. The chopper will pick us up there."

———

Sam's heart rate doubled as he watched the chopper hover momentarily and finally land in a clearing behind the Hotel.

The Schweizer 300C resembled a toy, with a tiny bubble of plexiglass held together by thin strips of fibreglass. The engine housing was open, and exposed to the elements and, worst of all Sam thought, it was located directly behind the cramped passenger compartment. If it could be called a passenger compartment, Sam thought. There were three seats, jammed up close to each other across the front of the machine, and that was the extent of the seating arrangements.

The control panel situated directly in front of the middle seat looked like a small box with seemingly less switches and knobs than a cheap household radio. Hardly enough to keep the thing in the air, Sam decided. As he watched the flimsy, twin rotor blades slowly turning to an eventual stop he was convinced, if this thing came down, everyone strapped inside the tiny capsule was undoubtedly doomed to a fiery end.

The pilot strode casually over to where Sam and Foley stood, and extended his hand. "G'day, Sounda's the name."

Foley shook the pilot's hand. "I'm Russell Foley. Sounda? That's an unusual name."

"Yeah," the pilot smiled. "My name's Grantley Sleep. My friends call me Sounda." He offered his hand to Sam.

Sam shook the pilot's hand, and studied his face. His eyes were hidden behind aviator sunglasses, and his face was covered in a beard perhaps three days old, making it difficult to determine his age, but Sam guessed it at about forty. His rough, knock-about look left Sam feeling even more uncomfortable about the prospect of flying than he already felt, and when he leaned in to shake hands, he was sure he detected a smell of stale beer on his breath.

Sam introduced himself. "Sam Rose. Been flying choppers long?"

"More years than I care to think about," the pilot smiled. "Fell in love with helicopters when I was a kid."

"It's small," Sam said, indicating the chopper.

"Great little bird though," Sounda said. "Bought her second hand about eight years ago. Haven't had her up much lately. I'm contracted to a mining company, but they've stopped work for the moment so she's been sittin' on the tarmac at Tennant Creek."

"When was the last time you took it up?" Sam asked.

"Ah... let me see... about three weeks ago, I think it was. The old girl coughed and farted a bit. Shit in the pipes I expect. But, she got me back down safely."

Sam felt his knees begin to buckle, but managed to hold himself together. *"Shit in the pipes!"* he thought. "I'm glad to hear it, he said."

The pilot turned to Foley. "Where do you blokes wanna go?"

"How well do you know this area?" Foley asked.

The pilot shrugged. 'Mostly I fly the Tennant Creek area, where the mining leases are. I have been down this way a few times, moonlighting doing tourist flights over the Devil's Marbles and stuff."

"We want to have a look at the country to the east, and west of here," Foley said.

"How far east and west?"

"I don't know. We need to get up there and have a look. We are looking for a house, or a building... a shed maybe. It will be off the beaten track... isolated... might even look abandoned," Foley answered.

"Which way first?" the pilot asked.

"It doesn't matter," Foley said. "Let's try east first."

"Okey dokey," Sounda smiled. "Just the two of you, is it?"

Sam's mind raced to formulate an excuse not to board what he saw as a flying coffin. He was about to say he would stay at Wauchope; maybe drive down to Wycliffe Well and make enquiries with the management and staff. However, before he could say anything Foley nodded to the pilot.

"Yeah, just the two of us."

"Whew! That's a relief," Sounda smiled. "She only

seats three. Let's see if the old girl gets off the ground without giving us too much trouble." Sounda turned and headed back to the helicopter.

Foley looked at Sam. "Are you okay?"

"Yeah, of course I'm okay. Why wouldn't I be okay?" Sam said a little too hurriedly.

"You look pale," Foley said.

Must have been the eggs," Sam offered.

––––––

Thank God for seat belts, Sam thought to himself, as the Schweizer lifted off in a thick cloud of swirling dust. His stomach churned as the pilot the left-hand side of the dropped the nose, turned towards the east, and sped away, the skids almost brushing the tops of trees bordering the far side of the camping ground.

Three grown men crammed inside the tiny capsule was a tight fit. Sam sat in the left-hand seat, with Sounda in the middle, and Foley on the pilot's right. Sam's knees rested against the base of the tiny control panel, his right shoulder touching the pilot's left.

When he dared to open his eyes, and look out of the window which seemed to be just centimetres from his face, Sam was washed with a wave of vertigo. For a brief moment, he thought he was going to throw up all over the floor, and closed his eyes again, tightly, until the feeling subsided.

When he finally found the courage to open them again, he looked at the tiny, box-like control panel. He knew nothing about helicopters, or indeed any type of aircraft, but he would have thought there would be a lot more gauges on the panel than this. The only gauge he could identify was the fuel gauge and he was relieved, albeit mildly, to see the tank was three quarters full.

Sam turned his head and saw Russell Foley looking around the pilot at him.

"Are you sure you are all right?" Foley asked.

"Yeah, I'm good," Sam answered. "This is fun, isn't it?"

Foley spoke loudly, so he could be heard over the noise of the engine directly behind them. "You wanna go back?"

"What?" Sam said. He leaned forward and looked across at Foley.

"I said, do you want to go back?" Foley repeated.

"No, I'm good," Sam offered an unconvincing smile.

The pilot turned his head, looked first at Sam, and then Foley. "What altitude would you prefer to cruise at?"

"Fuckin' ground level," Sam whispered to himself.

Foley leaned forward against the constraint of his safety harness and looked at the pilot. "What do you recommend?"

"Three hundred metres, about one thousand feet," Sounda answered. "That's high enough to see anything ahead, and it's low enough to identify anything below us."

"Sounds good to me," Foley acknowledged.

Ten minutes into the flight, Foley noticed something out to the right of the chopper. He leaned forward and tapped the pilot on the shoulder.

"What's that, out there to our right?"

Sounda looked out to where Foley indicated. "That's what's left of the old Wolfram mine. Nothing there now. It closed down decades ago."

Foley studied the old site. From the altitude the chopper cruised, the long abandoned mine site was now just a bare patch of ground with the crumbling remains of a once productive open-cut pit looking no bigger than a swimming pool size hole in the ground. There were no buildings at the site. Probably removed many years ago, Foley decided. He disregarded the site, and returned his concentration to the view in front, and to the left and right of the flight path.

Way off in the distance to their front, the outline of the Daveport Ranges appeared on the horizon. It all looked different from this perspective, Foley mused. The distant ranges could just be seen from ground level, but from one thousand feet in the air they appeared much more distinct, and obviously covered a far bigger area than he would have thought.

A short time later, the well where the bodies were discovered came into view.

"There," Sam said. "Out in front. It's the well."

Foley looked to the front, and saw the Task Force was still in position at the well site. Like tiny ants, the members of the elite unit were gathered around the remnants of a campfire, a short distance from the well.

"Look at the pussies, Russell," Sam said. "Those dudes are supposed to be tough, what's with the campfire?"

"Nights can get pretty cold out here," Foley said.

"Hmph!" Sam chuffed. "Should have just cuddled up together."

"Didn't you apply for the Task Force about ten years ago?" Foley asked.

"In one, brief moment of weakness," Sam muttered.

"You were rejected as I recall," Foley smiled.

"The OIC at the time was an idiot," Sam said, as if it explained everything. "Still is," he added.

"You don't think it might have had something to do with you bonking his twenty-two-year-old daughter?" Foley posed.

"He was an idiot long before I started bonking his daughter, as you so succinctly put it" Sam offered.

The pilot turned his head and looked at Sam. "Sounds like you've led an interesting life."

Sam glared at the pilot, and pointed out the front windscreen of the chopper. "Here's a thought. Might be an idea if you keep your eyes on the road."

Sounda ignored the advice and said to Foley, "You wanna put down here?"

"Maybe later," Foley said. "Let's keep going east for a bit longer."

"Roger that," Sounda acknowledged. He smiled at Sam, and turned back to his front.

After an hour-and-a-half flying in a grid pattern over the country to the east of Wauchope, the pilot executed a one-hundred-and-eighty degree turn, and headed back, over the well, towards Wauchope.

"We need to refuel," he announced.

"Where?" Foley asked.

"Back at Wauchope," Sounda said. "They've got drums of Avgas stored there. It's a slow, hand-pump process, but you chaps can have lunch while I fuel up."

"Sounds like a plan," Foley said.

"Lots of nothing out here," Sam observed as they flew back over the well.

"We'll have lunch and then try west of Wauchope for an hour or so," Foley said.

"This guy could be anywhere," Sam suggested.

"Even in Tennant Creek, or any one of the small one-horse towns up and down the highway."

"Yes, he could be," Foley agreed. "But, I'm more inclined to think he will be isolated somewhere, away from public scrutiny. He's holding women prisoner for weeks at a time, maybe more than one at a time. He can't be doing that where there are people nearby. Someone would have heard, or seen, something."

"What do you want to do if we have no luck out to the west?" Sam asked.

"Then we fly north, and then south," Foley said. "He's out there, somewhere."

If the thought of flying west after lunch wasn't daunting enough for Sam, the prospect of possibly flying north, and then south afterwards sent a shiver of apprehension through him. He looked out his window, and watched the earth hurtle by a thousand feet beneath him. What ever happened to the good old days when the police hunted down killers on horseback?

Just as he pondered his own question, the helicopter engine coughed twice, dropped a few hundred feet, and then regained its rhythm. Sam gripped his chair until his knuckles hurt.

"Whoops!" the pilot uttered as he fiddled with the fuel mixture knob. "Old girl's gettin' a bit uppity."

"Wha... what's the problem?" Sam asked, failing miserably to sound unconcerned.

"Fuel's runnin' a bit rich," Sounda announced. "Could have a lot of shit in it too," he added. "Bloody stuff's been sittin' 'round in old drums at Tennant Creek for months... years, some of it."

"Should we be concerned?" Foley asked.

"*Or maybe praying,*" Sam muttered to himself.

"Nah!" Sounda said. "She'll be right. Happens all the time. I'll just tweak the mixture a bit, and she'll be good as new."

―――

Lunch was a game of hide and seek with the media. The deception of the mysterious lead at Wycliffe Well played on them by Sam was not accepted with good grace. As soon as the pilot touched down, shut down the engine, and opened his door, they descended on the chopper as one. A clamoring, calling, protesting mob of frustrated journalists demanding answers.

Foley, and Sam ducked into the hotel through the back door, and took refuge in the kitchen. Eventually they ate their lunch sitting at a stainless-steel food preparation bench while the kitchen staff, which included the young Irish lass, and the publican himself, worked around them cooking and serving the handful of travelers who passed through Wauchope on their way to somewhere else.

"How you blokes gettin' on?" the publican asked during a short break in the lunch demands.

"We're good," Sam said as he chewed on his hamburger. "So's this," he waved the burger at the publican.

The publican smiled. "The best burgers you'll get between the Alice and Darwin," he bragged.

"I believe it," Sam said, taking another bite."

"You blokes going up in the chopper again?" the publican asked.

"Yeah, after lunch," Foley said. He nibbled on a celery stick he picked out of his salad bowl.

Sam looked at him. "Shoulda had the burger, mate."

"Yeah," Foley responded scornfully. "And then have a triple by-pass before I'm fifty because my arteries are all clogged up with grease and shit from eating too many hamburgers."

"Find anything of interest out there this morning?" the publican asked.

Sam looked at him suspiciously. "Those reporters got you on a kick-back for information?"

The publican looked horrified. "No... no. Shit no," he answered hurriedly. "They've been hounding me ever since they came back from Wycliffe Well, but I don't know anything."

"Good to hear," Sam said.

"Well did you?" the publican pushed.

"Did we what?" Sam asked.

"Did you find anything?"

"No," Foley said adamantly. He stood up, wiped his mouth with a serviette, and turned to Sam. "Let's go, Sounda must be ready by now."

As they prepared to leave, Sam's old girlfriend, Rebecca Anders, entered the kitchen from the front bar area.

"I wouldn't go out the back door if I were you," she warned Sam and Foley.

"How did you get in here?" the publican asked.

Rebecca smiled at him. "I'm good at what I do. I bluffed my way past the girl out there. Told her I was Sam's wife."

Sam groaned audibly.

Foley looked at Sam, and then at Rebecca. "Why shouldn't we go out the back door?"

"Because there's about fifty of them out there now.

This is big. The reports of missing girls, bodies in a well, Task Force members crawling all over the place, have gone nation-wide. There are news crews here from every state, and they're all out back, expecting you to get on board the helicopter out there."

"Anyone out the front?" Sam asked.

"There was," Rebecca said, "Until I let on you were about to fly out of here. I've seen my share of media scrums in my time, been in one or two myself, but this was a beauty. Tripping all over themselves to get around back."

"Any suggestions?" Foley asked Sam.

Sam faced Rebecca. "Can you stall them?"

"Maybe," Rebecca answered. "What's in it for me if I do?"

Foley answered for Sam. "An exclusive. We'll give you all the details before we announce anything officially to the media."

Rebecca looked at Sam. "Can I trust him?"

"Definitely," Sam said. Then to the publican he said. "Can you get a message to the pilot?"

"Yeah, no problem," the publican nodded.

"Tell him to be ready to go when we come out." He turned to Rebecca. "Go back outside, through the main front door. Hurry to the back where the media mob is waiting, and make a fuss about Russell and I leaving in our car. Hopefully it will get them back in front of the hotel and we can slip out the back."

"Another ruse? Rebecca said. Do you think they'll fall for it again?"

"Of course they will," Foley answered. "They're journalists, they'll fall for anything."

"I think I'm insulted," Rebecca frowned. "Can I come with you?"

"The chopper's only got room for three," Sam said.

Rebecca smiled seductively at Sam. "I could sit on your knee."

"As appealing as that sounds," Sam smiled. "I'm sure the pilot would not allow it."

————

The publican left first. He made his way through the pressing media throng, and walked briskly over to where the pilot leaned casually against his machine, watching the excited, impatient members of the press clamoring at the rear door of the hotel. The pilot listened with interest to the publican, and then climbed aboard the helicopter and began the start-up procedure. When the chopper was running in optimum take-off mode, Rebecca Anders appeared from around the side of the hotel. She acted excited and breathless.

"They're leaving!" she called loudly. She pointed animatedly to the end of the hotel from where she had just appeared. "Around the front! They're leaving in their car!"

The mob ran. Bumping, jostling, elbowing those who got in their way. They rushed as one to the end of the building, and disappeared around the corner. Instantly, Sam and Foley ran out the back door, raced for the helicopter, and scrambled awkwardly into the confined passenger compartment.

A few moments later, the pilot maneuvered the chopper, his hands and feet working in unison as it lifted off, hovered nose down for a few moments, and then sped away in a swirl of dust.

15

M andy slid out from under the bed. Cautiously, she tip-toed from the bedroom, hurried along the hallway, entered the room where she had climbed through the window, and peeked out at the front of the house.

The man's car was gone. Way off, in the distance, the dust cloud thrown up by his vehicle slowly dispersed in the still morning air. He was gone. He was driving fast, but he would be scanning the country on either side of the track looking for her. Perhaps assuming she would follow the road away from the house, he was back-tracking along the route searching for her.

Mandy breathed a heavy sigh of relief. She had time, she thought. As much as she wanted to be as far away from this place as she could get, as quickly as she could, she guessed she had time to get a few things together; things she would need.

She turned, and looked around the room. She decided it must be a small living-room. There was a small settee with a side table, and little else. She hurried from the room, and stood once again in the hallway. Her eyes were drawn to the bedroom she had just come from, and she shuddered as she looked at the open door of the most evil place she could imagine.

In that room, the man committed the most disgusting abuse on hers and all the girls who came before her. She did not want to go back in there. She swung her eyes to the kitchen on her left. She needed to get food to take with her. The sandwich she had brought with her on her escape from the room was back in the shed; it was wet and reduced to a mushy, inedible state. There had to be something more substantial in the kitchen; her captor had to eat, after all.

Inexplicably though, she was drawn to the bedroom. She also needed clothing; something more than the flimsy underwear she had been wearing since he brought her to this horrible place. Her clothes had to be here somewhere. She took a couple of steps towards the bedroom, and paused, steeling herself to continue. One more look behind her, at the closed main doors, and then she hurried along to the bedroom.

The wardrobe doors stood open, just as he had left them when he grabbed the rifle while she hid under the bed. Mandy moved across to the wardrobe and looked inside. Not wanting to touch anything, she leaned forward, her head very close to the opening. The man had very few clothes it seemed. One tatty, grubby overcoat, two pairs of jeans which might once have been blue but were now of indeterminable color, and three plaid, long-sleeve shirts, heavily creased, and very obviously unwashed seemed to be the extent of his wardrobe. Apparently, the man had little regard for the practice of laundering his clothes.

A large, cardboard box, on the floor at the back of

GARY S. GREGOR

the robe, the lid closed but not sealed, caught her attention. Mandy cautiously reached in and pulled the box out onto the floor. She opened the lid flaps and gasped in surprise. The box was filled with clothes; girl's clothes. Her dress was right there on top. Mandy sobbed loudly, threw the blankets from her shoulders, and pulled the dress over her head. Somehow, this simple act, the thing she had done a thousand times in her short life, brought her a confidence and sense of security she could not explain. With renewed enthusiasm, she fumbled deeper into the carton. Tucked down one side of the box, along with several other pairs, she found her sneakers. Mandy wanted to cry with joy. She was going to get away from this place. She had her clothes, her shoes, and she had water, more water than she could carry.

Fully dressed, and with her comfortable sneakers on, she was about to leave the bedroom when she decided to take another look in the wardrobe. She needed something to carry food in, if she happened to find any. Feeling bolder now, she stuck her head into the wardrobe and looked closer into the corners. And, there it was! a back-pack! Mandy smiled victoriously, and pulled it from the cupboard. The pack was empty, and it would carry everything she needed. It must have belonged to one of the other girls, she decided.

Clutching the back-pack to her chest, Mandy hurried from the bedroom and ran to the kitchen. She was immediately appalled at how dirty everything was. The sink, beneath a window on the far side of the kitchen, was filled with dirty dishes. In the centre of the room, a table, heavily scratched and covered in old, ingrained stains of unidentifiable origin, was held on a quasi-even keel by a block of wood jammed under one leg. A long bench, attached to the walls, ran around the perimeter of the kitchen.

Similar to the table top, sections of the bench not covered in discarded food wrappers, empty baked bean and camp pie cans, and old, yellowing newspapers, were scarred with deep scratches and covered in months, more likely years, of accumulated dust and grime. Mandy shuddered in disgust at the conditions the man chose to live in.

Above the bench, fixed suspended along one wall, a row of cupboards, two with the doors ajar and hanging by only one hinge, appeared mostly empty apart from a few chipped plates and coffee mugs. Mandy skirted the table, reached up, and opened one of the closed cupboards. She was greeted by several cans of food; tinned tuna, spaghetti, baked beans, camp pie, and an open, half empty jar of peanut paste. Hardly a nutritious, gourmet selection of food items, but food nonetheless. She hurriedly grabbed what she could, and tossed the items into the back-pack.

As she was about to leave the house and return to the shed to add water to her collection of supplies, she remembered the blankets she discarded in the bedroom. The day was already promising to be another hot one, but the nights were cold and she had only her light, summer dress for protection against the chill of the night and the heat of the sun during the day.

She did not know where she was, or how long it would take her to walk to safety, and she figured she might have to spend several nights out in the open, exposed to the icy chill of the desert nights. If she left the blankets, she knew she would regret it.

The last thing she wanted to do was go back into the bedroom, but she had to. She lifted the back-pack, heavy with its cargo of tinned food, and hurried from the kitchen. Determined not to linger, she stayed in the bedroom only long enough to scoop up the two blankets and then she left the bedroom as quickly as she entered. She opened the big double doors, and paused. Before she left the awful house behind her, she hesitated briefly, and looked long, and hard out at the road leading away from the house. She saw no sign of the man returning, and there was no longer any dust from his vehicle hanging in the air. Satisfied she was truly alone, she hurried out onto the verandah, down the steps and around the far corner of the house, heading for the shed.

After re-arranging the contents of the back-pack, Mandy managed to get one five-litre bottle of water jammed into the top. She grabbed a second bottle, and decided she would carry it in her hand. She would drink this one first, she decided. With ten litres of water, she estimated she could survive for ten days at least, maybe up to a fortnight if she was careful. Surely she could reach help in that time.

Satisfied she was ready, Mandy lifted a third bottle of water from the stock pile, unscrewed the cap, and drank lustily. She drank as much as she could, paused for a few moments, and then drank again, forcing it down even when she felt she could not possibly swallow another drop. Finally, she discarded the bottle, and watched for a moment as the water leaked out onto the floor of the shed, the irony of the precious water running to waste did not escape her.

Grunting with effort, the pain of the repeated assaults upon her, and the new, different aches she suffered as a result of her climb up the chimney cavity reminded her of how much her body had endured.

She struggled into the straps of the back-pack. When it was settled relatively comfortably over her shoulders, she was ready. She could finally leave this place.

As she walked from the shed, she fought back tears. A number of girls, she had no idea of exactly how many, were never going home again, not alive. Her thoughts lingered on Veronica; she was the one Mandy knew. Veronica was dead too, she knew instinctively. She also knew if she hadn't escaped she would be dead also, if not already, then very soon.

She decided to follow the road. Not right *on* the road, that would be foolish. If the man came back, he would see her and she was smart enough to know she wouldn't get away a second time. She would follow the road from a long way off. Far enough away so she would have time to react if she saw dust in the distance indicating a vehicle approaching.

Mandy figured she was on the western side of the Stuart Highway. When she was at Devils Marbles, she recalled, way off, to the east of the famous tourist spot, there were ranges that were a distant, low, pale lilac color against the blue sky. She remembered they looked magical, silhouetted against the eastern horizon as the sun rose in the morning.

The lovely couple in the caravan parked next to her in the camp ground said they were the Davenport Ranges. She remembered they said it was beautiful should you dare to take the four-wheel-drive-only road into the area where there were many large waterholes around which one could camp.

As Mandy walked as briskly as she could away from the house, she could only guess at which way she was headed. When she was locked in the room with Veronica, she determined from watching the sun set

GARY S. GREGOR

through the window, the front of the house faced
south. Therefore, she guessed the road to, and from,
the house ran in a north, south direction. If her calcu-
lations were correct, the Davenport Ranges should be
on her left as she followed the road.

To her right the Tanami Desert, thousands of
square miles of hot, dry, gibber plains and red sand
hills stretched away to the western horizon and beyond. Out there, unprepared, one would perish in a
matter of days. Bones, picked clean by eagles,
bleached white by the searing sun, and scattered far
and wide by wild dingoes, would likely never be
found.

Occasionally, Mandy stopped and peered intently
into the eastern sky, but there were no ranges on the
horizon. Out here, the east looked as arid and as devoid of landmarks as the west. Only an occasional
clump of stunted saltbush, or a small outcrop of
quartz, broke the vista of an endless, shimmering
landscape. Her only hope was to stay in touch with
the road. Close, but not too close. This had to be the
same road the man used to bring her to the house. It
had to lead out, eventually.

Mandy walked for a long time. Her pace was slow,
and the weight of the back-pack had her stooped,
head bowed, and laboring in the heat as the mildly
warm morning rapidly became a hot, and uncomfortable afternoon. Now, the sun was high in the sky, and
beat down mercilessly on her head. She could feel her
face burning, and she was tired. She had to rest. The
constant walking intensified the pain in her legs, her
back, and her groin. As she came to a quartz outcrop,
she sat down behind it, took a welcome mouthful of
water, pulled the blankets over her head and then lay

down on the hot ground. She would rest for just a few minutes, she decided. She was asleep in seconds.

———

Miranda woke, confused and disorientated. For a few moments, she wondered where she was. She threw the blankets aside, and sat, studying the terrain. She was free, she remembered. She looked back over the distance she had walked since leaving the house, more than a little happy she was away from the place and the evil monster who lived there.

Reaching for the bottle of water, she unscrewed the cap and took a mouthful. The water was warm, it had been sitting in the hot sun while she slept, but she drank it anyway. Staying hydrated was vital. With her background as a nurse, she knew the body needed water for survival more than it needed food.

Mandy looked up at the sky. She had no way of knowing how long she slept. The sun was to the west of where she sat, and lower in the sky now than when she stopped to rest. She guessed it was mid-afternoon, and she had probably slept for a couple of hours.

She wiped at beads of perspiration forming quickly on her brow; mid-afternoon was the hottest part of the day. The urge to rest more was strong, but knew she had to get up and start walking. The more distance she put between herself and the house the better, she thought. However, she knew the afternoon heat would sap her energy very quickly, so she decided to wait until sunset before she set off again. It would be much cooler walking during the night hours, and she would be able to cover a lot more ground, she reasoned.

She squinted into the sun, and focused on the road in the distance. She could just see it, and wondered how she would stay on course through the night if she could not see the road to guide her. She would have to move closer to it. When the sun started to sink in the west, and while there was still sufficient light to see by, she would move across the barren landscape and get closer to the road. The risk was substantial, but one she had to take.

Mandy suspected the road was the only access to, and from the house, and the man was out there now, looking for her. If she got too close, and he was traveling up and down the access road searching for her, he would see her. It would be dark, she concluded, assessing the risk.

She would see his head lights in the distance before he got close enough to see her, she decided. She would have time to drop to the ground, throw the blankets over her body and curl up into a ball. In the dark, if she was lucky, he would not notice her.

She laid down again, and pulled the blankets back over her body. Hidden from the road by the quartz outcrop, she believed only the closest scrutiny would give her position away.

16

As he had done when they searched to the east of Wauchope, the pilot flew in a grid pattern to the west. The sky was clear, and by maintaining an altitude of one thousand feet, vision was excellent for a great distance in any direction.

After thirty minutes into the flight, they had seen nothing of interest apart from the main railway line than ran from Adelaide, the capital city of South Australia, to Darwin, the northern most city in the Northern Territory, and one narrow, dirt, road beginning near the Devil's Marbles, and following a meandering route to an unknown destination far off to the west of the highway.

The road, or track as it should more appropriately be referred, traversed across the landscape in a winding, haphazard manner, incongruently, it seemed, given there seemed to be no obstacles in its path necessitating the somewhat aimless route it followed.

Russell Foley asked the pilot to follow the road for a while; ultimately it had to lead somewhere, he figured. They were flying over the eastern edge of the immense expanse of the Tanami Desert and, while he was aware attempts were made in the past to settle the fringes of the Tanami, all ended in failure. It almost never rained in this country, and he understood any underground water which was found had always proved unpalatable and not fit for consumption by man or animals.

As he studied the hot, dry land a thousand feet below, negative thoughts drifted into his mind. He began to feel they were not going to find anything. Nothing, and nobody, could possibly survive out here. As he considered asking the pilot to return to Wauchope, something up ahead, a dark shape against the horizon, caught his eye.

"What's that?" he asked. He pointed across the pilot's front. "Up ahead... eleven o'clock... what is that?"

Sam peered at the shape in the distance. "I don't know. It's too far away."

Foley tapped the pilot on the leg, and pointed again. "Over there," he said. "What is that?"

Sounda reached down, removed a pair of binoculars from the side pocket in his seat, and passed them to Foley. "Take a look," he suggested.

Foley put the glasses to his eyes, adjusted the focus, and a house filled his vision. "It's a house," he announced.

"A house?" Sam asked.

"Yeah, a big old homestead," Foley confirmed. He passed the binoculars to Sam.

"What the hell... " Sam said, as he zoomed in on the distant house.

Foley said to the pilot. "Let's take a look."

Sounda adjusted his course slightly, enough to bring the chopper on a direct flight path to the house.

———

The engine coughed once, spluttered, coughed again, then fired, and continued as normal. Sam watched anxiously as the pilot reached out and fiddled with knobs and switches.

Sam turned in his seat and asked the pilot, "Everything all right?"

"The old girl's runnin' a bit rough," Sounda answered as he tweaked the knobs again. The engine coughed again, and backfired loudly. "Come on you bitch!" he muttered. "Don't quit on me now."

Russell Foley leaned forward and spoke to the pilot. "What's the problem?" he asked.

"Dunno," Sounda announced. "Sounds like a fuel blockage. Bloody Avgas, probably been sittin' in the drums at Wauchope for years."

"Can you clear it?" Sam asked, deep concern etched on his face, and evident in his voice.

"Just have to hope it clears itself," the pilot said.

"And if it doesn't?" Foley asked.

"If it doesn't, I'll have to put her down." Sounda answered.

"Can you do it safely?" Foley asked.

"I've trained for it," the pilot answered. "Never had to do it 'though," he added.

Sam was convinced he detected a hint of concern in the pilot's voice. He looked out the window to the left, and then the window to the right of Foley.

Should I hang on tight and hope for the best, he wondered? Perhaps a quick prayer wouldn't hurt either. He saw nothing out there. Desert, all the way to the horizon. If they crash-landed out here, they were a long way from anywhere. Should have stayed at Wau-chope, he thought.

The engine spluttered, coughed again, and then stopped altogether. Suddenly everything went deathly quiet in the cockpit. The pilot tried frantically to restart the engine. It refused to fire. He knew the machine would drop under controlled autorotation at approximately seventeen-hundred feet per minute. They were cruising at one thousand feet, so he knew he had less than a minute to control the descent, and there wasn't enough time to persist in his attempts to restart the engine.

He immediately lowered the collective, taking the pitch off the rotor blades and initiating descent. Keeping the blades turning was vital, and the up-draft of air acting on the underside of the rotors should take care of that. He also had to keep the chopper straight and prevent the nose from dropping. Unfortunately, he was rapidly running out of altitude.

Sam glanced at Foley, and noticed he was gripping his arm rest and bracing himself for the inevitable. Foley glanced at Sam, offered a resigned nod of his head, and planted his feet hard against the floor.

"We're going in!" the pilot yelled over his shoulder. "It's going to be a rough landing! You need to brace yourselves!"

"Oh, shit!" Sam cursed. He stared wide-eyed out of his window as the ground rushed up at them. He had no arm rest to grip onto, so he reached between his legs and grasped the underside of his seat, his head almost touching the control panel. He gripped until his fingers hurt, and held his breath, anticipating the inevitable impact.

They were only a couple of hundred feet from

ploughing into the desert floor. The pilot yelled curses loudly as he wrestled with the control stick,, his feet working furiously on the large pedals.

As the earth raced up at them, the pilot continued struggling against the powerless machine's downward momentum. They were going to crash; now there was no doubt.

"BRACE YOURSELF!" Sounda screamed. "BRACE... BRACE... BRACE!"

———

The chopper hit hard. The pilot fought to keep the machine level but unfortunately, just before impact, the nose dropped and the Schweizer 300C went in nose first. The rotor blades hit the ground and sheared apart in a crunching, spinning confusion of tearing metal and flying dust and grit.

The force of the rotor impact with the ground, spun the body of the chopper violently before it flipped onto its back, continued to spin crazily for two complete revolutions and then finally came to rest in a thick cloud of dust.

Russell Foley opened his eyes, and felt the safety harness straps digging painfully into his shoulders. Everything was eerily silent, save for the crackling sound of the engine cooling. He shook his head in an attempt to clear the fuzzy confusion flooding his consciousness. He was upside down, strapped in his seat. He coughed as dust from outside flooded into the cabin, and rushed into his lungs each time he inhaled.

Foley turned his head, and looked across at Sam in the seat next to the pilot. He wasn't moving. His eyes were closed, and there was blood, a lot of blood. It seemed to be coming from Sam's forehead, just above his eye. As Foley watched, trying to focus, the blood dripped through Sam's hair, and onto the ceiling of the cabin, which was now below them.

"Sam!" Foley called. His voice was husky, and dry, from swallowing dust. "Sam! Are you all right?" He reached across, nudged Sam, and got no response. He focused on Sam's chest, and saw it moved as he breathed. Satisfied his friend was alive, he looked at the pilot.

Sounda's body hung suspended, limp and unmoving, in the command seat. He did not respond when Foley called his name, and there was no detectable movement in his chest.

What Foley did see was more blood, much more blood. It had pooled on the ceiling directly underneath the pilot's head.

Getting out was not going to be easy. Foley was held in his seat by his safety harness, hanging upside down, his body weight straining against the harness straps. Thoughts of a possible fire motivated him to move quickly.

Reaching up to his waist, he clasped his harness buckle and pressed the release catch. He immediately fell, his head contacting the ceiling, and his legs folding above him, jamming him awkwardly between the seat and the roof of the helicopter.

With difficulty, he managed to turn himself into a position where he was able to reach the door handle. Nothing happened when he turned it. Must be jammed, he decided. Turning and contorting his body again in the confined space, he was able to maneuver himself into a position where his feet rested against the door.

Drawing his legs back as far as he could, he kicked out at the door. It did not budge. He tried again, and this time he was sure he felt it give, just a little. He rested for a few seconds and then lashed out once more. The door flew open and banged noisily against the fuselage.

Foley crawled out of the wrecked chopper, and lay on the ground, catching his breath. He rested for just a moment, and then looked back at the chopper. He had to get Sam, and the pilot, out of the wrecked aircraft. He climbed to his feet and circled the chopper, stopping at Sam's door.

Sam was still unconscious when Foley reached in and unclasped his harness. He grunted with effort as Sam's body fell from the open harness and crumpled ungainly on the roof. Foley gripped him under his armpits and worked his way backwards out of the chopper, dragging Sam with him.

Once outside, clear of the fallen chopper, Foley dragged Sam a short distance from the wreck, and laid him carefully on his back, and then went back for the pilot.

Sounda was dead. Foley felt for a pulse and found none. A large, open wound yawned across the pilot's forehead, and on closer inspection Foley saw small pieces of skin, bone and hair stuck to one corner of the control panel. Sounda must have been hurled forward violently, and his head contacted heavily with the corner of the metal control panel.

Foley carefully unsnapped the safety harness and, as delicately as he could in the confined cockpit, lowered the pilot's body from his seat. The likelihood of fuel leaking onto the hot engine and creating a fire was still a concern for Foley; he wouldn't consider leaving the body in the chopper.

A few minutes later, Foley had the pilot's body outside on the ground next to Sam's unconscious form. He sat next to the two with his head lowered, breathing hard from exertion. Then, an audible moan from Sam attracted his attention and he looked at his friend.

Sam opened his eyes, and immediately closed them again. Intense pain raged like fire in his head, and he groaned again. He lifted his hand to his forehead, and felt a wet, sticky substance. The pain was sharper, more intense, where he touched. He heard a voice. It seemed to come from far away, and he tried to focus on the sound.

"Sam, are you all right? Wake up. Open your eyes."

Sam opened his eyes, and saw Russell Foley leaning over him. Slowly he realised he was lying on his back on the ground. His head hurt. Foley was calling his name.

"What?" Sam moaned.

"Wake up," Foley nudged Sam gently.

Sam tried to sit up. "What happened?" he groaned.

"We crashed," Foley answered. He pushed Sam back down.

"Wha... what?" Sam asked again.

"We crashed. The chopper crashed," Foley repeated.

"Jesus," Sam cursed. He tried again to sit up, and Foley pushed him back. "Let me up, Russell," he said, slapping Foley's hand away.

"Just rest a bit longer," Foley ordered.

"No, let me up." Sam ignored Foley, and forced himself to a sitting position. He looked around and saw the wrecked chopper. "Jesus," he said again. "What the fuck happened?"

"A fuel blockage I think," Foley said.

Sam turned his head and saw the pilot laying prone, an arms-length away. "Shit, is he okay?"

"No," Foley said. "He's dead. Hit his head in the crash. The impact killed him."

Instinctively Sam raised his hand and felt his own head; it came away covered in blood. "Shit that hurts," he declared.

"You hit your head too," Foley announced.

"Is it bad?" Sam asked, thrusting his head towards Foley.

"It knocked you out, but I don't think it's too bad. Typical head wound, they bleed a lot."

Sam looked back at the dead pilot. "Could have been me," he decided.

"Could have been," Foley agreed, "But it wasn't. You've got a skull like a block of wood." He got to his feet. "There must be a first-aid kit in the chopper. I'll have a look, see if I can do something about your noggin."

As Foley moved away towards the wreck, Sam called after him. "See if there's any water in there somewhere. My throat feels like a bloody sand pit. Must have swallowed a truck load of dirt."

"Okay," Foley called back.

"Coupla cold beers would be good as well," Sam joked.

Foley paused, and looked back at Sam. "I don't like your chances."

Sam thrust a thumb at the pilot's body. "Well, at least see if there's something in there to cover Biggles here with."

"Don't be disrespectful," Foley ordered.

"Disrespectful!" Sam scoffed. "Dis-bloody-respect-ful! I had to sit right next to him! He stinks like a brewery, the chopper looks like it hasn't been serviced since the day he got it, and it flies like a fuckin' tractor. Fuckin' nearly killed us both! Someone needs to tell *that* bloke about respect!"

"Too late for that," Foley said as he continued to the downed chopper. "Welcome back, Sam."

———

Foley found a first-aid kit, a blanket, and a large plastic container of water in the wreck of the chopper. He covered the body of the pilot with the blanket and held it in place with stones gathered from the immediate vicinity. In the first aid-kit he found a bottle of saline solution, a tube of antiseptic cream, and a bandage. He cleaned, and bandaged Sam's head wound, and stood back to admire his handiwork.

"Just like a professional," he said proudly.

Sam looked up at Foley, and the bandage slipped down, covering one eye. "Professional what?" Sam asked sarcastically.

Foley reached down and adjusted the bandage. "I could have been a doctor," he declared.

"Trust me Russell, the sick and the injured are very happy you chose to be a cop, and not a medical practitioner," Sam said.

"I'm going to ignore your ungrateful criticism," Foley responded. He fumbled in his pocket for his mobile phone. "No reception," he said. He turned back to the downed helicopter. "I'm gonna see if the radio still works, and get help out here."

Foley climbed into the wreck and examined the radio. There were no lights on the control panel indicating anything was working. He examined the panel, found the radio controls and attempted to send a mayday call. No sound came back at him. No verbal response; not even static. The radio was dead. He tried unsuccessfully one more time, and then tossed the hand piece aside in frustration.

"Any luck?" Sam called from where he sat waiting.

Foley climbed out of the wreck. "No, nothing," he answered. "It must have been damaged in the crash."

"If it ever worked in the first place," Sam suggested. "I never heard it working at any time during the flight." He nodded towards the covered body of the pilot. "I don't think old Sounda here was all that fastidious when it came to maintaining his helicopter in pristine working order."

Foley nodded. "Yeah, you may be right." We should have brought the hand-held radio from our car."

"If there is no telephone reception out here, there's not likely to be radio reception," Sam said. "So, what now?"

Foley studied the country around them for a few moments. "Well," he began. "We were heading north just before we came down. There's a road over there somewhere," he pointed to the west. "And, there was a house up ahead. Perhaps we should head for the house. Maybe we can get help there."

"How far away was it?" Sam asked.

"I don't know," Foley shrugged. "Twenty kilometers I guess."

"Twenty kilometers!" Sam said. "That's a long walk

in this heat." He shaded his eyes and looked away to the north.

"Do you think you can make it?" Foley asked, sounding concerned.

"Of course I can make it," Sam said indignantly. "I'm just saying... it's a long way. It's hot, and this is all the water we have." He indicated the water bottle.

"No one knows where we are, Sam," Foley explained. "We could sit here and hope someone might happen by and find us, or we can walk to the house and look for help ourselves."

"All the experts will tell you, you should never leave your vehicle when you are stranded in the desert," Sam insisted.

Foley shrugged. "Okay, we'll do it your way. We'll sit and wait."

Sam raised his hand, halting Foley from sitting down. "Wait... wait," he said. "Let's not be too hasty. You're right. No one knows we're out here. They'll miss us eventually, and come looking for us, but they don't know where to look." He indicated the dead pilot. "Old Biggles never filed any flight plans we are aware of."

"So, we walk to the house?" Foley posed.

Sam looked to the north again, and paused, considering their chances of making it to the house before the desert claimed them.

"Okay, we head for the house," he nodded. "Besides," he continued. "A couple of days in this heat and Sounda is going to be very unpleasant to be around."

"Good decision," Foley smiled. "I'm gonna search the chopper and see if there's anything we can cover the pilot with, and anything else we can take with us.

We'll look for the road and follow it north. The house will be at the end of it."

The road was further away than they thought. They stumbled across it after walking for two hours, stopping occasionally to have a drink of water and rest for a few moments. They walked for another hour before deciding they would stop and rest and then continue when the temperature dropped with the onset of nightfall.

Their water was almost gone. They took a small sip each, and lay back on the hard ground, the rough dirt road just a few metres away.

"How's your head?" Foley asked.

"I think my chakras are all out of whack," Sam answered.

"Your what?" Foley asked.

"My chakras," Sam repeated. "You know, those metaphysical, energy centre things. We all have them, even you Russell."

"I may have them," Foley said, "But mine are working just fine."

"Mine are out of whack," Sam repeated. "They need re-balancing."

"I think something needs re-balancing," Foley declared. "But I don't think it is your chakra thing-a-me-jigs."

"You need to get in touch with your inner self," Sam said.

"I need to get in touch with a bloody big steak," Foley said.

"Stuff the steak!" Sam announced. "I need a cold beer."

"How far do you think we've walked?" Foley asked.

Sam thought about the question. "I dunno, eight... nine kilometres... maybe."

"And the house when we saw it from the helicopter was twenty klicks away?" Foley continued.

"I'm guessing about twenty kilometres, yeah" Sam shrugged. "But, we walked about five k's due east from the crash site, looking for the road, and the house was to our north. I reckon we are still about fifteen kilometres away."

Foley picked up the water bottle and shook it. "About half full," he declared. "We need to reach the house before we run out of water."

Sam prodded Foley with his elbow. "Great deduction Einstein. That's another reason why they pay you the big bucks." he tucked his arm under his head and closed his eyes. "I'm gonna have a nap. Wake me when it's dark."

———

Russell Foley nudged Sam awake. "Come on old man, wake up. It's time to move."

Sam sat up and rubbed his eyes. "What time is it?" he asked.

Foley glanced at the luminous display on his watch. "Eleven thirty."

Sam looked up at the sky, aglow with millions of stars. He stared at the heavens, mesmerised at the view.

"It's late," he said. "Did you over-sleep?"

"No," Foley answered. "I've been awake for hours. You, on the other hand, slept like the dead."

Sam sat up and massaged an aching shoulder. "Why didn't you wake me?"

"You looked so cute, I didn't have the heart to," Foley said.

"You're so full of it, Russell," Sam said, getting clumsily to his feet. "Tell me why we are still friends."

Foley smiled in the dark. "Tough question, Sam, ask me one on sport." He paused. "Are you ready to go?"

"I just woke up. Can I take a leak first?"

"Of course," Foley said.

Sam turned his back and walked a few metres away. "No peeking," he called over his shoulder.

When he zipped up and returned to where Foley waited he said, "Bloody cold, isn't it?"

"Yeah," Foley agreed. "This is the desert. The nights are freezing."

"Maybe we should light a fire and warm up a bit before we go," Sam suggested.

"Look around you," Foley said. "There's nothing out here to burn. Anyway, how would we light a fire? Rub two sticks together?"

"It was just a thought," Sam shrugged.

"We'll walk the cold out of our bones," Foley said. "Come on, let's go. We should be able to make the house in three, or four hours."

"Maybe they'll have a fire," Sam wondered aloud as they started walking.

They walked north, stopping and resting for fifteen minutes after every hour. When they stopped to rest, the icy chill cooled them rapidly, and they found themselves eagerly anticipating setting off again, to maintain their body warmth. They continued the routine into the early hours of the morning.

At first, they talked animatedly about the missing girls, and the likelihood of them finding the perpetrator. Talking seemed to take their minds off both the trek and the distance they still had ahead of them. However, as the night hours passed painfully slowly, their conversations became less frequent. They were tired. The bitterly cold air was cruel, and even the warmth generated by walking seemed less, and less comforting the further they trekked.

They stopped again to rest at four-thirty in the morning. They each took a sip of water, and noticed the bottle was almost empty. Russell Foley looked into the eastern sky, hoping to see the first signs of an approaching dawn. He turned and spoke to Sam.

"Dawn can't be far away," he said, hopefully.

"At least an hour, maybe two," Sam said, somewhat absently. He was staring into the darkness ahead.

"What is it?" Foley asked.

Sam pointed to the north. "There, what's that?"

Foley squinted into the darkness to their front. "I don't see anything."

"There," Sam jabbed a finger forward. "Up ahead."

As Foley focused, an indefinable shape materialised against the slowly lightening sky. He stared at it, trying to figure out what it was. The longer he watched it the more solid in form it seemed to develop.

"I see it now," he said, finally.

"I think it's the house," Sam announced.

"Really?' Foley strained his eyes on the shape.

"Yes, really," Sam nodded. "It's close... maybe two, three hundred metres."

"Let's not stand here debating on it," Foley said. "Let's check it out." He started walking towards the shape, and Sam followed close behind.

The house was in complete darkness; Sam, and

Foley approached it stealthily. When they reached a set of steps leading to a wide verandah at the front of the house, they paused.

Foley inclined his head towards Sam. "Looks quiet," he said in a hushed tone.

"Sleeping," Sam suggested.

"Maybe," Foley agreed.

"I can't see any vehicle," Sam whispered, close to Foley's ear.

"There's a shed," Foley said, indicating a large, dark, square shape at the end of the house.

"Look at the door," Sam said, pointing at the house.

"What?" Foley asked.

"Look at the door," Sam repeated. "It's open."

Foley leaned forward and stared at the front of the house. "Yeah, it *is* open," he agreed.

"Let's take a look," Sam said. He moved forward, and started to climb the steps to the verandah.

"Wait," Foley said.

Sam turned and watched Foley as he removed his service pistol. "Do you think you'll need that?" Sam questioned.

"I'd rather be safe than sorry," Foley answered in a whisper. "We've been looking for an isolated house."

Sam paused, and finally decided a weapon might not be such a bad idea. He un-holstered his own Glock.

"Doesn't get much more isolated than this," he agreed. He waited for Foley to join him on the bottom step, and then they proceeded up onto the verandah together.

At the top, they stood side by side, and peered intently into the darkness beyond the open door, then in whispered tones,

"What do you think?" Sam whispered.

"I think no one's home," Foley offered.

"Should we go in?" Sam asked.

"Might be polite to knock first," Foley suggested.

"Why knock?" Sam asked. "The door's open. That has to be tacit consent to enter."

"I suppose you're right," Foley nodded. "You go first."

"Me?" Sam said. "Why me? You're the boss. You know what they say."

"No, tell me what they say."

"They say 'never ask your men to do anything you're not prepared to do yourself.'"

"Who says that?" Foley scoffed.

"It's in the manual," Sam said.

"It's not in *my* manual."

"You must have an old edition," Sam decided.

"Are we gonna stand here arguing the point about who goes first?" Foley asked.

Sam looked at the door. "It's double doors," he said. "We could go in together."

"Or, we could just knock," Foley said. He stepped forward and knocked hard on the closed half of the two doors.

"Police officers!" he yelled. "Anyone home?"

Foley paused, and waited for a response. When none came, he looked at Sam, and then knocked again.

"Police officers! We're coming in!" He waited again, and still got no response from inside the house. He looked at Sam. "You ready?"

Sam stepped up next to Foley. "Yep, let's do this."

Both men moved forward, stepped together through the door into the house, and stopped, waiting for their eyes to adjust to the dark. No sound came from inside, and they were unable to distinguish anything recognisable in the gloom of the interior.

Foley stepped to the side and ran his hand along the door jamb, feeling for a light switch. "There's no light switch on this side," he announced to Sam. "Try your side."

Sam followed Foley's lead and fumbled for a light switch on the opposite side of the door. He found one and clicked it on.

The room suddenly flooded with light. Sam, and Foley stood at the beginning of a long, wide hallway. Immediately to their right was an open door leading to what appeared to be a large empty room. On their left was another door offering access to a kitchen. Directly in front of them, the hallway ran the full length of the house. At the far end was a closed door they supposed led to the outside rear of the house. Other doors, on both the right, and left side of the hallway would presumably lead to the bedrooms and a bathroom.

"Hello!" Foley called loudly. His voice echoed around the large room. "Hello, police officers, is anyone here!"

"I don't think anyone is home," Sam decided aloud.

Foley agreed. "I think you're right."

Sam moved to his left and entered the kitchen. He found another light switch and flicked it on. Cockroaches, hundreds of them it seemed, scampered across the floor and the bench tops.

"Jesus!" he cursed.

"What is it?" Foley called from the hallway.

"Take a look at this," Sam called over his shoulder.

Foley joined Sam in the kitchen, and they stared at the disgusting sight before them. The sink was piled high with filthy, unwashed dishes. Cupboard doors hung open on broken hinges, and litter covered every available space on a waist high counter top around the perimeter of the room.

"Who would live like this?" Sam questioned.

"Someone does," Foley answered. "The power is still connected." He walked slowly around the room, careful not to step on anything undesirable. The floor covering, linoleum of unrecognisable color, was chipped, cracked and peeling in a dozen different places.

He paused at the sink, and looked at a pile of dishes spilling out onto the drain board. He shook his head in disbelief, and continued his circuit of the kitchen, looking into cupboards, and underneath a rubbish laden table standing askew, and supported under one leg by a piece of timber.

When he got back to where Sam waited in the doorway, he frowned. "Whoever lives here needs a few housekeeping tips."

Sam grimaced. "It stinks in here. I'm getting out before I gag."

"Me too," Foley said. He followed Sam from the kitchen.

They stepped through the doorway on the right of the hallway and paused in the centre of the room. Light from the hallway penetrated deep enough into the room to indicate it was sparsely furnished. A window, stark and unadorned with curtains, looked out to the front of the house, and an old, well-used settee in the center of the room faced the window. A small, wooden side table stood next to the settee. The top of the table displayed innumerable scars burnt into the surface from carelessly discarded cigarette butts. An ashtray, overflowing with butts and ash, balanced precariously on one edge. Sam, and Foley looked at the meager furnishings and then at each other.

"Not only do the home owners need housekeeping hints," Sam scoffed. "Some advice on decor also wouldn't go astray."

"Reminds me of your place," Foley observed.

"I don't smoke," Sam defended himself.

"Is this the main living room?" Foley speculated.

"Maybe," Sam suggested. "Or it might have been a dining room, it's close to the kitchen."

"Needs a woman's touch," Foley said.

"You don't think a woman lives here?" Sam asked.

Foley looked about. "Are you seeing the same things I'm seeing?"

"Some women are just not good housekeepers," Sam answered.

Sam, and Foley left the room and stepped back into the hallway. Beyond the kitchen, and also on the left-hand side of the hall, was a bathroom and a separate, smaller room which had to be a toilet. They walked cautiously along the hallway, pausing at every door they came to.

Beyond the bathroom and toilet, they stopped in front of an open door decidedly different from any other doors in the house. This one, slightly ajar, had a large, heavy bolt attached to it. An open padlock hung from the bolt.

"What's with the padlock?" Sam wondered aloud.

"Let's find out," Foley suggested. He reached out,

pushed the door open a little wider, and immediately raised his hand to his nose. "What the fuck is that smell?"

"Phew!" Sam responded from behind him. "That's foul!"

Foley pushed the door harder, and it swung wide open. "You wanna check it out?" he asked Sam.

Sam side-stepped around Foley. "Let's not start the 'you go first' shit again." He stepped into the room, and stopped dead in his tracks. "Oh, shit!" he exclaimed.

Foley stepped in behind him.

"I think we might have stumbled on the wolf's lair," Sam declared.

"What is that?" Foley indicated the upturned bucket in the middle of the floor.

"I think that's a toilet bucket," Sam answered.

The room was big; way bigger than the kitchen, and almost twice the size of the room opposite the kitchen. Sam spotted the mattresses on the floor, and crossed to where they lay on the floor in one corner of the room.

"This is where he kept the girls," he said.

"Girls... plural?" Foley pondered.

"There are two mattresses," Sam responded. He held his hand tightly over his nose and mouth as he crossed the room, stooped and picked up a set of car keys. Attached to the key ring was the broken body of a small torch. A small battery, along with tiny pieces of smashed lens, lay scattered about the floor. "These are Ford keys," he announced to Foley.

. Russell Foley crossed to where Sam stood, studying the keys. "Miranda Winters drove a Ford," he said.

"Could be a coincidence," Sam muttered.

"I doubt it," Foley said.

"Why do you think they were tossed aside?" Sam asked.

Foley moved across to the fireplace, squatted, and stared into the empty space. "Look at the soot, and ash in the bottom." He craned his neck and tried to look up into the chimney. "I don't think there has been a fire in here in a long time. So, how did all this crap get in the bottom?"

"Are you suggesting what I think you are suggesting?" Sam asked, as he joined Foley.

"She climbed out through the chimney." Foley stood.

"Seriously?" Sam asked.

Foley shrugged. "Why not? Do you have another scenario?"

Sam stood, turned and indicated the door behind them. "The door was open. Maybe the perp took her out."

"Maybe," Foley said. "Let's check the rest of the house."

Back in the hallway, they entered the room opposite, immediately recognising it as the main bedroom. As in the other rooms they had so far seen, it contained very little in the way of furnishings. In the middle of the floor, between an unmade, large four-poster bed and a wardrobe against one wall, there was a large, open, cardboard carton.

Sam walked across to the bed. The bedding was disarranged, and hadn't seen the inside of a washing machine for a long time, he guessed. Thin ropes attached to the head, and foot of the bed indicated a sinister purpose. He looked down at the confusion of ropes and bedding, and noticed the sheets, obviously once white, were stained with patches of red. They were stains just like those he had seen many times before in the course of his career, many old and faded, others recent looking. He knew instantly he was looking at dried blood stains.

Sam shook his head in disgust. "Fuckin' animal!" he spat.

From behind him Foley called. "Look at this, Sam."

Sam turned. Foley was on one knee, in front of the cardboard box.

"What is it?" Sam asked.

"Clothes," Foley said. He reached into the box, and took out a pair of lady's light, cotton slacks. "It's full of women's clothes."

"I think we've found our man... or at least where he lives," Sam suggested.

"The mongrel's keeping souvenirs," Foley concluded. "Check your phone, Sam. Have we got reception out here?"

Sam flipped open his mobile phone and checked the digital display. "Nothing," he said. He flipped the phone shut and returned it to his pocket.

"Let's check the rest of this place," Foley suggested. "It will be daylight soon. Maybe we'll get lucky."

"You think he'll come back?" Sam posed.

Foley shrugged. "Why not, he doesn't know we are here. Wherever he is, I'm sure he will be back sooner or later."

"Let's hope it's sooner," Sam said. "I'm looking forward to meeting this character."

———

Outside, Sam, and Foley rounded the corner of the house at the end of the wide verandah, and discovered the ruptured water bottle next to the rain water tank. Sam picked it up and examined it.

"Doesn't look like it's been here long," he said.

Foley stepped in front of Sam and squatted. "What do you make of this?" he asked.

Sam squatted next to Foley. There, in a small, damp patch on the ground, close to the water tank, was a very small, partial footprint. Just the front half of the print was visible.

"Looks like a child's print... or maybe a young girl. "Do you think she would have got far?" Sam stood and looked off towards the distant horizon.

"It would depend on whether or not she's hurt," Foley said. He got to his feet and looked across at the shed. "Let's take a look in there."

Cautiously, they approached the power shed and entered. They found nothing other than the battery bank, and a large supply of distilled water.

"This is the main power supply," Foley said. "Battery banks are used when there is no electricity grid to feed into. There will be solar panels on the roof charging these batteries," Foley said. "I'm guessing these have been here for many years."

"Why would anyone live way out here?" Sam wondered aloud. "This is a substantial house. Why build it in such an isolated place?"

Foley shrugged. "Who knows?"

Sam crossed back to the door, and stepped outside the shed, followed closely by Foley.

"We need to get a forensic team out here," Sam said.

"There's no mobile phone reception, and I never

saw a land-line phone inside the house." Foley swept an arm across the landscape. "There are no phone poles anywhere. Our hand-held radio is still in the vehicle at Wauchope. How are we gonna get forensics out here? No one knows where we are."

"Someone will miss us, eventually," Sam suggested.

"They might miss me; you I'm not so sure," Foley shrugged.

"Thanks, mate, I love you too," Sam said.

"They don't know where to look," Foley continued.

Sam started to walk back toward the house. "Then, we'll have to wait for the house holder to come back, and borrow his car."

"And lock his arse up," Foley added, following closely behind.

"And shoot him," Sam said.

"You might want to consider shooting him *before* we lock his arse up," Foley advised. "Too much paperwork the other way around."

"Good thinking, Boss," Sam smiled. "They teach you that shit in the Inspector exams? Come on, I'll make you a coffee."

"Do you think we can find any clean cups in there?" Foley asked.

"We might have to wash a couple," Sam suggested.

"Yeah, in acid," Foley scoffed.

They found coffee, sugar, and eventually managed to get two coffee mugs clean enough to satisfy them they would not contract an infectious, and possibly fatal disease. An open container of long-life milk, and very little else, sat on a shelf in an old, noisy refrigerator in the kitchen. On sniffing the open container suspiciously, Sam, and Foley elected to drink their coffee black.

They carried their drinks out of the house, distancing themselves from its suspicious, lingering odours. Before they sat, Sam picked up the filthy, overflowing astray from the small table on the verandah and dropped it over the railing, onto the ground.

"What if he doesn't come back?" Foley asked, sipping his coffee.

"He'll be back," Sam said.

"What makes you so sure?" Foley queried.

Sam shrugged. "He hasn't made the bed, or done the dishes."

———

Sam looked suspiciously at the contents of his coffee mug, raised the mug to his nose, and sniffed. He took a very tentative sip.

"What does this taste like to you?" he asked Foley

Russell Foley took another sip of his own coffee. "Dry roasted, Brazilian beans, grown on the north side of a gentle slope, taking advantage of the gentle, warm breezes drifting up from the fertile valley."

"Must be the dirty cups," Sam grimaced.

"You scrubbed them in boiling water so long you almost took the enamel off," Foley said sarcastically.

Sam place his mug on the table. "Doesn't taste like real coffee to me."

"Probably years past its use-by date," Foley said.

"The fuck-wit who lives here is past *his* use-by date."

"Don't forget to tell him that when he comes back," Foley suggested.

Sam sat upright, and stared at something which caught his eye. "What's that?" he said.

"What's what?" Foley asked, now peering into his own coffee mug suspiciously.

"That," Sam pointed to a dust cloud way off in the distance.

Foley focused on where Sam was indicating. "Speaking of him coming back, this might be him now."

"Shall we put the kettle on again?" Sam asked.

"Fuck the kettle," Foley answered.

Sam and Foley stood, stepped back inside the house and flattened themselves against the hallway wall. Surreptitiously they peeked out through the doorway at the dust cloud rapidly approaching the house. Both men reached for their weapons, un-holstered them, and held them at their sides, barrels down. If this was their man, they wanted to be ready. He would be armed, and he would not hesitate to fire at them to avoid apprehension, they figured.

"You think this is him?" Foley asked.

"I doubt it's the Mormons," Sam responded. "It has to be him."

"Forget the banter about shooting him," Foley said. "We need to take him alive."

"You would have to be the biggest fun spoiler of all time," Sam answered.

"We need to know where the girl is," Foley explained. "He can't tell us if you fill him full of holes."

"Can I shoot him after he tells us?"

"Maybe... I'll think about it," Foley said.

By now they could see the outline of the vehicle, still a way off, and its form no more than a dark shape in front of a swirling dust cloud rising high in the sky behind it, but it was definitely a car, and it was coming fast.

Eventually, the vehicle slowed noticeably, and finally stopped about two hundred metres from the house. Sam, and Foley could see the silhouette of the driver. He, or she seemed to be alone, just sitting, staring through the windscreen at them.

"What's he doing?" Sam wondered aloud.

"I think he suspects something," Foley suggested.

"Why doesn't he come on up and check?" Sam posed.

"Yeah, right," Foley chuffed. "He's killed at least six girls, maybe seven if Miranda Winters is another of his victims. Would you waltz on over and introduce yourself if you suspected you might not be alone?

"Good point," Sam conceded.

Suddenly the vehicle began to move slowly forward.

"Here he comes," Sam said.

"I don't think so," Foley said. "I think he wants a closer look. He's not sure what's going on."

"The closer he comes, the better," Sam murmured.

17

———

Miranda woke with a start. A bright light shone in her face, blinding her.

"Wha... what?" she stammered, shielding her eyes.

"Hello Miranda," the man said.

Instinctively, Mandy pushed away with her feet, sliding backwards across the hard ground. She tried to stand, got to her knees, and became tangled in the blankets. She stumbled and fell onto her back. "Oh no... no... no!" she cried, shielding her eyes from the powerful torch light burning brightly in her face.

"You didn't *really* think you could get away from me, did you Miranda?" The man stood over her, his legs straddling her body.

Mandy gave up. She simply surrendered. She had nothing in reserve to fight the man. Her energy levels were at rock bottom. She rolled onto her side, curled her body into the fetal position, and buried her face in the blankets, waiting to die. Death would be welcome, she decided. The pain would stop, and she would be truly free from the evil monster standing over her, smiling down on her broken and beaten body.

"That was very clever, Miranda," she heard him

say. "Very clever indeed, climbing up the chimney. Who would have thought of it? You are to be congratulated." He prodded Mandy with his foot. "Well done, girl."

Mandy whimpered, and buried her head deeper into the blankets. The strong, unpleasant smell of dirt, and body odour long ingrained in the material flooded her nostrils.

"Do... do... do it qu... quick," she stammered.

"Do what quick?" the man asked.

"Kill me," Mandy's voice was muffled in the folds of the blankets.

"Kill you? Oh, no, Miranda," the man said, a hint of pleasure evident in his words. "I'm not going to kill you, not yet. You have proved yourself to be a worthy adversary. You've shown an initiative, and daring far beyond what I would have expected from you, certainly far beyond that shown by all the other weak, spineless sluts. I have plans for you, my dear, big plans. You and I are going to have such a good time together, you'll see. You might even get to like me."

Mandy lifted her head from the blankets and looked up into the blinding torch light. She could not see the man's face; the light was too bright. She lifted her hand and shielded her eyes. "What do you want from me?" she sobbed.

The man remained silent for a few moments. "Your company, Miranda," he said finally.

From out of the darkness behind the bright torch light, Mandy saw a hand reach down to her.

"Here," the man said. "Let me help you up."

Mandy shuffled backwards. The man followed.

"You can't get away from me, Miranda," he said.

"You tried once, ingeniously I might add, but surely you know now there is no escape."

"How... how did you find me?" Mandy asked.

"Oh, please Miranda. You insult my intelligence. I've lived out here for a long time. I know every square inch of this country. I knew you would have to follow the road. It's the only way out. I saw something in the darkness that didn't belong... just a lump on the ground, behind the quartz outcrop. I almost drove straight past it. I've driven out here thousands of times, and I realised I'd never seen this particular lump before. I knew instantly it was my Miranda, my sweet, smart, daring Miranda." He offered his hand again. "Get up," he ordered.

"Why don't you just kill me now and have it done with?" Mandy whimpered.

"Miranda, I don't really believe you want to die. Why would you go to the trouble, and considerable effort of escaping from the house if you are prepared to die?"

"I'm ready now," Mandy said, resignedly.

"Be that as it may, I'm not ready for you to pass from this world just yet. I have plans for you... for us."

"Wh... what plans?"

"Don't worry your pretty self about the details, Miranda. That's my job. If you haven't already guessed, I'm pretty darn good at this sort of thing."

"You are a murderer!" Mandy said. "You killed all the other girls."

"They were passed their use-by date," the man chuckled.

Mandy buried her face in the blankets once again resigned to whatever fate awaited her.

"Get up Miranda!" the man ordered.

"No," Mandy muttered.

"Don't make me drag you up, Miranda. Trust me, you don't want me to do that. Now, get up."

"No," Mandy repeated.

The man leaned down, grabbed a fist full of Mandy's hair, and pulled her violently to her knees, and then to her feet. Mandy screamed, grabbed his hands, and tried desperately to make him let go. It felt like he was going to pull her hair out of her head. She fought hard, kicking out at him, and striking him in the leg, just below his knee. The kick served only to inflame his anger and incite him into yanking harder at her hair.

"Let go! Let go!" Mandy yelled.

Mandy struggled uselessly against his assault, knowing full well she could not fight him off, but gaining a small degree of satisfaction in knowing the resignation she felt when she woke and found him standing over her was gone, replaced now with a desperate urge to fight. If she was going to die at the hands of the monster, she was going to die fighting. She lashed out again with her foot, aiming for his groin. A hit in the right place might cool his ardor, she reasoned. She missed her intended mark, and lost her balance. If he hadn't such a tight grip on her hair, she would have fallen backwards.

The man yanked hard on her hair, and Mandy screamed. Then he hit her. He swung with the hand holding the torch. The punch was instinctive, and poorly aimed, but it still managed to connect with Mandy's face.

Mandy's eyes rolled back in her head. Her knees buckled, and her body began to collapse. The man tightened his grip on her hair, and held her upright.

GARY S. GREGOR

He hit her again. This time, as the torch connected, he let go of her hair, and Mandy's body flew backwards, landing with a dull thud on the hard ground.

The man stood over Mandy's prone body. Her dress had flown high as she fell, and the hem now lay above her waist, exposing her brief cotton panties. The man shone the torch light on her exposed abdomen, and he licked his lips in voyeuristic pleasure at the vision before him. A part of him wanted her, right there, and then, but he fought the urge. As nice as he knew it would be, it was far more fun when she was awake and enjoying the experience.

He set the torch on the ground, arranging the light so it illuminated Mandy. Then he squatted next to her and slid his arms underneath her body, braced his knees, and lifted her in his arms. Standing, he looked down into her closed eyes. A trickle of blood oozed from a wound under her chin where he had hit her, and already, even in the dull light thrown up by the torch, he could see the skin around the wound beginning to discolor. Soon it would be a swollen, dark bruise. Might have broken her jaw, he wondered.

Still, she had to do what he asked. If she continued to refuse, he would continue to hurt her. A pity though, he thought. She was so pretty, prettier than any of the others. Compared to Miranda, the others were nothing more than an interesting, amusing diversion. This one he *really* liked. She had spunk too, and it excited him. He had waited a long time for someone as exciting, as pretty, and as so damn sexy as Miranda to come into his life. This one was a keeper, at least for the moment.

He carried her over to his car, lowered her ungracefully to the ground and opened the rear door.

Pausing briefly, he ogled her disheveled and vulnerable body, and then lifted her effortlessly and bundled her roughly into the rear of his vehicle. He thought about tying her hands and feet but decided against it. She was out to it. He had hit her hard. She wouldn't come around for a while. He had time to get to where he was going. He slammed the door, hurriedly retrieved the torch, and climbed in behind the wheel. As he drove away, the first faint hints of dawn appeared in the eastern sky. He smiled, and found himself becoming aroused.

"Soon," he said aloud. "Soon, my pretty Miranda... once more it will be just you and me."

————

Mandy opened her eyes, and groaned. The pain in her face was excruciating. Radiating upwards from her jaw, it felt like a constant succession of red hot needles being thrust into the soft flesh under her chin. She touched her jaw gingerly, and her hand came away damp with blood. She closed her eyes as tears filled them and blurred her vision. A new wave of pain washed over her, and she groaned softly.

The pain was so bad she wanted to cry out, but she couldn't open her mouth without another hot, searing needle of unbearable agony screaming through her head. Instead, only a pitiful, low, moan escaped from her lips, and she prayed for the nightmare to be over, even if it meant her death. She had already accepted death was what the monster had in store for her, eventually. At least death would bring her peace and end the pain.

Through the suffocating blanket of pain, Mandy

arrived at the conclusion she was in the man's car, like the time he first kidnapped her from Devil's Marbles. Her body bounced uncomfortably. Each time the car hit a rut, or a corrugation in the road, her head struck the floor, and the pain intensified a hundred-fold. Fine particles of dust filtered into the rear compartment of the vehicle, irritating her nostrils and she fought hard to stifle the almost overpowering urge to cough.

Slowly she began to remember. The man had hit her. He hit her in the face with a torch. How did he find her in the dark, she wondered? It must have been like looking for a needle in a haystack. He had to be incredibly lucky, or he really did know this country as well as he said he did.

Mandy moved her legs, and suddenly it dawned on her she was not tied up. Her hands and feet were not bound. Carefully she lifted her head and looked around the tiny cramped space. She dared not lift her head above the rear seat in case he was checking the rear vision mirror and saw her. If he saw she was awake he would stop the car and tie her up.

Renewed, intensified pain shot through her face, and she stifled a sob as she turned her head and looked at the rear door. Guessing it would not be locked, she considered opening it, and jumping out of the vehicle. Her perception, laying uncomfortably in the rear baggage compartment, was the car seemed to be traveling very fast over the rough, corrugated dirt road. The fall would kill her, of that she was certain.

She stared at the closed door for what seemed a long time. Dying this way was something she had to seriously consider. There would be pain when she hit the ground, lots of it, but she was experiencing lots of pain right now, and there was lots of it as a result of the things the monster did to her. However, death would be quick, and any pain associated with the fall would be brief. She squirmed closer to the door, raised her hand to the release catch and touched it with her fingers. Then. she paused. The car was slowing.

Mandy felt the car slow, and eventually stop. As dust settled around the vehicle, it seeped through every tiny orifice it could find, and the urge to cough was strong as she breathed it. She waited for the sound of the driver's door opening.

He would come for her now. This was the last moments of her life, she believed. Her thoughts went to her family at home, and hoped someone would find her body and send it back home so her family could have closure. She missed her folks terribly. Her mother would be inconsolable, her father too. She was so close to them, and the thought of never seeing them again filled her with more fear and dread than the thought of dying.

Mandy could hear no sound other than the car engine idling monotonously for what seemed like ages. The man still had not gotten out of the vehicle, and she wondered what he was doing. She desperately wanted to take a peek and see why they had stopped. Slowly, carefully, she lifted herself onto one elbow. Her head was now just a few centimetres below the back of the rear seat.

Ever so slowly, she raised her head until her eyes looked over the rear seat. Just the top of her head and her eyes were visible. If the man looked into the rear vision mirror he would surely see her. He seemed to be staring out through the front windscreen, looking at something up ahead.

As Mandy covertly watched the man, the car started to move. Startled by the sudden movement, she dropped her head below the seat, and felt the vehicle moving very slowly forward. Gathering herself, she lifted her head once more and peeped over the seat. She glimpsed a house! *The* house! The bastard had brought her back to the house. She closed her eyes, and bit down hard on her lip, stifling the urge to cry out.

Then, the car stopped again, and Mandy saw two men step outside the house, onto the verandah. The two men, stood together at the leading edge of the verandah. The man had accomplices! Now there were three of them! What if there were more than three? Maybe there were others inside the house? Thoughts, fears and unanswered questions rushed at her, way too fast to comprehend.

Then she saw the guns. Both men were holding guns. Each was holding a pistol down by his side. They looked clean-cut and reasonably well dressed, in contrast to the shabby, unclean attire of the monster driving the car. They had to be police! Yes, they were police officers! They had found her! They were here to take her away from this awful place! She wanted to cry out with joy. She would get to see her family again.

Suddenly, the car started to speed up. It turned very suddenly, throwing her roughly about in the cramped rear compartment. It started to accelerate. Horrified, Mandy pushed herself into a sitting position, and looked out the rear window. The house was behind her now! They were speeding away from the house and the two men on the verandah!

Mandy screamed. It came out muffled, and dis-

torted, and the effort brought on a new wave of excruciating pain.

"Hhh... eelp meeee! Hel... pp meee! She waved furiously at the two men, rapidly growing smaller as the
vehicle sped away from the house; away from her sal-
vation. Believing it was finally over, Mandy slumped
to the floor and sobbed uncontrollably.

———

Sam stared at the girl's face in the rear window of the
vehicle. She was waving desperately at them. He could
see her mouth moving. She was calling to them.

"What the fuck?" he yelled.

"He's onto us," Foley said. "He must have seen our
weapons."

Sam raised his Glock, chambered a round, and
raced to the bottom of the steps.

"No!" Foley ran after Sam and grabbed his arm.
"Don't shoot. You might hit the girl!"

Sam lowered his weapon, and stared after the
rapidly retreating car. "He's getting away," he said
aloud.

"We've got no vehicle," Foley said. "We can't
follow."

Frustrated, Sam kicked at the dirt. "Jesus! Jesus
Fuckin' Christ! He's got the girl!"

"I know," Foley said. "I saw her."

"Was it the Winters girl?" Sam asked.

"Probably," Foley answered. He holstered his
Glock. "Unless he's grabbed another one."

Both men stared in silence at the car rapidly di-
minishing in size as it sped away. A dense cloud of

dust rose into the sky behind it. They watched it in silence until it was just a speck on the horizon.

"Where the fuck will he go?" Sam asked, finally.

"I don't know," Foley said.

"I've never felt so bloody helpless in all my life," Sam announced, bitterly.

"Tell me about it," Foley agreed.

"So, what now?" Sam asked.

Foley shrugged. "We wait."

"For what?"

"Eventually, when we don't return, they will come looking for us," Foley answered.

"And in the meantime?"

Foley turned, and stepped back to the open doorway. "Another cup of coffee?" he suggested.

Sam followed Foley up the steps. "I'm not sleeping here," he declared defiantly.

"We might have to," Foley said.

"There's only one bed," Sam continued. "And I'm not sleeping in that."

Foley stopped at the top of the steps, turned and looked out in the direction the car had fled. "We could walk out."

"Fuck that!" Sam responded. "We just walked a thousand fuckin' kilometres!"

Back in the kitchen, Foley sat down at the small table. "You know," he said. "I don't think I've ever heard you complain as much as this."

Sam sat in the other chair. "Yeah, well I'm just gettin' started."

"How about that coffee?" Foley asked.

"You want me to make it?"

"Yeah," Foley said. "That would be nice."

"I made it last time," Sam complained. "It's your turn."

"Have you forgotten, I'm the boss?"

"Oh, no, you're not going to pull the, 'I'm the boss' shit on me again, are you?"

Foley turned to face Sam. "Black. One sugar."

18

"SHUT THE FUCK UP!" the man screamed. "NOW!"

The car swerved dangerously on the loose gravel at the edge of the road, and he fought to save the vehicle from sliding into a perilous sideways skid. He was traveling way above the speed he would normally consider safe, and the steering wheel bucked, and spun unpredictably in his hands. If he lost it, the car was going to flip. Reluctantly, he eased off the accelerator, and slowed a little, gaining a little more control of the speeding vehicle.

He glanced into the rear vision mirror. Miranda was kneeling in the rear of the vehicle, staring out the back window at the house, fading and then reappearing through a thick cloud of dust thrown up behind the car, and getting smaller in size the further away from it the car traveled.

The man wiped sweat from his forehead with the back of his hand. His heart raced, and his mind flooded with questions. Cops! Where did they come from! How did they get there? He did not see a vehicle.

Were there others? Were they on to him? They had to be on to him, they wouldn't be at the house otherwise. "Fuckin' cops!" he muttered to himself.

From the rear of the vehicle he heard Miranda sobbing loudly. He could hear her over the noise of the screaming engine and the loud thumping of the wheels over the corrugated road. He glanced again in the mirror. Beyond where Miranda knelt, staring out of the window, sobbing inconsolably and banging her fists against the glass, the house was no longer visible but still she stared into the dust clouded distance.

"They're not coming for you, Miranda," the man called to her over his shoulder. "It's just you and me now." His eyes darted from the road in front of him, to Mandy in the back of the car. "You need to be quiet. I can't concentrate with you bawling your fuckin' head off."

Suddenly Mandy went quiet. The man saw her head drop. Perhaps she had come to the realisation no one was coming for her, he decided. He hoped she had not resigned herself completely to her fate; he liked it when she put up a fight. Then, the rear door flew open wide and Mandy started to lean towards the opening.

The man stood on the brake pedal, and the car began to slide sideways. For a few seconds the vehicle skidded dangerously. The speed bled off quickly, and the car slowed dramatically. With the sudden and dramatic loss of momentum, Mandy was flung backwards and she crashed heavily into the rear of the back seat. The man took his foot off the brake, and turned the car's front wheels against the direction of the skid. The vehicle rocked violently, but stayed upright. He wrestled with the vehicle, and eventually guided it to a stop. He took a deep breath, unbuckled his seatbelt and clambered from the car.

Mandy was in so much pain she could not move. The sudden stop had sent her crashing into the rear seats. The back of her head hit first, and her body followed a millisecond later. She lay in a crumpled heap, her knees drawn up to her chest, in so much pain she could not even cry out. Her jaw had to be broken. Every bone, every muscle, every sinew in her body screamed in protest. She could not even think clearly.

Then she screamed; a primeval, wretched, mournful sound, shattering the silence rapidly descending over the desert. She closed her eyes, and surrendered to the pain as blissful, pain-free unconsciousness settled over her.

The man reached into the rear of the vehicle and grabbed Mandy by one leg. He dragged her roughly forward until her legs dangled out of the rear luggage compartment.

"Wake up, Miranda," he ordered.

Mandy did not move. He looked at her closed eyes, and was unable to detect even the slightest movement of her eyelids. For a moment, he thought she might be dead. Perhaps she had broken her neck, he wondered. He looked at her breasts. His eyes lingered there while he waited for any sign she was breathing.

There! The slightest rise of her bosom against the constraints of her dress gave him renewed hope. She was alive. He stared at her breasts, his gaze lingering, once again, he found himself becoming aroused at the sight of her.

Miranda was not just pretty; she was also extremely sexy. The other girls were all pretty, and initially, it was always their looks, and their figures, he was attracted to, but he wanted more than looks and a nice body. He wanted a girl who oozed sex appeal. It had to seep out of her pores like the morning dew on a ripe peach.

The others simply resigned themselves early to the probability they were going to die. It seemed they all accepted it as though it were inevitable. Of course, it *was* inevitable, but they did not know that for certain. They could have fought, *should* have fought. They should have shown some spirit; at least offered token resistance.

They all elected not to fight. They chose instead to cry, and scream, like toddlers having a tantrum, and they continued to do so right up to the point he silenced them permanently.

Miranda was different. She was young, gorgeous, and incredibly sexy. In that regard, she met all his prerequisites. The difference between Miranda and the others was obvious right from the get-go. Miranda showed spunk. She fought him. Even when she was bound by her hands and feet to his bed, she bucked and writhed underneath him. It drove him wild. *That* was sexy. *That* was what he wanted in a woman. He wanted more of *that* from her.

As he looked at her crumpled body in the back of his car, he suddenly regretted hitting her in the face with the torch. At least he regretted hitting her as hard as he did. Her face, her pretty, pretty face was swollen and misshapen.

"Must hurt like hell, Miranda," he said softly to her comatose form. "It will get better. Soon, I promise, it will get better. Then we can be together again. You'll like that, I know you will."

He reached under Mandy's body, retrieved the ropes he kept in the vehicle, and tied her hands and feet. He almost placed a gag over her mouth, but decided not to. It would hurt her too much, and might mean it would take longer for her to get better.

He didn't want to wait any longer than he had to. He wanted to be with her again, as soon as possible. The urge was so great he found it difficult not to take her right there, in the back of the car. But, he needed to put distance between himself and the house, not to mention the two cops waiting for him there. Also, he had to consider Miranda was out cold, and could not possibly get the same enjoyment from it as she surely would if she were awake and participating with the same enthusiasm he had come to enjoy so much. He decided to wait. He pushed her legs back into the car and slammed the door.

As he raced along the road, putting even more distance between himself and the house, he noticed a vehicle approaching from the opposite direction. In all the years he had lived at the house, he couldn't remember ever seeing another vehicle using the road.

"Gettin' like a fuckin' freeway," he muttered to himself.

The oncoming vehicle was still a way off, but it was coming fast. Assuming it was more police, he slowed dramatically, steered off the track, and headed east, increasing his speed dramatically. With no designated road to follow, the going was extremely rough. The vehicle bounced, and careened dangerously across the hard, stony terrain. Glancing occasionally through his driver's side window, he fought to keep the four-wheel-drive on a course that would not end in disaster. As the oncoming vehicle neared the position where he turned off the road, he recognised it as one used by police SWAT personnel. He depressed the accelerator harder, attempting to put more distance between himself and the approaching police vehicle.

19

R e-assigned from the well where the bodies were located, Sergeant Wayne Donaldson and his Task Force members picked Terry Potts up from Wauchope, refueled, and headed for the area where they believed the helicopter carrying Foley and Rose had come down.

The Lenco BearCat slowed, and stopped. Sergeant Potts alighted from the passenger side of the vehicle, and walked around to the driver's side. He raised a pair of high powered binoculars to his eyes, and focused on the speeding vehicle, racing away to the east.

Donaldson wound down the driver's side window. "Do you want to go after him?"

"No," Potts answered. "I don't know who that is, but we need to get to the chopper. We don't know if it crashed, or the pilot chose to land for some reason. We have been unable to reach them by radio or mobile phone. Until we know what happened, we need to make them our priority."

"Okay," Donaldson agreed. "Jump in, we are almost there."

Fifteen minutes later, they found the downed helicopter. Terry Potts scanned the horizon to the north. Behind him, the task force members combed the wreckage of the downed helicopter. He was surprised, and relieved, to find Sam Rose, and Russell Foley were not with the downed chopper.

The pilot's body was discovered alongside the wreck, indicating Rose and Foley must have walked away from the crash, possibly one, or both of them, injured. They had to be out there somewhere, he decided, as he stared into the distance.

Something up ahead caught his eye. He fiddled with the focus wheel on the binoculars, and a dark shape filled his vision. A long way off, outlined against the horizon, a house appeared. A square, black, shadow against the pale blue sky on the distant horizon, the shape shimmered in the heat waves rising from the hot earth.

"Hey, Wayne," he called to the commander of the task force. "What do you make of this?"

Wayne Donaldson walked across from the wreck, and stood next to Potts. "What have you got?"

Potts handed Donaldson the binoculars and pointed to the horizon. "I think it's a house, maybe ten klicks away."

Donaldson focused the glasses, stared in silence for a few moments, and handed the binoculars back to Potts.

"It certainly looks like a house," he said. "Too far away to detect any movement... more than ten klicks, I think," he said. "You wanna check it out?"

"Yeah," Potts nodded. "Let's take a couple of your blokes with us. Leave the rest here to watch over the wreck, and the pilot. We'll pick them up on our way back"

The Task Force Sergeant returned to the chopper, delegated duties to his men, and prepared to set out for the distant house. "We're ready to leave," he said to Potts.

Terry Potts lowered the binoculars, and climbed into the passenger compartment of the BearCat.

"Let's hope we get lucky," he said.

———

Foley and Rose had completed a cursory search of the house and the outlying shed. What was needed was a forensic team to go over the entire property, they agreed. This was the place the man kept the women prisoner up until the time he killed them and dumped their bodies in the well, there was no doubt in either of them.

They were seated on the top step of the verandah when they saw the dust cloud of an approaching vehicle long before it arrived.

"I don't suppose this would be our man coming back?" Sam suggested.

"No, he's long gone," Foley said.

As they watched, out of a dust cloud the Task Force Lenco BearCat slowed, and pulled up in front of the house. Sergeants Terry Potts, and Wayne Donaldson alighted from the front of the big armoured vehicle, and two members clad in black jumped out of the rear and adopted defensive positions behind the vehicle.

Foley and Rose stood and stepped forward to the top of the steps.

"Well, well!" Foley smiled down at the two sergeants. "Are we glad to see you blokes."

Donaldson and Potts walked across to the foot of the steps. Potts indicated the blood-stained bandage wrapped around Sam's head.

"Tell me you've been drinking, and fell over," he joked.

"No, I haven't been drinking," Sam smiled. "But, I could use one."

"How did you find us?" Foley asked.

"When you weren't in the wreck of the chopper, we figured you walked away," Potts explained. He indicated the property with a sweep of his hand. "This is the only place as far as the eye can see for hundreds of kilometres. We assumed you would have seen it from the air and decided to make for it."

"How did you know the chopper crashed?" Sam asked.

"Ahh," Potts said. "Good old Sounda, may he rest in peace, had a GPS emergency positioning beacon installed in the aircraft when he got the contract with the mining company. He must have triggered it when he knew a crash was inevitable."

"He never said anything," Foley said.

"Probably too busy trying to keep the thing in the air," Potts suggested.

"Good old Sounda," Sam added.

Wayne Donaldson stepped forward, and rested one foot on the bottom step. "You blokes forgot the golden rule," he said.

"Golden rule?" Sam questioned.

Donaldson looked around. "This is the Tanami Desert. If you find yourself stranded in the desert, any desert, you *never* leave your vehicle."

"Thanks for pointing that out," Foley responded.

"We'll try to remember that the next time we are in a helicopter crash in the desert."

"There won't be a next time," Sam declared, fingering his bandaged head.

Terry Potts looked past Foley and Rose, at the house behind them. "Who lives here?" he asked.

"Did you pass a four-wheel-drive on the way here?" Sam queried.

"We didn't exactly pass it," Donaldson explained. "It turned off the road and raced across the desert to the east, before we got to it."

"You didn't see the driver?" Foley asked.

"Or the passenger?" Sam added.

"Passenger, what passenger?" Potts asked.

Russell Foley walked down the steps and stood in front of Donaldson and Potts. "That was our man," he said.

Potts shrugged. "What man?"

"The man who snatched the girls, killed them, and tossed them down the well."

"One of the missing girls was in the back," Sam said.

"You have to be kidding," Potts said.

"I wish we were," Foley answered.

"And, he lives here?" Donaldson asked.

"He kept them here before he killed them," Sam explained.

"Are you sure?" Potts asked.

Foley indicated the house. "In a bedroom, down the hall on the right, there's a large box filled with clothes we suspect belonged to the missing girls. And, there's a room opposite, where he kept them locked up."

"Jesus Christ," Potts cursed. He looked behind him at the wide-open spaces. "That was him?"

Sam nodded. "That was him."

"And one of the girls was in the car?" Potts asked.

"Possibly the latest girl to go missing, the one from Devil's Marbles," Foley answered.

"Winters," Potts said. "Miranda Winters."

"Was he here when you got here?" Donaldson asked.

"The house was empty," Sam confirmed. "The front doors were open, and no one responded when we called out, so we went in."

"Probable cause," Potts declared.

"Something like that," Sam nodded.

"After we found the room where he kept the girls, and the box of clothes, we came back out here on the verandah, and he drove up," Foley continued.

"You got a look at the dude?" Potts asked hopefully.

"No," Foley answered. "He stopped a couple of hundred metres out when he spotted us. We had our weapons drawn, and he turned and high-tailed it out of here."

"We saw the girl in the back of the vehicle," Sam said. "She was banging on the back window, and it looked like she was calling out to us."

"She looked terrified," Foley included.

Potts kicked the ground at his feet. "And I let the bastard go," he said disgustedly.

"Don't beat yourself up over it, mate," Foley said. "You weren't to know. You've been in the job long enough to know, from time to time, shit happens."

"If he kills the girl, I'll never forgive myself," Potts shook his head.

"We need to get him before he does," Sam said. "There's no mobile phone reception out here." He looked at Donaldson. "Have you blokes got a satellite phone?"

Yeah," the Task Force commander nodded. "In the truck." He inclined his head towards the BearCat.

"Good," Sam nodded. "Get onto Tennant Creek, and get a couple of road blocks in place... one in Tennant Creek, and one down South, at Barrow Creek. Then, have a couple of mobile patrols running up and down the highway between the two places. This prick has got to come up for air somewhere."

"I'm on it," Donaldson said as he turned away and walked quickly back to the Task Force vehicle.

"Also," Foley called after him, "We want a forensic team out here. See if you can get John Singh from Alice Springs up here with some troops. He's the best forensics guy we've got. We need to go over this place from top to bottom. Tell them to bring sleeping gear and supplies. They might be here for a while."

"Okay, got it," Donaldson waved.

Sam turned to Potts. "Terry, can we get a lift back with you?"

"No problem," Potts said. "We'll leave the Task Force chaps here to secure the house. The boss has set up a command centre at Tennant Creek. This case has hit the international media and there's news crews all over the fuckin' place, not to mention families of the missing girls have flown in from overseas. Fuckin' place is a mad house." He paused. "I don't suppose you got a vehicle description? I'll get a BOLO broadcast to all our patrols."

"Four-wheel-drive," Sam said. "An old model, maybe a Toyota covered in dust so the color was hard to pick... maybe beige. It was too far away to get a plate number."

"Okay," Potts nodded. "At least it's something." he turned away and followed Donaldson back to the Task Force vehicle.

"He's gonna struggle to get past not stopping the perp's vehicle," Sam decided.

"He's been around a long time," Foley said. "He's a tough cop. He'll get over it."

"As long as we find the girl alive," Sam concluded.

"That would help," Foley nodded.

"You hungry?" Sam asked.

"Yeah, let's slip out to McDonalds," Foley said sarcastically.

"Stuff McDonalds," Sam said. "We've got Baked Beans and camp pie inside."

Foley raised his eyebrows. "Sounds delicious, but I might hold out until we get back to civilisation."

Sam shrugged. "Suit yourself. I'm gonna rip the lid off a can of Baked Beans." He turned to re-enter the house.

"Wait!" Foley said.

"What?" Sam halted at the foot of the steps, and turned back to Foley.

"It's getting hot," Foley said. He indicated the Lenco BearCat. "We have to ride in that thing, shut in the back like sardines in a tin can, and you want to eat Baked Beans?"

"Do you have a problem with that?" Sam asked

"No, go ahead, knock yourself out, but you are riding on top on the way back."

"What are you suggesting?" Sam asked, feigning offence.

Foley threw his hands in the air in a gesture of sur-

GARY S. GREGOR

render. "I'm not suggesting anything apart from you sitting on the roof."

Sam pointed at the Task Force members deployed around the vehicle. "What about those blokes? They've been living on pack rations for a couple of days. They'll be farting a symphony all the way back. I'll be happy to ride on the roof."

"Task Force members don't fart," Foley explained. "They pass wind gently and inconspicuously."

"Bunch of girls, that's what they are," Sam chuffed.

"Don't let them hear you say that," Foley warned. "They are highly skilled. They can kill you with one finger."

"Only if they take it out of their arses long enough." Sam turned, hurried up the steps, and disappeared into the house.

20

Mandy opened her eyes. It took her a few seconds to realise where she was, then she remembered the house, and the two men standing on the verandah. They had guns and, at first, she thought they might be accomplices of the man driving, but there was something about the way they looked leading her to think they were police officers. The way the man turned the car and sped away indicated the two strangers were not people he wanted to see. She remembered staring at them through the rear window, and calling out, screaming at them, to help her.

She remembered the feeling of utter hopelessness which engulfed her as the man sped away from the house and the two men who could well have been her one chance of escaping the nightmare. A dark, heavy blanket of doom descended over her, cocooning her, penetrating every pore of her being until not the slightest glimmer of hope remained. She remembered looking down at the door handle, and considering jumping out of the car. It would be easy, and quick. She recalled reaching forward and opening the rear door. After that she remembered nothing.

Now, her hands and feet were tied. She lay awkwardly on her side, and her shoulder ached where it dug into the hard floor beneath her. She did not know how long she was unconscious, and she had even less idea where he was taking her.

Obviously returning to the house was no longer an option for her captor so, where were they going, she wondered? Rolling onto her back eased the pain in her shoulder, but the pain in her jaw, and face was as bad as ever. She ran her tongue around the inside of her mouth, and tasted blood.

The vehicle bounced, swerved, and swayed all over the place and occasionally, all too occasionally, her head slammed against the floor sending needles of red hot pain searing through her entire body. She closed her eyes tightly, and tried in vain to focus on something other than the pain.

When she finally opened her eyes, something in the corner, tucked in behind the rear seat, caught her attention. Her vision was blurred, and concentration on the object was difficult with the jostling of the vehicle across the rough terrain. She squeezed her eyes tightly shut, and then opened them again, trying to focus.

A tyre iron! At least that's what she thought it was called. Mandy had never had occasion to change a tyre in her life, but she had seen a tyre iron before; there was one in her Festiva, a much shorter one than the one she was looking at, but the shape was the same. It would make a handy weapon, she thought.

Suddenly, she was glad the man had tied her hands in front of her, and not behind her back as he had done before. Carefully, she reached out with her bound hands, and wrapped her fingers around the shaft of the tyre iron. Despite the stifling heat in the confines of the vehicle, it felt cool to touch as she lifted it a few centimetres to test the weight. Not too heavy, she decided, but heavy enough to do damage if she got the opportunity to use it against the man. Exactly *how* she was going to use it she did not know. She hoped she would have time to think it through before they stopped and he came for her again.

Mandy pulled the tyre iron in close to her body, tucking it into the folds of her dress. Satisfied he would not immediately notice it, she muttered a silent grunt of satisfaction. Attacking him with, or without, a weapon was never going to be easy trussed up the way she was.

She searched with her eyes, looking for something, anything she might be able to use to cut through the ropes cutting deep into her wrists and ankles. The ropes restricted the blood circulation. She wriggled her toes, and then her fingers, in an attempt to get feeling into them. She knew she had to keep her fingers and toes moving or else they would lose all feeling and she would not be able to use them when the time came to act.

Underneath where she lay, covered by the filthy carpet, there would be a compartment housing the spare wheel, she assumed. She could feel the lid of the compartment pressing uncomfortably into her back. Maybe there would be something in there she could use to cut the ropes, she wondered.

All she had to do was slide away from the lid, lift the carpet, lift the lid, and search the space beneath, all with her hands and feet bound, and without arousing the suspicion of the man driving the car. Easy!

She quickly abandoned the idea, realising she would never be able to do it; he would see her for sure, and it was important she controlled how this was going to work. If he suspected she was up to something in the back of the car, he would stop and investigate. The tyre iron was the only weapon she had, and if he found it, and took it from her, the consequences were something she did not want to think about.

An idea came suddenly, accompanying the urge to pee. It seemed they had been driving for hours, and now she needed to relieve herself. Should she call out to the man to stop so she could pee? If she did, and he stopped, would she get the opportunity to attack him before he realised she had the tyre iron?

He was far too strong for her, she had already discovered that following his vicious and prolonged sexual attacks. The tyre iron offered her a small measure of confidence. Losing it before she got the chance, was not an option.

She wondered how long she could resist the urge to pee while she formulated a plan of action. Not for too much longer, she decided. She would have to attack fast when he opened the rear door. If she hesitated, he would be on to her. With her hands and feet bound, she could not fight him off if it came to a tussle. All she had in her favour was the element of surprise, and the tyre iron.

From somewhere amongst the mouldy, dusty odours emanating from the carpet matting covering the floor, she smelled a faint hint of perfume. Just a whiff, a slight, diluted whiff of sweet perfume, and then it was gone, overridden by the much stronger smell of dust and mildew. It made Mandy think of the other girls who would have lain here in the back of this very same vehicle as the monster carried them to an unknown, terrifying fate. The faint odour spurred her on, like a message of encouragement from the grave.

She maneuvered herself so her feet faced the rear door, and her head rested against the back of the rear seats. In this position, her legs were bent at the knees so she was almost in the fetal position. Then, she rolled onto her back. Now her knees pointed at the roof and she was poised, coiled like a spring, ready to lash out with her feet when he opened the door. Her dress rode up high around her waist exposing her bare thighs.

She gritted her teeth painfully, and closed her eyes against the indignity of the position, wondering how her life had descended so quickly into the humiliating state she now found herself. She fought back tears and tried to focus instead on how much pleasure smashing the man across his ugly face with the tyre iron would bring her.

Silently willing herself to act, she called out to the man. "I need to pee!" Mandy grimaced as she tried in vain to close her mind from a renewed wave of pain searing through her damaged jaw.

The vehicle continued on, its speed unwavering as it bumped, and swayed over the extremely rough terrain, as though the man never even heard her; or if he did, he chose to ignore her.

"I need to pee!" Mandy called again, louder this time.

Still the car did not slow, and the man did not respond. He had to be ignoring her, Mandy thought. No way he didn't hear her. She had to try again. She had to get him to stop. He would stop eventually of course, she knew, but she wanted him to stop on her terms. If she waited until he chose to stop, and she did not know where that might be, he would control the situation. Mandy tried again.

"If you don't stop and let me out to pee I'm gonna do it right here in the back of your car!" she yelled as loud as her injured jaw would permit.

Suddenly the vehicle slowed dramatically. It skewed and skidded to a halt amid a cloud of choking dust, much of which filtered into the rear of the car.

"What are you yelling about, Miranda?" the man called from the driver's seat.

"I... I need to pee," Mandy answered.

"Hold onto it!" the man demanded.

"I can't," Mandy said. "I'm going to do it here, if you don't let me out."

"Don't you piss in my car!" the man called threateningly.

"I... I have to go," Mandy said.

A few moments of silence followed. Only the sound of the idling diesel engine filling the vehicle.

"I'm warning you, Miranda, if you piss in my car you will be sorry!" the man warned.

"I can't help it. I have to go... now!" Mandy said.

"Jesus, fuckin' Christ!" the man cursed.

Mandy heard the door open, and the man got out. She grasped the tyre iron, glanced down at it, and, confident he would not immediately see it, she prepared herself. This was it. The only chance she was going to get. She could not, would not, mess it up. It had to work. It had to. She braced herself, coiled like a spring, ready to strike.

The rear door swung open. The man saw her lying on her back, and his eyes were drawn immediately to her exposed thighs. He smiled, and his tongue snaked lizard-like across his bottom lip. Mandy waited, allowing his evil eyes to linger on her body.

"You better get out before you piss those pretty little panties," the man suggested, his eyes fixed and staring at her groin.

"Help me," Miranda said.

Finally, he looked up at Mandy's swollen face. "What?"

"You will have to untie my legs, and help me out of the car," Mandy said. "I can't pee with my feet tied together."

The man seemed to be considering her words for a moment and then, he reached down and yanked her sneakers from her feet. He tossed the shoes passed Mandy's head, and they thumped into the back of the rear seats. "Just in case you are thinking about running again," he said. "You won't get far in your bare feet, not that it wouldn't be fun chasing you down," he leered.

"Untie my feet," Mandy repeated, ignoring his threat.

The man leaned into the vehicle. His eyes swung from Mandy's exposed thighs, to the rope constraining her ankles. He fumbled with the knot and Mandy felt the binds loosening. His head was at exactly the right level. It was now or never, Mandy decided. She could not afford to think about it. She just had to do it.

Mandy kicked out hard and fast, with all the strength she could muster. Both her feet connected with the man's face, and she felt his nose crunch beneath them. He grunted loudly, staggered backwards, and stumbled into the open door. His hands flew to his face.

Mandy saw blood running freely between his fingers. She had to follow through. Waiting to see just how bad he was hurt was too risky. She had to disable him so he could not retaliate.

———

Mandy sat up, and slid forward on her backside until her legs dangled out the back of the vehicle. She climbed awkwardly out of the car, and stepped around the man who by now had collapsed to his knees. Mandy positioned herself behind him, and raised the tyre iron high above her head.

"You broke my fuckin' nose," the man cried, his voice muffled behind his blood covered hands. "You fuckin' bitch, you broke my nose!" He lashed out with one hand, grasping at the air where he last saw Mandy.

"I'm gonna kill you Miranda! You are dead, you fuckin' bitch. You fuckin' hear me? You're fuckin' dead!" He found the open door, grabbed it and tried to pull himself to his feet.

Mandy had to act now. If he got to his feet, he might be able to overpower her. She had hurt him, but she didn't know how badly, and she could not afford to wait to find out. She swung the tyre iron hard, aiming at his hand gripping the open door.

Mandy's aim was not perfect, but it was effective. She had intended to strike him above the elbow, but when she swung the tyre iron she closed her eyes tightly throwing her aim off. The bones in the man's wrist snapped loudly under the blow, and he screamed maniacally, collapsing again to the ground.

He grasped his broken wrist with his good hand, and writhed in pain in the dirt.

"Oh, Jesus!" he cried. "Oh, Jesus! Oh, Jesus! My arm! My arm! You broke my arm. Oh, God, help me! You broke my arm!

Blood flowed freely from the man's busted nose, and Mandy could see his wrist was cocked at an odd angle and already beginning to swell. She felt a small degree of satisfaction.

She raised the tyre iron above her head again, determined to hit him in the other arm this time if he looked about to retaliate. For a moment, she considered hitting him anyway. She hated him with an intensity, obscuring any hint of mercy which may lay just beneath the surface.

Mandy was a nurse. Her career focused on caring for the sick, and the injured, not causing them any more pain and suffering beyond which they already endured. This man, however, was sub-human. He was an animal who would kill without any compunction for his victims. Not for a second did Mandy regret the action she had taken.

What she did, she did in self-defense. Her career as a nurse, and her desire to help those who, as a result of illness or injury, were unable to help themselves, was of little consequence in the here and now.

The man's intention was to kill her, just as she was certain he had killed all the other girls. She was not going to die out here, in the remote, desolate, Australian outback at the hands of a sadistic madman.

Mandy looked down at the man rocking back and forth in the dirt, alternately crying in pain and cursing her loudly, and she smiled.

"You are done hurting people, you bastard!" she hissed. "Now I'm in control."

"You broke my arm... and my nose!" Blood ran from the man's smashed nose, into his mouth, and speckles of red sprayed as he spoke, his voice halting and nasal sounding.

"I should have killed you," Mandy responded.

Suddenly, in one lightning fast movement, the man lashed out with his good hand, grabbed Mandy by the leg, and pulled hard, attempting to bring her down. Mandy stumbled and almost fell. Regaining her balance, she swung the tyre iron from above her shoulder and connected with the arm gripping her leg.

Mandy heard the bone in the man's forearm crack. It could have been the radius bone, or the ulna bone, Mandy didn't care which. Indeed, she thought it might be nice if both were broken.

The man screamed, and let go of her leg. Now, with a broken wrist and forearm, he was unable to use either, and both arms flopped uselessly across his chest. He moaned pitifully with the pain and tears flooded from his eyes.

"Oh, Christ!" he moaned. "Oh, shit, you've broken both my arms!"

"Don't forget your nose," Mandy reminded him.

"You're fuckin' dead, bitch! You fuckin' hear me? You're fuckin' dead! I'm gonna kill you, you fuckin' bitch!"

Mandy scowled down at the man. "Really, and exactly how do you propose to do that?" she snarled. "After all, you have two broken arms and a broken nose. Killing me might not be as easy as you might think."

The man moaned agonizingly. "Help me up!" he demanded.

Mandy leaned over and stared down at the man. "What?"

"Help me up," he repeated.

Mandy reached down with her free hand, grabbed the man by the front of his filthy shirt, and hefted him roughly into a sitting position, giving scant consideration to his injuries.

"Oh, shit! That fuckin' hurts. Be fuckin' careful!" he screamed.

"Be careful?" Mandy said. "Be careful? I'll be as careful with you as you have been with me... and the other girls. You are an animal, a wild, rabid animal. Give me one good reason why I should consider your feelings."

The man looked up at her, his eyes pleading. "Because I'm hurt," he sobbed. "I'm hurt bad."

"Nowhere near bad enough if you ask me," Mandy snarled and hefted the tyre iron above her head.

The man tried to lift his arms to protect his head but the pain was too severe, and he was unable to raise them from his lap. He turned his head away from the expected blow, closed his eyes, and pleaded mournfully. "No! No! Please no!"

A few moments later, when no blow came, he opened his eyes and turned his head back towards Mandy. She had lowered the tyre iron, and held it loosely but threateningly at her side. She stood over him glaring down at him. Her eyes broadcast more hatred than he had ever seen in anyone.

He knew Miranda was capable of killing him, right there and then, and more than willing to do so. He was hurt bad. His wrist, forearm and nose were broken, and the pain was unbearable. As a result of his injuries, he was incapable of overpowering her, at least for the moment, but somehow he would.

"Where were you taking me?" Mandy asked.

"What?"

"You heard me, where were you taking me?"

"It doesn't matter now," the man said. "I can't drive anywhere with two broken arms."

"That's true," Mandy nodded. "You can't. But, where were you headed before we stopped?"

The man shrugged. "Nowhere."

Mandy lifted the tyre iron again. "Your legs are next," she threatened. "This is the last time I'm going to ask. Where were you headed?"

The man shied away. "I... I have... there's an old hut in the Davenport Ranges, I... I go there sometimes."

"You were taking me there?" Mandy asked.

"Yes," the man confirmed.

"Where are the Davenport Ranges?" Mandy queried.

"East of here," the man answered.

"How far east of here?" Mandy probed.

"Maybe two hours," the man confirmed.

Mandy paused, and looked around, paying particular attention to the country ahead of the vehicle. She shaded her eyes against the glare of the sun as it reflected off the barren desert landscape. Finally, she turned her attention back to the man.

"Where is the highway?" she asked.

"The highway?" the man questioned.

"Yes, the highway. The Stuart Highway, where is it?"

The man indicated with a nod of his head. "East."

"How far?"

"An hour... maybe."

Mandy stared again at the country stretching beyond the front of the vehicle. "Should take you... what... half a day to walk there?"

"Wha... what do you mean?" the man stammered.

Mandy glared stern-faced down at him. "I mean, I'm taking the car. You can stay here and die in the desert, or walk to the highway."

"I'll never make it," the man moaned. "I'll die of thirst. It's too far!"

"You said it was only an hour from here," Mandy said.

The man dropped his head and looked at the ground. "Maybe it's two hours," he murmured. "And that's driving. It's too far to walk... in this heat... without water."

It was difficult to smile with her injured jaw, and it hurt, but Mandy smiled anyway. "Then stay here and die." She slammed the rear door shut, turned away and walked to the front of the vehicle.

"No! No!" the man screamed. "Don't leave me here! Please don't leave me here. I can't walk that far. I need to get to a hospital!"

"Tell someone who cares," Mandy called back to him.

She was about to toss the tyre iron onto the front passenger seat when she noticed the rifle on the passenger side of the vehicle. The butt rested on the floor, and the barrel leaned against the front of the seat, pointing towards the roof. Mandy climbed into the car, and stared at the rifle. She had never in her life seen a firearm of any kind, other than in a newspaper or on television.

The very sight of it terrified her. Instinctively she knew this was the weapon the man used to kill the other girls, and with which he would have killed her had she not overpowered him. Ignoring the gun, she climbed into the car, adjusted the driver's seat position, pulled the door closed and started the engine.

Mandy was not used to driving a vehicle with manual gears, and as she drove away, the vehicle kangaroo hopped a few times, and finally stalled.

"Damn!" she cursed. She turned the key, and restarted the vehicle. From behind her she could hear the man screaming, begging her not to abandon him. Carefully, she slowly moved forward, gathering speed. She glanced into the rear vision mirror, and saw the man had struggled to his knees and was calling after her.

As the distance between them rapidly extended, Mandy glanced again into the mirror. The man was still on his knees but he was no longer calling after her in desperation. His head had dropped, and he was staring at the ground. Apparently, he had resigned himself to being left to die alone in the desert.

Mandy returned her focus to the front, but something made her slow and eventually steer the vehicle to a stop. For a long time, she stared out through the dust smudged windscreen, the only sound being the idling of the diesel engine.

She was not looking at anything in particular; it was more like she was enveloped in a fog of uncertainty, not seeing anything, just staring at the vast nothingness stretching unbroken to the far horizon to her front.

Eventually, she looked again in the rear vision mirror, and the man was now just a speck far behind her.

She could not do it. She could not simply leave him there to die, and die he surely would without food and water.

Something deeply ingrained in her psyche would not allow her to abandon him, despite the evil he was responsible for. She was a nurse. Every single fibre of her being was conditioned, perhaps even destined to care for people, not cause them pain and suffering.

As if emerging slowly from a fugue, Mandy sighed deeply, turned the car around, and returned to where the solitary figure knelt in the dirt, moaning softly with pain and despair.

21

Tennant Creek Police Station was situated mid-town, on the main street, and it was under siege. Media representatives from all branches of the media, from all corners of the country, and a few from international agencies, descended upon the police station demanding answers. In the absence of answers, they demanded at the very least, an official briefing as to the progress of the investigation.

Such a briefing was finally presented by the Assistant Commissioner Southern Command, Donald Jefferson. The "bodies in the well" case had captured the imagination and the curiosity of the plethora of media outlets, as well as the general public. The usually capable telephone system at the police station was in a constant state of overload. Officers who worked out of Tennant Creek had serious concerns whether they were going to be able to adequately and sufficiently service the needs of the local population.

The media was, however, in all its manifestations, an obstinate, passionate and determined group, and was never going to tread lightly when it came to informing the masses of the facts of something as newsworthy as the kidnapping and subsequent murder of six young girls in the heart of the Australian outback.

The story had all the hallmarks of the serial murderer, Ivan Robert Marko Milat, and the so called "backpacker murders", when seven young backpackers were brutally murdered, and their bodies dumped in Belanglo State Forrest in southern New South Wales in the nineteen-nineties. As it did with the Milat murders, the bodies in the well case attracted the media like sharks in a feeding frenzy.

Russell Foley, and Sam Rose, arrived at Tennant Creek just as Jefferson ended his media briefing. They waited in the station incident room where the investigation was being controlled. Jefferson stormed into the room, and angrily tossed his briefing notes onto a nearby desk, startling a young constable engrossed in cataloging statements and forensic reports.

"Sorry," he mumbled. "Bloody media! They're like vultures fighting over road-kill!"

Suddenly he noticed Foley and Rose at the back of the room. Both men were casually sipping coffee, watching him as he entered the room. "Sergeants Foley, and Rose, welcome back."

"Thank you, Sir," Foley acknowledged.

Sam simply nodded in the general direction of the Assistant Commissioner.

One of the positions held by Donald Jefferson on his way up through the ranks was Officer in Charge of the Task Force, way back when Sam Rose was dating his daughter. Jefferson did not like Sam. Indeed, he thought Sam was somewhat of a loose cannon, as well as a lecherous fool, and had no compunction about telling him so whenever an occasion brought the two of them into close contact.

Jefferson was discreet enough however, not to remind Sam of his dislike for him while in the presence of other members of the force, something he found difficult, but necessary in the interests of maintaining a degree of credibility given his senior position.

Sam did not always rigidly follow accepted procedure as laid down in General Orders, but he was a good cop with an excellent clearance rate, an operational statistic Jefferson could not deny, although he secretly wished he could. An undefinable thing about the younger man's gung-ho manner of getting the job done not only seriously conflicted with his own by the book way of doing things, but irritated the hell out of him. Then, of course, there was his daughter's broken heart, which served to exacerbate his intense dislike of him.

Sam was aware of his superior's disdain for him, but it was not something that kept him awake at night. Jefferson was one of a small number of senior officers in the job who got where they were as a result of intense study, and subsequent passing of promotional exams, as opposed to putting in years working the streets.

The job needed both types, of course; there had to be those who drove the ship. But the dizzy heights of commissioned officer rank had never been an attraction for Sam. His methods might be seen by those like Donald Jefferson as unorthodox, but he was not about to deviate from, or change the manner in which he went about his job.

Jefferson looked at Sam. "What happened to your head?"

Sam shrugged, and fingered the bandage on his head. "Just a scratch," he answered.

Jefferson turned to Russell Foley. "You two all right?" he asked.

"Yes, Sir," Foley reported.

"What happened?" Jefferson continued.

"Nothing much, just a little helicopter crash," Sam said sarcastically.

Jefferson glowered at Sam. "I was talking to Sergeant Foley."

Sensing an uncomfortable tension building between Sam, and Jefferson, Foley looked at the Assistant Commissioner.

"The chopper suffered an engine failure," he explained. "Fortunately we were not flying at a high altitude. We came down hard, and Sergeant Rose was injured."

"Pilot was killed," Sam added.

"Yes, so I am told," Jefferson scowled.

"I could have been killed myself," Sam continued.

Jefferson turned bodily towards Sam, and fixed him with a glare. "How very fortunate we all are you survived, Sergeant Rose." Jefferson's made no attempt to disguise his sarcasm.

Lost for an appropriate response, or perhaps accepting that offering one would be folly, Sam sipped his coffee and remained silent.

Jefferson turned back to Foley. "I understand you got a look at the suspect?"

"Yes," Foley confirmed. "He was a way off, too far to get a description, but he had a girl in the rear of his vehicle. He recognised us as police, and he turned and bolted. Obviously, we were on foot and were unable to give chase."

Jefferson turned his focus to Wayne Donaldson,

the Task Force commander. "You got a look at him too?"

"Yes Sir," Donaldson answered.

"And he bolted from you as well?" Jefferson asked, accusingly.

"Yes Sir," Donaldson confirmed.

"You were in the BearCat I assume?" Jefferson posed.

"Yes Sir."

"And you chose not to give chase?"

"We had a chopper down, Sir," Donaldson explained, "With two of our people on board, as well as the pilot. I considered our priority was to find the chopper, and see to the welfare of Sergeants Foley, and Rose."

"And the pilot," Sam interjected.

Jefferson glared disapprovingly at Sam. "Thank you, Sergeant Rose."

"You're welcome, Sir," Sam smiled.

The Task Force Sergeant continued. "We had no way of knowing the driver of the car was a suspect," he explained.

Jefferson turned away from Donaldson and addressed Russell Foley. "What's the deal with the house?"

"It's definitely where the suspect kept the women prisoner," Foley answered.

"What the fuck is a house doing way out there in the middle of nowhere?" Jefferson posed.

Sergeant Terry Potts stepped forward. "Perhaps I can shed light on that, Sir," he reported.

"Please do," Jefferson invited.

"I have done a bit of research into the house. It seems it was built there by the government about twenty years ago, as an experimental project aimed at opening the area to cattle production. A large shed was set up with solar panels for power, and to house a battery bank. Then, the government was ousted in an election, and the incoming government abandoned the project before it ever got off the ground."

"Why am I not surprised?" Jefferson said sarcastically.

Jefferson turned to Foley. "Sergeant Foley, you and Sergeant Rose get cleaned up and get back to Wauchope. I want you to co-ordinate a search for the mysterious car and driver from there. Road blocks have been set up north of Tennant Creek, and south of Barrow Creek. He has to be somewhere between those two places. Find him!"

"That's a lot of country," Foley said.

"I've got the two chaps from Ti Tree patrolling between there and Barrow Creek, and another car patrolling between here and Barrow Creek. I've also requested a helicopter from one of the tourist flight companies in Alice Springs. They are flat out with rubber-necking tourists at the moment, but as soon as they can spare one it will be sent up here."

He turned his attention to Sam. "You and Inspector Foley might consider conducting a search from the air."

Sam opened his mouth to protest but Foley interjected. "Can we reach you here, Sir, or are you returning to Alice Springs?"

"I'll be here until this is over," Jefferson said. "Right now I've got a room full of next of kin I have to placate." He turned to leave the room, paused at the door, and turned to speak again to Foley. "Keep me informed," he ordered. "Updates every time you have something I should know about.

Oh... and before you go," he thrust a thumb at Sam, "You better get him checked out at the clinic... duty of care and all that bullshit." He glared at Sam. "Sergeant Rose, I want this bloke alive so forget the cowboy tactics!" Jefferson turned briskly and left the room.

A few moments of awkward silence fell over the room as the Assistant Commissioner's footsteps faded into the distance. Finally, Sam looked at Foley.

"Who was that bloke again?" he asked, feigning ignorance.

"That's the man who is going to have your stripes if you fuck this up," Foley smiled. "Come on, let's get out of here. I've organised a four-wheel-drive, and we'll head back to Wauchope as soon as we get you checked over at the clinic."

"I'm not going to the clinic," Sam said adamantly. "And, may I also remind you, I'm not getting on board any more helicopters!"

"May I remind *you,* it's not a particularly good career move to go against the Assistant Commissioner's orders," Foley said.

"He's an idiot," Sam said.

Foley nodded. "Be that as it may, he *is* the Assistant Commissioner, and you are the lowly Sergeant. I would suggest he is in a position to make life very difficult for you should he choose to do so."

"He did that the day he was born," Sam huffed. He walked from the room, paused several paces out into the corridor, and looked back at Foley. "Are you coming?"

Foley hurried after Sam. "Yeah, someone has to keep an eye on you."

———

Russell Foley and Sam had just walked out the front door of the police station when Russell Foley's phone rang shrilly with the William Tell Overture.

Sam threw Foley a look which said for Christ's sake change the ring tone.'

Foley fumbled in his pocket, retrieved the phone, and flipped it open. "Foley," he answered.

"Inspector Russell Foley?" a voice asked.

"Yeah, speaking," Foley confirmed.

"Inspector, my name is Detective Senior Constable David Merritt. I'm with Major Crime, Police Headquarters in Melbourne."

Foley glanced at Sam and raised his eyebrows questioningly. "Hello David, what can I do for you?"

"I understand you are heading up the investigation into the, bodies in the well case up there," Merritt said.

"That's right, I am," Foley answered.

"I might have something for you," Merritt announced.

Foley tensed, his interest piqued. "Really?" he said.

"We may have a lead for you," Merritt responded.

"We could do with a lead," Foley admitted. "What have you got?"

Foley heard a rustling of papers on the other end of the line, and then Merritt spoke again.

"We have a runner from down here, a toe-rag by the name of Leonard James Williams.

"He served nine years for the kidnapping and rape

of a young twenty-year-old girl. Kept her prisoner for several weeks, and raped her multiple times over the period. He was out on parole, and skipped a couple of years ago. Rumour at the time was he headed up your way, but he has never surfaced. From what we're hearing down here, the MO of your chap up there sounds remarkably similar to Williams."

"Nine years for kidnap and rape, seems a tad light to me," Foley remarked.

"Yeah, tell me about it," Merritt responded. "This guy is a real piece of work. When he was fifteen-years-old he killed both his parents."

"Shit!" Foley exclaimed.

"He claimed his father slit his mother's throat, and then he wrestled the knife from his old man, and plunged it to the hilt into his chest in self-defense."

"Not right?" Foley asked.

"You could drive a truck through his story it had that many holes in it," Merritt explained. "It was a slam dunk for the prosecution. He was remanded to a state juvenile facility where he spent the next four years before he escaped. He was on the run for a couple of years. Stole someone's ID and lived on the street."

He paused, and Foley heard more rustling of papers.

"It was during this time we liked him for a series of sexual assaults in the Melbourne CBD area, but the police at the time were never able to find him."

"You weren't kidding when you said he was a real piece of work," Foley said.

"That's not all," Merritt continued. "He has a history going way back to his school days. He was expelled from two schools for inappropriate behavior toward a handful of female students."

"What exactly do you mean by inappropriate behavior?" Foley asked.

"Well, obviously, he was a juvenile at the time, and the records are sealed, but I can tell you I managed to track down one of his former teachers, and it seems he got his jollies grabbing girls, exposing himself, and shoving his hand down their knickers. Some of them he ejaculated on."

"Jesus!" Foley cursed. "Sounds like a real sick bastard."

"Yeah, and it never got any better as he got older," Merritt said.

"And no one twigged to his real identity?" Foley asked, astounded.

"Not until he came to our attention over the kidnap and rape I mentioned earlier. DNA from the victim matched with his DNA we had on record."

"Did the girl survive?" Foley asked.

"Yes," Merritt said. "She fled when he fell asleep following one of his rape sessions, but the general feeling at the time was he was more than capable of murder; we like him for the disappearance of a couple of other young girls who are still missing. It wouldn't surprise any of us down here if he killed them, and dumped the bodies somewhere they might never be found."

"There certainly are a few similarities with our case," Foley agreed. "Any chance you can send me a copy of your file on this character?"

"All I need is a fax number."

Foley provided Merritt with the fax number at Tennant Creek Police Station, thanked the Victorian detective, and disconnected the call. He dropped his phone back into his pocket and looked at Sam.

"That was interesting," he said.

"Tell me more," Sam said.

"There's a fax coming through from Melbourne. They have a possible suspect for us to consider. He did time down there for kidnap and repeated rape of a young girl. She managed to escape, and he was subsequently caught... did a runner while on parole. The chaps down south think he headed up here to the Territory."

"You think he might be our man?" Sam asked.

"Could be," Foley said. "When he was a teenager he killed both his parents, and he has managed to accrue a long history of sexual offences dating back to his school days. We'll get a better idea when we see the file."

"How does such a bloke survive?" Sam asked. "He has a vehicle... he has to buy fuel for it... he has to buy food etcetera... where's he getting his money?"

Foley thought for a moment. "I expect we'll find the vehicle was reported stolen, probably from down south. As for money, I can't answer that. Maybe he steals from his victims... they're backpackers, so they will have limited funds available. We've seen his food supplies, and there was nothing there costing more than a few dollars. Perhaps when we catch him you can ask him how he manages to finance his extravagant lifestyle."

Sam nodded. "I will. I'm looking forward to meeting this dude."

"Me too," Foley agreed.

22

Mandy slammed her foot on the brake pedal, spun the steering wheel at the same time, and the rear of the vehicle skidded broadside, stopping just centimeters from where the man kneeled with his head bowed. A cloud of dust and fine pebbles, thrown up by the tyres, peppered the man's kneeling form and settled slowly around him. Mandy threw open the door, climbed out, and hurried to the back of the car. She opened the rear door and stepped back.

"Get in!" she ordered.

The man did not move. He mumbled incoherently, giving no indication he even realised Mandy had returned. A thin, elastic-like, string of drool hung from his lips until it finally broke, and plopped into the dirt in front of his knees.

"Get in!" Mandy ordered again.

Slowly, the man lifted his head and looked through vacant, red rimmed eyes at Miranda. "You came back," he mumbled.

"I'll never understand why," Mandy answered. "Now get in the car."

"What?"

"Get in the car."

The man's eyes strayed slowly from Mandy to the open door at the rear of the vehicle. "The car?"

"Yes, get in the car."

"You came back for me," the man said. "You *do* care."

Mandy glared at the man. "Don't misinterpret my coming back for you as having anything to do with how I feel about you," she explained.

The man smiled weakly. "But you came back."

"Just get in the car, before I change my mind."

Pleading eyes fixed on Mandy. "I can't get up... my arms are broken."

Mandy paused. She looked from the man, to the interior of the car, and then back to the man. Then, she stepped behind him, and grabbed him by the back of his shirt. Just touching him caused her to shudder with revulsion, and she almost changed her mind. Deciding not to spend any more time thinking about the validity or otherwise of her actions, she hefted him, and he struggled to his feet, moaning loudly as jolts of pain shot through his arms. When he stood, he started to walk to the front of the car, and Mandy grabbed him again and halted his momentum.

"In the back!" she demanded.

"What?"

"In the back... get in the back!"

"In the back?"

"You heard me," Mandy said. "You get in the back of the car, or you stay here. Your choice."

The man hesitated, and then sat down in the back of the car, his legs hanging out of the open door. "Let me ride in the front," he pleaded.

"Not going to happen," Mandy said. "It's in the back, or nowhere. Lift your legs in."

"Please," he begged. "I can't hurt you, both my arms are broken."

"If you don't lift your legs into the car, I'm going to drag your sorry butt back out, leave you here in the dirt, and drive away. I will not come back a second time."

The man looked up at Mandy, and was instantly drawn to the set of her eyes, the way she looked at him with a steely, serious determination. He knew instinctively she really would leave him out here.

He could not hold her eyes without a tiny, almost imperceptible shudder of fear trembling through his body. He looked away, slowly raised his legs, and slid backwards into the vehicle until his shoulders rested against the back of the rear seats.

Mandy slammed the door, hurried to the front of the car, and climbed in behind the wheel. She leaned forward to start the engine when the man's voice came to her from the back of the car.

"Where are you taking me?" he called.

"You're going to prison!" Mandy called over her shoulder.

"You'll never find the way without my help," the man said.

"I'll just keep heading the way you were," Mandy said. "I'll come to the highway eventually."

"No you won't. The highway is not that way," the man said softly.

"What did you say?" Mandy asked.

"The highway is not that way," he repeated.

Mandy paused. She looked out the windscreen, and saw nothing but desert in front of her, all the way to the horizon. A prickle of doubt fluttered at the fringes of her mind. Was he playing games with her? She looked out the driver's side window, then out the passenger side window and finally she looked again out through the front windscreen.

Desert, nothing but desert as far as she could see. What if he was telling the truth? What if straight ahead was not the way to the highway? No, it had to be, she reasoned. If she kept driving straight ahead she would reach the highway and help. Then, there it was again... the flicker of doubt.

Mandy leaned forward, and rested her forehead against the steering wheel. In this position, she was looking directly at the dashboard gauges. Her eyes were drawn immediately to the fuel gauge. She blinked, blinked again, and stared at the gauge. It indicated under a quarter of a tank of fuel remained. How far would less than a quarter of a tank get her, she wondered? Would it get her to the highway?

As she stared at the gauge, she once again felt the familiar blanket of despair descending over her. She had to focus. She could not allow the fear of failure to overcome her. She had made it this far. She had escaped from the house. She had overpowered the man. She could not lose now that she had come this far.

Mandy needed to think. The car was facing the same way as it was when the man stopped, falling for the ruse she needed to relieve herself. Wherever the place was he was heading for, it had to be straight ahead... somewhere. How far, she wondered?

He must have known how much fuel he had left, and he was still prepared to keep going. Or, perhaps he didn't know. Maybe he was panicked, and flight was all that occupied his crazed mind. She stared again out through the windscreen at the endless, barren landscape. She had no choice, she decided. She had to continue.

"You're lying," she called back to the man.

"I'm not lying," he responded. "The highway is not that way."

"I don't believe you," Mandy said. She grabbed the discarded tyre iron, opened the door, climbed out of the car, and hurried to the back of the vehicle. She flung open the rear door and raised the tyre iron high above her head.

The man cowered back against the rear seats, and tried to protect his head with his broken arms.

"Don't," he cried. "Don't hit me."

"I'm not going to listen to your lies!" Mandy yelled. "If you don't shut up, I'm going to break both your legs next! Where's the highway?"

"Don't h... it me," the man stammered.

Mandy swung the tyre iron, and cracked the man hard on one leg, just below the knee.

The man yelped, grabbed at his leg, and screamed louder as the effort sent pain searing agonisingly through his arms.

"Oh, Jesus... oh, Jesus!" he cried.

Mandy raised the tyre iron again. "Where's the highway?" she asked threateningly.

"Straight ahead... straight ahead!" the man sobbed.

Mandy lowered the tyre iron. "Your leg's not broken," she declared. "But if you are lying to me, it soon will be."

"I'm not lying... I'm not... I promise," the man said. "The highway's ahead."

Mandy slammed the door so violently the vehicle

rocked, and dust fluttered from the body. She hurried back to the front of the vehicle, climbed in behind the wheel, her jaw ached agonisingly and a dull, throbbing pain behind her eyes began to grow in intensity. Determined to continue, she started the car, and drove forward, quickly gathering speed.

From the rear compartment, the sound of the man moaning in pain rose above the noise of the car engine. She tried to block out the pitiful sound, and fumbled with the radio, receiving only irritating static for her effort. Frustrated, she cursed loudly, slammed her hand into the 'on/off' switch, and silenced the awful, ear piercing crackle.

Ignoring anybody moaning in terrible pain, and doing nothing about it, was totally out of character for her. Helping to ease people's suffering had always been natural for her. Despite her loathing of the despicable creature in the back of the vehicle, it was difficult for her to ignore the sound of his pain.

Hot, humid air rushed into her face through the open driver's side window. She dared not wind it up or the heat would be stifling. She could feel the heat from the racing diesel engine radiating through the firewall, burning her bare legs. She looked down at the dashboard, searching for air conditioning controls. When she found them, she reached for the switch to activate the cooling mode.

She did not see the small, rocky, quartz outcrop until the front driver's side wheel hit it. The steering wheel jerked painfully from her one-handed grip, and the car swerved crazily, rode up on two wheels, and threatened to roll over. The car fishtailed crazily out of control, and Mandy was tossed like a pebble in a barrel.

She was not wearing her seat belt, and she screamed as she was tossed across the cabin. Hurled back into the driver's seat, her body crashed heavily into the steering wheel, then the door, then the dashboard. When the vehicle finally came to rest, it was pointed at an angle at odds with the direction the wheels were facing.

Mandy lay across the centre console, the upper half of her body sprawled ungainly across the passenger seat. She lay there for a few moments, catching her breath. Her head hung over the front of the seat, between the seat and the firewall, her mind racing as she struggled to comprehend what happened. She moved first her arms, and then her legs, relieved she seemed to have escaped any broken bones, although it felt as if she had fractured every bone in her body.

Slowly she pulled herself up onto the front seat, and looked out through the windscreen. Dust was still settling as she opened the door and stumbled clumsily out of the car. She stretched, flexing her arms, shoulders, and back, satisfying herself she was not suffering any adverse effects. Suddenly she remembered the man, and hurried to the rear of the car, grabbed the door handle, and wrenched open the door.

A sharp, burning pain stabbed in the fleshy part of her upper arm, just above the elbow. Simultaneously she heard the bang, and knew instantly she had been shot. She spun away from the open door, and fell to her knees, grabbing at her arm. She took her hand away and saw blood; lots of it.

The man had shot her. How did he get the gun? When she last saw it, it was in the front seat. It must have been flung over the seat, and into the back during the chaos of the spinning, skidding, and bumping of the car when she hit the rocky outcrop.

A loud, mournful moaning from the interior of the car focused her attention. She dared to look up and peek into the rear of the car.

The man had dropped the rifle, it lay on the ground at Mandy's feet. He was lying on his back, supporting his broken arms across his chest. Mandy moved instantly, seized the rifle from the ground, and tossed it aside, well out of his reach should he consider shooting her again. Gingerly she got to her feet.

"You bastard!" she screamed at him. "You shot me!"

The man tried to sit, managing to lift his head, and then fell back, his head banging against the floor.

"I'm hurt, Miranda. Help me... please," he sobbed.

"Help you! Help you! Why should I help you? You shot me!" Mandy spat. She looked down at her arm.

Miraculously, the bullet had just lightly grazed her upper arm, leaving a flesh wound, and, while it bled a lot, it did not appear to her trained eye to be serious. If not for two broken arms, his control of the weapon would have been much more effective and he might easily have killed her, she decided.

She clasped the wound with her free hand, and pressed hard in an attempt to stem the bleeding. She stepped back from the car, reached for the open door, and slammed it shut.

"You shot me, you bastard," she mumbled to herself as she walked to the front of the car.

What Mandy saw when she looked at the front of the vehicle filled her with dismay. The driver's side wheel was pointing at an angle, almost ninety degrees to the wheel on the passenger side, and the front driver's side of the car had collapsed. A jagged tear gaped in the tyre side-wall, and now the wheel rim sat on the ground.

Mandy was no mechanic, but she knew instantly something was very badly damaged underneath the front of the car, and it was going nowhere. She dropped her head in despair, fighting back tears of frustration.

Suddenly her frustration turned to fury. She lashed out with her foot, and kicked the lopsided wheel arch.

"Bloody hell!" she yelled. "Damn, damn, damn!" She clasped her head in her hands, and looked up at the cloudless sky. "Oh, God, why can't I get a break? Help me... please!"

The hot, relentless sun burned her face. A bead of perspiration ran down her forehead and into her eye. She wiped it away and looked down again at the damaged front of the vehicle. What now, she asked herself?

Mandy turned away from the vehicle, leaned back, and rested against the collapsed wheel arch. Through her light dress she felt the heat from the car body on her lower back. She stared out at the vast miles of barren desert stretching as far as the eye could see in every direction.

The reality of her situation did not escape her; she was alone, stranded in the middle of the Australian outback, a place so desolate, so alien, she struggled to imagine a place anywhere on the planet more depressingly lonely and isolated.

She didn't even know where the road leading to the house was in relation to where she was now. And, if that wasn't burden enough to comprehend, she was accompanied by a madman, a psychopath, who had killed before and was intent on killing her.

She looked down at her arm. The bleeding had eased a little. Clasping her hand tightly over the wound, she wondered if things could possibly get any worse. She opened, and closed her mouth gingerly, and winced with the pain of her injured jaw.

Mandy had a choice to make. She could surrender to the apparent hopelessness of the situation, and at this point the situation she found herself in really did look hopeless, or she could resist. As she stared off into the distance, from a place somewhere deep inside her she could not identify, a determination to survive flickered, and began to slowly surface.

The feeling was more an emotive thing than it was tangible. Just a feeling, a will to survive, slowly rising from deep within her, growing in intensity as it made its way to the surface of her consciousness. She would not succumb; giving up had never been an element of her character. She would get out of this mess. Somehow, she would make it out of the godforsaken desert, and she would see her family again. This was not her time to die. Not yet.

23

_____

With seven sutures in his freshly bandaged head, and a pocket full of pain killers, Sam left the medical clinic in Tennant Creek, anxious to get back to Wauchope. When he climbed into the four-wheel-drive seconded from the police station, Foley was waiting.

"Is that the fax from down south?" Sam asked of the file Foley was reading.

"Yes," Foley confirmed. "And very interesting reading it makes," he added.

"Do tell," Sam invited.

"How's the noggin?" Foley asked, indicating the fresh, clean bandage on Sam's head.

"The noggin's fine, thanks for asking. What's in the file?"

Foley closed the file, tossed it in Sam's lap, and started the car. "You can read it on the way back to Wauchope," he said. "I need a shower and a change of clothes, followed closely by a cold beer and a large steak."

Sam looked up from the file. "Did you say cold beer?"

"I see the chopper crash didn't damage your hearing," Foley replied with a mild, sarcastic edge to his voice.

"Any sentence with the words cold beer in it always gets my attention," Sam confirmed.

Fifteen minutes later, after driving in silence, Foley nodded at the file Sam was reading. "What do you think?"

"About the cold beer?" Sam asked.

"No you moron, about the file."

Sam dropped his eyes back to the file in his lap. "Well, obviously, I haven't read it all yet, but I've read enough to satisfy myself this... " he read from the file. "Leonard James Williams character sounds like he could be our man."

"I think so too," Foley said. "While I was waiting for you at the clinic, I ran a name check on him in our system. He doesn't appear."

"Not anywhere?" Sam asked.

"Nowhere," Foley confirmed. "He has no motor vehicle registered in his name here in the Territory. He does not hold an NT driver's license, and his name does not appear in the criminal data base. By all accounts, he is a clean-skin up here."

"Indicates the car was, more than likely, stolen," Sam commented.

"That would be my guess," Foley said. "There's a photo of him in the back of the file," he added.

Sam rifled through the pages to the back of the file, and looked closely at the photograph of Leonard James Williams. The man in the image wore a full-face beard, making it difficult for Sam to determine his age. He flipped back to the front of the file, found a date of birth for Williams, and quickly did the math in his head.

"Fifty-two years old," he announced to Foley.

"Yeah," Foley nodded. "With a penchant for much younger girls."

"He's not a pedophile," Sam noted, browsing the file. "His tastes seem to be for young women, not juveniles."

"He's a dirty old man, nonetheless," Foley stated.

"There's no law against having sex with a younger woman," Sam said.

Foley took his eyes off the road and looked at Sam. "If there was, you'd have gone to prison a long time ago," he joked.

"Oh! Oh, that hurts!" Sam complained. "May I remind you, every one of my relationships with ladies younger than myself was consensual."

"Point taken," Foley conceded. "And, of course, you didn't kidnap, rape, and murder any of them... did you?"

"Very funny," Sam closed the file and tossed it onto the dashboard.

Foley indicated the file. "The chaps at Tennant Creek are distributing the photo around town. We'll do the same at Wauchope... and down at Wycliff Well. The house is a long way from anywhere, and our perp has to be getting supplies somewhere. Hopefully someone will recognise him."

"Even if someone does recognise him, we still have to catch the bastard," Sam said.

"He's on the run," Foley explained. "He can't, and won't, go back to the house. He knows we are on to him. Unless he's got a back-up hide-out, he is out there somewhere, driving around trying to figure out what to do next. Sooner or later he has to stop for fuel... or food... or water."

"He's not going to stop for supplies while he's got the girl in the back of his car," Sam suggested. "He'll kill her first."

"If he hasn't already," Foley responded.

————

Sam, and Foley showered, changed into clean clothes, and met in the hotel front bar thirty minutes after arriving back at Wauchope.

Foley arrived first. He was nursing a beer and reading the Williams file when Sam entered. "Feel better?" he asked Sam.

"Much better," Sam answered. He sat on a stool next to Foley, and raised a finger to the publican who brought him a beer and put it down in front of him. At the opposite end of the bar where it seemed he always sat Kenny, the old bar fly, sipped at his usual rum, and nodded almost imperceptively in Sam's general direction.

The gesture was not something Sam expected from the old chap, but he nodded in response anyway, figuring Kenny must have nodded in a gesture of greeting; either that, or the old codger was falling asleep.

Sam moved to pay, and Foley said, "I paid already."

"You did?" Sam sounded surprised.

"Don't get too excited, you're paying for the next one," Foley said.

When the publican walked down to the other end of the bar, wiping the bar top as he went, Sam leaned closer to Foley. "Why do they charge so much for drinks in places like this?"

"Because they can," Foley shrugged. "There's no competition. You want a beer, you pay the asking price... or drink water."

"They charge like wounded bulls for water too," Sam noted. He took a long draught of his beer, smacked his lips loudly, and said, "Damn that's good."

Foley removed the photo of Leonard Williams from the file and waved it at the publican who was making his way back along the bar, still wiping as he came.

"Got a minute?" Foley called.

The publican wiped his way to where Foley and Sam sat, stopped, wiped at a non-existent smudge, and looked at Sam.

"Bump your head?" he asked.

"Yeah, something like that," Sam answered.

"Too bad," the publican said, and turned to Foley. "What can I do for you gentlemen?" he asked.

"We'd like you to take a look at this photo," Foley said, handing it to the publican. "Have you seen this bloke before?"

The publican fumbled with a pair of spectacles hanging on a chain around his neck, placed them on the end of his nose, and looked at the photo. He held it at arms-length, then brought it up close to his face and finally moved it back out to arms-length.

"I'm not sure," he said. "People come through here all the time. He looks kinda familiar."

"Maybe you need new glasses," Sam suggested.

"No I don't," the publican sounded miffed. "These are new. I only got 'em ten years ago."

Sam looked at Foley. Foley looked at Sam. They both looked at the publican.

"What does that mean exactly, he looks kinda familiar?" Foley asked

The publican shrugged, and handed the photo back to Foley. "It means I'm not sure if I've seen him before. I don't waste time studying people's faces when they come in. They stop, they buy fuel, maybe a drink, or something to eat, and then they leave."

"Okay, thank you," Foley said. He slid the photo back into the file. "What about Kenny, down the end of the bar, do you think he might recognise the photo?"

"You could always ask him," the publican suggested.

"Any chance you could ask him to come up here and take a look?" Foley asked.

"Kenny won't leave his stool until he's ready to leave the bar," the publican said. "He always sits in the same place... doesn't want anyone else sitting in his spot."

Sam looked past the publican at the almost empty room. Then he swiveled on his stool and looked behind him. "There's no one else here," he said. "Who's gonna take his seat?"

"You know that, and I know that," the publican replied. "But Kenny doesn't know that. He's a creature of habit is our Kenny."

"He's an eccentric old fart if you ask me," Sam mumbled.

"Thanks for your help," Foley smiled at the publican. "We'll wander down the other end and have a chat with him."

"That would be best," the publican said. He turned away, and wiped his way back down the bar.

"An eccentric old fart?" Foley said to Sam.

Sam sipped his beer. "Yeah."

"The man's a Vietnam veteran. He's a bloody hero. Where's the respect?" Foley insisted.

"Yes, he is a Vietnam veteran and, fifty years ago, when he was young and full of testosterone, he was undoubtedly a hero. I have the utmost respect for all our veterans, but his past achievements don't make him any less an eccentric old fart today." He stood. "Let's go and have a chat with the old digger."

Sam made himself comfortable on a stool on one side of Kenny, and Foley did likewise on the other side. Kenny sat hunched forward over the bar, a glass of dark rum in front of him, and he gave no acknowledgement to either of them. To one side of his glass, an old ceramic ashtray, badly chipped and stained with many years of nicotine build up, almost overflowed with cigarette butts. Carelessly discarded ash littered the bar around the base of the ashtray.

Sam looked at the ash scattered on the bar, and decided the publican was obviously not as particular about wiping the bar down this end as he was with the rest of the bar top. Perhaps he just got tired of cleaning up after Kenny every time he missed the ashtray.

The publican glanced at the three men, and Sam indicated Kenny's drink, ordering him another.

"G'day, Kenny," Sam greeted the old timer.

"I can buy my own drinks ya know," Kenny mumbled gruffly.

"I'm sure you can," Sam said. "But it would be my pleasure to buy you one."

Kenny turned his head and looked at Sam. "I've

learnt people who buy me drinks usually want something from me," he said suspiciously.

Sam raised his hands in a surrender gesture. "Sorry, I was just being friendly, I'll cancel the drink." He moved to signal the publican.

"You've ordered it now, might as well drink it," Kenny said. "Don't want to confuse old Bob there."

Foley opened the Williams file and removed the photo. "We wondered if you might have a look at this photograph and see if you recognise the man." He held the photo in front of Kenny who was slow to respond. Eventually he lowered his eyes to the photograph, and looked at it. His eyes lingered on the photo briefly, and then he returned his focus to his drink.

The publican had placed another rum next to the one Kenny was currently drinking, and Kenny moved it so it was behind his current drink and not adjacent to it. He seemed to be very particular as to how the two glasses were aligned and, finally satisfied both were positioned as they should be, he lifted the first glass to his lips and sipped surprisingly daintily.

Foley placed the photo down on top of the file. "Do you recognise the man in the photo?" he asked Kenny.

"Yes," Kenny answered. He lowered his glass, lining it up precisely in front of the fresh one.

"Yes what?" Foley asked.

"Yes I recognise the man in the photo," Kenny said.

"Do you know his name?" Foley probed.

"Yes."

"You want to share it with us?"

"I guess so," Kenny shrugged indifferently. "I don't suppose it's a secret."

"Well?" Foley pushed.

"Name's Len," Kenny said.

"Len?" Sam said.

Kenny looked at Sam. "You hard of hearing?"

"No," Sam responded. "Are you sure his name is Len?"

"Well I ain't ever seen any ID confirming it," Kenny said.

"So how do you know his name is Len," Foley asked.

"He told me," Kenny answered. He fumbled in his pocket, withdrew a pack of tobacco, and commenced the process of rolling a cigarette.

"You spoke to him?" Sam asked.

"Couple a times," Kenny shrugged.

"When was the last time you spoke to him?" Foley asked.

Kenny paused, licked the cigarette paper and sealed the tobacco in a thin roll. He plucked the loose strands of tobacco protruding from both ends, stuck the cigarette in his mouth, and lit it with a grubby, well used Bic lighter lying amongst the spilled ash on the bar top.

"Dunno," he said. "Month ago... maybe." He blew a thin stream of smoke across the bar top.

"Where was that?" Sam asked.

"Here," Kenny said. "I don't wander far from here."

"He came here?" Foley asked.

Kenny looked lazily at Foley, and then at Sam. "You two are a regular tag team. A man could get dizzy swivelin' his head between the two of you." He took another drag of his cigarette and chased the smoke down his throat with a sip of rum; a more generous sip this time.

"What did you and Len talk about?" Foley asked.

"Didn't talk about anything," Kenny said. "Just said 'hi' across the bar."

"And he told you his name?" Foley continued.

"That's what I said... I guess you must be hard of hearing too." Kenny drained the last of his rum, put the empty glass down softly on the bar, and moved the fresh drink forward, again lining the two glasses up perfectly.

Sam watched the little ritual with fascination. "Did Len tell you his surname?" he asked.

"I didn't ask, and he didn't say," Kenny answered.

"Did he mention where he was from?" Foley asked.

"I didn't ask, and he didn't say," Kenny repeated.

"That had to be a stimulating conversation," Sam suggested.

Kenny scowled at Sam. "You should consider keeping your facetious remarks to yourself, young fella."

"I apologise," Sam offered.

"As you should," Kenny added.

"Kenny," Foley interjected, trying to ease the building tension. "Did Len happen to mention where he lived?"

Kenny picked up his drink, sipped, put it down, dragged on his cigarette, and looked at Foley. "I didn't ask, and he didn't say."

Mildly frustrated, Foley opened the file, slipped the photograph inside, and rose from his stool. "Thank you for your time, Kenny."

"Hmmph!" Kenny grunted in response.

"Sam, let's get something to eat," Foley started walking away.

As Sam started to rise, Kenny turned to him. "What happened to your head?"

"I fell out of bed," Sam answered.

Kenny nodded as though he understood. "I remember doin' that meself, when I was about your age."

Sam turned to follow Foley.

"Oh, just so you know," Kenny said to Sam's back. "There ain't nothin' wrong with *my* hearing... for an eccentric old fart."

———

"That went well," Sam said as he, and Foley made themselves comfortable in the hotel dining room.

"Ahh, sarcasm! That's the old Sam I have come to know and love," Foley smiled.

"That's a sarcastic thing to say," Sam shot back.

"What do you think about Kenny?" Foley asked.

"I like him," Sam said.

"I don't think he's particularly fond of you," Foley commented.

"Baloney!" Sam scoffed. "Don't worry about good old Kenny. Kenny and me are birds of a feather. We're like that," He crossed his fingers in front of Foley.

Foley picked up the menu, glanced briefly at the fare on offer, and put the menu aside. "What would you be thinking right now if you were Leonard Williams?" he asked Sam.

Sam thought about his response for a few moments. "I'm guessing he doesn't know we stumbled across his house by accident, so he would be thinking we are on to him, we know who he is, and he may even be aware we found the bodies in the bottom of the well. He will assume we are watching the highway and will have road blocks in place. He will either be driving around out there in the desert, trying to figure out his next move, or he will be laying low somewhere, gathering his thoughts."

"What about the Winters girl?" Foley asked.

"I don't like to think about it," Sam said, "but I know we have to. I think she is probably dead. Williams is running, he won't want to be hampered by a girl who is almost certainly afraid for her life and desperately trying to escape. I'm afraid he might have already killed her and dumped her body in the desert."

"Unfortunately I think you are right," Foley frowned. He pushed his chair back from the table. "Suddenly I've lost my appetite," he said.

"Me too," Sam said. He also pushed away from the table and stood to leave. "Let's go out there and find this prick."

"I'm thinking the Tennant Creek chaps better find him before we do," Foley announced as the two men walked from the dining room.

"We know he's got a gun," Sam nodded.

"What are you suggesting?" Foley asked, suspecting he already knew.

"I'm not suggesting anything," Sam said. "But, sometimes the baddie with a gun gets shot by police defending their own lives."

"That's true," Foley agreed. "We hear about that sort of thing all the time."

Sam looked at his watch. "It's getting late," he observed aloud. "It'll be dark in a couple of hours. Where do you want to go?"

Foley paused. "Remember the road we saw from the chopper?"

"I'm not overly enthusiastic about remembering *anything* about the chopper," Sam mused.

"It seemed to start on the western side of the highway, near the Devils' Marbles," Foley continued.

"You are being somewhat over generous calling it a road, it was more like a bush track," Sam commented. "Eventually it led to the house."

"Right," Foley nodded. "When the perp took off from the house, he followed the road for a while, and then Potts and Donaldson confirmed he took off across the desert, heading east, when he saw the task force chaps approaching."

"You guessing he's still out there somewhere?" Sam asked.

Foley shrugged. "He hasn't been stopped by any of the roadblocks. The mobile patrols up and down the highway have not reported any sightings."

"There's a lot of country out there, Russell," Sam said. "He could have reached the highway at any point without being seen."

"Yes, you're right, but he will know we have road blocks in place, so he won't use the highway."

"Are you suggesting he either crossed over the highway and is now somewhere east of here, in which case he may be long gone by now and we'll never find him, or he is still out there, somewhere west of the highway?"

Foley slapped Sam on the shoulder. "I've trained you well," he smiled.

Sam ignored the remark and stepped toward the police four-wheel-drive. "We don't have a lot of daylight left. Let's get mobile. This bastard's not going to come to us."

24

Mandy looked up again into the cloudless sky, shielding her eyes against the glare of the late afternoon sun. The thought of spending the night out here frightened her. The desert nights were bitterly cold, the nighttime temperature consistently dropping to near freezing.

She no longer had the advantage of blankets to wrap herself in as the approaching darkness descended, and she shivered involuntarily in anticipation of the coming night. Being alone out here with her kidnapper was fearful enough at any time for her but, spending the night alone with him filled her with a dread she fought vainly to dismiss from her mind.

Behind her, low moans came from the rear of the car. She hurt the man badly certain both his wrists were broken. Instinct told her she should help him, but even if she wanted to, she had nothing to ease his suffering. Besides, despite his injuries, the bastard still managed to shoot her. If ever she had considered doing something, anything, to help him, the consideration was erased the moment he pulled the trigger.

Mandy looked again at her arm. Fortunately, the

bullet only grazed her, and now the bleeding had all but stopped. She really needed something to wrap around the wound to keep it dry, and free from the intrusion of dirt, dust, and grime, which there seemed to be no shortage of.

She moved to the rear passenger door of the car, opened it, leaned in, and felt around under the seat. Disappointed but not surprised, she found nothing she could use as a bandage, she stood, and slammed the door. Realistically, she supposed it was too much to expect the man to carry a first aid kit with him. She moved to the front passenger side door, opened the glove compartment, and peered in. A few old fuel receipts, a tattered, dusty road map, and a ballpoint pen were the only contents.

"Damn!" Mandy cursed as she stepped away from the vehicle. As she looked out over the endless, barren country, she was startled when the man called her name.

"Miranda... Miranda!"

Mandy turned and looked to the back of the car. The man called again.

"Miranda... Miranda! Where are you? Miranda?"

Mandy slumped dejectedly and stared at the ground at her feet. Although his voice seemed devoid of any menace and she no longer felt he presented a serious threat, she was reminded of the situation she found herself in every time she heard his voice.

Too frequently a burning, stab of pain, deep, and low, in her groin brought back the horror she had endured at the hands of the monster laying just a few metres away from where she stood. Every recurring thought of Veronica, and the other girls, reminded her of just how close she had come to sharing their fate.

Revulsion for the man now at *her* mercy came in waves as consistently as all the other horrific memories. Hatred of anybody was an emotion totally foreign to Mandy. Not for a moment in her life could she honestly recall feeling such intense hatred for anybody; until now. It both surprised and alarmed her how seemingly easily the emotion surfaced.

Prior to her kidnapping, she would have thought it impossible to ever feel so strongly repulsed by another human being. For this man, whoever he was, whatever the horrors he might have endured in his past that had brought him to this point in his life, Mandy could find nothing in her very being which might resemble compassion.

"Miranda! Where are you! Come here!"

Mandy stepped back to the passenger side of the car, reached in, and retrieved the tyre iron from where it lay on the floor. Then, cautiously and reluctantly, she walked to the rear of the vehicle. She raised the tyre iron above her head, reached out with her free hand, and opened the door. As the door swung open, she stepped back immediately; she was not going to be taken by surprise a second time.

Somehow the man had managed to get himself into a sitting position, and was slumped against the rear of the car's back seat. His broken arms rested in his lap. Already both his lower arms had swelled to twice their normal size, and mottled, dark blue bruising was evident from his hands to his elbows. One arm was so badly broken at the wrist the hand lay at an awkward, sickening angle. A large node, just behind the thumb where the bone threatened to break through the skin, appeared red, and inflamed. Dried blood from his badly broken nose caked his beard, and a thin strand of bloody spittle hung from his chin. The man was a sorrowful, pitiful sight but, despite his disheveled, injured appearance, Mandy was not about to take any chances.

"What?" Mandy snarled at the man.

"Wha... what's wrong with the car?" he stammered.

"Something's broken," Mandy answered.

"What's broken?"

"I don't know. I don't know anything about cars."

"Help me out, I can have a look," the man suggested.

"You've got two broken arms. What can you do?" Mandy asked.

"Nothing, but maybe I can tell *you* what to do to fix it."

"I'm not coming any closer to you than I am now," Mandy declared.

"Just help me out, Miranda," the man asked again. "We'll both die if we stay here. There's no water, and night is coming. We need to get out of here."

"*I* need to get out of here," Mandy said. "I don't care if you die here."

The man smiled weakly. "You don't mean that, Miranda. You can't let me die here. You care about me. I know you do."

"You mean nothing to me!" Mandy spat. "I hope you die... slowly!"

The man fixed Mandy with a stare. "We are both going to die slowly if we don't get out of this place. Now help me out of the car so I can see the damage."

Mandy stepped further back from the car. "Get out by yourself, I'm not helping you," she said.

Carefully, the man slid forward and lowered his

legs out of the door. Tentatively, he stood and leaned against the open door. "I don't know if I can walk, Miranda," he said. "You hurt my leg. Give me your arm."

Mandy stepped further away. Poised and ready to strike, she raised the tyre iron a little higher above her head.

"You have to be kidding," she said. "I'm not giving you my arm. You are on your own." She backed away and returned to the front of the car to stand next to the damaged wheel.

The man carefully put weight on his injured leg, waited a moment and then, leaning with his shoulder against the car for support, he limped slowly and ungainly to the front of the vehicle. He stopped at the driver's door, sucked in a couple of deep breaths as waves of pain washed over him, and looked down at the wheel.

"You fucked it, Miranda," he announced. "The wheel is fucked. The car is going nowhere. We are stuck here. You, and me. Alone." He leered at Mandy, and a drool of bloody spittle ran from the corner of his mouth into his filthy beard.

"You take one step closer to me and I'm going to hit you again," Mandy waved the tyre iron menacingly.

The man smiled crookedly. "It's gonna be a long, cold night, Miranda. We could keep each other warm."

"You disgust me, you filthy pig!" Mandy spat. "You keep away from me! You hear me! Keep away!"

The man took a step towards Mandy, and stopped. A hot needle of pain shot through his leg, he stumbled and almost fell. "Ahh, shit!" he mumbled.

Perhaps he was making a grab for her, Mandy

thought, or perhaps he was just testing his injured leg. Either way she reacted instantly, ducking low, and rushing straight at the man. She swung the tyre iron hard, and low, and felt it crack against his already injured leg.

The man screamed, his knees buckled, and he collapsed. A small puff of dust rose as he crashed headlong into the hard ground. Mandy stepped back, raised the tyre iron again, and held it threateningly above her head.

His first instinct was to clutch at his leg, which only served to painfully remind him his arms were badly broken. The pain was excruciating. His vision blurred, his mind tumbled, and spun, adding an uncontrollable dizziness to his already incapacitated state. The last thing he recognised was Mandy's bare legs, and thighs. Then, his eyes rolled back in his head and the painless, merciful blackness overtook him.

———

When the man woke, it was dark. He opened his eyes and tried hard to focus. He was on the ground, one side of his face resting in the dirt. The hard earth beneath him dug into his hip and shoulder and, every time he inhaled, a tiny puff of dust was sucked into his lungs. He coughed against the irritation in his nose and mouth, and more of the fine desert dust filtered downwards through his throat.

He rolled onto his back, grunting with the effort, blinked once, and stared up at the millions upon millions of stars winking down at him from the desert sky. He was cold, and shivered against the bone penetrating chill.

Slowly, ever so slowly, he began to gather his thoughts. He lifted his head and looked about him in the darkness. At his feet, he saw the dark silhouette of the car. As he stared at it, out of the darkness, the shape became clearer. He was laying close to the driver's door, and he was able to discern the door was shut. He remembered the car was badly damaged and he turned his head to the front wheel. Even in the dim light he could see the vehicle's front fender was slumped over the wheel which was skewed at a jaunty, unnatural angle to the body of the car.

Then, he remembered everything. Miranda had hit him with the tyre iron. More than anything, he remembered the pain. Must have passed out, he decided; must have been out of it for a long time because it was dark now. The bitch hit him. Why, he wondered? He liked her... perhaps more than any of the others, he decided. He thought she liked him too. The bitch hit him. How many times? Three? Four? Both his arms were broken, his nose was busted, and his leg hurt like hell.

No more mister nice guy, he declared silently. No more chances for Miranda. She had to die, just like all the others, and that was unfortunate. He wanted someone in his life he could keep forever, and he hoped Miranda might be that someone. He was wrong. She hurt him, and now she had to pay for it.

Where was Miranda, he wondered? He turned his head in every direction possible and stared long and hard into the gloom. He could not see her. Maybe she was watching him at this very moment. Watching, waiting for him to make a move, so she could hit him again. Bloody fuckin' tyre iron... should have kept it somewhere else... anywhere else but in the back of the car.

Maybe she was asleep. He looked again at the closed front door of the car. Maybe she was asleep inside the car. She wouldn't sleep outside on the ground; it was too cold. Besides, she was too fuckin' *la-de-da* to sleep outside on the ground...yeah, she had to be in the car.

Slowly, he managed to raise himself to a sitting position. He could see better now. He stared at the closed car door, less than a metre in front of his face. Wary it might fly open at any moment, and she would hit him with the tyre iron again, he was careful not to make a sound. If she was asleep he did not want to wake her, not until right before he killed her.

He would take her by surprise, but he wanted her to know what was coming. This time he would not fuck around. This time the bitch would die, and she wouldn't realise it until the very last moment. He shivered again; not against the cold this time, but with the anticipation of what he was about to do.

Suddenly, he remembered the gun. He stared away into the darkness behind the car. Miranda threw it away after she snatched it from him. He didn't remember her retrieving it. It had to still be out there, on the ground, somewhere behind the car.

How he was going to stand posed a difficulty he hadn't thought about until now. He couldn't grab hold of the car and hoist himself to his feet without the pain of his broken arms sending him headlong into another state of unconsciousness. How was he going to get up?

Slowly, so as not to make a noise and alert Miranda, he rolled onto his front and supported himself on his elbows. The pain was almost too much to bear and he struggled against the wave of nausea sweeping over him. With extreme difficulty, he pushed up with his elbows and raised his legs underneath him until he was resting on his knees, his elbows bearing the bulk of his body weight. He stayed that way for a few moments, sucking in deep breaths, and waiting for the pain to subside sufficiently to get to his feet.

Long, pain filled minutes later, the man stood facing the car. He waited, and watched the car for any sign of movement within. Satisfied Miranda had not heard him, he dared to move.

Walking was as problematic as the act of getting to his feet. Every step forward sent searing pain through his leg. Slowly, as quietly as he could, given his injuries, he limped to the rear of the car and stopped. He looked to where he thought Mandy threw the rifle. If it was out there, he could not see it. With difficulty, he edged forward, one slow painful step at a time, his head lowered, and his eyes focused on the ground in front of him.

"Gotta be here," he whispered to himself.

In the dark, every shadow on the ground looked like a rifle, and each time he paused to examine one of the shadows, it brought him more disappointment.

"Looking for this?"

Mandy's voice from behind startled him. He spun around instinctively, pivoting awkwardly on his damaged leg. The move sent savage pain through his limb, causing him to stumble and lose his balance. In a bizarre, animated, uncoordinated jig, he stepped forward, sideways, then forward again, desperately trying to keep from falling. Pain, like a series of high voltage electric shocks, knifed into the soft flesh behind his knee each time he stumbled. Finally, he went down, crashing face first onto the ground.

A wail, unlike anything Mandy had ever heard in her life, a haunting, thoroughly disturbing sound as though from a wild creature from a prehistoric time, split the silence of the desert night. The ungodly, loud, and hollow wail resounded in the enclosure of the night, enfolding her in a chill of terrifying dread. Even when the man finally stopped wailing, the sound seemed to continue, as though it had taken on a life of its own.

Finally, it stopped, but not abruptly. It seemed to fade into the distance, almost as if it was racing away towards a place far from here, wailing pitifully all the way until the sound could no longer be heard.

Mandy looked at the crumpled figure on the ground. He lay on his back, rocking back and forth, the ear-piercing wail now a subdued mournful, eerie half-moan, half-sob; the image of a broken, beaten man.

With caution, Mandy stepped closer to the man. She held the rifle awkwardly, with the barrel pointed at him. Mandy had never held a rifle before. She had never seen a rifle, or a firearm of any description, other than in movies and magazines. She had seen the damage firearms can do to the human body a handful of times but, holding one, aiming one, and firing one, was about as foreign to her as anything she could imagine.

If she had to pull the trigger, she knew where it was located, but whether or not it would fire was pure speculation. She didn't even know if she could pull the trigger.

Maybe if she felt her life was in imminent danger

she could. Or maybe not. Either way she did not want to be placed in a position where she had to make such a decision. Taking a human life had to be a whole different experience than saving one, she figured.

The man eventually stopped rocking back and forth, and became still. It seemed the more he moved about, the more acute the pain. He lay on his back, his eyes closed tightly as he waited for the waves of pain to ease.

"Oh! Oh, fuckin' hell!" he muttered through clenched teeth.

Mandy leaned cautiously forward, and prodded the man in the ribs with the barrel of the rifle. He started, and his eyes flew open.

"Miranda, you... ha...have to h... help me," he stammered. "Please."

Mandy stepped back a couple of paces. "You were looking for the gun," she said. "Why would I help you?"

"I'm the only one who can get us both out of this mess, Miranda. If you don't help me, we are both going to die."

"*You* might die," Mandy said, without any real compassion. "I'm gonna walk out of here."

"No!" he cried desperately. "You'll never make it without my help. I know the way to the highway."

"I'll take my chances," Mandy said.

"You can't just leave me here," he whined. "I don't think you have it in you to let me die."

"I'll send the police to you when I get to the highway," Mandy said.

"You'll never get to the highway, Miranda. Not without my help. You'll die out there, alone in the desert, we both will."

"You can't walk," Mandy reminded him.

"Yes I can," he insisted. "If you help me, we can walk out together."

"I'm not going to help you walk out," Mandy said. "If you want to try on your own, I can't stop you, but I'm going alone."

The man struggled awkwardly and painfully to a sitting position. "We should stay with the car, Miranda."

"You can stay with the car, or you can try to walk out on your own," Mandy proposed. "I don't care either way. You were going to kill me, just like you killed all the other girls. I'm not helping you, and I'm not listening to you." She turned abruptly and walked back to the car.

With only the interior light to guide her, Mandy searched the car thoroughly. She lifted the old carpet on the rear compartment floor, and searched the space where the spare tyre was housed, looking for water, or a torch, or both. She found nothing. All she had was a tyre iron, and a gun she didn't know how to use. She slumped against the body of the car and stifled a desperate sob.

She hated to admit it, but the man was right. The smart, sensible thing to do was to wait with the vehicle. That's what all the books and articles she had read before leaving for her adventure in Australia advised. The two men she saw at the house were police officers. She saw them only briefly, from a distance, but they looked like police officers. They had guns, she remembered. How they came to be at the house was a mystery but they would be looking for her, at least she hoped they were. They would have a better chance of finding her if she stayed with the car, she reasoned.

Staying with the car, however, meant staying with the man, and she was sure she couldn't do that. She was cold, it was dark. She needed to sleep, and she needed to get warm. Her medical training taught her hypothermia was a very real threat if she got lost out here in near freezing temperatures.

Suddenly she had an idea. If she stayed inside the car, with the doors locked, the man could not get at her. If she kept the motor running, she could turn on the heater and keep reasonably warm. Not a lot of fuel remained, but with the motor just idling over, she expected it would last until daylight. Not an ideal situation, and it meant the man would be nearby, albeit locked outside the car, but if the police were looking for her, she guessed they stood a better chance of finding the car than they did of finding her wandering aimlessly somewhere in the vast desert.

Mandy agonised over the decision for a long time before she finally decided she would stay with the vehicle.

She removed the keys from the ignition, walked around the vehicle ensuring all the doors were closed, and then she locked them using the key remote. Then, she walked around the car a second time, physically checking every door, satisfying herself each was locked.

She unlocked the car, climbed into the driver's seat, and locked the door behind her. Then she manually locked each of the remaining doors, even climbing over the front, and rear seats to lock the rear access door.

Back in the driver's seat, Mandy turned, replaced the key in the ignition, and started the engine. She fumbled in the dark, found the overhead interior light, and switched it on. Then she switched on the vehicle headlights; if the police were looking for her, the headlights might help guide them to her.

Making herself as comfortable as she could, she looked in the door mirror and saw the man was still sitting where she left him. In the darkness, he was nothing more than an indistinct shape but, as she looked at him, and even though she could not see his face clearly, she sensed he was staring back at her. A tremor of fearful apprehension shuddered through her and, as tired as she was, she dared not close her eyes.

————

Leonard Williams became enthralled, and eventually obsessed, with killing when he was just a young boy. He started with tiny creatures, small lizards and bugs he found in the back yard of the house he shared with his parents. Pinning lizards to the ground with a nail and watching them writhe in agony until they eventually succumbed was an endless source of amusement for him. Similarly, capturing bugs in his Bug Catcher, a second-hand Christmas gift, one of the very few Christmas gifts he could ever recall getting, pulling their wings off and watching them slowly die gave him almost as much pleasure as the lizards.

By the time he was ten years old, Leonard had disposed of countless such creatures and was rapidly becoming bored with the monotonous tedium of dispatching lizards and bugs. The desire to graduate to a larger species grew more, and more compelling. The all-consuming urge manifested itself into action when he was just twelve years old.

A neighbour's prize Burmese cat, who had never once in its five years of life ventured from its owner's back yard, was found partially skinned, and hanging by the neck from a tree less than one hundred metres from home. A post mortem conducted by a veterinary surgeon at the expense of the cat's owner determined the animal had been skinned alive before it was hung in the tree. The night of the cat killing, when he had snuck covertly back into his bedroom, Leonard masturbated for the very first time.

———

Leonard's parents were drunks and child beaters. They drank every day and night, and when they weren't beating the crap out of each other, they all too regularly meted out beatings to young Leonard. He had come to expect a degree of violence would be inflicted upon him by at least one of them, and sometimes both, almost daily. If by chance, or more often than not by incapacitation as a result of alcohol intake, he was spared a beating, rather than feel relieved, and welcoming of the respite, he felt strangely unwanted, and unloved, as if they had forgotten he even existed. At least when they beat him he knew they were acknowledging his presence in their lives.

Expulsion from a number of schools for beating on much smaller and younger students, and sexually assaulting some of the female students, aggravated Leonard's frustration. When he wasn't at school, he dreamed of killing a living, breathing person. The dreams would come to him at any time day or night. His mind would just drift, unsolicited, to thoughts of taking a human life. These reveries always carried him to a warm, pleasant place of contemplation where he would find himself physically aroused, longing to experience the sexual relief he was certain would accompany the act of killing a human.

At fifteen years of age, Leonard brutally murdered both his parents. He killed his mother first. She was passed out in her bedroom. His father, in a drunken stupor but still conscious, was staring numbly at a blank television screen when he stumbled to the bedroom to investigate the gurgling sounds.

Leonard was leaning over the bed where his mother lay with her throat cut from ear to ear. Leonard, still clutching the large knife, turned, and faced his father.

Mouth agape, his father looked at his dead wife and then at Leonard. His son smiled at his him, walked across the room, and plunged the knife deep into his chest.

———

Killing his parents ignited a passion in Leonard. As a fire that has burned down to ash but continues to smolder, it never died, and four years in juvenile detention served only to increase his desire to kill again.

Eventually, escape was easy; ridiculously so. Leonard was mopping the floor in the main reception area of the detention centre when a disturbance broke out in the in-mates social room, which sent the security personnel scurrying to that area of the centre.

The juvenile detention centre was not a prison, and the main front entrance doors were never locked during daylight hours. Leonard found himself alone in the foyer. He simply dropped his mop and walked out the front doors.

He spent the next few years living on the street, assumed a new identity, eventually stole a motor vehicle, and started kidnapping, raping, and killing young women. He kept them in an old abandoned farm shed on an isolated property far away from the city and those who were hunting him. If the last girl he grabbed hadn't escaped, he would still be down south doing what he loved.

Killing after violent, non-consensual sex, was as addictive to Williams as heroin was to a junkie. Fortunately, his addiction was much less expensive than the addict's drug of choice. Killing cost no more than the price of a bullet, and the sex was even cheaper.

———

Leonard lifted his head slowly, and looked toward the car. As he watched with curious interest, Miranda walked purposely around the car, checking all the doors. Then, she locked the car using the remote, and walked around the car a second time, checking all the doors.

Initially, he wondered what she was doing and then, finally it dawned on him. She had chosen to stay with the vehicle. Williams forced a smile.

Had she chosen to walk out as she had indicated, he knew he could not follow. His leg was so badly damaged he doubted he could walk a hundred metres, let alone the thirty, maybe forty kilometres of desert between them and the Stuart Highway.

Miranda would never make it either, he decided. She had no idea in which direction to walk, and he was not about to tell her. If she chose to ignore his advice, she would perish, and despite the injuries she had inflicted on him, he did not want her to die yet. When she did die, and she would, it would be by his hand and not at the mercy of the desert.

25

A few kilometres north of Alice Springs, a road often described as one of Australia's worst routes, traverses the Tanami Desert all the way to Halls Creek in the north of Western Australia. The Tanami road was nearly eleven-hundred kilometres in length, all of which was horrific bone shaking corrugations, dangerous wash-a-ways, and dense, red, bull dust as fine as talcum powder.

Huge cattle-carrying road trains, up to fifty metres in length, pulling three or more trailers, freighted livestock to the southern railhead along the Tanami Road, the most direct route between the Kimberly cattle region of Western Australia and Alice Springs, often adding to the damage done by mother nature.

Often impassable during the northern wet season, the Tanami Road, despite its treacherous hazards, was a magnet to the myriad of four-wheel-drive enthusiasts for the sole purpose of bragging rights over conquering the road. Many never do, and the number of abandoned, rusting wrecks dotted along the length of the road is testament to what many would say is the folly of those with bigger balls than brains.

In its current condition the track confronting Foley and Rose was worse than the Tanimi Road. A keen eye would discern that, in the distant past, it might have represented more of a road than it was now. The rough dirt road, stretching out to the west of Devil's Marbles and fading into the distance across the Tanami Desert was now nothing more than a very rough, un-maintained, single lane bush track.

Two wheel ruts, just centimetres deep and separated by a narrow strip of red dirt and flat, smooth, and sharp edged Gibber stones, snaked away from Devil's Marbles and disappeared into the west. On either side of the track, low, spiky Spinifex grass, common to the desert areas of the Northern Territory, grew right up to the edge of the wheel ruts and in some places threatened to obliterate any trace of the track. As far as the eye could see in any direction, it seemed nothing survived in this country save for the Spinifex grass.

Folks looked upon this country not as an inhospitable, unforgiving wasteland waiting for the naive and unwary to venture into it at their peril, but as a beautiful, untouched example of the famous Aussie Outback created by God. It was to be lauded, protected and preserved for future generations to admire. Such folk were almost certainly those who had never ventured beyond the comfort of their sitting rooms and the high definition, digital images beamed into their homes via the Natural Geographic Channel.

To more realistic folk, and the majority, the Tanami Desert was a barren, nuclear moonscape which would, for those foolish enough to enter, slowly and agonisingly suck the life from them, leaving bones that were bleached by the unforgiving sun, then crumbled to dust.

Foley stopped the police four-wheel-drive at the beginning of the track, stared out into the desert in silence for a few moments, and finally turned to Sam.

"Who would ever think raising cattle in this country might be a successful enterprise?"

Sam shrugged. "No doubt a shit-for-brains bureaucrat in a plush office somewhere decided it would be a good idea to waste our taxes on a hair brained scheme only shit-for-brains bureaucrats would believe would work."

"Very succinctly put," Foley nodded. "Shall we head out there and see what can find?"

"Do you really think he is still out there?" Sam asked, sounding mildly pessimistic.

"I don't know," Foley shrugged. "He's on the run, he knows we are looking for him, wherever he is, he will be planning his next move."

"Let's hope his next move is not to kill the girl," Sam said.

Foley leaned forward over the steering wheel. "I'm hoping he will keep her alive, as a hostage at least."

"A bargaining chip," Sam concluded.

"Exactly," Foley nodded.

Foley looked at his watch. "It's five thirty now. We've got about three, maybe four hours before nightfall. Donaldson gave us the waypoint of where the perp left the track and took off across no-man's-land. Let's see if we can find that point and re-assess the situation."

He keyed in their present position as a waypoint into the vehicle's dashboard GPS, brought up the spot given to them by the Task Force commander, and then started forward slowly along the track.

The enhanced suspension added to all police four-wheel-drive vehicles was no match for the deep corrugations delivering endless, shaking, and jostling. It slammed up through the floor into their legs and upwards along their spines, and into their necks. Their heads shook violently from side to side until it seemed their teeth rattled.

"These vehicles are smooth, aren't they?" Sam commented, sarcastically.

Foley gripped the steering wheel as it jerked, and wrenched in his hands, his knuckles white with the effort, as the car bounced along the track.

"Don't stick your tongue out," he cautioned. "You're likely to lose half of it."

Sam gripped the hand hold above the passenger side door with one hand, and braced the other against the dashboard. His knees tensed and locked against the firewall at his feet.

"This has gotta be the best country in the world," he chattered through clenched teeth.

Thirty minutes later, after enduring a ride which seemed to get worse the further along the track they traveled, Foley slowed to a crawl, braked, and finally stopped. He sat for a moment, breathing deeply.

"Why are we stopping?" Sam asked, silently pleased they had.

"I need to stretch my legs," Foley explained. "And I need to take a leak. This bloody endless shaking has stirred up my bladder." He undid his seat belt, opened the door and climbed out of the car.

As Foley walked to the rear of the vehicle to relieve himself, Sam undid his own seatbelt and climbed out of the car. He raised his hands high above his head and stretched.

"I feel like all my bones have been reassigned to different parts of my body," he called over his shoulder to Foley.

Foley zipped up and returned to the front of the car. He looked at Sam across the vehicle's roof. "You want to keep going?"

Sam looked again at his watch. "Yeah, we've only been out here half an hour, let's keep going. Do you think you can miss a few of the bumps this time?"

"You wanna drive?" Foley huffed.

Sam raised his hands in a surrender gesture. "No, I don't. Far be it for me to suggest I might be able to miss most of the bumps."

Foley climbed back behind the wheel. "I was never going to let you drive anyway," he mumbled half aloud.

"What?" Sam said as he too climbed back into the vehicle.

"Nothing," Foley said. He started the engine, slipped the transmission into drive and moved slowly forward. The bone shaking corrugations were still there.

———

When darkness fell, so did the temperature. As Foley concentrated on keeping the vehicle's wheels running within the existing ruts on the track, as opposed to lurching off into the razor sharp Spinifex grass, Sam reached down and fumbled with the vehicle's heater controls.

"Getting bloody cold," he declared.

"And late," Foley added.

"Do you want to continue?" Sam asked.

Foley glanced down at the dash board GPS screen. "We're pretty close to where he turned off the track," he announced. "A couple of kilometres I reckon."

"Let's stop and take a breather," Sam suggested. "We might be able to see more from outside the car."

Foley continued driving for a few minutes and eventually stopped. "I think this is it," he said.

Both men looked out of the window to the east. They stared in silence for a while, their eyes wide, and roving slowly back, and forth across a dark and shadowy landscape.

Outside the relative comfort of the car, nothing beyond ten metres of the vehicle could be identified other than dark, obscure silhouettes of stunted clumps of spinifex dotted across a carpet of black earth illuminated in the glow from the vehicle's headlights.

The cold, dark, night had settled quickly over the desert like a dense Autumn fog. Only an endless sky of twinkling stars, occasionally interspersed by the faintly glowing tail of a comet as it streaked across the limitless dark sky offered any indication there was a universe surrounding them.

Other than the crackling of the vehicle's engine as it cooled quickly in the frigid night air, Sam, and Foley might well have been locked in a soundless vacuum, such was the eerie, suffocating silence enfolding them.

Sam opened his door and climbed out, followed immediately by Foley.

Sam shivered. "Shit, it's cold."

Foley rubbed his hands together, stamped his feet a couple of times, and walked a few paces away from the vehicle. "I hope the girl is not laying out there somewhere, slowly freezing to death."

Sam walked around and stood next to Foley. "I hate to be the pessimist," he said. "But I think she might already be dead."

"You don't think he wants to keep her alive as a hostage?" Foley asked.

"Maybe at first I felt he might," Sam said. "But I've been thinking about it for the last hour or so. He knows we are on to him. The girl will slow him down. Alone he might get through a traffic stop. If he is stopped, and he has the girl with him, it's over.

"He doesn't know we have his description... and his photo. I think he will want to put distance between himself and us as quickly as he can. The girl will be a burden. I think he will have already gotten rid of her."

"I hope you're wrong," Foley said as he turned to walk back to the car.

Sam stood a few moments longer, staring out into the vast blackness. Something way off in the distance caught his eye. He watched it for a few seconds, and then it was gone. Dismissing it as insignificant, he was just about to turn and join Foley in the car when it appeared again.

Something was out there. A very long way off, and it only appeared for a second. Perhaps it was just his imagination, he thought. He stared long, and hard at where he thought he saw whatever it was, and now it was gone. Frustrated he closed his eyes tightly, and opened them again. Still nothing. A whole lot of cold, dark nothing.

Then, there it was; very faint flicker of light in the distance, and then it was gone. Sam raised himself on his toes, and stared. He saw it again; a light. It flickered once, twice and then it was gone.

Sam heard the car door open behind him.

"Are you coming?" Foley called.

Sam ignored his friend, and continued to focus on the vast expanse of darkness in front of him.

"Sam, get in here, its fucking freezing!" Foley complained.

"Come here," Sam called, without turning. He did not want to lose his focus.

"What is it?" Foley asked.

"I don't know. Come and look."

Foley climbed back out of the car, and crossed to where Sam stood rigidly staring into the darkness.

"What?" he asked.

Sam pointed. "Out there... there's a light."

Foley stepped up alongside Sam. "A light?"

"Yeah, a light... there... way off."

Foley stared in the direction Sam pointed. "I don't see a light," he said.

"It comes and goes," Sam explained.

"I don't see it," Foley said again.

The faint glow flickered again. "There... there!" Sam cried.

Foley saw it, just for an instant. "Yeah, I think I saw it."

"What is that?" Sam asked.

"A star?" Foley suggested.

Sam shook his head. "No, it's not a star. It's too low to be a star."

The faint light blinked twice, and then stayed aglow for several seconds before disappearing again.

"There it is again," Sam said. "That's not a star."

"What else could it be?" Foley asked.

"A car," Sam suggested.

"A car?" Foley said.

"Yeah, a car's headlights," Sam guessed.

"A car has twin headlights," Foley reminded him.

"When they're a long way off, headlights can look like a single light," Sam explained.

"It's gone again," Foley observed aloud.

"How far are we from the highway?" Sam asked.

"Too far. That's not the highway," Foley said.

"Keep watching," Sam instructed.

Both men stared in silence, waiting, hoping the light would re-appear. Many seconds went by without the light returning.

"It's gone." Disappointment was evident in Sam's voice.

"No!" Foley said excitedly. He thrust his arm out, and pointed at the light as it flickered on again.

"It has to be a car," Sam decided.

"Or a torch," Foley said.

"Why is it blinking on and off?" Foley asked.

Sam shrugged. "I don't know... maybe a trick of the light... the atmosphere."

"Or somebody signaling," Foley suggested.

"We need to take a look," Sam said. "But I'm afraid to turn away in case I can't find it again."

"I'll bring the car forward," Foley suggested. "You keep it in focus."

Sam stared intently at the light as it flickered on, and off, sometimes staying off for several moments, giving him concern it might not return. As he watched he heard Foley start the car and turn off the track. When the car stopped alongside him, he spoke through the open passenger side window.

"Can you still see it?" he asked Foley.

"No, I've lost it," Foley said.

"I need to get in the car," Sam said. He pointed to the faint glow on the dark horizon. "It's there... can you see it?"

Foley focused for a few moments, trying to locate the light. "Yeah... I've got it," he said finally.

"Keep watching, I'm getting in," Sam said.

Sam climbed into the vehicle, and both men sat for a moment, staring out through the windscreen.

"You still got it?" Sam asked.

"Yeah," Foley answered. "It's faint, and this is going to be a rough ride. We need to keep it in sight."

"I'll watch the light," Sam suggested. "You get us there."

26

Leonard Williams waited. He shivered as the bitterly cold night air closed around him, biting through his clothing, chilling him to his core. His arms, and his leg ached mercilessly, and he struggled to keep his mind focused on something other than the constant pain.

He stared at the car watching Miranda as she sat in relative comfort, sealed inside the vehicle with the heater churning a constant flow of air warmed by the running engine. The interior light was burning, and he could see her clearly. She sat in the driver's seat, her head back, resting against the headrest. Occasionally her head jerked forward, as if she might have briefly fallen asleep, and woke with a start.

"Ffff...uckin' bb...itch!" he chattered, his teeth clacking noisily.

She would be tired, he thought, but she would fight sleep. She was scared, and while she had the upper hand, at least for the moment, she would not want to risk falling asleep and face being taken by surprise.

Williams had to do something, and he had to do it quickly. If he waited too long the cold would get him.

The body-numbing cold seem to penetrate through to the very centre of his being. He tried to wrap his arms around himself in an attempt to get feeling into his body but the injuries to his arms made it impossible. He looked down at his hands, and slowly, tentatively tried to clench his fingers. One arm was worse than the other. His right wrist was definitely broken; he didn't need to be a doctor to diagnose it. The hand was skewed at a crazy angle to his wrist, and the fingers would not move.

On his left hand, however, the fingers slowly closed and clenched into a fist. He opened them, closed them, opened them again, and continued this ritual until he felt a modicum of feeling was returning, at least to that hand.

Although his left arm hurt like hell, he was satisfied it was not badly broken. He focused on clenching and unclenching his fist, taking his mind from the cold he knew would eventually overcome him if he did not take drastic action soon.

He stared at Miranda's profile. She had not moved in a long while. She had to be asleep, he thought, but he had to be sure. She had the tyre iron, and the rifle. If she was awake, and he tried anything, she would hurt him again, maybe even shoot him, and although the desire to get up and move about was almost overpowering, he fought against the urge. He had to be certain Miranda was asleep. So, he waited, and watched, clenching and unclenching his fingers, moving his toes inside his heavy boots, stretching and flexing his injured leg.

Williams knew exactly what he was going to do,

but the timing had to be perfect. Miranda had to be asleep, soundly and deeply asleep, and not likely to wake until he was ready. As he watched and waited, he spent the time moving his injured joints, trying to get as much feeling and movement into them as he could.

———

Mandy fought the very strong desire to close her eyes and drift off to sleep. Inside the car it was warm, and the urge to hunker down in the seat, lay her head back, close her eyes and sleep was all powerful. She even allowed thoughts of nodding off for just a few minutes to creep into her mindset. She would just nap, her subconscious told her. Just for a short while. It couldn't hurt. She was safe inside the car. All the windows were closed, all the doors were locked, the interior light was on, the headlights were on, what could go wrong?

She wouldn't see, or hear him coming for her, that's what could go wrong. She had to stay awake. A small... no, not small... a tiny amount of luck had gone her way, and she had to capitalise on it now. She was in control and she had to remain in control. The truth was, she didn't think she had enough strength, morally or physically, to resist the man again if he came for her.

He won't come for you, her inner voice imposed on her thoughts. *He's hurt bad. You hurt him bad. If he tries anything you will hear him. Go ahead, sleep. Just for a few minutes, you'll feel so much better if you do.*

Mandy slumped in the seat, laid her head back against the headrest, and closed her eyes.

Then, suddenly her eyes flew open, and she jerked

upright in the seat. "No... no!" she murmured aloud. "Don't fall asleep, damn it! Stay awake!"

She looked into the rear vision mirror on the outside of the door, and saw the man was still where she last saw him. He was sitting in the dirt, several metres behind the car. In the inky dark, his form was nothing more than a large, low, black shape against the backdrop of the night sky.

He hadn't moved since the last time she looked, she decided. That had to be a good thing. She knew she had really hurt him, maybe to such a degree he was incapable of moving. The assumption gave her little reassurance, reinforcing in her the desire to stay awake and alert. Falling asleep was simply too risky.

She knew the outside temperature would reach freezing, or perhaps below freezing, before day break. She also knew, if he remained exposed to the elements as he was, he would probably die. These thoughts gave rise to an inner turmoil she struggled to reconcile. Leaving him out there went against everything she believed in. It had never been in her nature, even as a child, to see another suffer and do nothing about it.

However, as difficult as it was for her to watch the man suffer, she dared not go to him. The alternative was to bring him into the car, into the warmth of the vehicle's interior, where he could, at the very least, enjoy a degree of comfort. That option was something she would not consider.

Mandy looked away from the mirror and shook her head as if to dislodge the burden of exhaustion weighing heavily upon her. She looked down at the dashboard and reached for the radio controls. Maybe if she listened to the radio it would help her stay awake.

Static, ear piercingly loud, burst from the speakers. Mandy started, and scrambled to turn the volume down. When she had it at a manageable level, she fiddled with the tuning knob. There must be music somewhere, she thought. Even inane, late night talkback would do. She had to stay awake.

Having wound the tuner up and back the dial, and finding nothing but static, she punched the on/off knob silencing the annoying hiss and crackle. Must be no radio reception way out here, she decided. Frustrated, she laid her head back again, and closed her eyes.

That's it Mandy... sleep. Just for a little while. You need to rest. You need to gather your strength to walk out of here in the morning. Just a few minutes... go ahead... sleep.

Once more she jerked, and opened her eyes. Her head lolled forward and fell against the steering wheel. The car horn blared in the night silence startling her.

"Damn it!" she cursed. "Stay awake!"

With her tongue, she probed inside her mouth and tasted blood. It had started bleeding again. She probed with her tongue, and pushed against a loose tooth in her lower jaw. Must have been knocked loose when the man hit her with the torch, she reckoned. She rubbed her jaw gently, and the pain eased moderately.

Thankfully, her arm had stopped bleeding. She was very lucky the bullet only grazed her arm, she thought. It could have been much worse. The bastard was trying to kill her. Probably would have if he had more control over the rifle. She touched the graze on her arm and examined her fingers. "No blood," she murmured. "Good."

She glanced again into the rear vision mirror. The man was still there. She watched him for a while and, finally, she dragged her eyes from the mirror and looked across at the passenger seat, finding a measure of comfort in seeing the rifle and the tyre iron close by.

Exhausted, she laid her head back once again, and closed her eyes.

———

Williams watched Miranda fighting to stay awake. He heard radio static blare loudly when she turned on the radio and fumbled with the controls, looking for a station receiving a signal. He could have told her there was no reception out here. All she had to do was ask. He dropped his head and smirked.

"Fuckin' bitch ain't likely to ask me anything," he mumbled to himself. As he watched, he saw her lay her head back. "Yeah," he murmured, "Go to sleep, Miranda."

She stayed that way for a few moments and, just when he thought she might have dropped off, her head snapped up and fell forward. The car horn blast loudly in the surrounding silence, startling him.

"Stupid bitch!" he cursed. "Go to fuckin' sleep!"

Once more, she laid her head back, and this time she stayed that way. Williams watched, his eyes fixed on Miranda. She was motionless. The minutes ticked by. He counted them in his head. One, two, three... and then it was five... and then ten. She was asleep, finally. He smiled and waited longer. Eventually he lost count of the minutes, but when he was satisfied she was not going to wake any time soon he decided to move.

He moved cautiously at first, shifting onto his side and drawing his legs up underneath him. Each time he moved he would stop, and look at Miranda, and each time she was still asleep. He had to move very slowly, so as not to alert Miranda, and movement caused pain to shoot through his arms and legs

Supporting himself on his good elbow, he very carefully got to his knees. Needles of pain shot through his injured leg, and he almost fell forward onto his face. Bracing himself and gritting his teeth against the pain, he pushed himself onto his feet.

He stood, unsteady at first. His legs were numb with the cold. He stumbled, almost fell, and then re-gained his balance. He stole a look at the car, relieved to see Miranda appeared to be still asleep.

Finally, getting feeling back into his legs, he dared to take a few tentative steps toward the car and the sleeping girl within. Agonising with every step and limping badly he moved closer to the car. Ever mindful Miranda might wake at any moment, he paused after every step, and stared at her still form through the closed window.

Then, he was there. He reached out, touched the roof of the car, and leaned against the rear door. Breathing deeply, against both the pain and the cold, he rested for a moment. In the dim light cast by the interior vehicle lights, his breath came in spasmodic, gasping puffs of condensation in front of his face. He looked through the rear window at Miranda. She was laying sideways across the seat, her head resting against the passenger seat headrest. He could not see her face, but he was certain she had not moved, and was still sound asleep. He smirked with satisfaction.

He leaned down, reached under the rear of the car, and fumbled about with his left hand. The first hint of unease began to flutter in his chest as he ran his hand back, and forth, under the rear bumper of the four-wheel-drive and found nothing. It had to be there! Somewhere!

A large clod of hard, dried dirt, dislodged by his fumbling fingers, fell and thudded softly onto the ground. He looked up quickly, hoping Miranda had not heard the sound. She was still sleeping. He leaned down again and continued his search.

Then, his fingers brushed over what he was looking for. It must have been covered by the dirt clod. He wrapped his fingers around it, pulled it free, stood, and brought the small, metal container close to his eyes and smiled.

"Yes," he whispered.

Way back, when he stole the car, he couldn't believe his luck at finding the keys in the ignition. The owner had stopped to fuel up at a service station and left his vehicle to pay for his fuel. Williams simply opened the door, climbed in, and took off.

He brushed accumulated dirt from the lid, and gently pried the container open. The key, a spare he hid under the vehicle, gleamed dimly in the light cast from the interior of the car.

He lifted the key from the container, and clenched it in his fingers; if he dropped it he might not find it again in the dark.

Satisfied Miranda was still asleep, Williams moved slowly, cautiously, along the passenger side of the vehicle, supporting himself by his left hand against the roof line.

He paused at the passenger side door, leaned down, and looked at the sleeping girl. Her head was turned towards him, her eyes were closed, and her eye lids fluttered softly every now and then. Must be dreaming, he decided.

As he stared at her face, her lips parted slightly. A tiny bead of saliva dribbled from the corner of her mouth. Williams found something about this natural, involuntary action extremely arousing.

Then, his eyes were drawn to Miranda's chest, and he watched it rise, and fall, as she slept. "You are so pretty," he whispered to himself.

He stood rigidly still, supporting himself against the passenger side door, and watched Miranda sleeping for as long as he dared before he finally dragged his eyes from her.

He lowered his eyes, and looked into the passenger seat. The rifle lay upright, resting against the seat, the barrel pointed at the roof. The tyre iron was on the seat. Both were within easy reach of Miranda if she should awaken. He had to open the door, get the rifle, and he had to do it without waking her.

Fortunately, the vehicle was an older model, and it had access for a key on both the driver's side door and the passenger door. As quietly as he could, he fumbled in the dark and slipped the key into the door. He glanced at Miranda. She had not moved. So far, so good.

Hoping the sound of the engine would cover the sound of the door lock disengaging, he held his breath and turned the key until the door unlocked with an audible click. He looked at Miranda. She stirred, lifted one hand, and wiped sleepily at the drool on her chin, and then dropped her hand into her lap. Her eyes remained closed.

Williams exhaled a sigh of relief. Now he had to open the door, reach in, and grab the rifle. He waited a few moments until he was satisfied Miranda was not about to wake up, and then he reached for the door handle.

The passenger door had not been used much since he had the vehicle, but he knew it squeaked on rusty hinges when it was opened. Nevertheless, he had to take the chance. He was gambling on getting the door open and removing the rifle before Miranda woke. If he was quick, he could do it.

He wrapped his fingers around the door handle, braced himself, and lifted the handle. Even with the sound of the idling diesel engine, the noise seemed to be extremely loud. He slowly pulled the door open wide enough to get his hand inside.

Miranda stirred again. This time she lifted her head from the head rest, and moved her body so she was now leaning across the centre console separating the two front seats. Although she did not open her eyes, she fidgeted in her seat, and then settled again.

Williams reached into the car, grasped the barrel of the rifle and, as he very carefully withdrew it, the barrel caught on the top of the door interior. He almost dropped it, but regained control and pulled it from the car.

He stood erect, held the rifle in his left hand, and supported the barrel in the crook of his broken right arm. He pulled the door open wider. It squeaked alarmingly, but Miranda remained asleep.

With difficulty, he positioned himself so he could

sit down in the passenger seat and lift his legs into the car. The process was slow, and painful, but he was finally seated. For a few moments, he studied Miranda, and listened to her softly snoring beside him.

He raised the rifle, and moved it so the barrel almost touched Miranda's forehead. Slowly, he moved it forward until the end of the barrel touched her skin. Satisfied, he smiled widely.

———

Mandy opened her eyes, and screamed.

Right there... just centimeters from her, was the wide mouth, the lips pulled tight into a gruesome smile exposing stained and rotten teeth. Gushes of warm, stinking, foul breath washed over her face, and she swallowed against the bile she felt rising in her throat. Then there was the eyes; the leering, demonic eyes of a mad man stared unblinking at her.

"Hello, Miranda," Williams said.

Mandy looked past the man at the wide-open door. "Hhh... how did you get in here?"

Williams smiled wider. "Spare key, Miranda. Every diligent motorist should carry one."

Mandy's eyes were drawn to the gun. The barrel was aimed directly at her face. She dropped her head and stifled a sob. "What are you going to do?"

"First I'm gonna get warm," Williams said. "Then, in the morning we are getting out of here."

"How?"

"We'll walk."

"Where to?"

"Don't worry yourself with trivial matters, Miranda. Get out of the car."

"What?"

"You heard me, get out of the car."

"It's freezing out there."

"As I recall, it didn't seem to bother you when you left me out there."

Mandy looked up at the dark, cold night outside the vehicle. "I'll freeze to death," she said.

Williams shrugged. "I hope not," he said. "It will be daylight in a couple of hours. I was out there much longer than you will be. I survived. You are a tough one, I'm sure you will too. Get out of the car."

"Please don't do this," Mandy begged.

Williams pushed the rifle forward. Mandy drew back until the back of her head was hard against the side window. The barrel touched the side of her face, and stopped.

Mandy whimpered. "Oh God... don't... please don't."

"I'm not going to ask again, Miranda." He slowly, and loudly enunciated his next words. "GET OUT OF THE FUCKING CAR!"

Mandy fumbled behind her, opened the door, and almost fell out of the car.

"Shut the door," Williams ordered.

Mandy slammed the door, and scurried backwards, away from the vehicle. She stared back at the man, his leering, smiling face mocking her. She saw him lower the rifle, reach behind, and close the passenger side door. Then she heard the door locks engage. He smiled wider at her, and settled down in the glorious warmth of the interior. He closed his eyes.

Mandy hid her face in her hands and sobbed loudly. Already, she felt the freezing air beginning to penetrate her light, summer clothing. She massaged her painful jaw, dropped her hands, and looked up at the clear, star filled sky.

"Please... please help me."

———

Leonard Williams hunkered down in the passenger seat. The doors were locked, he had the rifle, he had the tyre iron, and he had Miranda right where he wanted her. Well, not exactly where he wanted her, he would have much preferred it if she were inside the car with him. Sitting in his lap would be nice.

He peered out at Miranda. She was crying, he thought. Then she looked up into the sky and mumbled something he couldn't hear from his position inside the car. Was she praying, he wondered? Wasn't going to do her a lot of good if she was. Nothing could save her now.

Ages ago it seemed, but it was more like twenty-four hours or so, there was a time, when he could have, and probably would have, overlooked her aggressiveness. But that was then, before she broke one of his arms, severely damaged the other, and smashed his leg with the tyre iron.

He could not let those indiscretions go unpunished. A part of him would welcome the challenge of taming her. She had spunk, and that was exciting. But when spunk turned into physical violence, drastic measures had to be taken.

He could not trust Miranda anymore, and that was a shame. He had come to like her much more than any of the others; she was so much prettier. The freezing air outside the car might kill her, but he doubted it. It would be daylight soon, and she would soon be warm again. He wanted her alive. He wanted her to know he had no choice but to end her life himself. She had to know her dying could have easily been avoided if only she had done what he'd required of her. Her pending death was her own fault; she had to see that.

He could have killed her right then and there, when she woke up and found him sitting next to her. Probably should have killed her, he thought. But, he wanted to savour the experience. Right now, he was freezing cold, and he was tired. A couple of hours more wouldn't hurt. He would have a sleep and then, in the morning, he would have a little fun with her before he killed her. If she resisted, he would have his fun after he killed her.

He felt himself drifting off in the warmth of the car. No matter, he thought. He was safe in here. The doors were locked, the heater was pumping out beautiful warm air, and he had the weapons.

His injuries throbbed painfully, perhaps even more so now the warmth of the heater was thawing the numbness created by the freezing temperature outside. He wanted to sleep, badly, and very nearly dropped off several times, until another wave of pain washed over him, snapping him back to alertness.

Finally, he succumbed. His head dropped and he slept.

27

The police vehicle bounced and shuddered across the vast open expanse of desert. The headlights flickered crazily, like an old black and white silent movie, making it virtually impossible to spot any obstacles looming out of the darkness in front of the sturdy four-wheel-drive.

As one wheel, rode up over a hard clump of spinifex grass, it was followed immediately by another wheel, both Sam, and Foley were tossed about in their seats.

"Bloody hell, it's rough!" Sam announced.

"It's not exactly a freeway," Foley added, as he struggled with the steering wheel which seemed to have developed a mind of its own.

"It's interesting," Sam said.

"Interesting, what's interesting about it?" Foley asked through clenched teeth.

"This is probably the first time in the history of the planet a vehicle has driven across this land," Sam said.

Foley stole a quick glance at his partner. "And, you find that interesting?"

"Yes, I do. It makes me feel kind of important. Like

the explorers of old who trekked across the country from south, to north, and east, to west."

Foley chose to ignore Sam's line of the conversation. He had known Sam Rose long enough to know it was never a good idea to pander to his often-obscure direction of conversation which was, more often than not, totally unrelated to the current circumstances. Perhaps it was a sub-conscious defense mechanism... or perhaps not. Perhaps it was all just plain gobbledygook.

"Can you still see the light?" he asked.

"Of course not," Sam answered. "I lost sight of it ten minutes ago. Any chance you might be able to keep this thing on the straight and narrow?"

"I'm too busy driving to watch the light," Foley declared. "That's your job."

"Driving?" Sam scoffed. He bounced high, and hit his head on the roof. "You call this driving?"

Foley braked and brought the vehicle to a stop.

"*Now* you stop," Sam said. "I've cracked my noggin on the roof fifty times, on the side window fifty-eight times, my knees under the dash sixty times, and *now* you stop."

Foley sat in silence for a few moments, and then looked across at Sam. "You're such a fuckin' girl... stop fuckin' complaining and look for the light."

Sam looked back at Foley. "Two fuckins in one sentence. I don't think I've ever heard you use so much profanity in such a short time. Are you all right?"

"I'm fine, thanks for your concern."

"You're welcome. We're mates. It's what mates do... show concern for their mates."

"Look for the fuckin' light," Foley scowled.

Several minutes passed, and the two men sat in silence, staring out at the darkness. When the light did not re-appear, Foley began to consider turning back. He looked at his watch, and turned to Sam.

"It's two o'clock in the morning," he announced. "I think we should turn back."

"Why?" Sam asked, his eyes still focused on the darkness through the windscreen.

"Because we are chasing something we can't see," Foley said. "Maybe we should head back and regroup."

"What about the light?" Sam pointed to his front.

"We lost it," Foley shrugged. "It was probably just a mirage."

"That's no mirage," Sam said, jabbing his finger at the windscreen.

Foley turned his head sharply, and looked out to the front of the vehicle. "Where?"

"There," Sam said. "Ten o'clock."

Foley squinted in the direction of the distant, invisible horizon.

There! There it was. Closer now. A faint yellow glow, no brighter than a low lantern flame, way off in the black distance.

"How far away is it?" Foley asked.

Sam shrugged. "I don't know. Its pitch black out here. Distance is hard to determine."

"Do you think you can keep it in sight?" Foley asked, mild sarcasm evident in his voice.

"If you drive slower, and avoid all the bumps I can."

Foley shifted the gear lever, and the car moved slowly forward. "I'll do my best," he said.

He veered slightly left, bringing the distant light to the centre of the windscreen. The vehicle, traveling much slower now, rode up over obstacles with considerably less bumping and jostling, making it easier for Sam to keep the light in sight.

"That's better," he said to Foley. "Might be Wednesday next week before we get there, but at least I can still see the light."

"Sarcasm," Foley commented. "How very uncharacteristic of you."

"You said that before," Sam said.

"If I say it enough you might get the message."

"Remind me again... what is the message?"

"You can be a sarcastic SOB at times," Foley said.

"Oh, yeah, I remember now," Sam responded. "What if we get there, and it's just a trick of the light?"

"It's not a trick of the light," Foley answered. "It *is* a light."

"What if we get there and it's not him?"

"Better to get there and find out it's not him than not go and miss the opportunity to nab the prick."

"Or shoot him," Sam added.

"Or shoot him," Foley agreed.

———

One agonisingly slow hour passed, and Foley and Rose seemed to be getting no closer to the distant light. Then, the sky above the far distant eastern horizon lightened, heralding the approach of a new day. Sam, and Foley were still distant from the mysterious light, but it was brighter now, and it appeared to have divided into two lights, separated by the narrowest of dark space.

Foley stopped the car, and shifted it into neutral. The relatively quiet sound of the engine in idle mode was a welcome respite from the screaming, protesting racket which had accompanied the rough, bone jarring ride across the desert thus far.

"Not far now," Foley announced.

"I need a piss," Sam announced.

"Okay," Foley said. "We'll rest here for a few minutes, and then we'll go and introduce ourselves to Mister Williams."

"Sounds like a plan," Sam said. He climbed out of the car, and walked to the back of the vehicle.

When he was finished, he turned to get back into the car, and paused. Something about the distant light piqued his interest. He cocked his head and listened.

"Turn the motor off," he called to Foley.

"What?" Foley asked.

Sam walked back to the passenger door and leaned in. "Turn the motor off."

Foley reached down, and turned off the ignition. The engine fell silent, save for the crackling of the very hot engine rapidly cooling in the cold air.

"What is it," Foley asked.

"Listen," Sam said.

"Listen to what?"

"Shh... listen," Sam ordered. "Can you hear that?"

"I can't hear anything."

"You can't hear anything because you're talking too much. Get out of the car."

Foley released his seatbelt and climbed out of the car. "What can you hear?"

"Stop fuckin' yacking, and you'll hear it," Sam scolded.

Foley paused, and listened intently for a few moments. Then, he heard something, very soft, and a long way off.

"What is that?" he whispered aloud.

"*That* is a diesel engine," Sam answered.

Foley listened again. "You mean like a diesel car engine?" he asked.

"That's exactly what I mean," Sam nodded. "That's definitely a car out there. I'm betting it's a diesel four-wheel-drive."

"Like the one our perp was driving," Foley surmised.

"Exactly," Sam said.

"It hasn't moved," Foley said. "All the time we've been heading towards it, it hasn't moved. "Why would he sit there all this time with the engine running?"

"Think about it, Russ. He's on the run, he's had a big head start, he should be miles away by now, but he's not. He's sitting out there, in the dark, with his motor running, why would he do that?"

Foley thought for a moment, and suddenly he got it. "He's broken down!"

"Bingo," Sam smiled. "Go straight to the top of the class."

"It's freezing cold, the car's busted, but the motor still runs; he needs to stay warm," Foley continued.

"Now you're showing off," Sam declared.

"Don't stop me, I'm on a roll," Foley chuffed.

"How far away is he?" Sam asked.

Foley focused on the distant lights. "I don't know. Sound will travel a long way out here... four, maybe five klicks."

"Turn the headlights off," Sam said.

Foley reached into the car, and switched off the vehicle headlights. "Do you think he knows we're here?"

"We saw *his* lights," Sam said. "It's reasonable to assume he has seen ours. But, leave the lights off in case he hasn't. If luck is on our side, and he hasn't seen us, he may not hear us approaching while his motor is running. We might be able to get a lot closer before he knows we are here."

Foley nodded. "You're right, but even if he has seen us, he can't go anywhere if his car is stuffed."

"No, he can't," Sam agreed. "But we have to assume he is armed, if he has the rifle he used to kill the girls, he has us at a disadvantage, especially with these pea shooters," he tapped his holstered Glock. "We need to get as close as we can."

Foley moved to climb back into the car. "Okay, let's go. It's time we met this dirt bag."

Sam followed Foley's lead, and joined him in the vehicle. Foley started the car, turned to Sam and said, "You ready for this?"

"Oh, I'm ready," Sam nodded. "We've both crossed paths with a few bad dudes in our respective careers. This prick might just be the pick of the bunch. I don't think I've ever been more ready to confront anyone than I am to confront this arse-wipe."

As he steered the vehicle slowly forward with one hand, Foley un-holstered his Glock and handed it to Sam. "Check this out for me."

Sam took the Glock from Foley, released the magazine, checked the spring tension, and satisfied himself the nine millimeter rounds were seated as they should be. He handed the weapon back to Foley, and repeated the exercise with his own.

Both Sam, and Foley had faced off with armed offenders several times in their careers. Russell Foley had shot and killed a man in Darwin a couple of years previous, saving Sam's life, and the life of his then girlfriend, in the process.

Both had been lucky up to this point. Would the luck continue? Statistics would suggest the more something doesn't happen, the more likely it would. Was the approaching confrontation their time? The unspoken question was one both men silently asked themselves as their vehicle drew slowly closer to the now not so distant light.

28

Mandy wrapped her arms around herself, and shivered in the freezing air. Her body, so warm inside the vehicle, now chilled quickly. The cold was painful. She squatted on her haunches in an attempt to lower her profile; less of her body exposed to the chill, she reasoned. Still, the cold bit through her light clothing like thousands of ice needles peppering her skin. She lifted her head, and looked across at the car. The man looked to be asleep. His head had dropped, and he was not moving.

She dared to stand, and took a few tentative steps closer to the vehicle. She felt warmth from the engine reaching across the space between herself and the car. She took another cautious step closer, paused, and then another. She reached out, and placed her hand palm down on the bonnet of the car. The warmth was instantly wonderful.

Did she dare get closer? A quick glance through the window indicated the man was still asleep. An idea began to take shape in Mandy's mind. Deciding not to wonder about the consequences, she took one more quick look at the man, dropped to her knees, and peered under the front of the vehicle.

The warmth here was far too inviting to resist. Mandy sat down on the ground, and slid head first underneath the car. When her body was completely under the car, she lay on her back, and luxuriated in the heat radiating from the engine. The smell of diesel fuel was strong, and she gently covered her nose and injured mouth with her hand.

She rolled onto her side, folded an arm under her head, and closed her eyes. She was never going to sleep, the engine noise was too loud, and the fumes were almost overpowering. But, it was warm, and if she could manage to endure the discomfort for a couple of hours, at least until dawn, she could start walking out. She didn't know how far she was from the highway, and she had no food, or water, but she had to try.

The man could follow her, but if she could get a head start, his injuries would make it impossible for him to catch up to her. She was smart enough to know she might die trying, but dying on her terms had to be better than dying on his. She would not give him that pleasure.

———

Leonard Williams slept fitfully. One broken arm; possibly two, given the second arm was badly bruised and swollen, a broken nose, and a seriously damaged leg, were not maladies conducive to a restful night's sleep. As well as the pain accompanying his injuries, the ability to breathe naturally was severely hampered due to his broken nose.

He opened his eyes, and positioned himself upright in the seat; not an easy task in itself given his injured arms and leg, had stiffened considerably. He flexed his fingers on the least damaged of his hands until he was satisfied he had sufficient movement in the joints to use the hand. Then, he looked for Miranda.

From his position in the car, he could not see her. He checked the side mirrors, and the rear vision mirror, but Miranda was nowhere in sight. Probably laying down, he guessed... might even be dead. The clothes she was wearing offered such little defense against the freezing desert night air, she might just as well have been naked; it was a mind picture Williams lingered on for a moment.

It would be a shame, he thought, if she had succumbed to the cold, depriving him of the opportunity to dispose of her himself. It was something he had thought about a lot during the times he was awake during the night. So much so, he had reached a point where he was anxiously anticipating the break of day.

While he accepted Miranda had to die, he faced the task confronting him with mixed emotions. Just as heroin, cocaine, ice, or any of the other addictive chemical drugs brain dead junkies sniffed, snorted, swallowed or injected, killing had become Williams's drug of choice. The sexual abuse, and ultimate killing of young girls was, for Williams, the one thing he was really good at. He loved it. He craved it, and he could not imagine his life without those two components.

Miranda, however, was different from all the others. She had spunk. There were times when he seriously considered keeping her around permanently. He had moments when he thought he might be able to tame her, and she would eventually come to like him as much as he liked her; that she was so pretty, much more so than any of the others, didn't hurt either.

He would still have to kidnap, abuse, and kill, even if he kept Miranda. Would she eventually come to accept it was a strong physical need, and not a *cheating* thing? Would she be able to live with it as a necessary part of his, and ultimately her life? It would be a tough task, but he had never been one to shy away from a challenge.

Unfortunately, circumstances had changed. He could get out of the situation he now found himself in, but he could not do it with Miranda in tow. She had proved to be unwilling, and uncooperative. The police were looking for him and he could not hope to get away if Miranda remained with him.

Without her, he could get to the highway - it wasn't as far away as he led Miranda to believe - and then he could con a passerby into giving him a lift by feigning an accident, dispose of the unsuspecting good Samaritan, steal his car, and drive himself to a hospital far from the area, and offer a bullshit story about falling off a ladder by way of explaining his injuries.

He could make it work, but not with Miranda. Unfortunately, she had become a liability, one which had to be dealt with. While he had regrets about the need to kill her, he had come to accept that the necessity to get it done far outweighed any regrets.

Williams leaned across to the driver's seat, and switched off the engine. The silence was sudden. He sat for a moment, engulfed in the quiet, and wondered where Miranda might be. A small part of him admired her courage if she had indeed started walking.

He opened the door, and struggled awkwardly out

of the vehicle, stretched, yawned, and retrieved the rifle. Supporting himself against the body of the car, he limped around the rear of the vehicle to the driver's side. Miranda was not there. Maybe she was in front of the car, he thought.

He continued his awkward, stumbling way to the front of the vehicle and discovered she was not there either. He slumped against the bonnet, and stared off into the slowly lightening eastern sky. He could not see anything other than the open, desolate, barren landscape. She must have left in the middle of the night, he supposed. Then, he looked down and saw her feet. She was under the car. Must have crawled under there to keep warm, he guessed.

Supporting himself against the bonnet of the car, he kicked at Mandy's feet with his good leg.

"Good morning, Miranda."

Mandy yelped and yanked her legs further under the car.

"Come on out, Miranda," Williams ordered. "Like a good girl."

"No!" Mandy cried.

"I will shoot you, right where you lay, if you don't come out from under there," Williams promised.

"No, I'm not coming out!"

"Do you really want to die under there, Miranda?" Williams asked. "You know, no one is ever going to find your body."

"Someone will find the car," Mandy said, not at all confidently.

"Maybe," Williams agreed. "But from the air it's just another black fella's abandoned wreck, and no one ever comes driving out here. No one is going to think twice about it. Your dry and crumbling bones will still be under there fifty years from now. What about your family? Never knowing what happened to you. No body to bury. Do you really want to put them through that misery?"

Mandy's response came in the form of gentle sobbing.

"Come on out, Miranda. If you come out now I won't hurt you."

"You... you will," Mandy said.

"No, I won't... I promise," Williams lied. He paused, and waited.

Eventually, Mandy slid immodestly, and indelicately from under the car, her dress scrunched up under her backside. When she was out, and looked up at the man, he was staring at her near nakedness, a hint of a lecherous smile on his lips.

Clumsily she grasped the roo-bar attached to the front of the vehicle, hoisted herself to her feet, and flattened her dress around her legs.

"Good girl, Miranda," Williams smiled.

———

"There!" Sam indicated, pointing through the windscreen. "It *is* a car!"

Russell Foley adjusted the vehicle's direction of travel slightly. "Yeah," he said. "That has to be our man."

The vehicle's headlights were still burning and, as Sam and Foley got closer, they noticed what looked like a figure standing in front of the vehicle.

"Someone's there," Sam said.

"Yeah, looks like," Foley agreed.

"What's he holding?" Sam asked.

"I don't know, we are still too far away to be certain; it could be a rifle," Foley answered.

"Might be a good idea to assume it is," Sam suggested.

"Copy that," Foley said.

Foley eased off the accelerator, and approached the vehicle somewhat more cautiously. "Do you think he's seen us?"

"Might be a good idea to assume he has," Sam repeated.

"Looks like he has his back to us," Foley said.

———

Mandy saw the approaching vehicle moments before Williams heard it.

Williams saw Miranda's expression change, and then he heard the sound of a vehicle engine approaching from behind him. He staggered forward, lifted the rifle, and placed the barrel under Miranda's chin.

"Walk towards me, Miranda," he ordered.

Mandy flinched as the rifle barrel dug into the soft flesh beneath her chin.

"Wh... what?" she stammered.

"Walk toward me, now!" Williams demanded again.

As Mandy stepped forward, Williams stepped back, keeping the rifle firmly under her chin. His arm was beginning to tremble as the weight of the rifle aggravated his injured arm.

"Keep coming!" he ordered.

Satisfied Mandy had moved sufficiently forward, he removed the rifle from her chin, stepped behind her, and replaced the barrel, this time at the base of her skull.

"Don't move, Miranda. Not one step. If you do, you die. Do I make myself clear?"

"Ye... yes," Mandy stammered.

With difficulty, Williams snaked his badly broken arm around Mandy's neck, and pulled her back against his body. It hurt like hell, and he grimaced, and grunted, as the pain shot up his arm. But, with her head tucked tightly into the crook of his arm, he decided he could withstand the pain, for the moment at least. With the least painful of his two arms, he held the rifle firmly against her head, watched, and waited as the oncoming vehicle approached.

———

Foley suddenly thought better of the slow, and cautious approach, and pushed down harder on the accelerator. The four-wheel-drive bucked, and shot forward, bouncing treacherously across the rough ground separating the two vehicles.

"It's the girl!" Sam announced loudly, grasping the hand grip above his head. "She's alive!"

Foley braked, and stopped approximately fifty metres short of the man and the girl. Both men watched in amazement as the man manipulated the girl so she was in front of him, effectively shielding him with her body.

"The bastard's using her as a shield," Foley said.

"You think it's the Winters girl?" Sam asked.

"Has to be," Foley decided.

"Thank God she's still alive," Sam muttered.

"Now she's got to *stay* alive," Foley said.

"We can't help her sitting in here," Sam said. He opened his door, and stepped out of the vehicle, using the open door as cover.

Russell Foley reached down, and switched on the emergency lights mounted on the bar on the roof of the vehicle, and then followed Sam's lead and climbed out of the car.

Both men un-holstered their weapons, chambered a round, and lowered them to their sides, their index fingers resting outside the trigger guard.

"How do you want to do this?" Sam asked.

Foley paused for a moment, and then said, "Let's take a walk and think about it on the way."

Simultaneously, they stepped from behind their respective doors and began walking slowly towards the other vehicle. As they walked, they each moved outwards away from their vehicle as well as forwards, so they were separated by more than the width of the car. They needed to stay close enough together to be able to communicate with each other, but far enough apart so as to widen the target area should the killer decide to start shooting.

———

Mandy stared at the approaching car. The rifle barrel dug painfully into the back of her head, making it difficult for her to maintain a steady gaze on the vehicle, but she could see enough of it to feel a glimmer of hope fluttering behind the façade of terror which had descended upon her.

When the oncoming vehicle stopped, the flutter disappeared. She began to have thoughts of the car turning, and speeding back the way it came. She wanted to scream at it and whoever was inside it, but she feared if she did, the man behind her would kill her. She bit down on her lip and waited.

Then, Mandy saw the lights. Red and blue lights began flashing above the vehicle. Police... it was a police car. She whimpered a soft cry of both relief, and hope.

Two men climbed out of the car, and started walking toward her. They had guns held at their sides. As they came closer, she saw something about the two men she found familiar. Then it dawned on her! She was looking at the two men from the house!

She only got a brief, panic filled look at them before the monster sped away, but she was sure it was the same two men she saw at the house.

Thank you! Oh God thank you. You found me, she wanted to cry out to them. As difficult as it was not to scream out to the men, she held her silence. She had to let them do their job. They were police officers; they knew what they were doing... she hoped.

———

Leonard knew instantly it was the police. If he needed confirmation, it came when the roof-top emergency lights started flashing. He watched as the two men got out of the car and started walking toward him. He dared to let them come. Given his injured arms, he was not sure he could nail them unless they were up close.

"Fuckin' cops!" he muttered.

"You have to give up," Mandy muttered, surprisingly calmly.

"Ain't gonna happen, Miranda," Williams declared.

"They'll shoot you," Mandy said.

"The bullets will have to go through you first," he announced.

Mandy fell silent.

Williams waited. His eyes, alert, and filled with hate, darted from one cop, to the other, and then back again.

"Keep comin' you bastards," he whispered softly.

The cops kept coming. Slowly, and cautiously. Williams let them get to within twenty metres, and then he called to them.

"Stop right there!"

———

Sam and Foley were about five metres apart when the man ordered them to stop. Both men stopped, and stared at the girl and the man sheltering behind her. Like a well-rehearsed and synchronised dance, they both raised their firearms, and aimed at the place where the man and the girl stood.

Quietly, from the corner of his mouth, Foley said to Sam, "Have you got a clean shot?"

"No," Sam answered. "You?"

"No."

Foley addressed the man. "Good morning, Leonard," he called across the space separating them.

For a few moments, no response came from the man. Eventually he peered sneakily around Miranda's head at Russell Foley.

"You know my name?"

"We know everything about you, Len," Sam answered.

Williams's eyes swung to Sam. "Like what?" he called.

"We know you are a rapist, murdering piece of shit!" Sam answered.

Williams brow furrowed, and he stared at Sam through half closed eyes. "You think insulting me is gonna hurt my feelings?"

"You don't have any feelings, Len," Sam answered. "Let the girl go."

"Come any closer, and you're gonna have more than a sore head," Williams said, noticing the bandage around Sam's head.

Russell Foley took half a pace forward. "Forget about his head, Leonard. Do what he says and let the girl go."

Williams swung his eyes back to Foley. "One more step and she's dead."

Foley stopped. "You don't need to do this. Let her go."

Williams started the eye swinging thing again, from Foley, to Rose, back to Foley, back to Rose. He was displaying very obvious signs of a man highly agitated. Both Sam and Foley knew from experience, nervous, agitated, stressed, and strung out people with guns were the worst kind to try to deal rationally with.

"You two pigs drop your guns on the ground!" Williams ordered.

"We're police officers, Len," Sam said. "We don't surrender our weapons... ever."

"Drop them on the ground and step away from them!" Williams responded. "Or the girl dies."

"You won't shoot her, Leonard," Foley said.

Williams's eyes darted back to Foley. "You seem pretty sure of that."

"I am," Foley continued. "If you shoot her, she will fall, and we will shoot you. Are you prepared to die?"

"It wasn't in my plans," Williams smirked. "But, if it comes to that, so be it. Now, drop the guns!"

"What we have here, Len," Sam said, "Is a good old Mexican stand-off. Just like in the movies. We are not going to surrender our weapons, and I don't really think you want to die today. Let the girl go."

———

Miranda had to do something. The two police officers would not drop their weapons; the police in this country would be no different from those in hers, she supposed. She lowered her eyes and looked at the bent, and swollen arm just centimetres from her eyes, and suddenly an idea flashed in her mind.

The idea was fraught with danger, and it might very well be the last idea she ever had. But, she had to do something. The man was just crazy enough to go through with his threat to kill her. The cops would shoot him immediately if he did, but that would not help her.

The horror, the terror, the never knowing when she might be killed; it couldn't end for her now, not like this. She had survived on her own wits up to this point, and it was not right she should die with two police officers just metres away from her—not right, and not fair.

Mandy started blinking furiously, and kept blinking. She opened her eyes, closed her eyes. Open... close... open... close. The cops didn't seem to notice.

What are they doing? Can't they see I'm trying to tell them something? Panic threatened to overpower her.

———

Sam looked at Miranda. She was acting strange. Her eyes blinked, once, twice, three times, and kept on blinking. He could understand she was scared, she expected to die at any second. Perhaps the blinking was an involuntary, reflex reaction to the horrific situation she faced. He spoke softly to Foley out of the corner of his mouth.

"Look at the girl."

Foley dropped his eyes from Williams, to Miranda's face. "What is she doing?"

"I think she's trying to tell us something," Sam said.

Sam noticed Williams's badly misshapen hand. "Look at his arm," he whispered to Foley.

"Jesus!" Foley hissed. "It looks badly broken."

"You look hurt, Len. That arm looks bad. We can get you help... get you to a doctor," Sam called to Williams.

"The fuckin' bitch did that," Williams announced. "And she's gonna pay for it."

Sam smiled at Miranda. "Way to go, girl!"

"You have ten seconds to drop your weapons on the ground and step back!" Williams repeated.

"If we do that, you will shoot us... and then the girl," Foley explained. "We are not going to surrender our weapons. You need to understand that, Leonard."

"I understand you are running out of time," Williams said.

Sam, and Foley lifted their weapons slightly

higher, and took careful aim. They were aiming at Miranda's head. If Williams carried through with his threat and shot her, she would fall, and their weapons would then be trained at his chest. Centre mass; it's what all the training manuals recommended.

———

Mandy saw the two police officers raise their weapons higher. They were pointed at her head. She was staring down the barrels of two guns, and a third dug painfully into the back of her head. She could not wait a moment longer. She had to move.

For just a brief moment she lowered her eyes once again to the man's broken arm. The skin where the wrist bones threatened to break through had developed into an ugly, swollen, blue/black bruise.

This was it. Mandy lifted her eyes and resumed her blinking at the two cops. *For God's sake, don't mess this up*, she silently prayed. She braced her feet, and thrust herself forward, and down, her body weight falling against the man's broken arm.

Leonard Williams screamed. Involuntary reflexes kicked in, and he pulled his arm away from Miranda's neck. The rifle flew from his hands, and clattered in the dirt next to Miranda.

As Miranda fell forward, Williams looked up at the two police officers.

The first bullet hit him square in the middle of his chest, and the second a little higher. He staggered backwards, and crashed heavily into the car. He looked down at his chest as several more rounds plowed into his upper body.

―――――

In the few seconds remaining of his life, Leonard Williams found himself thinking how surreal it was to see the bullets killing him.

He felt no pain. Even his arms didn't hurt anymore. Slowly, his legs began to buckle beneath him, and he slid slowly down the body of the car until he sat in the dirt, staring wide eyed across the short distance between himself and the two police officers.

The very last thing Leonard Williams saw before his eyes closed for ever, was the cop with the bandage around his head. The bastard was smiling.

29

"I got him covered," Foley said to Sam. "Check on the girl." He kicked the dropped rifle away from the body, and stared down at Williams.

Sam holstered his weapon, and hurried to where Miranda lay in the fetal position on the ground, sobbing loudly. He knelt next to her, and touched her shoulder.

"Miranda, right?" he asked.

Mandy started, and shrunk away from his touch. "No... no... don't!" she sobbed.

"It's okay, you're safe now," Sam said softly. "It's over."

Mandy turned her face to Sam. "Is he... is he... ?"

"Yes," Sam said. "He's dead. He can't hurt you anymore."

Mandy pushed herself to a sitting position, and fell against Sam.

"Oh God," she whimpered. "He... he... he raped me."

"It's okay now," Sam said.

"He... killed other girls," Mandy continued.

"I know," Sam placed his arm over her shoulder,

and patted her gently on the arm. "He's gone now. He won't hurt anyone ever again."

Mandy stole a quick glance around Sam, at the body of the man, slumped against the car. He looked asleep. If it weren't for the blood, lots of it, on the front of his shirt, he could very well be taking a nap.

"Are you sure he's dead?" Mandy asked.

"Yes," Sam confirmed.

"I... I'm glad," Mandy said, and looked away from the body.

Sam helped Mandy to her feet. "Are you thirsty," he asked.

"Yes."

"Okay," Sam said. "We've got water in our car. Let me get you settled in there, and you can have a drink."

"Th... thank you," Mandy stammered. She allowed Sam to walk her slowly to the police car where he helped her into the back seat and gave her a drink of water.

A trickle of water ran down her chin. "I'm sorry," she said, wiping at the droplets. "He hit me in the face with a torch. It's hard to swallow."

"It's okay," Sam smiled. "Take your time."

"You were at the house, weren't you?" Mandy asked.

"Yes," Sam said. "I'm sorry we couldn't stop him there."

"I want to go home," Mandy said, tears welling again in her eyes.

"Soon," Sam said. "We'll take you out of here in a few minutes, I promise. I understand your parents are waiting at Tennant Creek for you."

"They... they're here?"

"Waiting for you," Sam smiled.

"I'm tired," Mandy sobbed.

Sam reached across into the rear of the vehicle, and grabbed a blanket. He spread it over her knees. "Why don't you lay down here on the back seat," he suggested. "I'll be back in a moment, and we'll take you out of here."

Mandy grabbed his hand, her nails digging painfully into his flesh. "Don't leave me... please," she sobbed.

Sam gently lowered her to the seat and covered her with the blanket. "Okay, I'll stay right here."

Seconds later, Mandy began to snore very softly. Sam watched her for a few moments, satisfying himself she was asleep, and then he gently closed the door and walked back to where Foley knelt before the body of Leonard Williams.

"Dead?" Sam asked.

"Well and truly," Foley confirmed.

"Got a few holes in him," Sam said.

"I feel like putting a few more in him, just for good measure," Foley stood.

"We need to get the girl out of here," Sam said. "But I don't think it's a good idea to take this prick's body back in the same car."

"I agree," Foley said. "There's a tarp in the back of our car. We'll cover him up, and send someone out here to pick up the body."

Sam turned to Foley. "Would you have dropped your weapon?"

"No, you?"

"No."

"Do you think he would have shot her?" Foley asked.

"It doesn't matter now," Sam shrugged.

Foley turned towards the police car, but halted when Sam grabbed his arm. "What?" he turned to face his partner.

Sam stepped closer to the car, and pointed to a bullet hole in the body work. "You missed," he declared.

"How do you know it was one of mine that missed?" Foley sounded suitably offended.

"It had to be you," Sam said.

"How do you figure?"

Sam slapped Foley on the shoulder. "Because I never miss."

THE END

Dear reader,

We hope you enjoyed reading *Bones In The Well*. Please take a moment to leave a review, even if it's a short one. Your opinion is important to us.

The story continues in *The Petticoat Gang*.

Discover more books by Gary Gregor at
https://www.nextchapter.pub/authors/gary-gregor

Want to know when one of our books is free or discounted? Join the newsletter at
http://eepurl.com/bqqB3H

Best regards,
Gary Gregor and the Next Chapter Team

LASSETER'S CAVE

It's hot, remote, desolate and dangerous; and about as deep into the infamous Australian outback as anyone would dare to venture. An eminent neurosurgeon, his loving wife and two adorable children, on the holiday of a lifetime, are shot dead, their shattered bodies left to the ravages of the desert sun and carrion-eating wildlife.

Detective Inspector Russell Foley, and his best friend and fellow Northern Territory cop, Detective Sergeant Sam Rose, are sent into the heart of the legendary Harold Lasseter, "Lost Reef of Gold" country to investigate the brutal murders.

Is it Gold Fever, or simply the twisted mind of a deranged killer protecting that which he believes is his?

http://bookgoodies.com/a/B01MXIKJVR

Bones In The Well
ISBN: 978-4-86745-162-5
Mass Market

Published by
Next Chapter
1-60-20 Minami-Otsuka
170-0005 Toshima-Ku, Tokyo
+818035793528

30th April 2021

Lightning Source UK Ltd.
Milton Keynes UK
UKHW040832290822
408009UK00001B/80